BATTLE SCARS I

MEN OF THE CROSS

Charlene Newcomb

This novel is a work of fiction. Names, characters, places and incidents are either the product of the author's imagination or are used fictitiously apart from those well-known historical figures. Any resemblance to actual persons, living or dead, is entirely coincidental.

BATTLE SCARS I: MEN OF THE CROSS

Published by Blue X Entertainment
Davenport, Florida

Copyright © 2014 by Charlene Newcomb

Cover art design by ProBookCovers.com

Maps ©2014 by Dennis Lukowski
Interior graphics by the Author

Title page art, Sword and Shield by angelfire7508
http://angelfire7508.deviantart.com
distributed under CC-BY-SA3.0

ISBN: 0692205942
ISBN 13: 978-0692205945

For my friends Al and Willie.

CONTENTS

ACKNOWLEDGMENTS

Writing is often a solitary journey, but a number of people encouraged and supported me on this adventure. My friends and fellow writers Jen Fitzgerald and Julie Durdin read and provided comments on my first draft. Several classmates in the University of Virginia MOOC *Plagues, Witches and War: The Worlds of Historical Fiction* had kind words for the opening scene and let me know I was on the right track. Janice Hardy critiqued the first page on her blog and offered thoughts on how to make it better. I read the first chapter to two different groups of librarians and they have been waiting patiently to see this novel published. Lastly, and most importantly, my Thursday night writing group, Cathy Hedge, Marie Loughin, and Mark Rogers, listened to me tell Sir Henry and Sir Stephan's story week after week. Mark also read the third—or was it fourth—draft and offered additional editorial comment. Marie and Cathy were the champs and provided extensive editing. The group's enthusiasm, questions, and observations made me work all the harder, and without them this novel might never have seen the light of day. They helped me find the words to share with you.

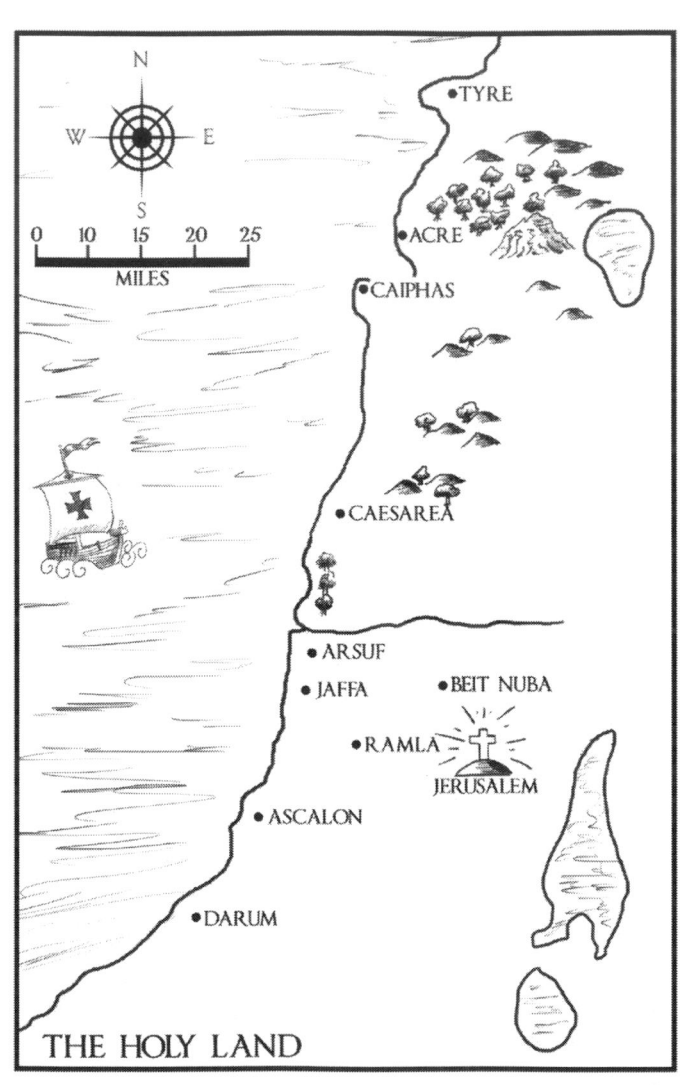

N
W   E
S

0 10 15 20 25
MILES

•TYRE

•ACRE

•CAIPHAS

•CAESAREA

•ARSUF

•JAFFA   •BEIT NUBA

•RAMLA
JERUSALEM

•ASCALON

•DARUM

THE HOLY LAND

Southampton
march1190

HENRY DE GREY PALMED the crucifix hanging round his neck. *This path, You have laid out for me.* His heart told him he'd made the right decision. He quieted the noise of his father's misgivings. What good was it to get your spurs and not answer the king's call? And what better service than to take the Cross, to free Jerusalem from the infidels.

"You do not know war." His father's words.

Henry's destrier shifted beneath him and pawed the ground. He stroked Sombre's neck, calming both man and beast. True, he was untested in battle. *But I have trained for this.* He would sail across the Narrow Sea and join King Richard's army at Tours. He'd journey with the Lionheart's men to Outremer, fight at their sides in the Holy Land, and if it were God's will, he would die for this noble cause.

A stiff wind tossed back Henry's hood. Waves of dark hair matted to his face and rain trickled into his eyes. He frowned at the column of wagons lumbering ahead through the Bargate, wares rattling and wheels groaning over the din of the driving rain.

Henry wished the storm could drown out that voice in his head. And this downpour, like his father's words, could easily drench his spirit—the galleys would never leave Southampton in this squall.

Riding alongside Henry, his servant Roger shifted from side to side to look ahead, anxious for a glimpse of the town. The fifteen-year-old tapped the pommel of his saddle, his frustration mirroring Henry's. When they finally passed through the city gate, Roger gasped in awe. Knights and soldiers crowded the High Street. There were hundreds, mayhap a thousand. Their colourful surcoats blanketed the road and obscured the mud beneath their boots. The storm, the delays, his father—none of that mattered to Henry compared to this. One look at these men erased his apprehension. He curled his hand around the hilt of his sword. He was one of them.

He urged Sombre onward. A score of tradesmen plied sword and bow, leather goods, and mail beneath pavilions set up in St. Michael's square. The rain slowed, and scents wafting from a baker's shop collided with the smells of stall after stall of fresh and salted fish. An argument at one cart drew stares. A fishwife with mussed gray hair haggled over prices with a customer. She waved a huge gutting knife.

"I'd place my silver on the old woman with the blade," Henry said.

"I gave my word to your father that I would remind you gambling only leads to trouble, my lord." Roger glanced sidelong at Henry. "She will win."

The pot-bellied customer shook his fist. "You foul woman." The fishwife crossed her arms across her chest, leaving a hand free to point her knife conspicuously towards his throat.

Applause erupted across the road. Four full-bosomed women crowded an upstairs window, cheering her and gesturing suggestively to men on the street.

"Holy saints in heaven." Roger's cheeks blushed like summer's strawberries. It wasn't the first brothel they'd passed on the road from Lincolnshire. Henry remembered Roger had stopped counting at ten. A boy growing up in the countryside wouldn't see that many in a lifetime. But a boy going on pilgrimage? That was another matter.

Mischievously, Henry asked, "Should I worry about you?"

"I *have* been to Lincoln, my lord." A grin settled on Roger's round face.

Lincoln did have its seedier quarters, but it was the memory of a trip to London with his father that made Henry smile. Lord Edward had answered his ten-year-old's wide-eyed curiosity with blunt honesty, and then added, "Not a word to your lady mother." Now at the age of twenty, Henry couldn't imagine being shocked by anything.

A shriek startled Sombre. The horse jerked, nearly throwing Henry. The fishwife was tearing around the cart. She shoved her customer. Her blade ripped his cloak. He flailed and stumbled back into Roger's horse.

"Whoa," Roger cried, trying to control the skittish rouncy.

The man stared at the fishwife wide-eyed, furious. He plucked a long blade from his belt and stepped towards her.

Henry whisked his sword from its scabbard and heeled Sombre between the combatants. "Enough, you two!" He planted the tip of his blade against the man's shoulder. People scattered. The voices from the brothel quieted.

"Put away your weapons," Henry ordered. "There's more than one merchant with fish."

The old woman snorted. "See if you find a better price elsewhere, thief."

Glowering at her, the man thrust Henry's sword aside with his long blade. "You are the thief, old woman."

"Go!" The force of Henry's voice drowned out the sound of his heart's pounding.

The fishwife flashed her knife again for good show, drumming up more applause from the enthusiastic whores. From the brothel's window, a dark-haired beauty called, "Come to me, brave knight." Her gaze swiftly left Henry. Her alluring smile faded, her eyes narrowed. Elbowing her friends, she pointed towards something on the street.

Henry tracked the aim of her slender finger. A slight figure slinked cat-like through the crowd.

"Thief!" the ladies chorused.

Hands reached for purses, outraged murmurs swelled. "Catch him!" someone shouted.

Darting through the crowd, the thief was hard to follow, but a soldier had taken up the chase. The brown blur darted towards Henry. Henry managed a good look. A young boy. A blue silk purse dangled from the sleeve of his filthy tunic. *God's bones, he is thin.*

The pickpocket charged into the gap between Sombre and Roger's mount. Sombre balked, head chopping the air. Without a second thought, Henry tightened his grip on the reins. He made a quick decision. He pressed his heels to Sombre's flanks. The destrier sidled into the other horse and the space between the two animals disappeared.

"Christ!" the soldier cursed, stumbling backwards to avoid bowling into the horses. "Out of my way."

Henry nudged Sombre but the pickpocket had shot away. The soldier manoeuvred around the horses and picked up his pursuit.

Roger twisted in his saddle to look after the chase. "If they capture him…"

Henry shrugged nonchalantly. "He is a thief. Stealing is against God's laws and civil law."

"They would cut off his hand?"

"Or hang him."

Roger bit back a trembling lip. "He is just a child."

"Man or child, woman—should the law provide exception?" Henry crossed himself.

Roger met Henry's eyes, studied his master's face thoughtfully. "You did that on purpose," he said, his voice near a whisper.

"Did what?"

The whores whistled and blew kisses to Henry before Roger could respond. "Brave knight, brave knight," the ladies chimed.

Henry blushed, glad for the ladies' distraction even though it meant they caught Roger's roving eyes again. Still, Henry was glad to see him smile. The fishwife with her knife and the young thief might easily dampen his eagerness for this journey.

Henry glanced from the ladies to Roger. Sheathing his sword, he said, "*You* are too young. And I am betrothed."

Roger sighed as Henry offered the ladies a salute and steered Sombre towards the sign of the Boar and Bear. No whores enticed customers to drop their hose and a coin or two there. It looked respectable, a refuge from temptation, and mayhap safer from the thieves and cutthroats on the street.

From somewhere up the road a swell of voices shouted the battle cry, "For St. George!" Six knights on magnificent warhorses galloped through the town, waving swords to celebrate their impending departure for the Holy Land. The crowds joined their chorus. "For St. George," they called, parting as the warriors passed.

Henry straightened in the saddle and unsheathed his sword. He lifted his blade in homage to the knights and roared, "Save Jerusalem!"

Exhilarated, Henry slid from Sombre. Behind him, Southampton Castle loomed on the motte, her banners flapping against the dark grey skies. The cool wind hinted that spring was no more than a dream but its bite bristled with anticipation, with hope. Pride swelled in Henry. He quickly quelled that feeling. God would not approve of prideful men.

He handed Sombre's reins to Roger. "Find a stable. Get a room. My bones ache. I am weary of the meager rations we've been eating."

They'd only two hot meals in six days, one a rabbit they'd caught, skinned and roasted. Mary, who ran the kitchen at his father's manor, had packed plenty of dried meat for their travels. "I will buy you an ale, and we shall have a fine meal."

He glanced westward where the clouds grew darker still. "God willing, we'll sail to Barfleur in a day or two."

Roger rubbed Sombre's snout, stealing another peek at the ladies. Henry shook his head. There were some things mothers did not need to know about their sons' education. "I will leave out Southampton's gritty details when I write home."

Henry strode into the Boar and Bear. He halted inside the door, eyes sweeping the smoky room, nose irritated by rushes on the floor that might have been fresh-scented hours earlier but now reeked of spilled ale and sour vomit. Nearly everyone in the tavern turned to inspect the new visitor. Henry's stomach knotted. Did he wear his inexperience like a halo? Grizzled older faces studied him but for a moment before returning to their business.

Henry pressed through the crowded tavern to a trestle near the hearth. Glad for its light and warmth, comforted by the ale that soaked his dry throat, he was content to sit quietly while conversation hummed around him. A handful of customers were merchants or tradesmen, all easily distinguished from the knights in their surcoats emblazoned with fierce-looking beasts and swords hanging from their belts. They shared bawdy jokes and tales of war.

"I fought with the king," a knight at the opposite end of the hearth told eager companions. "Does my family in Yorkshire welcome me back? No. What did I find there? My father dead. My older brother said 'be off.' The bastard offered me one meal and one goblet of his wine. It was the most putrid—" He shook his head. "Is that how a war hero is honoured? To us, my friends." The knight lifted his mug. His gaze caught Henry's. "And to you, sir!"

Intrigued by the knight, Henry nodded politely and sipped at his ale.

The knight kept his eyes on Henry. Firelight caught the deep blue of them. "I was at Chinon. Stormed the castle at King Richard's side. Fought with him from Toulouse to Maine, and was at Le Mans when we defeated his father. Queen

Eleanor personally thanked me at Westminster last year. Four years I have been with my liege lord."

Henry wondered how much of the knight's braggadocio was the drink speaking. He looked young, surely not more than a year or two older than himself.

The knight's companions grumbled their sympathy. "Well done, brave knight," one called. They toasted him again.

Across the dimly lit tavern Henry spotted Roger. He signaled to him. Amongst all these knights, he seemed just a boy. *Is that how I look to these men? To my father?*

Henry moved his cloak, quirked his head at the empty chair.

"Our room is passable, my lord," Roger said.

Henry nodded towards the brew on the table. "Sit. Drink up. I am sure the room will satisfy our needs."

Roger downed half his ale in one swig. A young maiden sashayed up to the table and placed a platter of meat and bread before them. She brushed the back of her hand against the blond fuzz sprouting on Roger's jaw but her gaze fixed on Henry. Bending close, her full bosom nearly spilled into Henry's lap. A blush crept up his neck. Roger's eyes widened. The girls back home weren't quite so blatant.

"Will that do for you, my lord?"

Henry swallowed hard. "It will."

"Are ye certain? I would be happy to—"

"Nothing more."

The girl sighed deeply and wandered to the kitchen, squeezing past the bragging knight who shuffled unsteadily towards Henry.

"The girls here can be accommodating." The knight gestured at the men across the room and added, "Or so my friends say."

Swaying, the knight grabbed the edge of the trestle. Henry offered him a seat on the bench before he fell into their dinner.

"I am Stephan l'Aigle. My father is...was Reynaud of Yorkshire," the knight said.

L'Aigle. The eagle. That explained the magnificent red bird of prey embroidered on Stephan's surcoat. "Henry de Grey. From Lincolnshire."

"My friend Robin…" Stephan scanned the tavern, and then laughed. "He is not here, but you will like him. He is from near Lincoln. And you—why are you familiar to me, sir?"

"We've not met, Sir Stephan. Mayhap you saw me at Westminster or in Poitiers."

Stephan pounded the table, rattling the trenchers. "At the coronation last year. That's it. It was grand, was it not?"

The intensity and passion in Stephan's eyes startled Henry. "I have never seen such a spectacle" he said, wondering why this battle-seasoned knight had singled him out. A scar on Stephan's jaw was visible through the dark blond stubble on his face. His hands bore signs that he'd been in many a scrape. And at King Richard's side?

"When were you in Poitou?" Stephan asked.

"Five years past, with my father. I wanted to be a squire in Duke, er, King Richard's household. My father had other plans. He felt I should return to Greyton to learn to manage our lands and the tenants' petty squabbles."

"And now," Stephan said, "you are answering the king's call to join the pilgrimage to Jerusalem." He pressed a finger to the patch of white cloth affixed to Henry's Lincoln green woollen cloak. The red cross on it marked Henry as a crusader. His mother had sewn it on with a prayer on her lips and tears in her eyes. And his father had argued…

You need not go to Outremer.

You served the old king. Why shouldn't I serve his son?

We can pay another to serve in your stead.

You think I am not able to wield a weapon in battle? It was you who denied me a chance to serve in Richard's mesnie where I might have honed my skills.

Edward de Grey stared past Henry, fists clenched at his side, eyes misted with concern. *You have nothing to prove.*

Henry grew angry. He drew himself straight. *Nothing but honour and duty—to my king. To God.*

Stephan stood, lifted his ale. "My friends, heroes all," he shouted, waving his mug across the room, oblivious to the ale spilling from the rim. "To the men who will take back the Holy City."

Cheers rippled through the tavern. Henry felt the excitement and counted himself lucky to be amongst these knights. When Stephan fell back into his seat, he tapped Henry's goblet with his own.

"For my God, my king, and my country," Henry said. He downed his drink. He stabbed a chunk of meat from the platter with his dagger. It dripped with thick brown gravy. He chewed it slowly at first and realised it was pork, near as good as the succulent roast that Mary made back home. Satisfied, he heaped a hefty portion onto his trencher. The crusty bread was stale but better than what was left in his bags.

Stephan waved off Henry's offer of food and launched into another tale of Richard's struggles against the barons in Aquitaine. He spoke of the cold and the rain, of times with companions around a warm fire. Men in the tavern dragged their seats closer. Whether they'd been on the campaigns or not, or were fresh to the coming struggles, they seemed entranced.

Names of at least a dozen or more men who'd not come back slid with respect from Stephan's tongue, his words acknowledged by other soldiers' nods. His gaze traced round the room but had a far off look, as if he saw these men gathered around desert campfires and wondered whom amongst them might meet their untimely end on the field of battle.

Roger listened, fascinated by the knight's stories. He'd pause mid-chew, swallowed hard. Henry thought he saw a hint of fear mixed with that wonder.

Stephan finished two more mugs of ale and finally quieted. His eyes fluttered. He ignored the throng of men around him and focused on Henry. That gaze unnerved Henry and he tightened his grip on his goblet.

"Good knight, good comrade," Stephan said. "May I ask you to help me to my room? I am not certain I will make it up the stairs on my own."

Henry tried not to grin. "Do you remember what room you are in?"

Stephan stared at him, frowning. "Of course. It is that way." He pointed towards the door. "Upstairs."

Henry lowered his head, chuckling. Before he had a chance to ask Stephan to clarify—if he could—Roger pointed to a short, balding man making his way to the bar. "We can ask the innkeeper." And with that, they learned that Stephan's room was the third door at the top of the stairs and right next to theirs.

Roger eyed the last chunk of bread.

Henry nodded. "It is yours."

Roger stuffed the food into his tunic. He helped Stephan to his feet, but it took both men to keep him upright. Stephan threw his arms across their shoulders and turned to Henry. "This weary knight thanks you, my friend."

Manoeuvring through the crowded tavern and avoiding arms flying animatedly was no easy chore. Stephan pressed himself tight to his companions but Roger stumbled against a table. A goblet crashed to the floor. Henry apologized to the drinker and pressed a coin into his palm.

Upstairs, they paused outside Stephan's room. The knight leaned closer, looked forlornly at Henry. "To my bed, please. I fear I shall fall over if you leave me here."

Henry couldn't resist a tease. "Do you always drink so much and talk so much?"

Roger pressed the latch down and shoved the door open with his foot. Walking three abreast was impossible in the tiny room. Backsides to the bed, they scooted inside, floorboards creaking beneath their boots.

Stephan fell onto the bed. "I swear I have few words when the sun is rising." Light from oil lamps in the hall illuminated his almost-boyish face. He tapped the coarse blanket, his eyes holding Henry's. "You should stay. Keep me warm."

The husky tone of Stephan's voice caught Henry off guard. Surely it was the drink speaking. Henry cleared his throat and tossed a blanket over Stephan. "This will have to do, friend. Sleep well."

Henry followed Roger to their room and waited until Roger lit a candle with a quick flick of his flint. The small space had two beds with barely a foot separating them. They looked clean despite the room's damp, musty smell. Cool spring weather meant the windows were shuttered against fresh sea air, though the smells of rotting fish, stale drink, and filthy locals might be all that wafted from the streets outside.

Roger found a corner for Henry's sword. He helped him strip off his tunic and hose. Someone stumbled outside their room and groaned loudly. When Stephan's snores bled through the wall, Henry said, "His head will be bursting on the morrow."

Roger winced. "He did have a bit of ale."

They both laughed, drawing a shout through the other wall. "Quiet!"

Settling on the edge of the bed, Henry stuck one foot out, and then the other, to let Roger remove his muddied boots while he dug through his pack. The wool blanket he found was softer and cleaner than the one on the bed. It brought back memories of home. He could hear his mother instructing Mary which herbs and flowers to use in his feather pillow, could almost smell the lavender and roses, though that pillow was near two hundred miles to the north.

Henry said goodnight to Roger, then lay down and tugged the blanket up to his chin, falling asleep quickly.

two

STEPHAN AWOKE NEAR NOON to a cold, damp, and dreary Southampton. The darkened skies matched his mood, a fitting way to end his days in England before sailing to the warm climes of the Greek Sea. Good riddance weather; good riddance, brother.

He made his way downstairs, where the smell of breakfast cooking sent him staggering for the exit. Leaning against the door of the inn, he rubbed his temples. Oh, the ale. He'd had far more than usual. Sleep helped, but he'd spent the morning attempting to piece together how he'd made it to his bed.

There was still a dull ache in his head and the rattling wares from a parade of wagons did little to help. Coopers, smiths, bakers—men of every trade imaginable jostled through the streets. "Three months?" "To Jerusalem..." "Ten or more thousand..." "The Saracens killed..." "Acre." That was one he heard repeated. Acre. It sounded harsh in his ears. Mayhap that was the effects of the ale? One thing was certain. The voices around him were filled with anticipation—and dread—about the long journey ahead.

Stephan had been seventeen summers the first time he sailed from Southampton to Barfleur. Brash and sure of himself. *Still am.* He'd honed his battle skills with the knights of Richard's mesnie in Normandy, Aquitaine, wherever his lord took him. When Richard took the Cross after Saladin's warriors killed thousands of Christians at the Battle of Hattin and captured Jerusalem, Stephan knew he must answer that call. Not for the Pope or the Church. For Richard.

Outremer would no longer be a place he'd heard described in song and legend. Somehow Stephan knew he'd see Jerusalem. At two and twenty, he was a cynic about the Mother Church and her servants. Whether he'd find salvation by confessing his sins and following the One True Faith, he was not so sure. He wanted to see the places this man—this Son of God—had walked. To do that at King Richard's side, to follow his liege lord until he took his last breath, would surely be the most honourable thing he'd ever do with his life.

A feminine voice called, "Hello, my sweet."

The driver of a two-wheeled cart tossed the woman a gap-toothed grin.

"Not you." She tossed her head back. Shouting above the braying of the tradesman's cantankerous mule, she leaned further out her upstairs window. "That one, Sir blond knight."

Stephan looked up, pointed to himself.

"You look cold and miserable, my lord." She smiled, dampened a finger with her tongue and held it against her lower lip. "I can help."

"I am afraid you have the wrong man, dear lady," Stephan said.

"Listen to him! He speaks the truth."

Stephan turned to the familiar voice of the rider on a grey courser. "Geoffrey!"

"I should like the arms of two such handsome knights around me," the whore said.

Geoffrey's hood flew back revealing hair the colour of a golden sun. As he reined in next to Stephan, he looked up at the woman and said, "*I* do not share."

She drew her hands to her bosom. "You break my heart."

Stephan bowed with a flourish. Blood rushed to his head. He grabbed Geoffrey's leg and straightened slowly.

The whore wasted no more time. Shouting out again, she aimed her flattery at other men wandering beneath her window and across the street.

Stephan asked Geoffrey, "Did you just arrive?"

Geoffrey swept the air with his arm, palm up. "Delivered through the gates of the city to you. It must be fate."

Stephan snorted. "The gates of he—"

"Do not say it. It was not my fault you lost that chess game."

Stephan planted a hand on the hilt of his sword. "You abandoned me." He patted his coin purse. "No coin, no horse, miles from camp, and breaking Richard's curfew."

Geoffrey flashed a smile. "You forgot to mention 'naked.' Winning the clothes off your back was a delight."

Stephan didn't let on that his loss had been thoughtfully planned and executed. He'd enjoyed every minute of that game and its aftermath.

"I'd be more than willing to apologize," Geoffrey added. "Mayhap another game of chess? Let me stable these beasts, find food and a bath."

Stephan sniffed at his tunic, turned his head aside. Last night's ale mixed with lavender from the washbasin in his room. An interesting combination. "There is a bathhouse just past St. Michael's."

Geoffrey urged his horse and pack mule up the road, calling back, "Meet me. What say you?"

Stephan felt as if there were more eyes than Geoffrey's on him. He caught the green of a cloak and a mass of dark, wavy hair.

Now he remembered. *Henry.* The handsome knight with a squarish, high-cheekboned face emerged from one of the shops.

Geoffrey followed Stephan's gaze. He sighed and imitated the whore in the window, laying his hands over his heart.

Stephan waved, laughing. "I shall see you at the baths."

"Do not make promises." Geoffrey pressed his heels to his mount and joined the throngs headed up Bugle Street.

A light drizzle began to spit. Stephan watched Henry tug his hood over his head. Lincoln green. Of course! He was from Lincolnshire. Sparse details of their conversation came back to Stephan. He suddenly recalled he'd asked the man to warm his bed. *Good Christ.* Searching his memory, he frowned. Had he forgotten if Henry had stayed the night? His head was in a fog. *Think man, think.*

Stephan smoothed his tunic, adjusted his sword belt. As Henry approached, he smiled—at least as much as the ache in his head allowed. Eyeing the packages Henry and his servant carried, he asked, "You are well-provisioned for the crossing?"

"We have purchased supplies to see us through for a few days. Sailing on the morrow, if this weather clears." Henry massaged his own temple as if he could see the effort it took for Stephan to be cheerful. His mouth twitched with a grin. "I did not think you would remember me."

"I was drunk, Sir Henry, but not that drunk."

Henry raised an eyebrow.

"Might I beg your indulgence?" Stephan asked. "Tell me what I might have said…or done."

Henry's eyes fell to mud splattered on Stephan's well-worn leather boots.

Then I did do something…

Behind Henry, Roger remained disinterested. Had he been there? Did he know?

Henry cleared his throat and looked up, almost shy. "There is not much to tell, Sir Stephan."

Stephan felt an odd sense of relief but wondered how he'd misjudged Henry's reaction.

A gust of wind sent Henry's cloak billowing like a sail. Henry gathered it close and rubbed a gloved hand over the soft wool. "My mother had this made at one of our mills. I would not be surprised if she chose the sheep herself, had a hand in the sheering—" Henry reddened, embarrassed. "I should not carry on so."

"It looks a fine make." Stephan found Henry's innocence refreshing. "You sound close to your mother. I envy you that." Stephan realised he'd not thought of his own mother in years, God rest her soul. She loved to sing and dance and play the vielle but despised the smell of sheep and cattle. "Breathe in," his father had said. "That's the smell of silver." She would scoff, content to let his father tease her about leaving the windows of the keep shuttered until the wind blew the stench of their herds away from the castle.

Henry shifted from one foot to the other. "We've one more stop at the farrier's, then back to our room to pack."

"Your horse?"

"Sombre threw a shoe north of London. He was re-shod, but no harm in one last look before we set out from Barfleur for Tours."

Stephan nodded searching for something more to say. He didn't want the conversation to end but any thoughts deserted him. Damn the ale. *If I ever drink that much again...*

Henry tapped the package under his arm and started into the inn. He let Roger pass and turned back to Stephan. "If you've not eaten, why not meet us at The Red Lion later? The innkeeper tells me the cook there makes a fish in almond milk with fresh herbs. We shall find no better."

Stephan ignored the churning in his belly. Surely he'd feel up to a meal in a few hours. "I will do it, but only if you permit me to buy you an ale. I am in your debt for your help last night."

Henry tipped his head. Watching him walk into the inn, Stephan decided he liked the young de Grey. He knew hundreds of knights from Normandy to Aquitaine, and would be glad to be in their company again. He'd lusted after some, had many willing partners. Henry seemed an innocent. The young noble showed no interest in a tumble in the hay, but mayhap in friendship? Stephan hadn't called many of the knights he knew true friends, save his mentor and confidant Robin du Louviers.

Melancholy overwhelmed him for a moment. Surrounded by a thousand of Richard's knights, how could a man feel so alone? Comfort in another man's arms was fleeting. It lasted only as long as that rush of blood and slipped away as quickly as the heart calmed.

Robin's friendship—for it had never been more than that—had kept him sane during the campaigns. He needed more friends like that. Like Henry de Grey.

three

TEMPÊTE SAWED HIS HEAD in the air and balked at the bottom of the unsteady ramp. He stamped and snorted, jerking away from the handler. The groom grabbed the bridle. He pressed his nose to Tempête's snout and ran his hand along the animal's neck.

Stephan watched from the deck, his jaw tight, his nails digging into the rail. *Calm, fiery one.*

Tempête turned as if he'd heard Stephan. The groom spoke to the warhorse as Stephan had suggested. That extra silver penny he'd shoved into the man's hand had been well worth it. Tempête calmed and pranced up the ramp.

Stephan stood transfixed at the stern, suffering along with each animal prodded aboard. Odd that it took his mind off the coming sea voyage, of the marches ahead, and sleeping on the cold hard ground. Around him, the crew made ready to sail. Sounds of knights' spurs scraped the deck. Carts creaked up the gangway. The discordant symphony rivaled the voices of tradesmen competing for last-minute business at dockside. The quay clamored with people. Stalls burst with goods of every kind, baked pies and pasties, and fresh fish. Fires smoking with roasting cod made his stomach growl. Breaking the fast might only bring regrets. Thinking of that fish lying heavy in his belly while the boat rode the waves made him forget his hunger.

The morning air was crisp, but the sun beat warm against Stephan's face. Wandering to the port side of the galley, he watched fishing boats manoeuvre through the maze of vessels in the harbour. They rode low, heavy with the day's catch. Gulls circled overhead like little thieves, waiting for the moment to strike.

"Good morning."

Stephan started. He hadn't heard Henry approach. "That it is." He was surprised the young knight's servant wasn't at his side. "Settled in?"

"Roger is stowing our supplies. I remember the last time I crossed the sea with my father. I am not anxious to spend time below-deck."

Stephan laughed. "Dark and dreary."

"And smells of too many men and beasts in so small a space." Henry's nose twitched. He stared at the water lapping at the side of the boat and then shot Stephan an inquiring look. "I was surprised I'd not seen you at The Red Lion yesterday. I had counted on that ale you promised."

Stephan rubbed his palm along the deck rail. He'd honestly meant to meet Henry at the tavern after his soak at the bathhouse. Geoffrey had insisted on a game of chess that led to a delightful, sweat-filled, heart-pumping afternoon—and evening—of antics. "My apologies. An old friend from the campaigns in Normandy arrived. We had many stories to share. The hour grew late."

"Time slips away easily," Henry said. "Is it true that men lose all sense of it in the heat of battle? My father claims it is so. He would say nothing more except that his closest friendships came from those campaigns with the late king."

"He speaks true of both. The men you fight alongside know what your family and friends from home will never understand. One soldier to another may speak of the campaigns. They are the lucky ones."

"Why do you say that?"

Stephan cast his eyes at some distant speck on the horizon. "I fear you will find out far too soon. Many only want to forget, mayhap like your father."

Henry smacked the rail with his fist. His shoulders tensed. "He told me I know nothing of war."

When Henry said no more, whether out of respect or disdain for his father, Stephan said, "Are you angry with him? Did you consider that he may be right?" He gestured towards the knights on the deck. "Look at these men. A few have been on campaigns. Others, like you, only think they know battle."

"I may be untested—"

"Oh, you will be brave." Stephan felt the twinge of an old battle wound and massaged his shoulder. "You will fight."

"Of course I will," Henry snapped.

But then what? Stephan knew cynicism bled through his words. He'd seen hundreds of innocents take up arms under King Richard's command. That rarely bothered him, so why now?

"I only meant—"

"To agree with my father?" Henry's frown quirked into a sarcastic grin, breaking the tension.

Stephan chuckled. "They *are* right at times. My father knew I would make a lousy priest. He sent me off to train as a squire with the Earl of Huntingdon when I was twelve."

"Your father sounds like a practical man. Mine? Stubborn. Pigheaded." Henry exhaled sharply. He turned his back to the water. Watching the nimble-footed sailors climb the rigging seemed to calm him. "What of your friend?" he asked. "Is he on board?"

"Geoffrey's plan to join the king must be delayed. A messenger arrived with grievous news of his father as we talked last night. He will be on the road to Leicester by now."

"God's bones. And here I complain when you have lost your father and spend time to comfort a friend about his own. How can I fault you for missing our dinner? It is not hard to talk into the wee hours when you are with a friend."

Talk. Yes, there was some of that. Stephan cleared his throat. "I did intend to apologize for anything I might have said when we first met. You did not see me at my best. You shall have my full attention on this fine boat. It will be hard to escape each other's company."

"You are a man of apologies today."

"Then I *did* speak of—"

Henry laughed nervously.

Stephan regarded Henry over the bridge of his nose, watched the red creep into his cheeks. He exhaled sharply. "If I offended you in any way—"

Wind swept Henry's dark curls into his eyes. He pushed them back, turning his face towards the horizon. "You suggested I might keep you warm."

"It *was* a cold night."

Henry rubbed his hand across his eyes. "Apologies if I mistook your meaning."

Of course Henry had understood his offer. Should he admit it or make light of it? "I am not so good a judge of men when drunk," he admitted.

"And when sober?"

Stephan leaned against the rail. He watched the deckhands readying the sail and observed the captain at the wheel talking with his coxswain. Angry with himself, he didn't want to look at Henry for fear there might be nothing but disgust on his face. He'd seen that look a hundred times over, even from those who preached one thing but practiced another. "You and I shall be friends and no more unless you say otherwise."

"So you truly meant..." Henry shook his head, embarrassed. "I am not...do not want... The Church condemns..."

Stephan raised a hand to interrupt Henry's stumbling admission. "As a friend, I would only ask one thing."

Henry could have inched away as some might do. He looked Stephan straight in the eye. "Then ask."

The sun slipped behind a cloud. Stephan would have seen that as an omen if he believed in them.

"Bishops, priests—they fling words like daggers. They would do better to mind their own. Do not speak of them to me. They do nothing more than corrupt God's words. He shall be my judge." *If he exists.*

"I will not repeat their preaching." Henry spoke so quietly that Stephan had to lean close. "I will not judge you."

No words had sounded sweeter to Stephan's ear. They were powerful words, blunt and honest, spoken from the heart by an honourable man. "Thank you. My shield and sword will be at your back to fight the enemy."

Henry clamped a strong hand on his arm. "And mine at yours."

That grip could have undone him. The temptation to stare at Henry's hand, to meet his eyes, was strong. *This will be one long journey.*

Stephan pulled away. He pointed to the weapon at Henry's side. "Are you any good with that thing?" It took strength to wield a sword, and there was sign of that in the way Henry had grasped him. He had potential, but would he survive his first battle?

Henry tipped his head from side to side. "I am, and with more practice I shall be the best."

"You've not fought *any* battles?"

"No."

"Rode the tourney circuit?"

"My father taught me everything I know."

"He would not talk of battle, yet trained you to fight." Stephan recalled his own service as a squire. Daily drills with sword and lance, mounted practices, and tourneys had honed his skills.

"He fought alongside the old king." Henry suddenly sounded proud of the man he'd called stubborn and pigheaded.

"And lived to tell about it," Stephan said. "Mayhap there is hope. We shall see how good you are when we work on your skills. We will need something to pass the time when we are not in the saddle. I shall ask Robin to give you special attention."

"As long as it is not the kind that might warm his body," Henry said with a grin.

"Robin?" Stephan laughed. "He is not inclined that way. He breaks women's hearts from England to Aquitaine. And what about you? Is there some fair maiden in Lincolnshire awaiting your return from the Holy Land?"

"Alys is my betrothed." Henry's words were cool, much like the breeze. He tucked his arms beneath his cloak for warmth. "Her father is Thomas Weston, a minor baron with a wool trade that near equals my family's. She is but fourteen. My father would gladly have seen us wed and her with child before I left, but her mother forbade it."

"A son and heir."

"If I should not survive."

"Do not speak of such things. We shall defeat the Saracens, take back Jerusalem, and return to England as heroes. Your Alys will have a handsome knight, and you shall breed like rabbits to appease your father's desire to secure his line."

Henry scoffed. "I should like to have more than that in marriage."

"What? You want love?" Stephan remembered his parents' arguments. He'd almost been glad to leave home at twelve. "Do you love another?"

"No," Henry said vehemently. He watched the clouds trail across the sky. The sun peeked out, illuminating the sadness in his eyes. "I should be happy that Alys would be my wife. She is a pretty young girl with golden hair and deep brown eyes. I do like her. It is just…I want her to accept me as more than a friend. Neither of us has a choice in this."

Both men knew there was rarely the expectation of love in an arranged marriage. From the moment they could walk, young folk of their class were married off to secure an alliance, for business, for property. They were no different from kings, like their liege lord. Richard had been betrothed as a young boy to the sister of King Philip of France, though many wondered when they might marry.

"Still, Alys should not be forced to marry someone she cannot come to love," Henry added.

"So *she* loves another."

"No. I do not know." Henry exhaled sharply. "She told me she was glad her mother would not permit the marriage."

"Mayhap you will come to love each other. And it may be years before we return to these shores. Alys will be more inclined to love and marriage by that time, and she risks her parents' scorn should she do something that would place her marriage to you in peril."

Henry gaped at Stephan. The thought that Alys might fall into another's bed shocked him. "She would not."

"Just as you will be faithful to her?"

Henry squirmed.

"Ah, I see. So you are not so innocent." Stephan chuckled. The more he spoke to Henry, the more he liked him. "Temptation is strong, especially when we are far from those we care about. You are not alone." He gestured towards the men ambling across the deck. "Many a married knight has found comfort in another's arms—man or woman—and gone home to wife and children. Even the late king had his share of mistresses, and King Richard is no saint though he is betrothed. If it shames you, and you feel it necessary, beg forgiveness and ask your priest to absolve you. Alys need never know."

Henry's brow rose. "You take love and marriage so lightly."

"Why should I feel guilty? I do not expect to have either. I may be dead tomorrow. I do what I want, take what I need, and hurt no one. My life beyond this world is between me and the God I pray to. You are free to remain chaste, my friend, if that is the life you choose."

Shouting along the waterfront interrupted their conversation. Henry followed Stephan to the other side of the galley to see the cause of the commotion. Laughing, Stephan pointed at the gathering on the quay. "See," he said, "the whores have come to offer themselves to the brave men of King Richard's army."

The women, who looked from fifteen to fifty, from beauty to beastly, protested when soldiers tried to herd them like cows, shooing them down the street. All they'd wanted was to pleasure the departing soldiers and earn a coin or two.

Four crewmen drew back the gangway. Ropes tossed from the quay sailed through the air, caught by rough, chafed hands that coiled them expertly. The captain ordered the oars into the water and the vessel lurched away from the docks. A cheer rose. Women wept and hands swayed to offer a farewell to the men who would save Jerusalem.

"Goodbye, sweet honeys." The noble standing next to Stephan waved a chubby hand at the ladies, one of whom blew him a kiss. "Victory will be ours."

"Lord Walter," Stephan said, "I am honoured to be in your company on this journey."

The older man nodded. "Sir Stephan."

An old friend of Stephan's father, Walter le Berviere had been a loyal supporter of the late king. Though he and Stephan had met on opposites sides of the battlefield, their friendship formed after Walter swore allegiance to King Richard.

The wake of fishing boats rocked the galley. Walter grabbed the rail. "How was Yorkshire?" he asked. "Your father is well?"

"No, my lord. Father passed before the king was crowned at Westminster last year and my dear brother did not think it worth sending word to me."

"Gilbert? That bastard. Your father was a good man. Left Castle l'Aigle to Gil, did he? I told him years ago he owned enough of Yorkshire to split it amongst his sons like old King Henry did with his four devils." Walter frowned. "What of your other brother?"

"Geoffrey joined the orders five years past. He is at the minster at Southwell."

"And you remain in the king's service."

"Aye." Stephan heard Henry shuffle his feet. "May I introduce you to Sir Henry, son of Edward of Greyton."

"Henry—I saw you knighted in Westminster this last September. A pleasure."

Henry straightened proudly. "My lord."

Walter rubbed a hand across his rounded belly. "My stomach tells me it is time for food. Would you goodly pilgrims care to join me?" He pointed towards the bow. "They've set a table for us."

Before either man could respond Walter sneezed. He rubbed his nose against his sleeve. "I fear I start this trip with an ague. As if rolling on the waves for days is not bad enough."

"Let us hope the sea is calm and the journey short," Stephan said.

Henry's face had paled. "My lord, I think I shall wait to eat. I must check that my manservant has stowed our things properly." He tipped his head to both men, "Until later," he said and headed below.

Food still had no appeal to Stephan, but he'd keep the man company. "After you, my lord."

Walter winked at Stephan. "Age before beauty, though my good wife Jane would disagree."

"I have heard it is best to keep the wife happy."

"Truer words were never spoken. Remember them well and you will find a woman who will love you when you grow old and fat like me. Now tell me, young Stephan, you have not yet made a match?"

Stephan shook his head. "Who would have a penniless knight, my lord?"

"Serve the king well and you may find yourself with lands and wealth when we return." Walter paused and eyed him up and down. "My daughter Mary is twelve, hmm?"

"A bit young—"

"She will grow older."

"As will I. Mayhap she would not like a husband nearly twice her age."

Walter laughed, started towards the bow. "Let me tell you about her."

Stephan watched the older man pace along the creaking deck. Odd, he'd never considered being more than a hearth knight in service to the king even when he knew that his friend Robin had been granted lands near Rouen. Might he find himself in a position where he'd need an heir? A man did not have to bed a wife regularly—he shuddered—only long enough to get her with child. A son.

Stephan shook off thoughts of married life and followed Walter. A future like that seemed a long way off. A future that might never be, with war looming ahead.

Tours
april 1190

four

HENRY WAS COLD, HIS tunic damp, and dark skies threatened more rain, but none of that mattered. A sea of tents flanked the town of Tours and warmed his body and spirit. Eyes sweeping the valley, he guided Sombre to the side of the road to let the caravan of wagons lumber past. After three weeks of travel, weary faces brightened when the king's camp came within their sights. Conversations grew lively. The pilgrims were anxious to unpack their belongings and stay in one place for more than a day.

King Richard's call to arms stirred fresh in Henry's mind. Another voice, his father's, made him twist his hands round Sombre's reins. "You will be like the thousands Saladin slaughtered at Hattin. Dead on the sands of Outremer." Henry smoothed the horse's mane to stop his trembling.

"Master, master!" Roger drew up beside Henry breaking the dark thoughts. "Look at all the tents and the banners. Is that King Richard's pavilion?" Everything remained new and wondrous to his young servant, a grand adventure; from the bustling port of Southampton, with its galleys of every shape and size, to this caravan that had grown as they'd journeyed south from Barfleur. Roger relished every sight and sound, whistling as tents sprung up like flowers blooming in a field. "I have never seen so many cows and pigs." He breathed in and made a face.

Henry chuckled. That was no sweet scent wafting up from the valley. Livestock crowded corrals scattered from one end of the camp to the other.

"We'd not have pasture to hold them all at home. And the horses," Roger added. A chorus of brays answered him.

"Do not forget the mules," Henry said.

Roger rolled his eyes. "They shall not let us, my lord."

"Good day to you, Sir Henry," a middle-aged woman called from atop a barrel on a wagon rolling past.

"And to you, Maude."

"I hear we shall be here a few days, my lord. Have the boy bring your clothes for a wash."

Henry could almost smell Maude's lavender soap. "I will send him by on the morrow," he said with a smile. He greeted other pilgrims he'd come to know. "This is home now," he told Roger. He palmed his cross and whispered, "For God, for my King."

Roger frowned. "But we are going to Outremer, my lord."

"We will live, eat, and sleep with these pilgrims from here to Jerusalem. It seems right to call this home."

Arching his back to stretch weary muscles, Roger's gaze followed the web of paths through the massive tent city. "Will there be room for us all?"

Henry laughed. "I am sure there will be. Why don't you go ahead and find a place for the tent."

"On my own?"

"Aye. Go on."

Grinning, Roger nudged his horse down the hill.

Henry felt as much in awe of the massive gathering as Roger. Twenty knights, their squires, and a host of men-at-arms had boarded with them to cross the sea. Hundreds more joined the pilgrimage south from the Normandy coast. The army and its entourage stretched like a colourful blanket before him, thousands strong, obscuring what had been pastures and farmland. There was no smell of tilled earth here this spring.

High above it all, the Lionheart's banner, a golden lion snarling on a red shield, fluttered on the breeze. The king's pavilion occupied a promontory with a commanding view of the castle and the city that flourished beneath it. Henry's throat tightened with emotion. *I have made the right decision. I belong here.*

Shouts erupted behind Henry. He turned. A familiar black destrier galloped within a finger's breadth of people walking alongside the wagons. Stephan brought Tempête to an abrupt stop at Henry's side. The horse seemed to smell the camp. Familiar with the sights and sounds of war, it flared its nostrils. It shifted restlessly, wild and rowdy like his name. Stephan kept the reins taut in his gloved hands.

"Magnificent," Stephan said, eyeing the flurry of activity in the valley. "Five years at King Richard's side—"

"I thought you said four," Henry interrupted, recalling their first meeting at the Boar and Bear.

"Did I?" Stephan rapped his hand against his thigh. "Too much ale."

Henry chuckled. He'd not seen Stephan drunk since that day in Southampton. They'd swigged many an ale in the weeks that followed and imparted numerous tales. Henry laughed at Stephan's jokes. The man could not sing to save his hide but took the other knights' teasing with grace. Sober Stephan was still a braggart, but he was honest and fair-minded.

"It is five." Stephan's face wrinkled in concentration. "Yes, five years at the king's side and I've never seen anything like this. Not even at Westminster when he took the crown."

A knight on a warhorse rivaling the size of Tempête drew up beside them. "York? It is you!"

Stephan gripped the older noble's arm and laughed. "I wondered if you'd stay away after you fell back into your wife's bed."

Edwin of Wiltshire shoved back his hood. He chuckled, the lines on his face deepening. "She'd prefer not to deal with me any more than needed." Tossing the wine-coloured cloak off his wide shoulders, he threw Stephan a mock look of despair. "Apparently I am no longer needed."

Stephan offered a sympathetic sigh. "I have told you before. Women will break your heart."

"True, but she is a good woman. And a good mother."

"The boys are well?"

"Healthy, strapping lads, the two of them. And Juliana is with child again, which she is none too pleased about." He waved his hand from one end of the caravan to the other. "I thank God my boys are too young for this nonsense."

Henry followed Edwin's gaze. The king's call—nonsense? Soldiers and the common folk like the coopers and tanners—these people had set out on a holy mission to secure Jerusalem from the infidels. How could this be nonsense?

Edwin leaned close to Stephan. "Besides, I enjoy your company fifty times over hers. The woman has no sense of play. Mayhap you and I might share memories of Poitiers later."

Was that the sixth or seventh time Henry had heard that line? He couldn't be certain if the knights were good comrades or had been intimate, and try as he might, he couldn't keep a blush from creeping into his cheeks.

Edwin turned to Henry. He brought his hand to his chest and nodded. "Edwin, of Wiltshire."

"My lord." Henry tipped his head. "I am Henry de Grey of Lincolnshire."

Edwin cleared his throat. "Ah—from up north like our Stephan." Eyes mischievous, he sized up Henry and then cocked his head towards Stephan. "You shall find no better than this one. And if he has called you friend, you must be as brave and noble a man as he." Edwin spurred his horse, shouted back over his shoulder, "God be with you both."

"*Our* Stephan?" Henry said. "Does everyone assume I have fallen to your charms?"

Stephan shrugged. "Do not worry. It's just his way of speaking." He dug his heels into Tempête and galloped down the hill.

~ ~ ~

STEPHAN HAD INTENDED TO find Henry after the caravan unpacked, but Edwin lured him away until the early morning hours with food and drink. No warm bed. Their playfulness extended to games of chance only. Now, after many had been to morning mass, and with the sun struggling to bleed through gray clouds, he'd found Henry's tent.

Settling on Roger's cot, Stephan watched the servant fold and stow Henry's woollen blanket. The boy proceeded from one chore to the next, and finally sat next to Stephan to remove the dirt that muddied his master's boots.

"That is good work you do, Roger," Stephan said, making up for all the times he'd not thanked the men and women who'd served his family.

The compliment made Roger brush the boot all the harder. "Thank you, my lord."

"When I was twelve, I became a squire in the Earl of Huntingdon's household. I had to shine mail, clean boots and brush down the knights' coursers. It is hard work."

"You were a servant?"

Stephan remembered that Henry hadn't followed the same path to knighthood. His father, Lord Edward, had hired a tutor to educate both Henry and his younger sister Beatrice. Both could read and write Latin and French, and were versed in music, mathematics, and in the art of warfare. And unlike many knights, Henry was quite adept with the bow.

"Aye, that is part of a squire's training in a large household."

Henry stepped over a puddle between the two beds. It hadn't been there when the tent was raised. Steady rain during the night created sapling-thin streams and pools of water throughout the camp.

Sitting across from Stephan, Henry tugged on a clean pair of boots, waving away Roger's help. "Have you spoken to the king?" he asked. "Will we be here long?"

"I have not seen him yet." Stephan wondered what he'd said to make Henry think he was privy to the king's inner circle. "But I found my friend Robin. He tells me that Richard and his advisors have been in council these last two days. There is to be a meeting with King Philip in Vézelay. We shall be here until midsummer's day, if not beyond."

"That long?" Henry's voice cracked with disappointment. "I thought we would see Outremer by summer's end."

Roger nodded, apparently under the same impression.

"You have been listening to camp gossip."

"I should only pay heed to you?"

"Of course!"

"But you've not yet spoken to the king. Can I trust your word?" Henry laughed.

Stephan treasured Henry's sense of humour and was glad of the friendship that had grown between them. The impression he'd left with the young lord from Lincolnshire that night in Southampton could have plunged any chance for friendship into the depths of the cold waters between England and Barfleur. Yet Henry stood by him.

The muddy road outside Henry's tent bustled with tradesmen selling their wares. Women called out, peddling warmed baked breads and meat pies. That aroma couldn't hide the smell of animals damp from the rains. Silver clinked as it exchanged hands. There was a clank of swords nearby. A practice drill had begun.

Stephan cocked his head towards the noise. "I hear we are near four thousand strong. With all the wagons, progress will be slow. Do you know how far it is to Marseille?"

"No," Henry said.

"Nor do I."

Henry's brow crinkled and Stephan laughed. He was being honest. His campaigns with Richard had never taken him that far south. "Robin will know."

Outside, a trumpet blared. Stephan recoiled. Henry was startled, too, but his eyes had locked on Stephan's face. Just as quickly, Henry turned away.

"It will take weeks to travel south," Stephan added. "Nobles must be cajoled. The king must ensure his lands remain in good hands whilst he is away. They collect his taxes after all. And more than a few shillings will be needed to feed and support this army. Those who remain loyal may be rewarded when he returns."

Henry scoffed. "I seek no reward. Those of us who have taken the Cross will have God's gift of eternal salvation. That will be more than I deserve."

Stephan hated to think how such noble intentions might be shattered when Henry learned the true nature of war. He worried for his friend. "For your sake," he said, "that is one thing I hope the priests speak true."

"You should not make them all out to be evil," Henry chided. "Many are good, devout men. What did Jesus say— judge not, that ye be not judged."

"I do not judge. I only curse their foul words." Stephan rubbed his temples. Thinking about priests made his head ache. "Enough. Robin is anxious to meet you. He has invited us to sup with him."

Henry chuckled. "Does the man know you have placed him on a pedestal?"

"Have I?" Stephan thought of the times he'd mentioned Robin when he spoke of past campaigns. Henry was right. Robin had served Richard near nine years and was a great knight. "Do not tell him. His ego is as high as the clouds as it is."

Henry grinned. "That explains why the two of you get along so well. If yours were any higher it would touch the stars."

Stephan pointed to himself. "Me?"

Henry cocked an eyebrow and whistled innocently. He turned to his servant. "Roger, deliver the washing to Maude when you are done here."

"Yes, my lord," Roger said, looking up without skipping a beat as he brushed a stubborn spot on Henry's boot.

Henry ruffled the boy's hair. Stephan studied the exchange between master and servant. Roger understood his duty. He'd tend to Henry's every need. But Henry, only five years older, looked after the boy. He'd have done so even if Roger's mother hadn't made him swear her son would come to no harm.

Henry stood and stretched. "Robin must be curious of news from Lincolnshire."

"I would not be so certain of that," Stephan said, remembering the few times Robin had spoken of home. "I know little of Robin's life in England but I do know he and his father did not part on good terms."

Henry caught the puzzled expression on Roger's face. "Did I not tell you that Sir Robin grew up in Ringsthorpe?"

"But Sir Stephan calls him Robin du Louviers, my lord."

"A title bestowed upon him by the king," Stephan said. "His father is a carpenter named William. And Robin was called Robert when he was younger. Do you know him?"

"The carpenter William has the biggest shop in the village! I do remember…" Roger looked from Henry to Stephan as a child would, wondering if his words might bring him trouble. He cleared his throat. "Robert—er, Robin was a show-off."

"He still is!" Stephan laughed, nearly choking.

Roger blushed furiously. "Apologies, my lord. I speak out of turn." He shifted his attention back to the stain on Henry's boot and feverishly worked the soft leather.

Henry pursed his lips to conceal his amusement. "You remember him? You were a small child when Robin left England."

"Aye, my lord. At least, it must be the same Robin. There's only one carpenter named William in the village. I remember him chasing Robin with a switch." Roger placed Henry's cleaned boot beneath the cot. He bit his lip, looking askance between the two knights before summoning the courage to speak. "When I was little, I wanted to be like the older boys. I followed Robin and his friends everywhere."

Stephan nodded. He'd done the same with his older brothers.

Henry's brow narrowed. "You overheard things?"

"Aye. Robin had nothing kind to say of his da'." Roger folded the cleaning cloth, stared at it a moment. A wry grin crossed his face at other memories. "Robin climbed higher, shot better, ran faster. Impressed the girls."

Stephan chuckled. "That is Robin."

Henry tapped Roger's chest. "You'll not speak of this to anyone."

"No, I would not, my lord."

Stephan stood up and looked pointedly at Roger. "Hand Sir Henry his blade."

"You expect trouble?" Henry asked.

"You and I will share a few ales with Robin," Stephan said as Roger handed Henry his sword belt. He ran a hand along his own scabbard. "We shall see if he has fond memories of home."

Henry adjusted the belt round his waist. "Will we?"

Stephan smiled broadly. "Carefully," he said and pounded Henry's back. "With any luck, Robin will not desire to cross swords when you speak of his father."

Worry crossed Henry's face. "Truly?" he asked.

"One of two things—mayhap he becomes drunk and melancholy, or he shall be angry and lash out at anyone within reach of his blade." When that didn't appease Henry's consternation, Stephan laughed. "Do not worry, my friend. It will be fine. We shall ply him with ale, get him to sing. You think *I* cannot carry a tune? Wait until you hear Robin."

Stephan sidestepped the puddle in the tent and ventured outside. Henry brushed past him. The smell of roasting meat from the pavilion wasn't nearly as intoxicating as the scent of sweat and grime of Henry. Stephan booted that thought from his mind and struck off after his friend.

Stacks of hay lined a section of the road leading towards the pavilion. Two boys bounded from one bale to another and onto a wagon. The wagonmaster shouted, "Out of here!" Nimble-footed, the boys sprang across a narrow gap, landing on a second cart.

Stephan laughed at their antics until the urchins leaped again and careened into Henry.

Henry staggered back. The smaller dark-haired boy caught his arm. "Sorry, my lord," he said, vigorously brushing non-existent dirt from Henry's clothes. The older of the two, a blond with green eyes, reached out to help.

Henry didn't feel the hand slide beneath his cloak but he felt the tug at his belt, saw the blur of the withdrawn hand and a blade. The boys shot away. "Thief!" he cried.

Stephan shouted, "Stop them!" and was on their heels with Henry a few steps behind.

The boys darted through the crowds. Carts toppled. Vegetables spilled to the ground. Onions, leeks, and some green and yellowish things disappeared into many a bystander's tunic as Stephan and Henry zigzagged past the mess. Curses flew through the air like arrows.

The blond boy drove into a lanky fellow with curly red hair. The man hit a puddle face first, sending clods of mud into the air. It splattered the well-endowed breast of a modestly-dressed woman. She shrieked and staggered back directly into the other thief's path. Arms windmilling, unable to stop, the boy plowed into her. She toppled into the mud with an unladylike oath. Entangled in her skirts, the boy landed on top of her. He waved his fleeing comrade onward. "Allan, run!" he cried.

Stephan hurdled over the bodies on the ground. The blond thief slowed, glanced back. His eyes flickered between Stephan and his friend. Stephan overtook him and grabbed his scrawny neck. He dragged the boy back to his accomplice and seized a fistful of dark, greasy hair.

"Ow, ow, ow!" the smaller boy whimpered when Stephan yanked him to his feet.

"God's blood, let us go!" Allan shouted.

Struggling, the boys tried to squirm away. Stephan held them tight.

Henry stopped to help the woman in the mud. When he caught up to Stephan he looked disapprovingly at the thieves, one hand firmly wrapped around the hilt of his sword.

Stephan presented his catch to Henry like they were fish hooked on a line. "These young ones found your purse, good sir."

"Found—?" Henry stared at Stephan, astonished.

Stephan was all for justice but there'd been no great harm done, just a couple of muddied pilgrims. The thieves had been caught with the purse. Henry lost nothing. *They are so young. No need for them to lose a hand—or worse.*

"Lad?" Stephan interrupted Henry. His voice was stern. His fingers raked into Allan's stringy golden hair and gave it a jerk.

The boy winced. "Yes, m' lord." Grubby hands produced a deep green pouch from a torn and ragged shirt. Trembling, he held his haul out to Henry.

Henry's eyes were fiery.

"Why, look, Sir Henry," Stephan exclaimed. "Never thought you might see that again, did you? No need for a hanging today."

Henry looked up sharply, blinked as if he'd been struck by some revelation.

Stephan took a deep breath. The boys did the same.

Henry palmed the purse, eyes cutting between Stephan and the thieves. He looked every bit the noble ready to pass judgment, to insist they be dragged away and locked in irons. Placing his hands in the small of his back he paced back and forth then finally paused before the smaller boy. "Actions like these will not be forgotten."

He sidestepped, placing himself directly in Allan's face. "When times are hard, it is easy to fall into habits that might lead you to the stocks or cause the loss of a hand. It would be a shame for that fate to meet two bright young men such as yourselves." He looked from one to the other. "Good deeds should be rewarded. A man should be thankful for what he has, grateful to those who help him." Digging into the purse, Henry handed the boy a coin.

Stephan released them, pleased that his faith in Henry's goodness hadn't been tarnished.

The boys looked at the sparkling coin, at each other, then at Henry. "Thank you, sir. Thank you!"

"No more stealing," Stephan said.

"No, sir knight," the younger boy said, trying to make himself more presentable by combing a hand through his dark hair.

"Won't need to, not with this," Allan said, fingering the coin. "I can double it soon as I find a game of dice."

Stephan shook his head. "You might lose it, boy."

"Go," Henry said. "Help pick up that mess you made, and then go home." Henry's face turned gentle with a smile that made Stephan shiver.

"Allan never loses," the younger boy called back as they scampered up the road.

"Stay out of trouble," Henry shouted.

Stephan clapped Henry's back. "You are a good man."

Securing the purse on his sword belt, Henry looked past Stephan towards the guards manning the castle towers. "I am not so certain that's true. Those two boys are old enough to know right from wrong. I was ready to see them both punished."

"But you were merciful, Henry. You let them go."

Henry rubbed his brow. "There was a thief in Southampton. He was younger, but God's bone, those two looked like him. Ragged, filthy clothes. Thin and hungry-looking. A soldier nearly caught that one. There would have been nothing I could do but follow the law. I might not have been so kind today had your actions—your words—not reminded me that there are times when we can do something. Forgiveness is the true telling of a man." Henry found Stephan's eyes. "Let me thank you, sir."

Stephan bowed. "I believe in second chances. They will mend their ways."

"I had not seen this side of you." Henry smiled again. "I like it. *You* are the good man."

Stephan felt heat rise in his cheeks, glad his skin was flushed by the dash through the camp. His heart was pounding. "Watch those sweet words, Sir Henry," he teased, trying to make himself believe that too was from the chase.

Henry feinted a punch and laughed.

Stephan cocked his head in the direction the boys had disappeared. "You told them to go home. Their accents. They are English. I think this *is* home."

"Camp-followers?" Henry asked. The boys would be two of hundreds, many who earned a barely passable wage performing odd jobs like washing clothes or cleaning out the animal pens. "Do you think they crossed the sea with their families?"

"That or stowed away, figuring they would live off scraps and thieving." Stephan steered Henry towards the pavilion. "Robin will wonder what has kept us. He is anxious to see your skills with sword and bow."

"I thought we were to dine."

"Yes, of course."

Henry tugged him back. "What have you been telling him?"

Stephan nocked an imaginary arrow and pulled back on his imaginary bow. "That we worked on technique whilst on the road from Barfleur but you are nowhere near as good a shot as me."

"What?"

"It's true." Stephan tried to suppress a grin. "And Robin is a far better archer and swordsman than I will ever be. We both have much to learn."

Henry laughed and shoved Stephan, and they weaved their way through the crowds.

~ ~ ~

"SIR HENRY." ROBIN BOWED.

He was taller than Stephan. Broad through the chest and shoulders. And weaponless, Henry noted.

"I am honoured, Sir Robin."

"Stephan said a knight named de Grey from Lincolnshire had befriended him. I know your father, Henry." Robin cast a wary glance from Stephan to Henry. "Choose your friends carefully, my lord."

Stephan pressed his hands to his heart. "You wound me, sir," he said, feigning a mortal injury, and then laughed, his shoulders shaking.

Long trestles lined the crowded tent. Henry stared at the lavish spread. He'd not seen so much chicken, pork, and beef, dried and fresh fruits, and biscuits since the great banquets after the king's coronation. The air smelled of garlic, ginger and spices he didn't recognize. His mouth watered when a serving girl placed a basket of warm bread in front of him. He grabbed the loaf and ripped off a piece. The leg of roasted chicken he culled from the platter of meats dripped with a thick brown sauce.

Robin wasted no time filling his trencher. His blue eyes followed the girl making her way past hands that weren't just reaching for food. Her girlish squeals and the clanking of platters and goblets shifted his attention back to his friends.

Henry took a bite of chicken and chewed, and then pointed the leg at Robin. "Greyton is only a few miles from Ringsthorpe. It is odd our paths never crossed."

Robin shrugged. "I was a mere carpenter's son. You, a noble, heir to a grand estate."

"Grand, is it? You never told me that," Stephan said.

Henry waved him off.

"You are also a year or two younger," Robin added.

Stephan laughed again. "A year? Didn't we celebrate your twenty-seventh summer October last?"

Robin chucked a chunk of bread at Stephan. Stephan elbowed Henry. "I may be a braggart but you must watch this one closely."

Robin and Stephan lifted their ales. Both took long swigs, eyeing each other over the rim of their mugs like two competitors racing to see who'd finish first. Empty goblets smacked the table at the same moment. In unison, they swiped their arms across their mouths then pressed fists together.

Henry washed down the chicken with a gulp of ale, envious of the knights' easy friendship. He tipped his mug towards

Robin. "My father told me of your skills with bow. He'd seen you win first prize at a festival."

Robin nodded. "Lord Edward presented me with one piece of silver for winning that contest. I used it to buy a horse to leave Ringsthorpe."

Robin's voice held no regret, no animosity. Henry doubted Robin might grow angry if William Carpenter's name came up, but he shifted slightly to check one last time that no sword hung at the knight's waist before venturing down that path. "My bow was made by your father's hands."

Stephan stilled beside him.

Robin stared into his empty goblet. He let out a long sigh. "Then you have the best-made bow in England, no, in all the king's realms." He looked up. "My father is a fine bow maker and a skilled carpenter. He was disappointed I had no desire to take up his trade."

Henry refilled their ales. "I would have brought news of your family had I known you served King Richard."

A shadow seeped into Robin's eyes. He turned away, his hay-coloured hair falling around his face. "My father would have nothing to say to me."

"Why? Because you left home?" Henry shook his head in disbelief. "He should be proud that you are one of the king's finest knights."

Stephan stabbed a piece of bread with his dagger. "Well spoken, my friend."

Robin pushed the food around his trencher. The serving girl he'd been watching a moment earlier ran her hand along his back. She leaned past him to grab the empty tankard. Her generous bosom brushed his arm but he didn't seem to see her, nor feel the squeeze she gave his shoulder.

"Do not trouble yourself with my father," Robin said.

Henry gave an impatient snort. "I shall set him straight when I return to England. Mayhap you will accompany me?"

"I have no reason to return except..." Robin's voice softened. "There was a beautiful young maiden. I am certain she has long since married, has a child or two at her knee. You might know her. Marian Fitzwalter."

"Fitzwalter?" Henry frowned, trying to place the name. "There is a Marian in my father's household these last six years. She'd left the village some eight or nine years past to marry but when she returned to become my mother's maid, she was a widow."

"Nine years?" Robin's face showed he was turning the numbers round in his head as Henry did. That would have been the same time he'd left England. "Would she have dark hair and deep brown eyes? Round, rosy cheeks, and long fingers as delicate as a flower?"

"I cannot say that I looked at her in quite that way, but aye, her hair is dark." Henry thought of Marian as a sister. She was older and had a child. Robin's description made Henry think of other girls in the village. Heat crawled up his neck. At fourteen, he'd tried to convince his father he was in love with one of them and was summarily reminded of his responsibilities as future lord. "These peasant women are sprung from Eve, the great temptress," his father had lectured sternly. "It would be far too easy to fall prey to them and breed bastards." It was good Lord Edward had been in Lincoln the day before when Henry had lost his virginity to a pretty green-eyed maid with ginger hair.

Robin chuckled at Henry's discomfort. "Marian has a mark," he pointed to a spot beside his nose, "here."

Henry nodded slowly. "She does."

"It must be her." A pained expression suddenly crossed Robin's face. "A widow? Poor Marian. I loved her. Never had a chance to good-bye. She must despise me. I have no reason to return to Greyton. She is better off without me."

Henry took a deep breath. "She has a child who just passed eight summers. A boy…named Robert."

Robin stared at Henry. "What?" His eyes narrowed, his breathing grew rapid.

Henry drew back. He looked nervously from Stephan to Robin, checking a third time that the knight had no sword.

Robin stood abruptly. He lunged across the table. Food spilled from his trencher and ale splattered. He fisted his hands in the fabric of Henry's tunic and jerked him upright. "Are you sure? Eight years you say?"

Stephan jumped up. He grasped at Robin's arms, ready to separate his two friends.

Flustered, Henry choked out an "Aye."

Robin released his hold on Henry and dropped back into the chair. He plastered his hands to his face. Henry and Stephan sat down slowly, exchanging worried glances.

Robin looked more incredulous than angry. "I have a son."

"Can you be sure he is your own?"

"Surely she would have told you?" Stephan asked.

"That boy is my own blood. I know this. Henry says Marian left after I did—" Robin grinned. "A son."

Robin reached for the heavy-bosomed girl who'd come up behind him with a new jug of ale. He kissed her soundly on the mouth then turned and set Henry's goblet upright. He poured more ale for each of them.

Stephan offered a toast. "To Robin and his son!" he shouted. "To King Richard! To the men of the Cross!"

The knights in the pavilion raised their mugs. They cheered and drank. "God bless the king!" "Jerusalem! Jerusalem!" They shouted until their voices grew hoarse and the candles sputtered and the night fell.

east from Tours
june-july 1190

five

AWARE OF THE HOOFBEATS of a half dozen coursers at his back, Henry spurred Sombre within a boot's width of the cart near the far end of the tourney field. He gripped the reins tightly, determined to skim as close as possible to the next obstacle on the course. His shook his hair away from his eyes, pressed low on Sombre's back, and felt the rush of the wind against his face. Just like racing against his sister Bea along the old Roman Road to Lincoln, hearing his parents shouting for them to hold back.

Banners of gold, red, and green marked the course, stretching the length of a pasture. Tournaments testing the knights' skills sprang up without planning on days when the army made camp well before the sun set. Everyone welcomed the break. The slow-moving caravan bred boredom. A broken wagon wheel or a cart mired in mud could be the highlight of the day, and the pilgrims took bets to see how quickly strong-armed men could mend a problem.

Nobles and common folk lined the course and blurred past Henry's vision. Shouts made him turn. Stephan beat the track six lengths back, but Ancel of Hertfordshire flew only a few paces behind Henry. Ancel had given rein to his Spanish stallion and might be the only one to catch him. But a sheen of sweat gleamed on his courser's neck, his ears flattened when heels dug into his flanks.

Henry knew Sombre well. The three-year-old destrier responded to his slightest movements. The narrow turn at the far end of the course was child's play. Henry spurred Sombre and stretched his lead at a full gallop.

Cheers resounded across the valley. Henry charged towards the Lionheart's banners that signaled the finish. He took one last look back. Ancel and Stephan had lost ground to him. He crossed the finish line with Roger whooping and hollering. "That's my master!"

Henry jumped from Sombre. He stroked the animal's snout, and then tossed the reins to Roger.

Stephan and Ancel were neck and neck coming towards the finish.

Henry squirmed to the front of the crowd, cupped his hands round his mouth to cheer. "Go, Stephan! To victory!"

Stephan shot past the last banner a few moments later. He leaped from Tempête, nuzzled his neck. Tugging the gloves from his sweaty hands, he strode up to Henry. His eyes gleamed as he pounded Henry's back. "Well done, Sir."

"Look at us, one and two," Henry said as others congratulated them.

"Now, my question, can you shoot an arrow and hit a target whilst at a full gallop?"

Henry nodded. "That will be the true test."

"Aye. One that might keep us alive." Stephan pointed towards the food and drink stalls, most serving from wagons hastily arranged to take advantage of the festival atmosphere. "Let's get an ale to celebrate your win, and then we shall see just how good you are."

"I'd be lucky to nock an arrow and hold my bow straight, let alone hit a mark, if you get me drunk."

"Me? Get you drunk? I would never do such a thing." Stephan winked. "Who'd carry me back to my tent?"

"A sign of true friendship."

"Indeed."

Stephan dragged Henry towards the ale cart.

~ ~ ~

THEY'D HAD THEIR ALE to celebrate Henry's victory and within moments the sky opened sending all the revelers scrambling to find cover. Stephan and Henry retired to the king's pavilion with a score of other knights. King Richard had not returned from a hunting expedition in the woods nearby, but squires and servants had scrounged up succulent venison and lamb and laid them out on one of the long trestles. The fire had been warm, the food plentiful, and the games exhilarating though Stephan lost at chess—twice.

"Mayhap you should give up the game," Henry said.

Broad-shouldered William of Abingdon slapped Stephan's back and laughed. "Listen to Henry. But dice? You've not played with me since we left Tours."

Henry looked between the knights. He'd learned that "play" might have multiple meanings and merely smiled shyly. "I cannot watch you lose another penny," he said. "I bid you goodnight."

"Victory!" Stephan shouted as Will turned him round and steered him to the dice table. Will plopped down beside Stephan and fingered the cubes as a crowd gathered. He tossed them with a quick flick of his wrist. Their audience groaned at Will's first roll, but cheered at Stephan's pair of fours. Ultimately, Stephan won, but that might have been because Will's hand was more interested in the muscles of Stephan's thigh than in the toss of wooden cubes. Stephan thought his own restraint admirable, especially when Robin stopped to talk and Will grew more daring in his exploration. Stephan was more than ready when other knights departed for the evening or bedded down in the pavilion and Will asked him back to his own tent.

Creaking wagons woke Stephan a few hours later. Will snored softly next to him, his hand resting at Stephan's waist. Stephan rose and shook off his exhaustion. He pulled on his hose and tunic and tugged aside the tent flap. Yawning, he stretched in the cool morning air. He wagged his head to clear it, tried to focus on the hum of activities around him. Where one tent after another lined the road five or six deep in both directions when he'd gone to bed, there now were empty, trampled plots of dirt. Hundreds of tents had been dismantled. A few campfires smoked and sizzled with breakfast but goods had been stowed and the pilgrims were making ready for one more day on the road.

Stephan called over his shoulder. "Will, get out of bed and I shall help you pack up the tent. We'll be left behind."

A horse whinnied and Stephan turned. The young thief from Tours came around the side of Will's tent. He held Tempête's reins out to Stephan. "I saddled him up for you, my lord."

Stephan eyed the boy suspiciously—what mischief was this? Straightening, he walked toward boy and horse, inspecting Tempête from nose to haunches. He stroked the destrier's neck. He checked the saddle, pleased to see the boy had tightened the straps perfectly. His saddle bag was packed tightly. Had the thief replaced its contents with useless rubbish?

Allan looked wounded. "It's all there, my lord, including two pennies loose at the bottom."

An honest thief, Stephan thought. Still, what was he after? "Sorting through my bag, were you?"

"Just to pull the wineskin you'd stuffed there. You'll need some ale on the march today."

"I do not remember asking you to see to Tempête."

"You did not, my lord. Me and Little John saw you speaking with the one they call Sir Robin last night. Heard that you were to ride at the vanguard this morn."

Stephan slapped his thigh. "Christ!" He gaped at the eastern edge of the valley where wagons were already kicking up dust.

"Sir Robin was looking for you when the sun came up. Told him we'd hurry you along. I talked it over with Little John. We thought it best to retrieve your horse first and then wake you."

"Little John?"

"My friend."

"The dark-haired lad?"

"Aye, my lord," Allan said, pointing to the boy peeking out from behind a nearby wagon. Little John held chunks of bread and cheese out to Stephan.

"Wait right here." Stephan hurried back into the tent. "Will?" He shook the naked knight and then tossed him a grey tunic carelessly thrown to the ground when they'd come in during the night. He slipped his surcoat over his head and then found his sword belt beneath Will's cloak. "There are two boys outside," he said as he secured the belt round his waist. "I shall give them a coin to help you. Mayhap one can find your squire."

"It cannot be daylight."

"It is, and Robin is waiting for me."

"I hardly slept, no thanks to you."

"Complain, will you? See if I warm your bed again." Stephan grabbed his cloak. Outside, he handed Allan a half penny. "You heard?"

"We shall help Sir William with his things."

"Good. Then I shall be off."

Allan handed him Tempête's reins and fingered the frayed edge of Stephan's cloak. "Little John is good at mending, my lord. He knows how to smooth the nicks in a sword, and shine it so bright that it might blind someone who intends you harm."

"And you know horses."

"That and much more, my lord. I would be glad to teach you a trick or two at the games."

"You were watching me at the pavilion last night?"

"Aye. You should be wary playing that knight from Rotherham."

"Oh?"

"He cheats."

"You know how to beat a cheater, do you?"

"Aye, my lord."

"Allan, is it?"

"Aye."

Stephan encouraged Little John to come forward. He ripped a chunk of bread from the loaf in the boy's hand. "Thank you." He bit into the bread, studying the two boys. Rough around the edges. Thin and filthy. But this Allan—he had some useful talents. And a good heart. He could have escaped from Stephan in that chase, but he'd slowed down, concerned about his dark-haired friend. Stephan imagined he'd learn if Allan exaggerated Little John's skills in time. "Find me when we camp for the night," he told the boys. "I have a job or two you might help with." He mounted Tempête and pivoted towards the vanguard. Pressing his heels to the horse, he called back, "And I just might take you up on those tricks."

~ ~ ~

THE WARM DAYS OF June turned warmer in July. The pilgrims—crusaders some would call them—packed up their city each morning and lumbered closer to Vézelay, which lay more than one hundred fifty miles east of Tours. Henry wished an army could move faster. He understood the need for the kings to meet there, but it only meant more delays on the road to Jerusalem.

The routine of the march made Roger happy, even if it did mean packing and unpacking Henry's belongings every day. Roger had found friends amongst the other servant boys. He shared camp gossip with Henry in between a never-ending barrage of questions, most of which Henry could not answer.

"Ralf—"

"From Sussex?" Henry interrupted.

"No, my lord. Bernard is from Sussex. Ralf is from Wiltshire." Roger slid the brush beneath Sombre's mane and stroked downward, repeating the move along the horse's neck. "His master told him that there are no trees in Outremer. The land is sparse and brown. And when the wind blows, the ground appears to move."

Sombre chewed on the grain in Henry's hand. "Moving ground?" Henry asked. "How can that be? Mayhap it is like the leaves blowing across the roads at home."

Roger looked past Henry's shoulder. A lush green forest surrounded the camp. "I cannot imagine a place without trees."

Henry rubbed his hands to dust off the last traces of feed. "I think we will see trees there." He palmed Sombre's forehead, looking up when two young girls skipped past. Arms linked, the dark-haired beauties studied him and Roger, their whispers caught on the breeze.

For a moment, Henry's thoughts turned to home. He remembered the quiet places there. He and Alys would lie on a hillside and watch clouds drift overhead, listening to birdsong and the buzz of insects. They shared their first kiss on one of those lazy summer afternoons. It was barely a peck on the lips, yet Henry—who'd turned eighteen that day—hoped for a sign of her feelings and his own. She'd giggled, shy, twitched her nose, and then scurried away. From his own observations of courtship rituals and his limited experience with the fairer sex, Henry thought that was good. Alys was but twelve after all. Still young. He watched her skip down the hill, felt nothing. Two years later, they tumbled playfully in the snow and Henry kissed her deeply. She'd studied his face a moment when he broke the kiss, and then sat up and began talking of her embroidery. Her stitching, by God! Henry tugged her back to the ground spiritedly. He kissed her again, wanting to feel passion and a fire in his groin. That memory would keep him whilst he was on crusade. But there was nothing in that kiss that stirred him.

Blacksmiths pounding metal at the forge brought him back to the camp. Animals in the corral snorted, cows bellowed and sheep nearby bleated a chorus. The silky voice of a troubadour suddenly echoed above the din of the tent city. Not quite birdsong, but Henry smiled.

The tempo of Roger's brush strokes slowed. He leaned slightly to get a look at the girls. They turned around, waving, and Roger returned their greeting. Sombre twisted to nip at his hand, reminding him who was boss.

Henry studied his servant. Roger was of an age when a girl would stir his feelings. Roger, like Henry, surely had been privy to the village boys' conversations about sex, but in Henry's experience those discussions rarely tied it to the Church's teachings. For good measure, Henry should sit the boy down like his father had done with him and talk about women and swiving.

Roger returned to his task to Henry's relief. "I liked the way the sun slipped down to meet the sea when we sailed," Roger said. "We never saw the sun on the horizon in Greyton."

"Wait until you tell these stories to your friends back home."

"I am glad you will be there, my lord, else they would call me a liar."

Henry heard a hint of worry in Roger's voice, but the boy just worked the brush along Sombre's back to his haunches. What else might they see on their travels that others would doubt?

He uncorked his wineskin and got a whiff of the sweet mead. He took a short gulp, wanting to save some of the day's ration for the long night ahead.

Up the road a path opened like Moses parting the sea. A young boy darted around people, sidestepped animals, carts, and equipment.

"Pardon, sir! Excuse me, ma'am!" The piercing voice echoed above the sounds of bartering, of gear being stowed or cleaned, of the smith working his trade. "Sir Henry!"

Henry eyed the boy. He'd not forgotten that face. It was the younger of the thieves who had stolen his purse in Tours. His dark brown hair looked clean and fell in waves around his face.

The boy grabbed an apple from a vendor's basket and flipped a coin at her. Vaulting over a bucket of feed, he tossed the apple to a little girl watching her mother chase an escaped chicken. In one swooping action, he captured the chicken and handed it to the woman before coming to a halt next to Henry.

"Sir Stephan sent me, my lord," the youngster said, trying to catch his breath.

"Are you running errands for him now?"

"Aye, my lord," he said with surprising enthusiasm. "And cleaning his boots and mail."

Henry eyed the boy's immaculate tunic and the black leggings that no longer bagged from his waist. Stephan had not only given him work to keep him from trouble, but also had outfitted him with new clothes. The knight was generous beyond measure.

"Good jobs for a young lad," Henry said. "What message have you from Sir Stephan?"

The boy squared his shoulders and took a deep breath, his face scrunched thoughtfully. "He said, 'remind Sir Henry that he had promised a game of chess in order that I might take his pennies one more time.' He is waiting for you at the pavilion, my lord."

Roger chuckled, drawing a smirk from Henry who fingered the pouch on his belt. "He is far too fond of my money. What is your name, boy?" Henry asked.

"John, my lord, but they call me Little John."

Henry looked him up and down. He was short and wiry but already looked like he'd added a bit of meat to his bones since they'd first run into each other. "How old are you?"

"Thirteen...I think."

Surprised, Henry frowned. He would've guessed ten. "You are small for so many summers."

"Aye, my lord. That's why they call me Little John."

Henry smiled. "Where is your friend? The one with the golden hair?"

"Master Stephan sent him off to help Sir Robin. Shall you come along with me now, sir, to let him have his go at you?"

"Have his go?" Henry sighed. "I must stop agreeing to these amusements with Sir Stephan. I cannot seem to win. It gets tiring."

Little John cleared his throat. "Allan is good at games, my lord. He often wins enough to buy us a meat pasty."

Henry smiled. "Why does that not surprise me?"

Little John shrugged. "He's already shown Master Stephan a trick or two. Mayhap he can teach you."

A breeze from the northwest pushed the scent of the cooks' fires to Henry's nose. Meat pasty. His stomach rumbled. The king's army would eat well tonight.

"Tell Sir Stephan he can share a meal with me first if he expects to get my coin."

Little John bowed. "Yes, my lord." He scrambled up the road, dodging in and out of the crowd.

"Roger, after you've stabled Sombre, enjoy the evening with your friends." Henry started past him towards the pavilion but stopped. "Do you miss home?"

Roger pressed his lips together. "Is it all right if I do, my lord?"

"Of course."

Roger sighed. "It feels so very far away. Sometimes I think I might never see it again. I miss my bed. And Mary's roasted lamb." He laughed. "I even miss your father's voice."

Henry ruffled Roger's hair. "So do I. So do I."

the River Rhone
10 july 1190

six

SOMBRE DRIFTED TOWARDS THE barely perceptible sound of water rushing over rocks. Henry caught a glimpse of the river when the trees aligned just so, and he understood the tempting call. He couldn't remember feeling so miserably hot. Dampness blanketed the air and clung to his skin. Sweat dripped down his neck. His tunic was soaked, plastered to his body. It was July and Vézelay was long behind them. By the end of month the army might reach Marseille, and finally sail towards the Holy Land.

Henry reached for his mead and took a gulp. The last drops dribbled onto his tongue.

"Have mine," Roger offered.

Riding abreast of Roger, Henry turned to take the flask. There was a flush on Roger's cheeks. His eyes were red, accentuated by dark circles beneath them. "You look like you need the drink more than me. Are you feeling well?"

Roger perked up but grimaced when he straightened in the saddle. "I am fine, my lord. We do not have warm days such as this at home." He took a deep draught of the cider he'd bartered for at breakfast.

"Warmer still when we get to Jerusalem," said a knight who overheard the conversation as he passed them on the road.

~ ~ ~

LITTLE JOHN FOLDED HIS arms across his chest. "He told me to wait right here, Allan. I'm not movin'."

Allan was quiet for a moment, his attention focused on tents rising on the opposite bank of the River Rhone. "Sir Stephan would tell you to come with me if he knew Master Robin already crossed the bridge. I could use a hand setting up his tent. You help me, and I'll help you with Sir Stephan's." He turned a roguish eye on Little John. "Mayhap buy you a pasty with my winnings from last night."

Little John's stomach growled, but he had his orders and ignored Allan's offer. "Look at them pilgrims. Packed so tight on the bridge they can barely move. All to find the driest spot for their tents. What's the hurry? A day or two and they will be packin' up again."

Allan scratched his head and nodded. "Where is this Marseille the knights keep talking about?"

"Too far," a squire with a blue and black surcoat called. His horse whinnied and tossed its head as another beast next to him balked and sidled into him. The squire's horse shifted, crowding a group of pilgrims. One man grabbed the side of a wagon and leapt aboard to the ire of the wagon driver, whose chickens bickered and clucked at the intrusion. Tempers were rising along with the heat of the day.

"Far, is it?" Allan asked.

"Days away or so I've heard." Little John made a map with his fist. He pointed to the space between two of his knuckles. "Sir Stephan said this is where our boat landed." Tracing a line to his wrist, he said, "And Marseille is way down here."

"That's a long way. But look at us." Allan beamed. "Serving two great knights. Honest jobs. I'll never go back to thievin' again." He clapped Little John on the back. "I'm off to find Master Robin."

Little John watched his golden-haired friend dart past a blacksmith's wagon. Little John lost sight of him amongst the crowds on the bridge. Allan was right. What incredible fortune they'd had. The London streets they'd once roamed were just bad memories.

~ ~ ~

"MAYHAP WE CAN TAKE a plunge in the river after we get the camp set," Henry said, looking through the trees towards the water rushing downstream.

"That would feel heavenly, my lord." Roger blinked away the sweat in his eyes. "Is that Sir Stephan?"

Stephan trotted in their direction. He'd been spending most of his days with Robin and others in the vanguard at King Richard's side. He appeared to have some official business today, inspecting the state of the caravan and sharing a word or two with other knights and the common folk. His face lit when he laughed at someone's joke. He had such an easy way with everyone.

Stephan saw Henry and spurred Tempête. "A few more days and we shall see the blue waters of Marseille," he said after drawing rein beside him. He took in a deep breath. "I can almost smell the harbour. Remember Southampton?"

"Dead fish along the wharfs?" Henry scrunched his nose remembering some of the rancid odors.

Roger's face mirrored his and then he sneezed. "Worse than pig slop, my lord," he said.

"You had better get used to that smell," Stephan said.

Henry grimaced. "I know, I know. Marseille, Naples, Messina, Acre. All sit by the sea."

Dark clouds blotted out the sun. The wind picked up and Roger shivered. Henry looked at him worriedly. It wasn't just the heat that brought that flush to his servant's face. He glanced skyward, hoping the rain would hold for Roger's sake until they'd set up their tent for the night.

Stephan pointed down the road. "The king's pavilion will be on the other side of the river. We must suffer another meeting between our liege lord and King Philip. Another ceremony," he said sarcastically. His disdain for politics—or was it just for the French king—rivaled Henry's.

Tempête pawed the road, his head cutting the air with the same impatience his rider showed. "Calm, fiery one," Stephan told the warhorse. "You like Philip Capet as much as the Lionheart does."

Henry chuckled. "Who dislikes who more?"

The rivalries, wars, and alliances between the king of France and the Plantagenets existed long before King Richard took the throne. Richard's betrothal to Philip's half sister, arranged some twenty-one years earlier and still not consummated, was only one rift between the rulers.

Stephan soothed Tempête with gentle strokes to his neck. "At least we will soon hear plans for the next part of our journey." He stretched in the saddle and looked at Roger. "You do not look well."

"It is nothing, my lord."

Stephan eyed him skeptically, frowning. "I will have Little John find a healer and send him round after we set up camp."

Stephan's compassion touched Henry. Before Henry could thank him, Stephan added, "You must be strong to serve your master's needs in the Holy Land."

"Yes, my lord."

Stephan turned back to Henry. "I am jealous."

Henry wondered if he should expect a tease, but there was none of the usual mischievousness in Stephan's look. "Of what?" he asked.

"You may think I came to while away the time in idle chat about politics, but I am here to deliver a message to you from Robin."

Henry raised a brow. Roger shot Henry a *should-I-ride-ahead* look. Neither of the men waved him off.

"He has been bragging about your skills." Stephan's voice remained nonchalant. "The king has invited you to dine at his pavilion tonight."

Roger grinned broadly.

"Me?" Henry had seen King Richard many times since Tours but never spoke with him, let alone shared a meal. He felt a thrill that lasted all of two heartbeats. "But I am no better than you."

Stephan threw his hands in the air. "I told Robin the same thing. He reminded me that the king already knows of my *superb* prowess with sword and bow."

They laughed but Henry felt awkward. "You have fought alongside him for years."

Stephan's eyes blazed, caught by sunlight piercing the clouds. "I was at Ballan when the old king surrendered to him. And before that at—" He shook his head. "No matter. Robin is right. The king knows your family has lands near those Count John has been granted in Nottinghamshire. It's all in the game. You will be one of King Richard's closest allies before this pilgrimage is said and done. He will need your loyalty when we return to England."

"He need not invite me to dinner to gain my allegiance. He is our king, Stephan."

"Somehow I knew you would say that." Stephan studied the long train of wagons coming up behind them to cross the river. "We shall follow him to Outremer and do all manner of good things in his name. Let us pray that our swords are true and that Saracen arrows bounce off our shields like the rays of the sun."

Henry's heartbeat quickened. Stephan's words made Henry feel like Saladin would fall to his knees before them.

~ ~ ~

CANTANKEROUS AND JOSTLING EACH other after another long day, the pilgrims crammed the road like cows being herded through narrow streets. What had been an orderly progression became a jam of wagons, pack animals and people. The width of the road shrunk on the approach to the bridge. The humans complained more loudly than the animals, their scowls and curses increasing in intensity, as the crush grew tighter.

Little John twitched at the thought of being pressed from all sides. His chest tightened and he realised there was a change in the air. It grew still. Not a sound could be heard except for wheels grinding against wooden slats.

A low rumble sounded. Little John glanced towards the overcast skies. The noise drummed again.

"That's not thunder," he said.

Crack!

It was the sound of timber splitting.

A half-mile behind Little John, Tempête shifted. He brushed Sombre's flank. Henry and Stephan stared at the hills listening to the echo of that rumble. It didn't fade like thunder but grew to a dull roar. Mules brayed and caged hens clucked. Shouts rang out. Boots pounded the ground. The world seemed to tremble. Panicked screams resonated from the caravan, sweeping up from the river crossing. Suddenly there was an ugly crash, then another, like trees in the forest being felled. But the noise wasn't coming from the hillsides or the skies.

Roger's face paled.

"My God," Henry cried.

"The king!" Stephan dug his spurs into Tempête and charged towards the vanguard.

"Stay here," Henry told Roger. He took off at a gallop after Stephan.

The bridge over the Rhône River was collapsing, taking tradesmen, knights and men-at-arms, horses and wagons, with it.

~ ~ ~

LITTLE JOHN KNEW THE cry of a wounded animal in the forests back home. He'd heard the wail of a mother at her son's hanging. But he'd never heard shrieks of sheer terror like those from the people plunging into the swollen river far below. Wagons shattered as they hit the surface. Baggage and war supplies floated downriver.

Allan! Little John took off at a dead run. His eyes scoured every face, from the pilgrims on the far bank of the river, to those still scrambling in both directions. Like a pack of wild animals they kicked, shoved, and shouted. Little John didn't call on God's help often, but he asked Him to let Allan be safe.

Fighting through a current of people racing in the opposite direction, he ignored the curses, ignored those appealing to the good Lord. He clambered towards the section of the bridge that collapsed. The remnants of the wooden frame shook. Another loud crack bent the air and one of the remaining pine trusses splintered.

The earth rolled beneath Little John's feet reminding him of waves tossing the boat on the crossing from England. The smell of rotted wood and the sight of so much destruction made him gag.

Little John grabbed the side of a wagon to steady himself. He pressed closer to the precipice. One beam hung precariously, groaning as it splintered by a finger's width every second.

"Hurry." A woman screeched at her husband, who struggled to save the contents of their cart. Pots and racks and a huge piece of dried, salted meat flew past her head towards solid ground. "Get out! We don't need no more."

Her husband paid no mind to her pleas, determined to save his goods before their cart tumbled to the water below.

Little John ducked when a stew pot whooshed within inches of his head. A coarse woollen blanket hit him square in the face. He tossed it aside and swayed, thrown off balance as the bridge dipped. Animals nearby suddenly quieted. Little John heard the wood crack over the woman's screams. The cart slid towards the edge. He grabbed her, pulling her to safety. Her husband jumped as the cart turned vertical.

"Thomas!" she cried.

The man's boot swiped the jagged edge of the bridge but he got no foothold. He reached out, hands grasping for anything, fingernails digging into rough wood.

Ignoring his own danger, Little John bolted towards him, dove to the ground, and captured his wrists.

"Help them," the woman shouted.

Hands damp with sweat, Little John grunted. Thomas was not a huge man, but he was taller and heavier than Little John. Sword practice with Sir Stephan had strengthened him. Muscles in his back, stomach, and arms tightened as Thomas' fingers started to slip. His arms burned but he imagined Thomas' hand was the hilt of his sword, the river the enemy, and he held fast. He felt himself begin to slide after the heavier man. He hooked his foot in the wheel of a heavy wagon on the road behind him. Just as he thought his arms might be ripped from his shoulders, someone grabbed his calves.

~ ~ ~

PANICKED PEOPLE AND ANIMALS backed away from the bridge, creating a solid barricade on the road. Stephan spurred Tempête into the woods to skirt the clogged highway. Henry thundered after him. A tree branch scratched his face as they blazed a trail towards the river's edge. He batted at the blood trickling into his eye, never letting up his pace a horse's length behind Stephan.

The steep hillside rising from the riverbank was strewn with rocks and blanketed in shadows by trees. The bridge loomed ahead and Henry's stomach clenched at the sight of people and goods being sucked downriver by the strong current. Scanning the pilgrims on the opposite bank, he spotted King Richard pointing and barking orders at his subordinates to help with rescue efforts. Robin and Allan were at his side. Something had captured their attention.

Henry followed their gaze. Two men—one dangling over the raging river, the other clutching him before he fell to his death. Henry blinked, looked closely. "That is Little John!"

Stephan had already spotted his young servant. "Hold him fast," he shouted.

Even if they'd been closer, Little John wouldn't have heard Stephan over the chaos. Henry ached at the sight of Little John's struggle to save the pilgrim. The man's legs dangled over the river. He kicked at the air like a murderer on a hangman's noose.

A cheer resonated from the bridge and from both sides of the river when the men were pulled to safety. Stephan punched the air, smacked his fist to Henry's. They shouted when Little John stood and was embraced by the rescued man, his wife, and dozens of others.

"Stephan!" Henry pointed to the innocents caught in the river. Not waiting for Stephan's response, he barreled down the hill on Sombre. At the river's edge, they swung down from their horses. Henry shed his sword belt. Stephan wrapped a rope around a tree and tossed it to him. Wading into the water, Henry tied the rope to his waist and moved into the current.

Stephan took another rope from Henry's pack, tied one end to the tree, the other round his own waist. He splashed into the river, just in time to grab a young woman. He dragged her to shore, leaving her coughing up water while he scrambled to aid others.

The next few minutes were a blur of water and noise as Henry plunged repeatedly into the water to rescue struggling pilgrims. He just retrieved a half-drowned dog when he spotted a large wagon drifting towards Stephan. It was picking up speed like a driverless carriage on a hill.

The upside down wagon was far too big for one man to stop. Stephan couldn't move from its path fast enough. He dove below the surface. The wagon raked over him.

Henry rushed into the river. "Stephan!" Pacing in knee-high water, he looked about frantically. *He must be all right.* The wagon jerked, then twisted in the current. Stephan's rope stretched from the tree, caught in the spokes of a wheel.

"Stephan!" Henry cried out again. He untied the line from his waist and dove beneath the water, following Stephan's rope. The line wound around one wheel at the front and one at the back. Stephan was trapped.

Henry came up for air. He shouted for help from people gathering on the shore. He took a deep breath and dove again. Grabbing Stephan's face, he pressed his mouth over Stephan's and blew. He kicked off the river bottom to surface, gulped down another lungful of air, grasped his dagger and dove. He slashed at the rope close to Stephan's tunic. He sawed frantically, but the blade slipped from his hand and disappeared in the murky water.

God's wounds!

Stephan's hand found his and pressed it against the handle of a dagger in his belt. Henry struggled to loose it. The belt held the blade fast.

Stephan touched Henry's cheek, shook his head. Dark spots appeared before Henry's eyes. His lungs ached. Anchoring one hand on the wagon, he seated the other on Stephan's dagger. With a final jerk, the weapon slid free.

Henry sliced through the rope, felt Stephan's head loll forward onto his shoulder. He lifted Stephan away from the watery prison. When they surfaced, a knight and his squire dragged Stephan to shore.

Henry stood in the shallows, his arms and legs weak. He shook violently. Two strong men grabbed him and led him to Stephan.

Stephan reached for his hand shakily and held it like the lifeline that it was.

seven

BY THE GRACE OF GOD the pilgrims buried but two men that day. But the final leg of the journey to Marseille saw one more death.

"Ne reminiscáris, Domine, delicta fámuli tui…"

Henry had barely been aware of Little John peering over his shoulder while the priest offered last rites. He would not have known what to say to him even if he'd been able to speak. He saw the boy swipe at his eyes before he ran away.

Exhausted by his vigil at Roger's side, Henry could barely stand. In the last few days, his young servant's flush had spun into a high fever. Remedies offered by the healers were futile. Roger grew weaker. Henry's prayers went unanswered. Roger stopped eating when he could keep nothing down and he withered away, his cheeks sunken. The ardor in his dark eyes disappeared like the sun behind thick clouds.

Henry moved beside him, ran his fingers along his damp brow. Roger fought to lift his hand. Henry smiled softly and palmed it in his own.

"Must I go home?" Roger asked haltingly, struggling for breaths between each word.

Henry shook his head, bit back tears. "Stay with me. Your mother—she's so proud of you. You're a brave young man. Do you remember her telling you that?"

Roger didn't respond, only closed his eyes.

The priest droned on.

Hoofbeats pounded the road outside. A horse snorted when its rider reined him in abruptly. Henry felt certain it was Stephan. He could hear him dismount, hear his scabbard brushing the stirrup with a light scraping sound. Words were mumbled, to whom he wasn't sure and didn't care. He did not—could not—turn around.

Stephan drew up beside Henry and rested a hand on his arm. "Little John told me that you had sent for the priest."

"Why must he die? This cannot be." Henry clenched his fists. "He was fine a few days ago."

The priest finished his recitation. The old man stood and departed with a solemn nod to the two knights.

"I am sorry." Stephan tugged on Henry's arm. "Come outside. Let Roger rest quietly."

Henry jerked away. "The healers and their potions—they are useless."

"You cannot blame them. The king sent his own healers to you. Roger has had the best of care."

Henry startled when thunder rumbled. "Surely there is something else to be done." Henry's fist found his palm, pounded it so hard he grimaced. "I told his mother I would watch over him."

Stephan reached for Henry's hand and unclenched his fingers. "You have."

Thunder boomed. Pilgrims hurried past the tent seeking refuge from a steady rain that began to fall.

Stephan pulled the tent flap closed. Sweat-soaked blankets and the tallow candle burning on the chest smelled so pungent, the air so stifling, it could almost be touched. He knelt next to Henry. "I have no words to comfort you, friend," he said quietly. "Think of the joy Roger had these last few months. The things he saw."

"Better he should have stayed safely in Greyton. He'd not be at death's door."

"You could not know that. We live and die and not at a time of our own choosing. For someone whose faith is strong—like you—is it said that God's will is done? You find comfort knowing Roger is in His hands?"

Henry ran his fingers along Roger's damp brow. God's will? Roger had such a spark for life, for the adventure that lay ahead. He was a good boy. Why was it his time?

Only the thunder answered his question.

The candle sputtered, burning lower, and shadows enveloped them. The wind howled. Rain pattered slowly against the tent like a man tapping his foot to a troubadour's sad song. Then the tempo changed, the rain pouring hard, beating incessantly like a drum. It drowned out everything but Roger's labored breathing.

Stephan shifted beside him. Henry nodded a quiet thank you, knowing he wouldn't face Roger's passing alone. He watched the rise and fall of the young man's chest, noticed his pale but peaceful face in the dim light.

Roger opened his eyes for one heartbeat. He caught Henry's gaze and took a breath. His last.

Henry touched Roger's cheek. Tears streamed down his face. He turned to Stephan and collapsed into his embrace. He listened to whispered words of comfort drifting into his ear.

Stephan brushed his forehead with a soft kiss and stroked his back.

Henry finger's tightened in Stephan's tunic, calmed by the compassion and strength of the knight's gentle touch. Henry tipped his head. Somehow, Stephan's lips found his. Warm, tender.

Henry's breaths grew ragged. A moan escaped his throat.

Stephan's hand slid along his jaw, behind his neck to pull him closer. Their kiss was desperate, needy.

A thunderclap stabbed the air. Lightning crackled nearby, close enough that Henry jerked from Stephan's arms like he'd been struck. His eyes locked on Stephan's, confused.

"Christ." Stephan turned away but Henry could see anguish marking the longing on his face. Stephan raked his fingers through his hair. "I am sorry, Henry. I did not...I should not have—"

Henry's heart beat wildly. *What am I doing?* He wasn't like the men who buried their pain in lust. No, he would not. "Please go." He fixed a blind stare on Roger's peaceful repose. "Just go."

"I will send some men to...to take care of Roger."

Henry waved the knight away without looking back. He laid his head on Roger's chest but this time, his tears would not come.

~ ~ ~

STEPHAN KEPT HIS DISTANCE. For that, Henry was glad. He could not help but notice that Stephan watched him at every turn, that he shunned the attention of more than one handsome knight in the days that followed.

Marseille's blue-green waters did nothing to erase the scars Henry felt. Losing Roger. Losing himself in a moment of sorrow. Three weeks passed before they boarded the ships for Outremer. Three lonely weeks despite daily drills and the numbing routine of waking, of eating. He felt disgusted with himself when he remembered how he'd responded to Stephan's kiss. He prayed when he rose each morning; he prayed before his head found the pillow each evening.

It didn't help when sounds permeating the night kept him awake. Sounds of passion, of men finding comfort with each other. Henry wanted comfort, wanted to be close to...

NO! It is a sin. This will pass.

But why did his heart tell him that lust had nothing to do with that kiss he'd shared with Stephan? He knew lust. He remembered his father's lectures and the whispered conversations with boyhood friends about women. He knew the ache in his groin when one of the village girls at Greyton took him to the hayloft.

This was a different ache. An affection borne of a treasured friendship. Was it more than the affection a person felt for a brother or a parent? How could that be?

Oh God, that night... Stephan had been there as a true friend to offer comfort when Roger died. Henry could still hear the words Stephan uttered, words filled with compassion and the heartache he felt for Henry.

Henry pinched his eyes closed. These feelings were like none he'd felt for anyone. It was more than physical desire. When Stephan wasn't there, he felt something missing in his soul.

What did that mean? Was that what a man felt for a woman he loved? *Is this what I should feel for Alys?*

Henry palmed his cross. "Dear God, help me."

toMessina
august-september 1190

eight

HENRY STARED ACROSS THE water. The sea stretched endlessly. A man could feel so alone out here. Thank God dozens of other boats stayed in sight. When had they last seen land?

The galley dipped and rose on the swells. Waves slapped the sides of the craft. Oars smacked the water in a dull steady beat. Gulls circled overhead, spotting their prey and diving beneath the sea. For once, Henry wished clouds hid the brilliant blue sky. The colour reminded him of Stephan's eyes.

Shouts on the deck distracted him from thoughts of the knight.

Stripped to the waist and deeply tanned, Little John flapped his arms wildly to shoo away a gull. The boy had grown in the four months since he'd schemed to steal Henry's purse. He stood near as tall as his friend Allan. Battle-practiced muscles in his arms and chest glistened with sweat. The bird dove again, snatching breakfast from Little John's hands. It alighted victorious on the rail. Little John cursed. He unsheathed the sword Stephan had given him and swung. The frightened gull dropped part of its meal and flew off. Little John took a final swipe at empty air. "Do that again," he shouted, "and I shall not miss!"

Henry smiled as Little John fetched the scrap of bread the gull dropped and plopped it into his mouth. He rested the sword against his shoulder and walked over to Henry. "It is nice to see you in good spirits, my lord."

"Did the creature leave you anything to eat?"

"Enough for a bird." He wiped his mouth across his bronzed arm.

"Roger would have laughed at you fighting off that little thief," Henry said.

"I'd have heard no end to it." Sadness choked Little John's voice. "I miss him, I do," he added. "Not near as much as you, I suppose. He served you well."

Henry swallowed hard. "He was more than a servant."

"Aye, he was a good friend." Little John pointed at a galley cresting a wave just ahead and to their starboard side. The king's shields decorated her bow. "Thank the good Lord that Allan is on Sir Robin's boat. I will not have to listen to his teasing."

Henry chuckled, wiped the sweat from his brow. He pulled the wineskin from his belt and took a swig. The heat felt oppressive, like they were standing next to a red-hot forge. The breeze helped, but it pushed the stink of sweaty men and beasts in its wake. Henry wrinkled his nose and held out the flask.

Little John took the wineskin when Henry offered it and gulped down a mouthful. "Aye, and that's the thing, my lord," he said, handing it back.

"What thing?"

Little John slid his sword back into the scabbard. "Allan and me, we tease each other. Fight one minute and get past it." He cleared his throat, shifted awkwardly from one foot to the other. "Master Stephan is feelin' mighty sad. I do not know what happened with you and him, but you both need to be friends again. Friends are what we need."

Henry grabbed Little John's wrist. "Did he put you up to this?"

Little John drew back, surprised. "No, my lord. I just see things, see the way you act 'round each other."

What did he mean by that? Henry released Little John, looked past him at Stephan deep in conversation with the coxswain. Henry quickly averted his eyes when Stephan saw him watching but he'd have no escape. Stephan padded across the deck. He waved Little John away with a tip of his head. "Henry, we must talk."

Henry remained rigid like one of the standing stones he'd seen to the west of Greyton as a boy. If he kept his eyes on the birds in the sky, his feelings could remain locked away. "Shall you just tell everyone?" he asked, his voice barely audible above the creaks and groans of the boat.

"I would not."

Henry pounded the rail. "Yet you send a young boy—"

"Little John? I've not said a word to him."

Two of the galley's crewmen stepped up to the rail nearby and inspected the long oars cutting the water. Stephan waited until they moved on before he spoke again. "I thought you knew me."

Henry's shoulders sagged. He did know Stephan, and that made it all the more difficult when that night remained so vivid. He'd been as much to blame as Stephan. "You are right. I am sorry. I have nothing more to say. I will defend you with my sword, my life, but I need not be in your company."

Stephan turned, his back to the sea. He leaned against the rail. "Our friends wonder why we do not speak."

A gust of wind tousled Henry's hair. He fingered the dark strands away from his face then grasped the deck rail so tightly that his knuckles turned white. "I wished I had been given a berth on a different galley. It is difficult to see you after…" He punched the rail again. "I told Robin I wanted to be alone. Let me grieve for Roger."

Stephan blew out a sharp breath. "It has been weeks—"

"Do *not* tell me how to remember him!"

"Dwelling on your grief serves no one. Not you, not Roger. You will see more death than you have ever imagined in Outremer. You must go on. Your friends depend on you."

Henry sighed deeply. "And I shall be there for them, for you, when we fight the Saracens." He squinted towards the east where clouds now lay low above a strip of land visible when the ship crested each wave. The tall masts groaned, a sound that could have been his heart. The memory of Stephan's lips against his sent an ache through his body. "It was wrong, Stephan." His voice cracked. "We must leave it at that."

"I know. I am sorry. I never intended…" Stephan scuffed his boot against the deck. "Once again I will remind you of words I spoke. I ask nothing more than your friendship."

Henry watched the whitecaps on the sea. He desperately needed to believe Stephan. Was he relieved Stephan offered no argument? Had he wanted to hear something more? No matter. His heart ached for the intimate bond between two people—for love. Two men could not love each other. Not that way. It was wrong. Against everything he'd grown up believing. Friendship was all they could have and it would have to be enough.

Stephan turned, tapping his fist on the rail and breaking the tension. "And so, my friend, a game of dice? Sir William and Thomas of Winchester have shillings to lose."

The galley swayed suddenly, tossed by a wave so high Henry wondered if the sea would swallow them. Stephan braced himself against the rail. Henry lost his footing and careened into him. The knight's muscular arms held him fast. Warmth rose in Henry's cheeks. Their gazes met, tangled like two swords crossed in heated battle. Henry could have sworn he saw desire brush Stephan's face.

When he found his footing, Stephan released him. Somehow, Henry needed to be able to look at Stephan, enjoy his company, and forget his body's sinful betrayal. Stephan seemed to push it aside so casually. He needed to do the same.

Henry managed a smile. "They will not be the only ones to lose a coin or two. You know I have not had much luck with games of chance."

Stephan viewed him suspiciously. "You say this, but I know you were playing with Allan before we left dry land. I have watched that boy. He is quite the gambler." He puffed out his chest. "Even I learned a bit from him. So, come. Watch the master."

Henry laughed. It felt good to laugh. "And just how much did you lose in Marseille?"

"Enough to buy a fat cow and a pig. But that was against David of Rotherham." Stephan leaned closer. "He cheats you know."

A shout from the wheel made them both turn. The coxswain pointed towards the eastern horizon.

Henry frowned. The clouds there had darkened and appeared to rise straight into the air like the tallest trees of the forests back home. They reached for the heavens from the land itself.

Little John trotted up beside them at the rail. "Look, my lord," he said. "It's the fire mountain."

"What?" Henry asked. "Is that smoke?"

"The locals call it a volcano," Stephan said.

"Does it really spit fire into the sky?" Little John asked.

Stephan nodded. "One of the crew told me about a hot flaming river that flowed down its side."

Henry shielded his eyes to get a better look. "Is there any danger to the ship?"

"We are in good hands." Stephan threw a mischievous look his way and then prodded Little John with his elbow. "But you know King Richard. After we disembark, he may want a closer look."

The king's galley cut the deep waters several hundred yards ahead. Even at this distance, Henry could see Richard pacing across the bow with Robin at his side. A slight figure hung by the rail—Allan, Robin's shadow.

Henry studied the sides of the volcano as the ship crested another wave. "Do you believe these stories about flaming rivers?"

Stephan shrugged. "As much as I believe the ones of King Arthur and Merlin." He cocked his head towards the king. His voice sobered. "We must always listen, Henry. And learn. This is the reason why you must not keep to yourself. It can be dangerous if we fail to heed the words of others. That failure could get you—or the king—killed."

Henry turned to Stephan, startled. It was a lesson his father tried to instill when he was younger. Knowledge was power, strength. Whether it was about the land, or about an enemy. The more you knew, the better chance you might survive.

"You are right." He grasped Stephan's arm.

Stephan looked down at his hand with obvious relief. Henry wanted to pull away, but Stephan found his eyes. Henry remained steady. He *did* trust Stephan. He needed to trust himself.

~ ~ ~

HENRY WAS EAGER TO learn more about the volcano known as Mt. Vesuvius but glad not to venture closer than five miles to it when Richard's fleet anchored under its watchful eye. The more he heard, the less eager he was about Sicily, which had its own smoking monster, the one they called Etna.

Three weeks later, when the galleys finally passed through the Straits of Messina, Henry could almost imagine the heat from the fiery mountain. Its summit nearly touched the clouds. Undaunted by the potential destruction Etna could release, King Richard stood at the bow of his galley as it entered the harbour, the sun reflecting off his bejeweled crown. The spectacle must have sent a shiver through even the bravest of men. Red lions on golden shields snarled from the bow. Banners fluttered in time to the beat of the oars. People thronged Messina's waterfront, crammed shoulder-to-shoulder. They peered from upstairs windows and from rooftops. Drums pounded out a steady rhythm and trumpets blared to welcome him. The people of Sicily knew the legend of the Lionheart. Now they saw the man.

Henry's admiration for the king grew a bit more as he watched Richard, steady and proud, greet Messina. The king's face didn't betray his concern for his sister Joanna. She should be amongst the crowds waiting to greet him. But there'd been little word of her since her husband, the king of Sicily, had died. There were rumours she'd been placed under house arrest. King Richard expected to find the dowager Queen Joanna well taken care of.

And if he did not there might be hell to pay.

"Messina is ours!"
october 1190

nine

HENRY FROWNED AT THE shop owner. "A shilling? For a loaf of bread? Not on knight's pay." From the moment they'd stepped off the boats, rumours about ridiculous prices for everything from food to equipment to services assaulted their ears. Their first excursion after setting up camp outside the city gates proved to be quite eye opening.

Messina was a busy seaport in normal times. With Christian armies using it as a gateway to the Holy Land, it had become like a pot of water on a fire, near ready to boil over. It was a pot with many unfamiliar faces, darker-skinned people like Saracens, Greeks, and others from the East—some local, some passing through—and despite the unethical business practices, Henry was intrigued.

"Enough!" Stephan lifted the small sack he carried, waving it at the plump, dark-haired baker at the counter. "The merchant up the street charged that for this meat and cheese."

"That will last us all of a day," Henry muttered.

Stephan chuckled. "Less if Little John gets hold of it. God be praised that King Richard helps feed us all. When he hears of these prices, baker and butcher best turn their voices to the good Lord and ask to be spared his wrath." He turned back to the bread maker. "Two pennies."

Henry kept a straight face, hiding his amusement that Stephan invoked God's name. True, the king would not be pleased, but he couldn't imagine that swords would be drawn.

The shop owner nudged the girl by his side. She winked at the knights and repeated Stephan's offer in her native tongue. Her eyes gleamed like onyx against a pool of olive-coloured skin. Soft black curls fell to her waist. Her translation went on longer than Henry expected. He wondered what she'd said when her cheeks reddened and her father batted at her hand, and leaned to whisper to her.

"He say ten."

Henry shook his head.

"Ten," the girl repeated, reaching across the counter to run her hand down Henry's arm. "With special treat." She cocked her head towards a tattered curtain that separated the front of the store from a back room.

"She must like the ones with dark hair. Good thing I've not a jealous bone in my body." Stephan's eyes were sparking with mischievous lust. "But ten? Mayhap four—"

"What? I am not—" Henry shoved the girl's hand away. "Three pennies. No more."

The dark-haired beauty studied Stephan, smiled at Henry. She nodded knowingly.

"What?" Henry asked innocently.

"Just trying to help," Stephan said, covering a grin with his hand.

Henry looked at the girl, shook his head. "I do not...we are not..." His face went a darker shade of crimson.

"Three," she said with a sigh.

Henry's stomach growled. The shop's fresh-baked goods and the aromas wafting from the stone hearth made his mouth water.

Stephan leaned close and whispered, "We will find no better."

Henry hadn't realised he was clenching his fist when Stephan pressed his fingers apart and slipped two coins into his hand. Taking a deep breath, Henry reached for another from his own purse and handed them to the girl.

The baker glared at the three of them but relinquished the warm loaf. His daughter rounded the counter. She slid her arms through the knights' and walked them out into the summer sunshine. Pecking each one on the cheek, she grinned and slapped their buttocks to see them on their way.

"Friendly, aren't they?"

"Some help you are," Henry said. "Not only do they cheat us with high prices, they sell their own daughters' services. What madness."

"They will not be lacking offers with the king's army camped just beyond the city walls. She *was* a pretty girl." Stephan stopped in front of a fruit cart admiring the pimpled skin of the plump oranges.

"You noticed?"

"I am not blind, Henry. Even I might admire a young woman's beauty though I have no desire to bed one. And you? Or is your Alys the only one who fills your thoughts?"

Henry kicked at pebbles in the street. "She will turn fifteen on Michaelmas. She was barely a girl when I left home, a head shorter than me, and skinny as a sapling. I like her hair. It is golden and looks like fresh-sown hay when the sun strikes it, like yours. Better than this mane," he said, pointing to his own head.

"So *that* is why you like me."

Henry's eyes flew wide. He opened his mouth to protest but nothing came out.

Stephan laughed. "Do not worry. I remember my promise. Besides, I am partial to men with *blond* hair." He whacked Henry's back playfully and took off at a full run.

"You!" Henry shook his head, and then began to run, darting through the streets on Stephan's trail.

The sun peeked between the shops and lodgings. Shadows wrapped Henry in their cool cloak, a safe harbour hiding the confusion in his eyes. Chasing Stephan reminded him of the forests back home where he'd chased Alys. She would hide but he'd hear her giggles and find her easily. Tickle her until she fell wriggling to the ground. She'd turn serious and her girlish spark would fade. He'd run his finger along the bridge of her nose, across her cheek, her lips. He looked into her brown eyes, wanting to feel something more.

Nothing. He felt...nothing.

There was an empty space in his heart and Alys did nothing to fill it.

But there was Stephan. Giving and caring, gentle, and so full of life. Stephan made him forget that emptiness.

Henry stopped running. He stared after Stephan. He shouldn't have these thoughts. His shoulders slumped and he rubbed his eyes, reached for his crucifix. He'd say many a *Pater Noster* tonight.

~ ~ ~

HENRY SETTLED INSIDE THE pavilion, which had been set up a short distance outside Messina's city gates. The flaps of the tent were pulled back. It wouldn't have taken much effort for the locals to hear raised voices extolling the maltreatment of Richard's army. The day wore on and one tale after another was told about the taunting and violence turned deadly. Indignation flared on the faces of the men around Henry. Whispered curses and the calls for justice grated on his ears.

Two breathless and bloodied squires charged into the tent. A great breeze swept the room and a chill seeped into Henry's bones. Richard's face turned stone cold as the two young men fell to their knees in front of him.

"A dozen of them came down on us, sire." Reginald, the older of the two, tugged at his ripped tunic trying to hide the blood and grime on his clothes. His deep voice rang strong though his hands trembled. "We would not hand over thirty shillings for a mule."

"Your lord would keep you in service for twenty more summers if you had!" someone shouted.

The knights in the room roared with laughter. Reginald and his companion both managed to smile as the king bade them to rise.

Standing behind Richard, Robin leaned forward. "Salisbury reported the same cost yesterday, my liege, which he refused to pay."

"For a mule?" Henry whispered to Stephan.

Stephan gave a low whistle. "I could buy three good pack horses in Poitiers for that."

For three days Richard had listened stoically to report after report of the price gouging, of knights and tradesmen voicing accounts of being doused with rotten food or piss tossed from upstairs windows. At first he was inclined towards moderation. He sought negotiations with Messina's governor, and asked for the French king's support. Philip, who'd arrived in Sicily a week earlier, refused to lift a finger, claiming Richard's unruly troops were the problem, not his.

"We offered a fair price, and would have gladly paid," Reginald said. "They sought to argue with us. We walked away, seeing no chance to reason with them. Had barely gone more than a few paces when their tongues spat the most vile utterances about you, sire."

Richard's brow shot up. He almost looked amused.

"We could not abide their words and drew our swords."

"You fought off twelve of them?"

"Not at first, sire. There were three, but they were joined quickly by their friends. We fought most bravely. If Sir Roger's squire had not stepped in to help us, we might not stand before you with this tale."

"We should raise a toast to you. Where is the squire?" Richard asked, shifting to look past them.

Reginald hesitated a moment and then spoke. "Eudo is dead, sire."

Angry murmurs swelled from one end of the pavilion to the other. Henry crossed himself. The clink of mail and swoosh of fabric said hundreds of others in the room did the same.

Richard clenched his fist, his face grim, his mouth a stiff hard line. "First, they will not return my sister to me, and now they kill my men." He stood abruptly. His chair flew from the dais. Broad-shouldered with long muscular limbs and a tan from Messina's sun, the king looked like a golden warrior ready for a fight.

"My patience is at an end." Richard pulled his sword from its jewel-encrusted scabbard. Eyes flaming with anger, he raised the weapon above his head. "We shall take this city."

Shouts swept the room. A hundred swords were unsheathed in a sound that would have caused the bravest of men to pause. Word of the king's declaration spread from the pavilion.

Henry shoved his way through the chaos of the camp to get to his tent. He fumbled with his gambeson and suddenly missed Roger. He'd not anticipated needing a squire until the fleet anchored in the Holy Land. Fighting against the citizens of Messina—some fifty thousand strong—had been the last thing he'd expected. Outremer was a thousand or more miles east, but King Richard had roused his army. The enemy was here—now.

Little John appeared at his door. *Stephan. Always looking out for me.*

"There's to be a battle?" the boy asked as he tightened the laces of Henry's gambeson and helped him don his hauberk.

"If God wills it." Henry adjusted his sword, bow, and daggers. Outside, he could hear the thunder of knights on horseback and battle cries resounding, harsh, like screeching crows. "Stay far from the line of fire," he added.

"Those were Master Stephan's same words," Little John said with a disappointed sigh. "God be with you, my lord."

Sweat beaded on Henry's brow. His pulse raced. He hefted his shield and charged towards the corrals to get Sombre. He snaked around wagons jammed with equipment rumbling along the road. Soldiers laden with bows, lances, and axes hastened towards the city gates.

At the stables, squires from the king's mesnie had readied the horses. Henry seated his shield and bow on the saddle hook. He swung onto Sombre's back and urged him down the road. Hastily constructed trebuchets, massive stone throwers on wheels, were being cranked back as he made his way to the line of Anglo-Norman knights. When the first boulders flew, Henry instinctively ducked, watching the arc of the missiles and stroking Sombre's neck when the destrier's head sawed the air. The unceasing pounding began, steady like the beat of a drum. Huge stones flung against the walls shook the ground.

The knights observed the action behind the archers, their arrows arcing in deadly flights across deep blue skies. A part of the wall crumbled from the trebuchet actions. Men-at-arms surged forward, turned back when crossbow darts flew from the wall walk.

Clouds gathered and cast the land and sea in and out of shadows, chasing the sun until midday when it began its descent towards the western horizon. And the pounding continued.

Henry fidgeted, feeling useless. The knights could do nothing until the walls had been breached. He exchanged a glance with Stephan who perched atop Tempête. Stephan watched the action calmly until he shouted, "Here comes the king!"

King Richard galloped towards them from the front lines. Sweat glistened on the haunches of his white warhorse. He reined in the magnificent animal, stopping beside Robin and a group of his trusted knights.

Richard's face was determined and calculating. He pointed to the gates then whisked his hand to the west. Henry and Stephan were too far away to hear his words but there appeared to be no disagreement from his knights.

A moment later, Robin trotted up beside them. He waved his hand towards smoke rising from the waterfront. "Our men have attacked their ships and we control the harbour. This assault on the main gate will continue. It will keep the locals distracted."

"Distracted?" Henry asked as a boulder smashed against the city wall.

"There is a gate on the western wall that is not well defended," Robin said. "Come. We are with the king."

Robin tugged his stallion's reins and spurred him on. Stephan donned his helmet and followed. King Richard and several of his Knights Templar shot past. Henry urged Sombre in their wake, leaving the noise of the siege engines and bolts whooshing through the air behind them.

The road skirted south and west, beyond the view of the city's defenders. Emerging from the wooded and hilly terrain, the twelve horsemen were observed by one lone guard at the western gate. The soldier on the tower raised the alarm to his comrades. Seconds passed. More men appeared on the battlements.

An arrow flew past the king. Another bounced off Robin's shield.

"Robin," the king shouted, "they are yours."

"Stephan, Henry—with me," Robin called.

"The rest of you—shields!" the king ordered. "To the gate!"

Richard and the other knights dismounted. Shields held high, they charged forward.

The hair on Henry's neck prickled. He rode forward with Stephan and Robin, nocking an arrow to his bow. The setting sun glinted off mail on the tower above the gate. A soldier with a crossbow. Aimed effectively, that weapon could pierce a shield.

Henry pulled back on the cord, loosed. His arrow sailed between the merlons. It sliced into the man's neck. Henry heard the scream, didn't look to see the man fall. He reached for a second arrow and mayhap for a heartbeat let himself think—he'd just killed a man for the first time in his life. Beside him Stephan and Robin moved smooth and swift and deadly, arrows sailing against red-tinged clouds. One man, then a second, screamed from the wall walk.

Two of the king's Templars chopped the gate with their axes. The others used their shields to protect them. The defenders had to expose themselves to loose arrows on the king's men at the foot of the wall. Each time one did, Henry released an arrow. There was no time to think. Aim and loose. Sight another. Aim. Loose. Enemies' bodies slumped over the wall, falling to the assault.

Movement on the tower caught Henry's eye. A crossbowman targeted Stephan. Nocking an arrow, Henry took in a breath, loosed the shaft.

"God's bones!" he cried. Missed by a hair's breadth, just enough to cause his enemy to hesitate.

Digging his spurs into Sombre, Henry charged. Shield up, he barreled in front of Stephan to block the man's shot, his eyes still tracing along the wall walk. "Another to your left," he shouted as his shield absorbed the blow meant for Stephan.

In one smooth movement, Stephan twisted in the saddle, grabbed an arrow from his bag, aimed, and loosed. There was an ungodly scream from the wall. Another man plummeted to the ground. The rain of arrows ended and a strange quiet loomed, the horses' hoofs on the rocky road the only sound. Two heartbeats later, wood splintered. An axe cracked the gate, a solid blow unlike anything Henry ever heard. They were through.

Two knights moved cautiously through the breach. When no one challenged them, they signaled to the others. Remounted and brandishing his sword, King Richard led them forward like a tempest.

Resistance grew as they approached the main city gate but the knights' rampage was swift. Those who stood in their path were shown no mercy.

Henry slashed his sword down as Sombre nimbly swept past foot soldiers and common peasants wielding lances and swords. His sword deflected one blow after another. When it ripped flesh, he heard the cries, saw the blood. He slashed again, not thinking. If he stopped to think he would be dead.

The defender who pounced on him came from nowhere. His momentum sent them both to the ground. Henry's sword flew from his hands and skittered a few feet away. He couldn't breathe. His head rang.

Stunned, Henry moved awkwardly under the weight of his hauberk. His attacker rolled away. Unarmoured, the man moved as fast as a rabbit. His fingers latched onto Henry's sword as he stood.

Henry struggled to rise. He saw sunlight glint off the bloodied blade. The soldier stood over him snarling with dark, crazed eyes. Heart pounding, Henry kicked. His boot grazed the man's groin. Grimacing, the man raised the sword to deliver a deadly blow.

"Die, bastard!" The shout came from behind the sword-wielding man. Henry heard a thud, the distinct sound of a bolt piercing flesh. His attacker's eyes widened. Blood spewed from his mouth. Dropping the weapon, the man pitched forward and smacked into Henry like a huge sack of grain.

Stephan tossed aside the crossbow he'd snagged from a fallen soldier. He rushed to Henry's side. Shoving the dead man from his chest, he asked, "Are you all right?"

Henry nodded, still breathless from the fall. He grasped Stephan's outstretched hand and struggled to his feet. Stephan swung his sword and brandished his shield, daring the onlookers peering from windows and alleyways to attack.

Henry retrieved his blade and they backed away slowly.

"My lords," a familiar voice called. It was the baker's daughter who'd wished to sell more than bread to Henry. She held a wineskin out, approaching them cautiously. Henry started to take it from her, but Stephan batted it away.

"What—"

"It may be poisoned," Stephan said.

The girl frowned. "I am friend." She reached for Henry, dabbing at the cut on his cheek.

Henry jerked back, seizing the girl's hand, his eyes flaring angrily. He saw the fear in hers and his expression softened. She meant him no harm.

Stephan tugged his arm. "No time for women now. Let's go. The king is nearing the gate." He darted towards their friends.

Henry followed, calling back to the girl, "God bless you."

King Richard's knights had formed in two rows, five abreast, and charged towards the bailey. The locals scattered, shouting to alert the defenders, but not before Robin loosed a shaft that sent one man on the wall walk tumbling to the ground.

The enemies' attention was suddenly divided. Boulders from stone throwers and flights of arrows flew at them in never-ending waves. The king's army assaulted them from one side of the wall; his band of infiltrators was at their backs. Either way they turned, chaos.

King Richard was in the middle of it all atop his spirited destrier, shield in one hand, bloodied sword in the other. "Robin," he shouted, "the signal."

Henry had lost sight of Robin until a fireball arced into the sky from his left flank. Robin loosed two more blazing arrows. The rain of flights from Richard's troops on the other side of the wall suddenly ceased.

But the fighting wasn't over. Enemy soldiers stormed down into the bailey brandishing swords, clubs, and lances aimed at the king and his men. Still unhorsed, Henry and Stephan trained arrows at men on the wall walk. An archer there might risk killing one of his own to strike King Richard. If anyone aimed a shaft into the bailey, the two knights would ensure that would be the man's last.

Richard confronted one attacker after another. He struck down, his sword slicing a deep gash in a man-at-arm's sword arm. He blocked the swing of an axe with his shield. His stallion reared, forcing the axe-wielder back a few steps. Undaunted, the man struck again.

Stephan unsheathed his sword and shouted, "St. George!" He rushed towards the king leaving Henry to mind the defenders on the battlements. Two men intercepted Stephan. Three blades tangled in the damp warm air, came apart, struck again. Stephan delivered a powerful blow. His attackers fell back but Stephan pressed them, sent one reeling to the ground, the other scrambling for cover.

Kicking up dust and rock, Stephan raised his sword for the final blow.

"Mercy!" the man cried, tossing his sword aside.

Skirting round the man, Stephan booted the weapon away and turned to the king. Richard's attacker had crumpled to his knees, arms hugging his chest. Blood seeped through his tunic.

Stephan saw that the king needed no help. Robin and three Templars fought their way towards the gate and were embroiled with twice their number. Stephan started after them. More swordsmen stepped in his path. Stephan roared a battle cry. Sweat pouring from his face he swung his sword.

Planted behind an overturned cart, Henry jerked towards Stephan. His arrow was nocked on his bow. The cord sang as he loosed an arrow at one of Stephan's attackers. The man lurched sideways and fell into the other, sending them both to the dirt.

"Surrender!" Richard waved his sword, hefted his shield, daring the enemy soldiers to attack him.

One took the challenge, raised his sword and charged the king. Henry's aim was true. He cut the man down at Richard's feet.

Archers and men-at-arms tossed their weapons to the ground. One of the Templars pounded Henry's back and handed him the king's standard. The knight turned and rushed to the gate to help Robin and the others lift the beam that secured it.

Henry and Stephan scrambled up the tower with the banner. It caught on the wind as the gate flew open. A tremendous cheer rose when the king's men spotted the red and gold flapping above the wall.

Richard spurred his destrier forward through the gate. He raised his sword to his army. "Messina is ours!"

ten

HENRY WINCED. HIS BODY ached. He was bruised in places he'd never imagined possible. Moving slowly, he inspected the mail the young squire from Richard's mesnie had cleaned and laid out meticulously. The boy fiddled with a bloodstained cloth, wadding it into his fist. Henry praised his hard work and sent him on his way. The boy's quick step reminded him of Roger. *God bless him.* Had he lived, Henry would not have wanted Roger to see the bloody turn of events in Messina.

Henry reached for the clean tunic on his cot. Pulling it over his head, he groaned again. He smoothed back his hair, then rubbed the scruffy growth on his face. His hands trembled. He remembered the soldier with dark, crazed eyes holding Henry's own blade over his head. *My God. I am still alive.* He crossed himself with effort, quietly thanking the good Lord and Stephan.

Music drifted on the evening air. The king's villa hummed with the sounds of victory. Messina had been looted and ships burned in her harbour. The victors reveled in the spoils of war, including finding pleasure with willing and some not-so-willing local women. Henry covered his face with his hands, confused. *Dear God, how many did I kill? This is victory?*

Thirst stung his throat. He wanted a drink—with Stephan. He could talk to Stephan.

He wandered outside. Stephan was down the road, his arm draped across the shoulders of a young man Henry didn't recognize in the dim light. Henry shrunk into the shadows, watching. Stephan and his companion shared a laughed and slipped into Stephan's tent.

Henry looked away. He chewed his lower lip, sucked in a breath. He needed that drink now more than ever. One to celebrate the victory. A second to forget the blood on his hands. And three or more more to drown the loneliness that crept into his thoughts.

~ ~ ~

NOT A CARE IN the world. That was Stephan, sitting outside his tent smoothing the nicks on his sword. Henry frowned, kicked at the ground, and finally wandered up to him.

"I looked for you last night."

Stephan didn't lift his head. "I left early."

"I had hoped to celebrate with you." Henry's cheeks reddened when Stephan looked up from his work. Those blue eyes were soul-piercing. Henry swallowed hard. "To thank you...for saving my life."

Mercifully, Stephan looked away to acknowledge the greetings of three knights walking towards the scent of the cooks' fires at the villa. He tipped his head at Henry. "You would do the same for me." He smiled and resumed rubbing his sword.

Henry shuffled his feet. He had no right to ask Stephan whom he'd been with. Why did it bother him?

Stephan lifted his sword. He twisted it back and forth admiring the sunlight that reflected off the blade. "Ready for another day in battle."

Henry shivered, remembering the blade that nearly took his life. "Surely the king does not believe the locals will attack us again?"

"They'd be fools to try, wouldn't they? We have given them a taste of our strength. They have conceded defeat and will be lucky if the king does not sentence their leaders to a hangman's rope."

Henry scoffed. "Politics."

"For a future lord, you truly are cynical about the ways of kings." Stephan laughed and stood up. "Ready for that drink? I think I am due more than one for saving your hide."

"I will not carry you back to your tent," Henry said.

Stephan's eyes lit with a grin. "You shall never let me forget Southampton, will you?" He sheathed his sword and started towards the villa.

Henry stared at his back. *He does not realise I am speaking of last night.*

Stephan looked over his shoulder when Henry didn't follow. "Coming?"

Henry trotted up beside him. What Stephan thought, who he'd been with—it did not matter. But if that were true, why couldn't he stop thinking about it?

The roasting meats weren't fragrant enough to overpower the stench of burned buildings inside the city walls. Henry cringed at the scent of death lingering in the air. Muffled wails echoed through the streets. The living mourned their dead. Inside the pavilion, the din of boasting knights and strumming troubadours drowned out those sounds.

The previous evening, Henry's stomach had been twisted as tight as the braid in the serving girl's hair. He'd taken one bite of chicken and tossed it aside. He felt much better now and filled his trencher with bread, roast pork and beef, before settling at one of the tables.

Stephan didn't join him right away but stopped, bumping shoulders with Benedict of Poitiers. He whispered something to the fair-haired knight, which made Benedict laugh. Henry paused mid-chew, suddenly feeling cold. He recognized that laugh—Stephan's companion the previous evening. His lover.

Henry dragged his dagger through the gravy on his trencher. He wished he'd not seen Stephan with Benedict headed into the tent.

Stephan plopped onto the bench. "Ale. I need ale." He grabbed the jug and poured them each a mug. Smiling, he turned to Henry and lifted his goblet. "To the man you cannot live without. Me!"

A raised sword flashed in Henry's mind. One second more and that soldier would have pierced his mail, severed his neck. He shoved the thought away and mustered a grin, tapping Stephan's mug. "To you!" he said. Taking a long slow swig, he let the brew coat his throat, hoping it would dull his mind.

The pork smelled of garlic and basil, and tasted even better than it smelled. Henry couldn't remember when he'd had a full meal—yesterday morning? And that had been some dried beef and an egg a servant had bartered for. He felt ravenous and shoveled food into his mouth. Amused, Stephan stopped to watch him before stabbing a piece of meat with his dagger.

Henry downed a second and then a third ale. He reached to refill his mug but Stephan caught his arm. "You will not be good for drills if you keep that up."

"Practice? Today?"

"Aye. Robin called for us to meet. Did you not get the word this morning?"

"No day of rest? Of course I am always ready when called," Henry said, eyeing the other knights' indulgence in food and drink. None of them would be sober if there was another attack. "The locals are calm, though I cannot say I would feel the same in their position. Why did the king allow the men to loot the town?"

Henry saw a flash of surprise—or was it fear—in Stephan's eyes.

"Christ, Henry." Stephan scrubbed a hand through his hair. "I knew you were an innocent—"

"These people are supposed to be our allies!" Henry snapped. "And I am not so naïve."

"This is war, Henry. We were wronged. Our soldiers murdered." Stephan's eyes strayed across the room, landing on Benedict. "We took what we felt should be ours."

Henry looked from Benedict to Stephan. "It is wrong," he said vehemently, lowering his head when Stephan faced him. Henry rubbed his fist across the rough wood of the tabletop. He thought of the men he'd killed, the smell of the slaughter. "We are no better than the enemy. We're all savages."

A knight across the room cackled, and as if to drive Henry's point home, the men gathered round him beat the trestles like drums.

Henry flattened a chunk of bread with the blade of his dagger. He waited for the noise to die down. "We have forgotten that God teaches compassion. Does that mean nothing in wartime?" His voice grew soft. "Will God forgive us for pillaging? Innocent women—girls—God's blood, they were raped."

Stephan fingered his mug, tracing the intricate design etched in the silver. "The men have rights to the spoils of war, Henry. Don't the priests claim God forgives because we fight for Him? For Jerusalem?"

"This is Messina. I did not take the Cross to fight the people of Sicily." Henry scoffed. He'd suddenly lost his appetite and shoved his trencher away. "And when did you become a religious man?"

Stephan waved his hands emphatically. "Not me. I would never make that claim."

One of the serving girls placed a fresh platter of meats and fruits and another jug of ale on the table. She smiled at them with crooked, yellowed teeth and brushed Stephan's arm, disappointed when he ignored her.

Henry stared across the room. "I should have stayed in England."

"What?" Stephan groaned. "Behind the safe walls of your manor house?"

"My father was right. I know nothing, understand nothing, of war."

"You know that Saladin slaughtered thousands of Christians. Is that not enough?"

"Killing people in Messina will not bring them back." He rubbed the ache in his temples. If Saladin's atrocities were all he had to know and supporting this pilgrimage was the right thing to do, why was his mind in such turmoil? He finally met Stephan's eyes. "It makes my stomach churn. Others seemed to revel in it."

Henry had barely said the words when Thomas of Winchester spouted off in agonizing detail how it took two slashes to sever the head from the body of one of their enemies. "His eyes bulged like the young maid who saw my engorged cock and nearly fainted with fright." Thomas imitated his victim's death throes then cupped his groin with a grunt. He grabbed one of the serving girls and pulled her into his lap.

Thomas' companions laughed. Henry snarled, finding nothing funny in the man's actions or words.

Stephan rubbed a hand across his back. Henry flinched. He turned fiery eyes on Stephan. "And you—"

"War is ugly, Henry." Stephan's gaze drifted across the room where Thomas sat. "Some brag. Or pray. Some get drunk to forget. Others find solace—"

"In another's arms?" Henry asked.

Stephan turned to him and nodded, no hint of regret. "Yes."

Henry grabbed Stephan's ale and downed it. He slammed the mug onto the trestle. Gravy slopped over the side of his trencher. Heads turned their way but only for a moment. These men had seen it before. Just another soldier frustrated or grieving, angry at war.

The fire in the hearth crackled and blotted out the hum of voices around them. Stephan reached for Henry again but stopped. "This is who I am. You know that." He leaned close, his warm breath brushing Henry's face. "I needed to fuck someone last night."

Henry covered his eyes again, rubbed his temples. "I am sorry. I cannot…it's not natural. Two men should not…"

"Nothing happened," Stephan said.

Henry locked gazes with him, surprised. "You just said—"

"I said I needed a fuck. I did not say I got one."

"I—I—" Henry fumbled for the right thing to say. This was Stephan. His friend. He'd accepted him as he was. What was he thinking? "I am sorry. I'd sworn I would never judge you."

Stephan poured himself another ale. He lifted it to his lips studying Henry over the goblet's rim. He took a swig and set the drink down. "I had every intention of taking that man in ways the priests say will require many *Pater Nosters* for forgiveness. When your groin aches and your soul feels it is on fire, you do not think about Hell because you are already in one. You cannot control the way you feel, the way you are." He exhaled sharply. "Damn it, I wanted him."

Henry fidgeted, his face reddening. Why hadn't Stephan swived the handsome young knight from Poitou? And what did it matter? He shouldn't care…but he felt relieved.

"But you did not give into that temptation. Why?"

Stephan's eyes fixed on the fire. "I do not know. We kissed—once—and it was pleasant as kisses go. And then he left."

"Once?" Henry asked, telling himself one last time that Stephan's liaisons with other men did not matter.

"I swear it." Stephan ran a finger across his lips, perplexed, turned towards Henry and shrugged. "Let's talk of something else. You look tired."

Henry thumbed his mug. "I did not sleep well." He cringed. "Nightmares." *God's wounds. And thinking of you with that man.*

"Reliving yesterday's fight?" Stephan asked.

Light streamed through the doors from the courtyard. Robin and another knight walked in, a golden hue cast round them. Henry watched the dust particles dance, shimmering against the light. It was calm and peaceful, unlike the memories that haunted his dreams.

"I can picture it so clearly. When I was in the thick of battle, I did not think. I acted." He found Stephan's eyes. "Is that how it goes for you?"

Stephan stared into his ale. "It is an instinct, I think, that keeps us alive."

"I remember feeling the blood pulse through my veins, my heart pounding so hard I could barely hear the screams of dying men, the grunts of horses, or bolts sizzling past my head." Henry took a long deep breath. "But when I lie down, my eyes so tired, my body crying for sleep, I see their blood—on my hands, on my sword, coating my armour.

"I hear flesh split, bones crack. That coppery smell of fresh blood brings bile to my throat. Is this what we live with the rest of our days?" Moisture pricked Henry's eyes. "Is this what my father meant?"

Stephan reached across the table and grasped Henry's hands. This time, Henry did not flinch. "The nightmares may never leave you," Stephan said quietly. "Speak of them. It will keep you sane."

"I thought all I needed to survive was faith in God and a strong sword arm. I was wrong. It is your friendship that may save me."

Stephan relinquished his hold on Henry and struggled to find a smile. "I have never been accused of saving anyone's mind."

"Better that than being the downfall of my mortal soul," Henry said lightheartedly.

Guilt—or was it regret—crossed Stephan's face. Henry regretted his words and said, "I did not mean—"

"Say no more, friend." Stephan looked relieved when knights around them stood and murmurs swept the room. "The king, the king…" Stephan and Henry drew to their feet and lowered their heads.

King Richard tromped through the door waving his hands like a blessing. He shouted, "These brave knights! Messina's bounty is ours!"

Acre
8june 1191

eleven

WEAPONS CLANKED ON THE deck behind Henry. Swordplay today. War tomorrow.

Henry forced back the dread in his gut as Acre's city walls came into view. His heart no longer burned with the passion he'd felt when he'd first left England. Roger's death—*my God, has it been near a year?*—had hit him hard but he'd lost more than his servant. He'd lost a bit of innocence that day near Marseille. And the rest of it disappeared in Messina.

Fingering his crucifix, Henry shifted his gaze to Little John's lesson with Stephan.

"Again," Stephan told his sparring partner. He took a step backwards, sword raised. Slicing the air with the blade, he teased Little John. Sidestep, lunge, a block.

God's heavens. Had he missed the boy becoming man? The seven months Richard's army spent in Messina had been good for Little John and Allan. Henry marveled at the change he saw. When they'd met in Tours fourteen months earlier Little John had been barely chest high, skin and bones. Now he stood a half head shorter than Stephan. Broad-shouldered, chest and stomach muscled with well-fed flesh. His enthusiasm for the adventure of serving the knight hadn't dimmed.

Little John paced, twirled his staff, frowning. When Stephan glanced towards the harbour, Little John chopped the air with the staff, catching Stephan's sword with a clang.

"Good, good, well done!" Stephan shouted.

Little John followed with another downward blow, a lunge, and then swung the staff round. He caught himself just before the hard wood met Stephan's temple. He gasped. "Sorry, my lord."

Stephan laughed. He pounded Little John's back. "No harm done."

Henry turned away not wanting to watch any longer. *No harm?* What lay ahead for Little John? For the king's army?

The galley drew into the harbour. The city of Acre had been under siege nearly two years. The pounding of the stone throwers drew Henry's eye. Jerusalem's fall had been the rallying cry for this call to arms, but the crusaders needed to secure Acre as a gateway. Without the great port, the desire to hold the Holy City in Christian hands would be nothing more than a dream.

Henry saw the smoke darkening Acre's late morning skies. His mood blackened. He'd expected to see his first battle here, not in Messina. He hadn't lost any friends that day, but he couldn't forget that he'd come within a dagger's width of an enemy blade. If it hadn't been for Stephan's true aim, he wouldn't be looking at the land that had given a Savior to all Christians.

Stephan. God help me. One regrettable moment. Why couldn't he let it be? Henry struck the deck rail, wishing away the ache in his heart. *What is wrong with me?*

~ ~ ~

STEPHAN SIGNALED LITTLE JOHN and paced back and forth, teasing him with the tip of his sword. He peered past Little John's shoulder, saw Henry beat the rail. *What are you thinking, my friend?*

The army had wintered in Messina and, for Stephan, it had seemed the longest—and strangest—six months he could remember. Queen Joanna had been released. Tancred, Sicily's king, recognized the wisdom of an alliance with a powerful warrior king like the Lionheart, especially when enemies from the north questioned Tancred's right to the crown.

King Richard's mother, Eleanor of Aquitaine, arrived with Richard's future wife. And oh, what storm clouds that had stirred, for the young woman wasn't the French king's half-sister to whom Richard had been betrothed. It was Berengaria of Navarre. The match, plotted by Richard and Eleanor before he'd left on the crusade, would secure the southern borders of Richard's beloved Aquitaine.

It was Lent, so the marriage had to wait. The fleet had finally sailed east in April, but storms at sea nearly destroyed the chance for Richard to make Berengaria his queen. The ships were scattered, some wrecked in Cyprus. Berengaria and Queen Joanna were within hours of being taken prisoner by enemies there when Richard found them. That threat had been met with the king's wrath, and within a month, he'd taken control of Cyprus and then married his bride.

Politics, as Henry would say.

Stephan looked at him again, remembering his shy smile when he'd danced with Queen Joanna at King Richard's wedding.

Oh Henry... Why does my life feel like it has been turned on its head?

Henry's close brush with death in Messina replayed in his mind. If he'd loosed that crossbow bolt one heartbeat later...

Little John's staff stung Stephan's sword. The blow traveled up his arm. Stephan recovered, blocked the next swing. Sweat beaded on his forehead and stung his eyes. The sun crept higher, barely a quarter above the horizon. It was not yet midsummer's day, but the bright orb beat down like fire as the ships edged slowly into Acre's harbour. Black smoke billowed from a dozen places in the city, dark and ominous, like an oncoming storm.

Darker still was the ache plaguing Stephan's body and soul. He knew what it was. He'd not been with a man since…when was it? Before Marseille? Not that there hadn't been willing partners. Like Benedict in Messina. He'd known then why there'd been no more than a kiss with that one. But he hadn't been able to admit it to himself for weeks after the encounter. And he'd never tell Henry. *It is because of you…*

Christ, what are these strange feelings?

Stephan's casual liaisons never involved feelings, except the pure bodily pleasure of being ravaged by another man. Of doing wonderfully unspeakable things with another man. And now he couldn't think of touching anyone else.

Henry, what have you done to me?

Stephan took a step back. He lunged at Little John. His sword sliced the air but Little John blocked it.

Stephan had never only wanted one man. And women? Growing up, he looked at the village girls with an uninterested eye. When he was squire in the Earl of Huntingdon's household, an older serving girl introduced him to sex on his thirteenth birthday. It was pleasant enough, but it was the tanner's son who'd made him see stars. Stephan breathed deeply, remembering the way he smelled of leather. His hands, calloused and rough, urgently pressed to Stephan's skin.

Life with Richard's army from Normandy to Aquitaine provided ample opportunity to forget the pitched battles in the arms of men who just needed a fuck. Sometimes it was driven by grief as he'd tried to explain to Henry. A way to release the energy and the passion stirred by war. To bury the pain. Sometimes it was pure lust. It felt damn good.

The men he'd been with meant nothing. He'd never dreamed of them. The sex, yes, but many of the men were nameless faces.

Now he only imagined Henry. Stephan's heart swelled. From the corner of his eye, he spied Henry again. His breath caught. What was this feeling when you could think of being with no other?

"Master Stephan?" Little John held his staff in mid-air.

Stephan waved his sword in the air, and then planted the tip against the deck. He leaned on the hilt and smiled. "Enough for today. You've much improved. Get cleaned up for we shall dock soon." He looked across the harbour at the siege machines pounding Acre, eyed smoke rising from fires in the city.

So much like the flames consuming his heart.

This could not be love. Men like him didn't love.

Damn you, Henry.

He glanced sidelong at the man he could not have. While his heart could live with the knowledge they'd never be more than friends, it would break into a thousand pieces if he ever lost him to a Saracen blade.

~ ~ ~

THE WIND SHIFTED TO the west. Acrid smoke from the city drifted towards the ships, but Henry hardly noticed. Stephan had come up beside him, the sweat of swordplay glistening on his chest and back. He thwacked Henry on the buttocks with a cloth. Henry jerked, allowing only a half-hearted glare.

Stephan dried his face and rubbed down his body with the cloth in deliberate and slow moves. His stomach muscles tightened and the biceps in his arms bulged. Little John mimicked him, flexing his arms to show his budding physique. Stephan jabbed his fist at the boy, then tossed the dirty cloth to him in exchange for his tunic.

Fidgeting, Henry looked past them both, well aware of the grin on the boy's face.

"Allan plans to take bets on Little John," Stephan said, tugging the light brown shirt over his head. "He thinks he will beat any of the knights' squires. Did you see how he feinted to the left then brought his staff up under my sword?"

Henry smiled as Little John disappeared below deck. "He has a good teacher."

Stephan tilted his head back proudly. "So I've heard."

Henry ignored the boast, focusing on the land beyond Acre's impressive stone walls.

Stephan followed his gaze.

"Are those Saladin's troops?" Henry asked. "There must be thousands of tents."

Robin's earlier report became a reality. Acre jutted out into the sea like a thumb on a hand. Water surrounded it on three sides. Mountains to the north, plains sweeping towards forested hills in the east and southeast. Henry remembered how Roger thought there'd be nothing but desert and blowing sands. He would have liked the trees, though they were nothing like ones in England.

"Saracens to the north," Stephan said, and then nodded his head to the east and southeast, "and more of the infidels there."

Henry shivered. Tents of every shape and size scarred the landscape, boasting the colours of sunsets and clouds. It was nothing like his first sighting of the king's camp back in Tours. Here, Saladin's army surrounded the crusaders.

"Shall we make quick work of it?"

Stephan and Henry startled. Neither had heard Richard and Robin approach. Bowing, they said, "Sire."

Henry added, "God willing."

"One look at you, my liege, and they shall scatter like rabbits with wolves—or lions—on their tails." Stephan rubbed his hands together, anticipating the enemy's fearful introduction to the legendary warrior known as Lionheart. "Surely word of Messina and Cyprus has reached them."

Richard chuckled. "I shall wave my banners over my head and they shall be off."

"They would be wise to do so," Robin said.

"If only it were that simple." Richard glanced at the galley's crew and the two familiar figures climbing the masts to secure the lines. "That boy is as agile as any of these seasoned crewmen, Robin. Better watch him. They are likely to keep him on board."

Allan dangled his legs, perched on the rigging as steady as a bird. Little John climbed more slowly, but he joined his friend, every bit as determined.

"I'll not let them, sire," Robin said. "He has proven his loyalty time and again."

Henry felt a tug on his heart. Robin's voice held a note of pride. The boy had become like a son to the knight.

Richard nodded. "And he is good at games of chance."

"He cheats." Stephan smiled.

Richard cleared his throat. "He knows when to call a bluff. That is not cheating. Did you know he has been teaching the queen and my sister his games? They are delighted. My lady wife bested me in a round whilst we lay anchored outside Tyre. If these sailors do not kidnap him, she may." He laughed and wiped a hand across his brow. "This ungodly heat. Come. Join me on the bow. Let us greet Acre."

Richard's reddish-gold hair gleamed in the mid-morning light. Sunlight reflected off the sword he held across his chest. Tall and statuesque, he looked intimidating yet calm. His enemies should take heed, Henry thought. The Lionheart had arrived.

Acre
july 1191

twelve

BREATHLESS, ALLAN RAN THROUGH the camp, vaulted over supplies and wagons, over people. "They're coming! The Saracens are coming!" He ran headlong into Stephan. "The wall—the French stone throwers have breached the wall."

Parts of Acre's wall had tumbled before, and, without fail, Saladin's troops would sweep down from the hills. While the French turned to hold back that horde, the city's defenders repaired the breach. Men died for nothing. The infidels maintained their control of the city.

King Richard knew the danger of the crusaders' exposure to a two-front war. Time and again he'd asked the French king to wait. Richard refused to commit his own army until he had more firepower. His fleet, with equipment to build more stone throwers and siege engines, had not arrived.

Stephan heard the sense of urgency cracking Allan's voice. "Calm down."

"It is different this time, my lord."

Another round of boulders smashed into the walls. The noise reverberated across the camp and out towards the plains. Drums pounded and trumpets blared from within the city.

"The French, my lord—all of them—they are going to charge."

"All of Philip's men?" Stephan asked.

"Aye. The knights are mounted and the men-at-arms, they have the scaling ladders. This is bigger than before." Allan waved towards the hills. "There are thousands of Saracens—"

"I see that black blanket moving towards the French line." Stephan blew out an impatient breath. It was no different than any other day in Acre, but if Philip had ordered a full assault on both fronts, they'd not succeed without the help of King Richard's men. "Where is Little John?"

"He is down there watching the French."

"What were you doing in their camp?" Stephan shook his head. "Find Robin. Tell him what has happened."

Allan shot away like a wolf on the chase. Stephan headed towards the French lines.

~ ~ ~

LITTLE JOHN CROUCHED BEHIND one of the wagons. Frantic, he looked around for a shield, aware that he'd wandered directly between the line of French knights and their men-at-arms. He and Allan only meant to get close enough to get a good look at the siege engines because there'd been so much talk of them in the English camp. Just a look. Neither had realised the French would choose this moment to launch an assault.

The Saracens charged across the plain towards the knights' menacing defensive barrier. Dust and dirt choked the air to the north and east. Horses snorted, shuffling, their reins held tightly by the knights before the charge.

"Shields," a captain shouted.

A rain of arrows from the wall walk pelted the men. Grumbling, they spat curses in their native dialect. Little John knew those words but little else they spoke. From the tone of their voices, he heard no fear.

Arrows bounced off shields, a steady beat. Little John had heard those sounds before but never been in the middle of it. He wouldn't let himself be scared. But he would have felt better if he'd a sword and shield in his hands.

French commanders shouted orders up and down the line. They strained to be heard over the boulders pounding the wall and the clink and scrape of armour as men prepared for the charge.

A missile struck a cracked section of the wall, gouging a hole as wide as a man is tall. Huge chunks of the wall split and crumbled, crashing towards the ditch. The ground shook.

Cheers swelled from the troops. The mounted knights blocked Little John's view of the approaching Saracens; raised shields and dust, the city. He couldn't see more than two horses' lengths in any direction.

Trumpets blared. "Charge!" The battle cry reverberated through the ranks. Little John felt their hoofbeats beneath his feet. A thousand or more horses thundering into battle wasn't a sound to forget.

The knights rode out to meet the approaching enemy while the men-at-arms charged into the breach. Arrows and crossbow bolts screamed from the wall walk and the sky turned black. A few feet in front of Little John, a man-at-arms took a hit. Little John paled. He'd seen men hanged, but never saw someone pierced by an arrow before his eyes. The man fell back and writhed on the ground. A moment later, he lay still, eyes frozen in horror, blood coating the fleur-de-lis on his tunic and pooling on the rocky soil.

Little John clenched the wagon wheel. Screams sounded all around him. Another man fell nearby, struck through the calf by an arrow. His face twisted in pain as he pulled himself towards the cover of the wagon.

Little John could almost reach the man. He held his breath, waiting for a pause in the shower of arrows, then lunged to reach the soldier's hand. He heard a *thunk*, saw the man's body quiver in a death throe. He jerked his hand back. "God keep you," he said. An arrow struck the ground in front of him and he pulled back again. He saw the dead man's sword and the shield he might use for protection and cautiously extended his hand when someone suddenly grabbed him from behind.

"What do you think you are doing?" Stephan shouted.

Little John wrenched free, pointed towards the dead French men. "I need something to fight with."

"You've no business being here."

"They weren't fighting when I first arrived. As long as I'm here, I can help."

"That is beside the point. The king holds us back for a battle we can win. If you are going to die, make it count for something."

Little John harrumphed. "I have no intention of dying."

Stephan smiled. "Good. Now let's go." He moved behind the wagon, his shield hefted above his head. Little John drew up beside him and they scrambled away from the wagon and towards the safety of the English camp.

~ ~ ~

RICHARD WAS ON HIS feet, eyes fiery. "Philip did what?"

Allan startled at the force of Richard's voice. Across the room, Queen Berengaria looked up from her dice game with Queen Joanna and turned worried eyes on her husband. He might sound fierce, but he'd barely recovered from a high fever that had kept him abed for days. He swayed and planted his hands on the trestle to catch himself.

"Please, Richard, sit down," Berengaria pleaded.

Allan wondered what King Richard's young bride truly thought of this place, of her confinement here. He always imagined queens and kings living in splendour behind castle walls. A tent in the desert—even one as lavish as the king's— seemed an odd place to bring his bride of two months.

Robin looked at ease and leaned on his sword. "Philip ordered a full assault despite your warning that it would fail."

"I will not order my men into battle. Philip—that fool. He has been here nearly three months. Has he learned nothing?"

Joanna must have sensed Allan's thoughts and patted her sister-in-law's hand. The late morning sun flooded the pavilion with light and reflected off her ruby ring. She smiled at Allan and pointed towards the dice. "Pay them no heed. Join us. I need your advice. I have two two's, a three, five and six. Do I roll again?"

Allan wanted to oblige but looked warily at Robin.

"Come along," Joanna repeated.

Robin prodded Allan with a stiff nod, and Allan scooted across the room. He settled in between the two queens, leaned forward and half-whispered to Joanna, "He just called the French king a fool, my lady. Is that...proper?"

Joanna smiled. "In certain company."

Allan shrank back. "I will not repeat it to anyone."

"We know that," Berengaria said, patting his shoulder.

Allan relaxed under the royal ladies' watchful eyes, Berengaria's dark like her hair; Joanna's brilliant green like an emerald. Joanna smelled of almonds and roses. Ringlets the colour of her brother's reddish-gold hair fell to her shoulders, and the jade gown she wore revealed creamy white skin. Berengaria's deep red gown was trimmed with pearls and gold. Allan's face grew warm in their presence in spite of the servants fanning the royal ladies. To think this former thief who once scrabbled with the rats for a meal now enjoyed the company of queens and the King of England.

"Now, come, Allan." Joanna tapped the table with her long slender fingers. "I aim to win this round. Show me that secret twist of the wrist again?"

"What?" Berengaria cried. "Allan's not shown me any special tricks and I won the last two games."

"There is no secret, my lady. I promise. Just a quick move is all." He cupped his hand, twisted his wrist to demonstrate.

Joanna practiced the move. "What shall we wager, Berengaria? If I win, Allan shall forego his duties with Sir Robin until the Sabbath."

Robin looked up, shrugged, when he heard his name. Allan grinned. He started to ask the consequences if Joanna lost when Berengaria waved a servant over to refill their goblets.

She sipped at the wine, her face suddenly serious. "Look at my lord king, Joanna. He has not fully recovered. I worry for him. If Philip's rash decision should cause Richard to do battle today..." She twisted the golden chain that held her crucifix. "Look at how he hides his pain."

Joanna studied her brother. His face was pale and stone-like, eyes narrowed, mouth tight. "He will not risk his men. It is too soon and he knows that. As for his health—the healers say he must rest." Her lips curled mischievously. "Mayhap the army can hold him down."

Berengaria rolled her eyes. Allan stifled a chuckle.

Richard ignored the whispers at the game table. "Have we any news of the fleet?" he asked.

Robin moved to the map spread out on a long trestle to one side of the pavilion. "Messengers from Tyre spotted them headed south yesterday. If the weather holds—"

"Damnable storms." Richard strode across the pavilion and sat next to Berengaria. He pressed his hand atop hers. She smiled shyly at him.

"God's grace, and we should see the ships in the harbour tonight," Robin said.

Richard grunted, downed a full goblet of wine. "Too late for those poor French souls." He threw the jewel-encrusted cup across the room.

Allan cringed and swallowed the lump in his throat. His da'—well, the man he thought was his father—threw things when he was upset. Or drunk. Allan rubbed his leg. He could feel the scar where a scalding kettle of stew had landed.

"Allan?" Joanna said.

"Ye—yes, my lady." Allan glanced at the dice on the table, sucked in a breath to calm his nerves. "Roll the three, five, and the six."

"One day," Richard said, glancing at Robin. "If only Philip had waited one more day. My ships would be here. We'd have another dozen or more stone throwers with his by tomorrow night. Twice that number in two days. Damn him."

"Yes, sire."

"Why in God's Holy Name does he think it will help to throw more of his men against the city's defenders and the Saracens? He has already tried and failed."

"He does not think, your grace. Shall I tell our men to stand down?"

Richard nodded. Robin bowed and departed.

Richard looked drained, his face paler. He closed his eyes a moment, smiling when Berengaria squeezed his hand.

Joanna rolled the dice.

"Sorry," Allan said when a one, three, and four appeared on the table. "You lose."

Richard's eyes flew open. "Let us pray not, young Allan. Let us pray not."

thirteen

THE KING HAD BEEN RIGHT. The French were left with defeat and counted a hundred or more dead and wounded amongst the knights and men-at-arms. Carcasses of dozens of magnificent warhorses littered the plains. Tens of thousands of arrows loosed and for what? Henry's cynicism climbed as another day dawned and temperatures rose.

He tugged at the hood of his hauberk. His hair dripped with sweat and clung to his neck. "Let the archers on the city walls hit me. In this mail, I might die from the heat at any moment."

Stephan shook his head, raining sweat on Henry and their horses. "Death might be a blessing."

Henry patted Sombre's neck. "I suppose the heat here is better than being cooped up below deck, isn't it, boy?"

Sombre bobbed his head up and down. Stephan's horse nudged his snout and both animals whinnied. Stephan urged Tempête forward along a track that wound through supplies off-loaded from the busses. As predicted, these very large boats, or dromons, had arrived shortly after the failed French assault.

"Nothing like a bit of spying on your friends," Stephan said, referring to the assignment given to them by Robin.

Henry gulped mead from his flask. "Is reconnoitering the same as spying?"

"According to Robin? No. We merely keep an eye on our French allies." Stephan chuckled. "Assess their strengths and weaknesses after their stupid assault."

"Keep your voice down."

"Don't you agree it was—"

"Yes, but that is not the point. Our knights will not argue with you, but it is not something we should blurt out from one end of the camp to the other."

Wagons lined up three to four thick and as far as the eye could see in either direction. Some were stacked high with barrels that held dried meats, grain and ale. Large wooden crates were filled with arrows, clubs, and lances. Timbers were fit in others.

"Can you imagine what this heat will be like by summer's end?" Stephan asked.

Henry stared at the light haze of dust kicked up by the men unloading the wagons. "At least we shall be trudging across desert sands towards Jerusalem by then. Better that than this idle time on patrol."

The smell of heated metal stung Henry's nose. The clangs from the forge rang until the blacksmith paused to inspect his efforts. Workers grunted, settling heavy wooden beams across their shoulders from the wagons. They trudged carefully on the uneven road to an area where the stone throwers and siege engines were being assembled.

"The knights are taking bets."

Henry laughed. "Is Allan behind that?" Robin's young servant had developed quite the reputation for games of chance, and not just among the royals. "What do they say?"

"Many predict Acre will fall soon but we shall be here until Christmastide. Later, if the winter weather is sour."

Robin had spoken of winter the previous day. Miserable rains, muddied roads and snow seemed unimaginable given the heat of July. Henry found this Holy Land strange and foreign, beautiful in its starkness. But oh, how he longed for the forests and the greens of England.

"We shall take the city, find rooms with soft beds, and wile away long winter nights at the palace," Stephan said.

"The palace?"

"Where the king will stay with his lady wife and sister. Ha!" Stephan chuckled. "To think I shall not need to sleep fully clothed with sword gripped in my hand. Acre might be quite the pleasant place."

"If there is anything left of it when this siege ends."

Up ahead, French stone throwers hurled huge boulders. Just before they hit the city walls, activity around Henry and Stephan stopped. The blacksmith paused. Workers froze. A collective breath was sucked in, held.

Crash! The earth trembled. A corner of the one they called the Cursed Tower crumbled. The wall remained intact.

Clang, clank. The blacksmith resumed his steady beat.

Stephan trotted ahead. He shouted out a greeting to Ralf Walter, one of King Richard's engineers.

Walter had cuffed a young boy by the ear, dragged him to rolls of thick cloth that would be stretched like a roof over a siege engine. "The men need these now. Move them down by Alard, and then get those hides and the netting from the wagon. Do not be late again else you'll not be working for me."

The boy's eyes were lowered. "Yes, sir. Thank you, sir." He struggled with the oversized tarp, slowly managed to lift it to his shoulder.

"Good work there," Stephan said. The youngster smiled and trudged towards Thomas. "Walter, will this engine be completed by day's end?"

"Yes, Sir Stephan. This, and three more of the stone throwers. The men will move them in place a'fore they get fed tonight."

Henry watched the workers. Their clothes were dirty, their faces covered with sweat and grime. Two men plunged their heads into a water-filled barrel and emerged dripping wet. Some looked ready to collapse.

"Do not starve them," Henry said. "They shall be too weak to finish the work."

Walter's lips pursed, but he nodded. Inhaling deeply, he cocked his head down the road. "Smell that, my lord? We break for the midday meal soon enough. I know my business. They work hard. I feed them well."

"We shall report your progress to the king," Stephan said. "He will be pleased."

Stephan prodded Tempête down the road. Henry drew up beside him and grimaced. "Shall we report our estimate of how many of his workers will be dead within the week?"

"Walter is no fool, Henry. He needs those men if he wants to stay in the king's good graces and on the payroll."

They trotted to the point where Richard's camp ended and Philip's began. Not quite a line in the dirt, but the French soldiers eyed Henry and Stephan suspiciously when they reined in their mounts.

"English," a mounted Frenchmen snorted.

The others half-turned to look at Henry and Stephan, grumbling. The French were fully armoured, some in heavy mail, others with lighter mail over padded tunics. All in golds and blues with the fleur-de-lis emblazoned on highly polished shields.

One man met the English knights' gazes. "Your king lacks the courage to join us in a full scale assault."

Henry wrapped his hand tightly around Sombre's reins. "King Richard does not run into battle. He is no—"

Stephan caught Henry's arm before he insulted the French king. It was too late. Two knights whisked their swords into the air and nudged their mounts towards Henry.

A third knight straightened to full height in his saddle. He exuded authority. Resting his hand on the pommel of the sword at his waist, he glared at his men. "Put those away." The man was huge, at least as tall as King Richard. His face was pockmarked and scarred from battle, his nose crooked.

Grudgingly, his subordinates complied but not before the knight added, "Watch your tongue, English, before one of my men cuts it out."

Stephan's hand found his own sword. "When our stone throwers are completed and our siege engines are in place, we shall add them to yours. Together we will bring those walls down. We'll be invincible."

The captain of the knights scoffed. "Tell your king to send sappers to the tunnels with our men. The walls won't crumble without undermining."

"None of your Englishmen are helping in the tunnels," someone spat to the murmured assent of a dozen of his companions.

Henry glanced at the tunnel entrances near the front of the French lines and cringed. Common in siege warfare, the tunnels would be stifling, especially by midday. They snaked beneath the ditch separating the camp from the city walls. The men who dug them—the sappers—looked more haggard than the builders in Ralf Walter's crews.

"King Richard is well aware that undermining operations and the steady crush of missiles will bring down Acre's walls. It is only a matter of days now that the Lionheart is here."

The French knights snickered at Stephan's bravado. "Days? Have not near three weeks passed, and how many of our people have died? Where were you when we attacked?"

The others grunted agreement.

Henry had seen the king's strategies in action. He wasn't about to question his decisions. King Richard might have great disdain for the French king, but military experience drove his motives. To tell these French that their king was an impatient arse would be pleasing, but Henry knew better than to rile their "friends" a second time.

Stephan sat straighter in his saddle. Fire brewed behind his eyes but he chose his words carefully. "Have you forgotten that we fight the same cause, good sir?"

The groan of the nearest stone thrower distracted them all. Another boulder sailed through the air. It smashed into the wall with a tremendous boom. The sound jolted Henry. He should be used to round after round of firing. The din kept him awake deep into the night.

Stephan bid good-bye to the Frenchmen and they started back to the English camp.

"The king did not look well this morning," Henry said.

Stephan glanced at him. "The queen beat him at one of those games Allan taught her."

"I am serious, Stephan."

The knight gave him a soft smile. "I know. I saw it in his eyes. His mouth and lips are covered with sores and fever has left him weak. He pretends his illness is not so bad."

"I had hoped it was sleepless nights, nothing more."

"The healers told Robin it is the Arnaldia."

Henry heard the French king had suffered the same malady but not near so bad as King Richard. Many English had been ill with this fever, had lost hair and fingernails.

Henry chewed on his lip. He watched defenders on the wall walk loose arrows on men loading the slings of one of the stone throwers. "What will happen if the king dies?"

Stephan took a long slow breath. "Many of the knights would go home."

One of Philip's siege engines destroyed by Greek fire was being cleared away. The charred remains were blackened like Henry's passion for this war.

"What would you do?" Henry asked, turning to Stephan.

"I will follow Robin. He and a few of the others—they would safeguard Queen Berengaria and the king's sister."

"Dear God. I had not even thought—" Henry crossed himself. "This would be a dangerous place for them without the king."

Stephan nodded grimly. "We would need to see them safely back to Poitou. Others might push on towards the Holy City. I am not certain there would be much of an army."

Henry tried to imagine Richard's men taking orders from the French king. He rejected that thought, his mind on the queens at the pavilion with a small contingent of guards. And Little John. He chuckled.

"What?"

"Little John. He is quite taken with Queen Joanna."

"That he is." Stephan laughed, drawing stares from the men taking a short break by the horse trough. One dunked his head into the water. Coming up for a breath, he splattered his friend. Only Ralf Walter's angry glare kept them from a water fight.

"Do you know he finishes his work for me in half the time? I have not seen someone clean boots and polish a sword faster than Little John," Stephan added. "And you'll not hear him complain about the chores Robin has given him in the royal household. He and Allan are already favorites of the queens."

Another boulder smashed into the city wall with an explosive thud followed by a barrage of missiles. The wall cracked with a sickening sound, like that of bone splitting flesh. Pea- to pig-sized pieces of the shattered wall slid into the ditch, the noise deafening. Dirt and dust rose like a thick curtain.

The English stopped work, cheering as French soldiers charged the breach. When the dust dissipated, the number of enemies on the wall walk had more than doubled. Men, women and even small children scurried to seal the opening from inside the city. A hail of arrows rained down, and French bowmen answered them with flight after flight.

Then the drumming began, an ugly steady beat joined by the familiar blare of trumpets from within the city. The French rear guard watched the wooded slopes to the north and east.

Henry shivered. He exchanged a *here-they-come* look with Stephan. Sombre stamped his hoofs nervously. The Saracen hordes swept down from the hills like waves pounding the shore. Their crescent moon and star banners rippled in the wind like mighty black or yellow sails.

The English cheers faded beneath the clang of armour. French men-at-arms turned back from the breach, forced to prepare for another repeat of the assault on the rear guard.

Stephan seated his shield in his left hand, looked at Henry. "I know we were ordered to observe, but I do not like watching my allies being slaughtered even when they ignore sound military strategy."

"Their knights did say we English had not helped," Henry said.

Stephan cocked his head towards the line of French knights. "They could use two brave knights like us. Shall we?"

Both men tugged their hoods up and seated their helmets. Stephan hefted his sword. He urged Tempête forward.

Palms sweating beneath his gloves, Henry unsheathed his sword from its scabbard. He spurred Sombre and took his place next to Stephan, ignoring the flutter in his belly. He touched a hand to where his crucifix lay next to his pounding heart. *Keep us in Your arms, oh Lord, that we might do Your work.*

Henry glanced sidelong at Stephan. "Robin and the king will not be pleased when they hear what we have done."

"Let's plan to tell them ourselves, shall we?" Stephan smiled, eyes lit with mischief. "You know the king would do it if he were here. Our punishment will be listening to him complain we charged without him. And worse, I will have to deal with Little John. He shall chastise me to no end after I lectured him about rushing into the thick of battle."

Henry laughed and then tapped Stephan's sword. This was the right thing to do.

~ ~ ~

THE FRENCH MEN-AT-ARMS STOOD shoulder-to-shoulder, lances pointed towards their foes, axes or clubs slung over their backs or hooked through their belts. Crossbowmen, one row kneeling, another behind them on their feet, planted their bolts in the ground, placed one and cranked back their bows. The line of men and horses stretched near a thousand paces along the edge of the plain, taut like a rope.

No one spoke, their eyes held fast on the cloud kicked up by the charging infidels.

A commander with a golden crest on his surcoat shouted, "Hold!"

The sound of hoofbeats approaching unnerved the horses. One reared, nearly throwing its rider.

The enemy cavalry—thousands strong—was half the distance between the hills and the French army. Still not close enough to send arrows into their ranks.

"Hold!" the call came again.

Three hundred paces. Almost there. The horsemen were now at a full gallop, pressed so close that light could not be seen between them.

"Loose!" the captain shouted.

The cloudless sky turned black with a thousand bolts. The first wave arced high. A second and a third followed, straighter. With each volley, men fell. Horses stumbled. The enemy lines broke. The fallen became obstacles to manoeuvre around. Yet still they came.

"Now!"

The French knights advanced. Philip Capet watched his army from a mounted position a safe distance behind the bowmen. As the knights kicked their warhorses to a canter, the air turned brown from the dust.

Enemy arrows bounced off French shields. Hundreds of lances were leveled.

And then, the Saracens were on them.

Mounted warriors collided in a mass of steel, wood, and flesh. The first blows killed many, sent others reeling. Lances splintered by the impact littered the ground. Swords were unsheathed.

Blood sprayed.

~ ~ ~

STEPHAN CHARGED INTO THE fray surrounded by men sporting the fleur-de-lis. English and French, the distinction disappeared. They fought as brothers—aware of each other, yet not, as the battlefield became a massive sea of men and horses. The neat, coordinated line of the charge had disappeared. Knights chose an adversary, or one found them.

The foot soldiers advanced, fighting unhorsed enemies or thrusting at the animals' unprotected legs. Swords and clubs and maces, arms swinging, shields raised. Philip's soldiers beat at the Saracens, weighed down by once-gleaming hauberks over padded gambesons and chausses made of mail. Lightly armoured, the enemy soldiers moved swiftly. They died easier when a blade got past their shields. But there were more of them, at least two for every Frenchman.

Stephan blocked one downward slash of a sword, deflected another. Tempête answered the press of his heels, a knee, his thighs. Stephan found flesh too many times to count. Men and horses screamed. His sword was drenched in blood.

Henry quickly lost sight of Stephan in the melee. Sunlight glinted off a raised blade. Steel against steel, he met a swift swing meant to sever his head.

A French knight thundered past, nicking Henry's attacker's arm. The enemy cavalryman did not slow, shouting, "Allah Akbar!" as he charged the French foot soldiers.

A crossbow bolt slammed into Henry's shield. He deflected it, his arm trembling from the blow. To his right, another bolt pierced the mail of a French knight with a *thwump*. The knight slid from his destrier, one foot caught in the stirrup. His head smacked the ground. The frightened animal dragged him until he broke loose from the strappings, his body still.

It was never quiet. Yet the screams, grunts, and the chorus of enemy voices, so loud and abrasive, became indistinct and faded into the desert dust. Henry could hear his own heartbeat. He heard Sombre, felt the animal's strength beneath him.

Another enemy soldier charged him. The man's horse pressed nose to nose with Sombre. Henry angled his shield, deflecting the blow from the rider's knobbed club. He nearly missed seeing another lance leveled at his body; the rider came hard on the heels of the club wielder. Henry jerked Sombre to his left. The club came so close that its wind brushed his cheek. Curses erupted behind him. There was no time to look back to see who'd been struck.

Ahead, a horse threw its Saracen rider. His French adversary had pivoted to finish him. The lanky Saracen jumped to his feet. The Frenchmen's sword missed him by an inch. Twisting, the Saracen ripped his blade across the leg of the man's mount. The horse screamed and crashed to the ground.

The knight rolled free from the animal's crushing weight but another enemy horseman bore down on him and the Saracen who'd attacked him was charging on foot.

Henry shot towards the Frenchman to intercept the horseback rider. There was a blur of a blade. Henry felt a sting as he leaned forward in the saddle, but he whipped his sword around to slice into the horseman's neck.

Jerking on Sombre's reins, he spun and saw the French knight sink his red-stained sword into the other Saracen. The knight looked up at Henry and his battle-enraged eyes suddenly softened. "Thank you," he called.

"Stay close. A dozen more are headed our way." Henry didn't need to point out that they'd strayed to the furthest edge of the fighting. At their backs, other enemy troops retreated, beating a path towards the hills.

The knight pushed back his hood. "We cannot take them all, friend." He swiped at his eyes. Sweat mingled with blood from a nasty gash above his brow. He looked so young, surely not any older than Henry. "Go, save yourself."

"We only need hold them a few moments." Henry tipped his sword at the Saracens. A sharp pain rippled along his arm. Blood covered his mail, some of it his own. Warmth crept down his flesh. A slight wound, nothing more. He ignored the throbbing and added, "Your knights are on their heels." *But are they close enough to help?*

One of the infidels charging them plucked a shaft from his arrow bag. He nocked and loosed it—at a full gallop no less. The arrow sizzled past Henry's head. The archer unsheathed his sword. His compatriots split off to force the French knights behind them to separate.

Heart pounding, Henry raised his sword to meet his foe. Their weapons crossed, locked together. Both men swayed in their saddles. Henry's muscles weakened. He grabbed the pommel of his saddle to stay upright. His fingers slipped on blood and sweat on the hilt of his sword. He strained with effort to keep hold of it, glad that his adversary chose to flee towards the hills as a few of the French knights drew closer.

Henry sucked in the hot desert air. He wiped the sting of moisture from his eyes. The Saracen's arrow had missed him, but the French knight he'd saved only a moment before was face down in the sand. Trembling, Henry closed his eyes and crossed himself. *God have mercy on his soul.*

The other knights had abandoned the chase, not daring to trail the retreating Saracens. Henry spurred Sombre to follow the French towards their own lines.

His mind started to clear as dust settled on the plain. His wounded arm suddenly throbbed. He heard himself breathe, then stopped, breath caught in his throat. He searched the field of battle looking for Stephan. *Oh God...*

Henry shielded his eyes from the afternoon sun. *Stephan...where are you?*

Henry saw no sign of Stephan amongst the men headed to the camp. He slowed, eyed the fallen. Bloodied bodies. Severed arms and heads. More Saracen dead than French. So many lives cut short.

Reining in Sombre, he looked for Stephan's white cloak. Nothing. Only the blue and gold of King Philip's troops and the desert-coloured ones of the Saracens lay scattered on this field of death.

Henry forced back the bile rising in his throat. His hands shook violently but he pressed Sombre ahead.

A lone figure walking on the plain caught his eye. "Stephan!" Henry shouted out joyfully.

Stephan saw him and smiled wearily. His cloak was tossed over one shoulder, his sword rested against the other. Blood splattered him from head to foot. He looked nothing like the braggart Henry had met in Southampton in what seemed a lifetime ago.

Henry's breath caught again. Something was wrong. Stephan was on foot. Henry shook his head. "No, not Tempête."

Stephan lifted his sword. It looked afire, reflecting the scorching sun. He waved it at Henry, a sign of victory despite his loss.

fourteen

THE ONLY VICTORY THAT day had been that they'd both survived. When next the sun rose, the battle still raged and Richard's men, siege engines and stone throwers joined the French efforts.

Henry lost track of the days. When they fought, he watched Stephan alert atop a roan charger. How strange not to see him on his beloved Tempête.

The pounding of the city walls was like a bad dream, constant, day after day and into the night. A nightmare with no end in sight. The same events, predictable, deadly, bloody. A portion of the wall would crumble. Cheers. Men rushed forward, some with scaling ladders, others to remove debris in the ditch to make their passage manageable. There would be wave after wave of arrows. Greek fire—a frightening, flaming weapon—rained down on them from the walls. The wounded and dying screamed. The drums. The trumpets.

Dear God, that noise. Henry closed his eyes. Beating, blaring, the sounds emanating from the city would awaken the enemy in the hills. Then thousands of the infidels attacked the crusaders' rear guard. They kept coming. Again and again. Every day.

Stephan always looked fresh, fierce, ready to throw himself into battle, unmarred by the glazed looks of the knights around him. King Richard, barely recovered from his illness, looked tired. Each day's battles wore more heavily on him.

Henry admired both men. He struggled through his own exhaustion. How could he let it take him when the king directed the battle from his sickbed? Henry wouldn't have believed it if he'd not seen it himself. Squires trotted Richard out on a litter, placing him beneath a lattice-framed cover, a cercleia, that repelled darts as well as any shield. The squires would set and hand the king his crossbow. In between issuing orders, he'd fire at the Saracens on the wall walk. A goodly number fell under his aim.

Though the noise of the stone throwers grated on Henry's nerves, he watched their destructive firepower with the same fascination as every other man in the camp.

"Turn," a black-clad captain ordered two men cranking a windlass on one machine. The beam of the stone thrower bent back with a groan as the firing position was set.

Henry followed the snap of the beam and the arc of the large boulder when it launched from the sling. Its perfect trajectory sent it sailing at the turret the men called the Cursed Tower. The impact sent shards of rock and dust into the air. The knights around him cheered.

Still, Henry cringed. "Will this ever end?"

Stephan heard the frustration in his voice and tried to make light of it. "I hope your sword arm is not as puny as your voice."

Henry ignored the jibe. "It aches, but I did beat Allan at arm wrestling last night."

"That gives me great confidence." Stephan's mirth was short-lived. He pointed at Henry's arm. "Did the healer's salve help that wicked cut you suffered?"

Watching the stone thrower crews load another sling with huge rocks, Henry dismissed the question with a wave of hand.

He wouldn't admit that the wound he'd suffered days earlier still ached.

"Acre will surrender," Stephan said.

Henry wasn't so certain. "Saladin's garrison commanders brought terms to King Richard. He rejected them. I do not understand. It sounded a fair offer to me." Politics still frustrated Henry. The money and suggestions of hostages had not been enough to satisfy King Richard.

"First offers are always ignored." Stephan's longer experience fighting had made him indifferent to wartime negotiations. He accepted that the winners would do things in their own way and in their own time. "They shall come around. Saladin knows their fate is sealed. We have blocked all supplies going into the city. The garrison's contact with Saladin has been cut, except for those damn trumpets and drums. And at least they have offered terms. This will be over soon."

"Hold," a stone thrower captain shouted to his crew.

Henry glanced at them, turned sharply as the sounds of battle ceased and orders rang out from the lines of bowmen. "Hold! Hold!" Arrows did not paint the sky black. Soldiers stopped whatever they'd been doing and looked at the city gates. A single white banner rose. A rider emerged when the gate opened.

"A messenger," Henry said. "Mayhap this one will bring new terms that King Richard will accept."

Two days later, on the twelfth day of July, Acre surrendered.

~ ~ ~

TWENTY-SEVEN HUNDRED PEOPLE were imprisoned, held for ransom in accordance with the terms of the surrender. The rest of the Acre's defenders were allowed to leave with nothing but the clothes they wore. Saladin would have thirty days to free Christians he had imprisoned during his campaigns, return the fragments of the True Cross his forces had captured at Hattin, and to pay two hundred thousand bezants to Richard and Philip.

The king's retinue moved into the palace. The crusader armies found housing in quarters throughout the city. Life on the ships and in the camps became unpleasant memories.

In the great hall of the palace, Stephan rearranged his food for the third time. Something soft hit his forehead and he startled. A grape bounced into the juices on his trencher and splattered his tunic. He looked across the table and rolled his eyes at Robin.

Robin tossed another grape into the air and caught it in his mouth. Grinning, he chewed it up and snatched another handful from one of many platters decorating the table. "The king already speaks of moving back to the camp. He must set an example for the men."

"We've been inside the city walls but for two days," Stephan said.

Robin shot a third grape skyward but Allan ran past and grabbed it mid-air. Robin stood as if to give chase, then laughed and stretched muscles still weary from wielding his sword in skirmishes with the Saracens.

Deepening shadows crept across the great hall. A dark-haired beauty serving the knights had caught Robin's eye. She hugged loaves of fragrant bread to her generous breasts. Without breaking his gaze, Robin bit into a cluster of grapes greedily, smiling when she pursed her lips and blew him a kiss.

Thirty knights in varying degrees of drunkenness enjoyed the late afternoon meal. Henry waved his hand from the men to the platters overflowing with meat, fish, breads and fruit. "Giving up all this and soft beds so soon for tents, snakes, tarantulas, and the harsh desert sun? They will not be pleased."

Stephan winced, rubbed the ache in his shoulder. "I would prefer the soft bed myself," he said as a serving girl leaned over him to light candles on the trestle. She drew back sharply expecting that a stray hand might find her buttocks.

Robin allayed her fears. "You are safe with that one," he said and then gleamed greedily. He reached for her hand. "But let me—"

She blushed and smacked Robin's hand playfully.

Robin laughed and shooed her away. He clapped Stephan's back. "Sorry, my friend. We might have another week or two to enjoy the soft beds."

"It is more than food and beds," Henry said.

Robin nodded cheekily. "It's the whores."

Stephan waved his hands. "I will not miss them."

"More for the rest of us," Robin said with a chuckle.

Stephan smiled until he met Henry's eyes. He knew Henry would not judge. He was as true to those words he'd spoken after they'd met as he was to his Alys. Henry had no interest in loose women. Or men. Stephan sighed. *More's the pity.* He swallowed what was left of his ale in one long gulp.

Henry stared into his empty goblet. He grabbed the pitcher of ale, poured another round. "The king is right. The men will be spoiled the longer we stay in the city. Have they forgotten we came to free Jerusalem from the infidels? Are they so anxious to stay in Acre?"

"Yet we cannot begin that journey, not with nearly three thousand prisoners underfoot," Robin said. "The king will not leave a small force behind to guard them. We shall be here until Saladin pays the ransom."

Hostages—their prisoners—and ransoms. Both were spoils of war and there was nothing unusual in Richard's demands.

Henry groaned. "That is near thirty days more if Saladin waits until the deadline."

Robin's hay-colored hair framed the frown on his face. "And he will not pay a day sooner than he must. Why should he? He can watch our men while away their time. A few nights to celebrate our victory are fine. But week after week?" He downed his ale. "They grow lazy. An army needs routine. Drills need to continue. Discipline maintained. The road to Jerusalem will be dangerous. The sea to our west. Harassed from the north, east and south by the enemy."

Stephan eyed Robin over the bridge of his nose. "So tell us. Does the king have a plan to convince his army to return to the camps?"

Robin rubbed his thumb to his forefingers. "A little coin in their pockets for their service might just do the trick. Did you see how the men flocked to remove debris when the wall fell, and under fire from the Saracens?"

"Two gold bezants per stone buys more than a wash in the bathhouse and a fine meal. King Richard is quite generous...and knows that bribery works." Henry lifted his mug to his dry, cracked lips.

"Whores!" Robin laughed.

Candlelight from the table reflected in Henry's brilliant blue eyes. Stephan shivered. *Henry. A bathhouse.* Laughter at the other end of the trestle interrupted Stephan's pleasant thought.

"To Leopold!" someone shouted.

"To the duke," another called. The knight pounded his goblet against the table, a slow steady drumming that others joined. They repeated the duke's name, sneering contemptuously.

"Unbelievable," Henry said. "He is our ally after all."

Robin thumped his goblet. "Henry, my friend, Leopold had no right to raise his banner over the city. It was an insult to King Richard. The duke's troops contributed little to bringing an end to the siege."

Henry didn't look convinced. "I hope the king does not regret ripping it down," he said.

Robin chuckled. "You worry too much."

"He upsets the Duke of Austria and has a mortal enemy in Philip, who feigns to be our ally. And I should not worry?" Henry tapped his drink to Robin and Stephan's mugs and gulped down the brew.

Stephan swirled his ale. Henry's concern didn't surprise him—he expected that—but he gave about as much consideration to the incident as Robin. That was the least of the problems they faced. When he stifled his vision of Henry and a bathhouse, his thoughts fell to the hazards of the coming march to Jerusalem.

Robin eyed him suspiciously. "You are far too quiet, my friend. Have you tamed that new destrier? If he is not to your liking, I am sure King Richard would offer another."

"He is fine, Robin. It was generous of the king to provide me an animal every bit as magnificent as my Tempête."

Henry reached across the table and patted his wrist. Stephan returned that comforting touch with a nod.

"Tell me, what is on your mind?" Robin asked.

"Little John's training. His education. The boy shows promise but he is a bit rough around the edges. Would the king be agreeable if I offered Little John's service to the queen?"

"Are you getting soft, Sir Stephan?"

"Yes, I am."

"I have been thinking of this for Allan." Robin planted his chin on his hands. "Both boys grow more skilled with sword and bow. They have the makings of young squires, don't they? For that, solid instruction in reading, writing, horsemanship, and the ways of the court will serve them well."

Henry laughed at them.

"What?" Robin asked.

"You know the battle for Acre was nothing compared to what lies ahead. They will be out of harm's way here." Henry grinned at the two knights. "I approve. They will be excellent squires."

"Neither one will be happy," Stephan said.

"I would not be so sure of that." Robin chuckled. "Little John blushes and falls all over himself when he is in Queen Joanna's presence. Both queens delight in learning Allan's gambling tricks. We shall make it clear to the boys that the royal ladies would miss them sorely and might need their protection should anything happen to the king."

Henry crossed himself. "God forbid."

"Indeed," Robin said. "I will talk to Queen Berengaria on the morrow."

"Not the king?"

Robin clasped Henry's arm. "Strategy, my friend. Learn it well."

Stephan laughed, lifting his goblet to toast his friends. "With the queen on our side, the king will be convinced that is one battle he should not take on. Better to face the infidels than the wrath of his wife."

fifteen

HENRY LUNGED, TRIED TO anticipate Robin's next move. Robin sidestepped, twisted, his sword sweeping low and up in a wide swath that set Henry off balance. He caught himself before his face hit the ground. He dared not look back at Stephan. Stephan's laughter echoed off the stone walls encircling the courtyard.

Robin wagged a gloved finger at Henry. "Again," he said.

Henry swabbed his brow. He tapped Robin's sword and circled around. Lunging, he thrust the blade at Robin's heart. Robin blocked the blow, pressing their weapons towards the ground. Henry swept both swords up and then countered, one blow, a second, forcing Robin back. His third blow sent Robin's sword skittering across the stone.

"Good work," Robin said. "You are as fine a swordsman as Stephan, and in half the time it took me to train him."

"What?" Stephan cried.

Henry bowed to Robin and offered Stephan a lower and more dramatic bow. From the corner of his eye, he spotted the gold fleur-de-lis on a deep blue tunic. One of King Philip's men watched them from the arched gateway into the courtyard. Henry straightened quickly.

Robin approached the elderly knight, one of the French king's trusted advisors. "So the rumours are true?" he asked.

"No rumours, Sir Robert." He handed a sealed letter to Robin. "My lord king sends his intentions to King Richard."

Henry sheathed his sword and exchanged a look with Stephan, surprised by the resignation on Robin's face. The city had been rife with gossip about Philip's plans within days of Acre's surrender, and Robin had said, "Pay them no mind." Yet here was proof.

Robin stared at the parchment, frowning. King Philip would return to France. Henry felt indignant. But not Robin. He wouldn't accuse the French of betrayal, or wonder aloud if Richard's army could take Jerusalem without them. When he looked up, a hint of regret filled his face. "I will miss our chess games, Jean."

"Only because you win all the time." Jean de Charny's heartfelt smile highlighted the lines in his face. "And I will regret that returning to France means we may one day meet on the battlefield as enemies."

"Mayhap our kings will find a way to keep the peace," Henry said.

Jean turned to Henry. "There is nothing I should like more."

"Jean de Charny," Robin said, "this is Henry de Grey, and you may remember Stephan l'Aigle of Yorkshire."

Jean tipped his head. "My lords. Sir Stephan—you accompanied Robert to Paris with news of the late king's death. He spoke highly of you then, and I understand why." He looked from Stephan to Henry. "Ranulf, one of our commanders, told me of your bravery fighting alongside our knights. More would have died had you not raised your swords that day."

"We stand together as allies against Saladin, my lord," Henry said.

"A common enemy." Jean turned back to Robin. "Something we no longer have at home."

Henry remembered the stories his father told about a sixteen-year-old Richard waging war against the late King Henry and making deals with Philip. Henry had had his share of disagreements with his own father, but he never understood how a son could take up arms against his own father.

"Politics and intrigue. Dowries and duchies. Old hates." Robin shook off those thoughts. "Will we have time for one last game before you depart?"

"On the morrow, before King Philip requires my constant presence for the arrangements to be made before we sail."

Robin clasped the man's arm. "I do envy you going home."

"God be with you, Robin." Jean bowed and departed.

Robin studied the letter. He cocked his head towards the doors into the palace, encouraging Henry and Stephan to follow. "Come with me."

Henry wiped the sweat from his neck and straightened his tunic. Nothing like accompanying the bearer of bad news into the lion's den.

~ ~ ~

RICHARD READ THE WORDS. He took a long haul from his drink and crushed the parchment in his hand, letting it fall to the floor. "The bastard." He flung his goblet across the room and smashed his fist on the trestle.

Robin retrieved the message. "Philip offers to leave his army here under the command of the Duke of Burgundy. His share of the hostages' ransom from Saladin should be more than enough to pay any of his men who will accompany us to Jerusalem." He glanced down at the paper though the words were ingrained on his tongue. "He plans to depart within a week."

"What a kind offer." Richard's voice bit like a blade.

Henry was glad the matter of Allan and Little John had been settled days earlier. If a large number of Philip's supporters departed, the road ahead might be worse than he'd imagined. He leaned close to Stephan. "After all we have been through. The Holy City is within our grasp, and the French leave."

Stephan shrugged. "There will be no dispute about who gives orders. We shall be better off without them."

Before Henry could respond, the king shouted, "Good riddance." He waved his hand at Robin. "Sit. We must plan. And you," he pointed at one of the servants, "get me more wine."

The days ticked away towards the negotiated deadline for the payment to release the prisoners. King Richard was determined to march south before the end of August. Twenty-seven hundred hostages. A large ransom. Time was running out for Saladin.

Acre
20august1191

sixteen

NOBLES AND KNIGHTS FILTERED into the council chamber. Tunics looked freshly pressed. Mail sparkled in the light pouring into the room through the arched doorways.

Henry was glad he'd arrived only a few minutes before the appointed hour. Near midday, the chamber was stifling, the breeze hot.

Stephan acknowledged him with a nod, but he cornered Little John, who'd come up behind Henry. "Head to the stables and have my horse and Henry's saddled," he said. "When you are done, remain at the palace until I return."

"Would it be all right if I wait until Allan comes back?" Little John asked.

"Allan?"

"Yes, my lord. He was tending to Sir Robin." Little John gestured past Stephan's shoulder.

"Stephan," Henry whispered. "The king."

Richard had entered the room from doors behind the dais. Robin accompanied him but Allan was nowhere to be seen.

"Robin has sent Allan on." Stephan herded Little John towards the courtyard "Now, go. Do as I ask."

Little John nodded solemnly and left.

Henry and Stephan snaked through the crowd and settled in a spot near the front of the room. "Thank you," Henry said. "Young ears do not need to hear us debate the fate of the hostages."

"I doubt there will be much debate, but the outcome will be gruesome," Stephan said.

The debate amongst the king's advisors began with harsh words that heated the air like Acre's summer winds.

"Saladin has defied you, my liege."

"He feels you are bluffing."

"We cannot wait another day. He will think us weak, sire."

Their faces looked adamant but bleak. The joy of their recent victory was buried beneath the burdens of war. King Richard sat stone-faced, listening intently. Behind him, Robin intercepted messengers coming and going, read their communiqués. Some he ignored; others were whispered to the king. Richard would signal him whilst the advisors pressed their case and Robin offered his ear when beckoned.

Henry gripped his cross. He knew what was coming. That didn't make it any easier. When King Richard stood, Henry brought the crucifix to his lips.

Richard's face was hard, resolute. "The deadline we negotiated in good faith has passed. We do not know Saladin's thoughts, though his actions speak for him. If he wishes to see that we do not bluff, that we shall not sit here in Acre and delay our pilgrimage to the Holy City, then we shall do what is our right. Saladin has condemned his followers to die."

Henry's stomach knotted, his thoughts filled with despair. *This is war?* He struggled to understand. The king refused to wait a moment longer. The army would face harsh winter conditions if the march to Jerusalem did not get underway. But without the ransom, the hostages could not be released. What message would that send to Saladin?

"Prepare the prisoners." Richard dropped heavily into his chair, his face still stern.

Voices washed across the room, a discordant chorus from anguish to joy. The song, or to some, the lamentation, swept into the courtyard and to the streets beyond. Richard's supporters whispered prayers, thanks-be-to-God-praises, and shouted for revenge and justice.

Stephan rested a hand on Henry's arm. "Are you well?"

Henry felt numb. *You know nothing of war.* "All those people. We will just execute them?"

"What is the king to do, Henry? Saladin has given him no choice."

"Have we truly waited as long as—"

"You heard the testimony." Stephan clapped his back. "Come. We must saddle up. The Saracens may rush down from the hills when this blood bath begins."

Stephan and Henry followed the parade of knights from the room. Men-at-arms rushed to round up the hostages. A festive mood gripped the city. Troubadours played and young girls danced in the streets. Henry had never seen such glee on the soldiers' faces. He tried to understand. The siege had been long and many Christians had died, but still, it made him ill to watch the soldiers prod their bound prisoners towards the open plain.

King Richard took his place with the knights on the line. If Saladin watched from the hills with his army, he'd not see Richard's face but he would recognize him sitting atop Fauvel, the dun warhorse Richard had taken as spoils when he toppled the ruler of Cyprus.

Henry wondered what went through the king's mind. The snarling golden lion on Richard's red surcoat contrasted with his stony expression. Could he order this mass execution and not feel something? Regret? Remorse? These enemies were not Christian. Did that make any difference? *Am I the only one sickened by what is about to happen?*

Archers stood three deep in front of the knights, crossbowmen on either flank and behind the archers. Men-at-arms knelt forming a fence of steel. Their lances stabbed the ground, angled towards the hills. Saladin's army stirred like ants scurrying madly when their colonies are disturbed. Saracen riders took to the saddle and headed further into the hills. Were they scrambling to notify Saladin?

A horn blared. Sombre pawed the ground nervously. Richard signaled the commander of his men-at-arms. The first sword was swung. A man's head hung in the air for a moment.

Henry cringed. He was too far away to see the prisoners' faces but their screams echoed across the plain. Sunlight glinted off a thousand or more raised blades. Blood sprayed against crystal blue skies with every slash of a sword.

The hills grew quiet, unmoving, but only for a heartbeat. The enemies' horses smelled blood and stirred. Curses punched the air from Saladin's camp and from the crusaders, barely audible over hundreds of ignored cries for mercy.

It was too late for the hostages but that did not stop the Saracens' charge across the plain.

"Here they come!" Robin shouted.

Henry steeled himself. Richard's archers loosed wave after wave of arrows. Enemy soldiers fell, yet they did not slow. And suddenly, they were upon Richard's men-at-arms. The enemy cavalry plunged headlong into sharp-pointed lances. Their horses screamed. Many got through that barrier, swinging their swords and knob-headed clubs. And the first of the crusaders cried out.

Richard ordered the knights forward. Henry followed Richard's charge. Blocking a lance, knocking the sword from another man's hand, severing an arm, slicing a leg, a throat, a head. Henry swung his blade to survive, but each swing was bitter. Saracens fell beneath each cut. He swung for Jerusalem. "For God," he shouted repeatedly until he was hoarse. His shield and sword arm kept him from death's door. It wasn't until the sun started to sink on the horizon that he found a moment to think about what he'd done. The Saracens were retreating, and Henry spurred Sombre away from the battlefield and towards the site of the executions.

~ ~ ~

"WHERE ARE YOU GOING?" Stephan called, trotting up beside Henry.

Henry slowed Sombre to a walk but did not stop. He'd wrapped the destrier's reins round his blood-soaked gloves. "I do not want to believe what happened here today. I think I must see it."

"Henry, no." Lines creased Stephan's brow and he looked at Henry worriedly. "Let's go into the city. We should get drunk."

"I cannot, Stephan. The thought of drink and food makes me ill." Henry reined in Sombre. His desert-tanned face was pale and streaked with sweat and blood. He sagged in the saddle, looked broken and weary. "You go," Henry added. "There will be many knights to celebrate this...victory. But I cannot be one of them."

"You shall need something to eat. If you will not come to the hall, I'll meet you at your room with some food after I have an ale. Just one ale. You will feel better, and hungry, later."

Henry shook his head and galloped off across the bloodied plain.

~ ~ ~

KNOWING HENRY WANDERED AROUND on that bloody battlefield squelched Stephan's appetite. He still wanted to get food and drink for Henry, but he'd not even wandered halfway to the palace when Robin intercepted him.

"You are filthy!"

Stephan looked Robin up and down. "You do not look much better." Robin nearly toppled into him. Stephan got a whiff of ale. "And you are drunk."

"I am not. I had a round or two...or three...with the king. Not one drop more." Robin slid his arm around Stephan's waist and pressed him away from the palace and into one of Acre's narrow alleyways.

"Where are we going?" Stephan asked.

"Why, to the baths, my lord."

"But I promised to bring Henry some food and ale."

"You shall want to be sweet smelling when you see him, aye?" Robin's grip tightened. He had no plans to let Stephan escape.

Smelling of lavender was the last thing on Stephan's mind when he remembered the look on Henry's face. The day's brutality would not be easy for Henry to put aside and he doubted a relaxing soak would turn his own thoughts from Henry.

The public bathhouse should have been heaven. So many naked bodies, water droplets gleaming on their skin. Stephan's groin ignored the signals sent by glistening muscles, bare arses and cocks. His heart did not pound. He could blame Henry for that.

Ale and wine flowed freely. The room reeked of dirt, sweat and blood mixed with fragrant herbs.

Robin let one of the girls strip away his tunic and hose and stepped naked into the steaming water. Stephan scraped at a darkened spot on his hauberk with his dagger, its scratch against the steel grating even amidst the raucous conversation around him.

Robin splashed him with water, but Stephan didn't move. "I am worried about Henry, Robin. If you had seen his face…"

"His pain is as real as any cut from a blade."

"I know. He knows," Stephan said. Robin told him nothing new. Both men had seen others' reactions to battle, had felt it themselves. Fear, revulsion. Everyone experienced it, but thoughts like these were consigned to the back of the mind and rarely spoken. For who would want to have others see them as cowardly?

Two young male bath attendants, each with only a cloth wrapped round their waists, tugged at Stephan's hauberk. He lifted his arms, stood frozen while they unlaced his gambeson and hose and removed his clothing.

"He will learn to deal with the deaths. The blood."

Stephan swallowed hard. "And if he does not?"

Robin shrugged. "Tell him to go home. Many have, including the French king. Henry is in a better position than most. He has lands, a title. Look at me, at you. At least Henry has something, and someone, to go back to."

Stephan dipped his foot into the bath and kicked it hard, sending a stream of water into the air. He hated to think of Henry in England. With her. He wasn't certain if Henry's loyalty to the king and to this holy crusade would trump his horror of war.

Robin clapped the water. "Get in. Take your mind off him." Robin closed his eyes, breathed in deeply. "Remember the smell of the lavender fields in Poitou?"

Stephan climbed into the bath and turned the conversation away from Henry. "Speaking of home—what about Marian? And that boy who might be your son?"

Robin opened his eyes. A faraway look brushed his face. "Oh, he is my son. I am sure of that."

"Have you sent word to Marian?"

"No."

"Why not?"

A young woman clad in a flimsy white floor-length tunic offered them ale, bent close to hear their conversation. Robin's gaze met hers, traced lower to the outline of her breasts through the fabric. He took an ale from her hands and stared at the dark brew. "It would not be fair to Marian. I could be dead tomorrow." He turned back to Stephan. "How could I give her any hope that I might return? Am I so bold to think she will want anything to do with me?"

Stephan swallowed his own ale, studying the knight. "She never remarried. You should tell her that you are alive."

"If we leave this place, if I set foot on English shores again, I will go to her."

The serving girl's mouth curled into a smile. "She would be a fool to turn you away," she said, and then wandered towards the kitchens.

Stephan clasped Robin's arm. "I will be glad for you."

"And what about you?" Robin slid his hand around Stephan's neck to tug him closer. "Henry?"

"A better friend I shall never have." Stephan's voice cracked. "His betrothed waits for him."

Robin pushed back but kept his voice low. "And you will just let him go."

"What choice do I have?" Stephan cried out a bit too loudly. Several knights turned, but he ignored them. He was angry. Not with Robin, but with himself for not putting his feelings behind long ago. Lowering his voice, he said, "Even if he could accept what I offer, there is no future of a life of love and happiness for men like me."

"There is always a way."

"Don't even let me wish. Cut me with your dagger. It is less painful."

Robin splashed his face, ducked beneath the water to clean the dirt and blood matted in his hair. When he surfaced, he gave Stephan a long, penetrating look. "Does he know that you are in love with him?"

Stephan buried his head in his hands. Was it that obvious? If Robin and Little John could see it, what went through Henry's mind? "I do not know. I think so."

"Shouldn't you be completely honest with him?"

"Not if I want his friendship."

Robin sighed. "Suffer him by your side but not in your bed."

"If I must." Stephan swallowed the rest of his ale.

Robin grabbed Stephan's mug and threw it across the room, startling one dozing knight and causing another to spill his ale. Robin cupped Stephan's face in his hands, kissed his cheek. The knights applauded the gesture and Robin grabbed a washing cloth from the side of the bath and waved it in the air with a flourish.

"What was that for?"

"You are a good man, Stephan." Sitting back, Robin reached for his own ale and brought it to his lips. He let it sit there before he placed the goblet down without taking a sip. "Send him home. It will let you forget, and there's no shame in it for him. He might keep his eye on the king's devilish brother."

Stephan had heard there'd been messages from England about Count John, the king's youngest brother. Rumours hinted that John had been consolidating his power. He had always been the old king's favorite. There'd been little love between the brothers. Would John ally himself with the French king to take advantage of Richard's absence?

"The king shows no concern that John wants to usurp his throne," Stephan said, watching Robin soap up the washing cloth.

"To the men, no." Scrubbing his chest with the sweet scented cloth, Robin added, "But he recognizes the danger is far greater now that King Philip is returning to France."

"Queen Eleanor will keep John in line."

Robin chuckled. "To the queen mother." He lifted his goblet, took a gulp, but his face turned stoic. "She has her ways with her sons. A powerful woman. But I do not trust John, and I trust the French king even less." The rush torches that lined the walls illuminated the dread in Robin's eyes. "Mind this. We fight a war for Jerusalem today and will go home to England and fight another."

Thomas of Winchester smacked Stephan's back. He slipped into the water beside him but did not sit. Holding his drink aloft, he swayed and started to sing a lewd ballad. His voice was deep and gravelly, off key, and he was plainly drunk.

Robin poked Stephan's shoulder and gestured at Thomas. "If we must listen to that, we all may soon desert the king."

Stephan laughed. Around him, a drumming on the sides of the baths began, uneven and off tempo. Many of the knights were in worse shape than Winchester. Drinks were raised to him; more spilled to the floor and in the bath waters.

A buzz from one corner of the room turned into loud heckling. Robin grabbed another mug of ale from one of the serving girls and stood. His torso dripped with soapy water. He extended his arms, waving them in the air, slopping ale over everyone nearby.

Thomas stopped singing and stared at him. The heckles ceased. Robin downed a huge gulp of ale. "Winchester," he said, "you sing like a wild beast whose leg is caught in a trap." The knights applauded. "And you are drunk."

Winchester reached for Robin's arm, nearly dragging them both underwater. "You can do better?" he asked.

Robin's brow arched beneath sun-bleached hair that fell across his forehead. "Me?" He cleared his throat.

"Soldiers at war
We fight evermore…"

He was every bit as bad as Winchester. Stephan buried his face in his hands. Robin would never live this down. On the other hand, so many in the bathhouse were drunk that few would remember the performance by daybreak.

"For king, for God and country
He will see us through this Hell to Heaven above."

"What song is that?" someone at the far end of the room shouted.

"That's no song," another barked. "Let Winchester sing!"

Robin ignored the intrusion. His voice grew louder. Winchester joined in and a massive groan swept the room. A handful of figs sailed through the air and smacked the older knight's face. Flying dates pummeled Robin. He stumbled over the words but finished strong.

Taking a bow, Robin grabbed Stephan to steady himself and plopped down into the water. He took a swig of his ale and looked at the knight. "Not a word."

Stephan shook his head, chuckling. He scrubbed his body with rose-scented soap then stood, beckoning the male attendants. After they dried him, he bid Robin goodnight and dressed quickly. He'd send Little John to retrieve his hauberk in the morning. There was enough food in the outer chamber of the bathhouse to fill a plate for Henry. He started down the road with a trencher in his hand, a wineskin tucked beneath his arm, and with the sounds of celebrations from the palace at his back. A shopkeeper swept out the dirt and dust at his doorway, closing his shop for the evening. Another retrieved breads and pies from a bank of shelves to put them away. Everything seemed normal but the baker's eyes were reddened and children wailed from a room over the shop. Young and old held tight to each other and scurried indoors as Stephan walked past.

The sun dipped towards the horizon but heat rising from the ground encased Stephan like a cloak. The cooler air at Henry's lodgings was a welcome relief, and he decided he should convince Henry that a long soak would let him relax. A long soak with Henry. That would be even better.

"Henry," he called, knocking on the door to Henry's room. He pushed the door open with his elbow. Empty. No sign Henry had been there. No bloodied clothes or shield. Nothing.

Alarmed, Stephan laid the food and ale on the chest next to Henry's bed. Back outside, he looked up and down the street. Two men on horseback trotted past. Stephan stared after them. *The stables.* Mayhap Henry would be there tending to Sombre. He ran through the alleyways.

Squires brushing down their masters' horses looked at him questioningly when he barged into the barn. He spotted Sombre contentedly munching away at a pile of hay. But no Henry.

He never should have left him alone.

seventeen

WHERE ARE YOU, HENRY? Stephan climbed a ladder of one of the camp's siege towers. Mayhap he'd see Henry from that bird's-eye view. The camp was almost ghostly, pockmarked with a fraction of the life inhabiting it when the city had surrendered. Corrals empty, others only half rebuilt. A handful of men had returned in the wake of the king's announcement of the army's move south in a few days' time. Still, enough supplies lay about—a more cunning enemy might have quite the haul should he choose to attack while so many celebrated in the city. Siege engines could be destroyed. Ships in the harbour could be looted and burned.

The ships. Stephan turned sharply. Henry might be down by the water, staring towards England.

He scrambled down from the tower. The run to the waterfront left him breathless. Galleys and busses looked as deserted as the camp. But still no Henry.

Think. Not in the camp. Not by the boats that might take him home. Stephan rested his hand on the hilt of his sword, his mind racing.

He hurried south along the water's edge. Encircled by clouds, the sun hung on the horizon like a teardrop. Nearly set, it splayed fiery reds and oranges across the water and against the sky, like blood splattered across a canvas. Stephan would welcome the darkness grabbing hold of the coastline.

At a loss, he was thinking of turning back to the city when he saw Henry staring at the sea. Henry's face was drawn and pensive, his brows pinched. Stephan drew towards him, and each step closer revealed all traces of Henry's youth and innocence had vanished.

"You are a hard man to find," Stephan said.

"I have been standing here a long while." The wind whipped Henry's dark hair into his eyes. He combed it back with trembling fingers. He'd not shed his bloodied mail and boots.

Stephan shuddered. He'd walked through battlefields where men lay sprawled, eyes blank, staring at the sky with lance, bow, or sword at their sides. He'd never really seen those men, never felt their deaths or thought twice of the carnage until he'd met Henry and felt Henry's pain.

Henry tipped his head to the south. "We will head to Jerusalem along the sea." He sounded matter-of-fact, almost casual.

Stephan knew the look in Henry's eyes. Putting on a brave face when, in fact, he was trying to make sense of it all, wanting to justify what was to come.

Stephan nodded. "With the Saracens shadowing us and the sea to our west, at least until we take Jaffa." The plan was etched in his mind after Robin's briefings. The crusaders' control of ports along the coast was vital. King Richard's ships would parallel the army south to Jaffa, bringing fresh supplies to replenish the troops, taking the sick and wounded to Acre to be cared for.

"Then east to Jerusalem," Henry added.

"Across desert, mountains, and plains," Stephan said. "A difficult journey, but we shall be within sight of the Holy City soon." He almost wished he hadn't said anything when he saw Henry's shoulders sag.

Henry took a deep breath, closed his eyes a moment. "I wonder if we will ever pass through its gates."

"Either Jerusalem's or the gates of Heaven if you believe what the priests say." When Henry didn't respond, Stephan added, "Of course we shall see Jerusalem. It is within our grasp. It's our right."

"And our might." Henry looked at his boots. "And the blood of thousands of innocents on our hands."

Stephan placed his palm on Henry's shoulder. "They are the enemy. You must remember that." He shifted, wrapping his arm around Henry's waist, and was glad when Henry didn't flinch against the comfort of a friend's touch.

Henry's head remained lowered. Waves lapped the sand at his feet. "It is one thing to defend your life against a soldier with bow or sword. Another to sever the head of a weaponless, bound prisoner. How will God forgive us? Why should He let us walk victorious into Jerusalem?"

Stephan chose not to answer. It wasn't the first time Henry had asked these questions, and surely he expected no response.

The sun slid into the sea and the silence lengthened between them. Stephan tightened his hold, resting his chin on Henry's shoulder. Henry reeked of sweat, dirt and blood. Those smells comforted Stephan—the man he loved was alive. "Come back to the city," he said softly. "I brought food and drink as I said I would. And you must sleep."

"That will only bring nightmares." Henry's voice trembled.

"Then we shall talk through the night. Come."

Stephan led Henry back. Neither spoke a word. Henry stood at the door and stared at his Spartanly-furnished room. Stephan clamped a hand on his shoulder, encouraged him forward. Pulling the door closed behind them, he quickly lit a candle on the chest beside the bed.

How could a man look lost in so small a space? Henry did. He'd stopped near the chest and froze, looking around as if unable to decide what he should do.

The quiet of the house unnerved Stephan. He was more accustomed to the sounds of comrades drinking and whoring. Or to the groans, screams, thuds and clanking of battle replaced at the end of a day by boisterous joy, grunts, and moans of pleasure. They'd pass out like the dead and he'd never wasted a moment thinking of them. He'd enjoyed their company and was done with it. He'd only been thinking of himself. He did not love those men.

Noise from the street filtered into the room and broke his reverie. A breeze tickled the flame of the candle.

Stephan filled a mug with ale, handed it to Henry, willing him to drink with a nod.

Henry forced down a swig. Taking it back, Stephan drank the rest, poured another and pressed it towards Henry.

Dried blood on Henry's hands showed harshly against his sun-browned skin. They both stared at it. Seeing it painted on his flesh was somehow more jarring—more personal—than the blood that stained his mail and hose. Lighting that candle had been a bad idea. Stephan found a cloth by the washbowl and scrubbed the blackish-red streaks away. If only erasing them could remove the memories.

Stephan set the cloth aside and reached to unbuckle Henry's sword belt. Fingers trembling, he fumbled with it. *What is this?* It wasn't like he'd never removed a man's belt before. It seemed like minutes before the strap released. He leaned the sword against the side of the chest and then tugged at Henry's hauberk.

"My servant—"

"Shhh. He is not here. Let me help you."

Henry lifted his arms. Stephan peeled away his mail, gambeson, and tunic, each piece of clothing removed more slowly than the last.

Stephan's throat grew thick and dry. Heat radiated from Henry's body. His crucifix lay on his bare chest, rising and falling as with his breath.

Bells pealed in the city. Men on horseback trotted past the window shouting, "Victory, victory!" Stephan turned towards the noise, avoiding Henry's eyes. He didn't dare look at his face or that body. He couldn't help that his feelings ran so strongly. All he wanted was to pull Henry close. To shield him from the gruesome thoughts of war.

Stephan grabbed a piece of chicken from the plate. "Eat," he said, handing it to Henry. "And sit."

Henry shifted his weight from one foot to the other. Tension in his shoulders seemed to wane. He didn't protest but bit into the meat and smiled.

Stephan rubbed his sweating palms against his tunic. He knelt and pulled off Henry's boots. Blood there had dried and only the scent of leather and Henry's sweat mingled in the air. He could get drunk on that smell alone.

Breathing in deeply, he shoved the boots beneath the cot and sat back on his haunches. Henry had demolished the leg of chicken and was chewing on a chunk of bread. Stephan hefted the ale and drank, offered it to Henry, and watched him tip the mug to finish the last drop.

"Do you want to talk?"

"No." Henry's mouth tightened. "I do not know. But stay." He shed his hose and lay down, grabbing the cover a servant had left folded at the foot of the bed. He slid as close to the wall as possible, his face turned towards it.

Stephan blew out the candle, plunging them into darkness. He stripped off his tunic and boots and crawled onto the cot.

Henry's hair was plastered to his neck. Running his hands through the dark tangles, Stephan pushed them aside and shifted closer, his bare chest pressed to Henry's back. Henry shivered but he relaxed against the touch. Stephan spooned his body, slid his arm over Henry and pressed his hand to his heart. He planted a soft kiss on his shoulder.

Within a few minutes, they'd both fallen asleep.

eighteen

SUNLIGHT BLED INTO THE room but Henry refused to open his eyes. The smell of bread baking tickled his nose. Unusual spices and the warmth of the morning reminded him he wasn't in Lincolnshire. No robins chattered. No smell of dew-covered leaves. Instead, the squawks of gulls grated on his ear. Acre.

Go away, Acre. Henry burrowed his head deeper into the bed. He caught the smell of musk and roses and his eyes flew open. His face was buried in the curve of Stephan's shoulder.

Henry's heartbeat quickened. He should pull away but he could not. Stephan might awaken and take this physical contact for more than it was.

Couldn't pull away? *Fool.* He didn't want to pull away.

Henry risked looking up. Stephan smiled down softly at him and there was nothing in the world he'd trade for that. Familiar sensations coursed through him. Heat. A good ache. He'd pushed them away before. He wasn't certain he wanted to this time. He needed something—someone—to hold onto in this insanity.

"I did not mean to wake you," he finally said.

"You did not." Stephan had been watching him. "Did you sleep well?"

"I had no nightmares, if that is what you ask." He glanced across Stephan's chest at the remains of the food and drink they'd shared. He found himself thinking of Stephan's arms encircling him when they'd stood by the water's edge. That strong chin resting lightly on his shoulder. Warm breath against his neck. He'd felt safe in Stephan's arms. But was it more than that?

He liked the way his arm lay across Stephan's chest, his groin pressed to Stephan's hip. Shyness almost overtook Henry, but the knight's heart beating beneath his palm gave him pause. He swore it pounded in rhythm to his breathing. What a wondrous feeling.

Without thinking, Henry traced the line of an old scar on Stephan's muscled chest.

Stephan drew in a breath. He lay perfectly still, avoiding Henry's eyes. "We should dress. We have much to do today." His heartbeat rose further beneath Henry's hand. "I'd told Little John to pack my things and wait at my lodgings. Poor boy must wonder what became of me. He might not have slept a wink, though if he did, he will be hell to awaken. He hates to get out of bed."

Henry chuckled. "So many words spilling from your mouth at this early hour."

"What do you mean?" Stephan asked, clenching the edge of the bed. "We must go to the palace. Robin might be looking for us."

Henry tilted his head, listening. The streets still slept. The only sounds in the house came from the kitchen and the creak of the bed. "No one but the cooks and gulls are stirring." He yawned again, looking up into Stephan's eyes. "Do you really think anyone would miss us after a night of drunken revelry?"

Stephan smiled. "Mayhap you are right. We could sleep away the rest of the morning."

Henry drew up on one elbow. "I was not thinking of sleep." He stroked Stephan's chest, grinned when Stephan's breaths grew short. Henry's fingers danced along the curve of his neck to his lips.

Stephan grabbed his hand. "Henry—"

Henry leaned over and captured Stephan's mouth, tasting the ale they'd shared. The stubble on his face smelled of salty sea air and hints of rose-scented soap. Henry pulled back slightly, dragging his tongue across lips chapped by Outremer's unforgiving sun.

Stephan groaned. Pushing Henry away, he sat up and threw his legs over the side of the bed. He crushed the bed coverings in his fists. "I have wanted this, wanted you, since the first night we met in Southampton."

"You did not even know me."

"That did not matter. I was a different man back then."

"So was I." Henry traced a scar on Stephan's back.

Stephan uttered a strangled moan. "Why…why are you doing this? Why now?"

"Don't you want me?"

"Of course I do. That is not what I meant." Stephan looked away, pained. "I have used so many men. I do not want that with you."

The uncertainty in Stephan's voice sent a glad ache through Henry. He sat up and tipped Stephan's chin, forcing him to meet his gaze. "I realised that a long time ago."

"I have never loved another man." Stephan's breath rattled in his throat. "What have you done to me?"

"Shouldn't I be asking that? Why is it that I can think of no one but you?"

Stephan's eyes sparkled. He slid his fingers from Henry's temple to his closely cropped, dark beard. He pressed their foreheads together. Henry sighed, melting into the warmth that brushed his mouth. Cupping Stephan's face in his hands, he nipped at his lips and then kissed him again deeply.

When he pulled away, Stephan whimpered. "Oh, Henry…"

"Is this all right?" Henry asked.

"Yes, yes. For all the stars in the heavens, yes! Do not stop."

Henry silenced him with another kiss. Stephan's hand trailed down his arm. His fingers twined through Henry's, the caress so tender that tears pricked Henry's eyes.

Stephan shifted abruptly. He pushed Henry back, pinning him against the hay-filled mattress. Stephan's kisses grew urgent. On Henry's neck, along his jaw. Calloused palms gripped his shoulders. Henry's groin twitched, every nerve in his body awakening.

Outside, a horse clip-clopped down the street. Voices drifted on the sultry morning air. Men shuffled along the marbled floors in the hallway, but those sounds disappeared behind the rush of growing desire that took Henry's breath away. New sensations assaulted him, his mind wrapped in nothing but Stephan.

Henry palmed Stephan's hand. Trembling, eyes locked on Stephan's, he dragged their hands over his belly, snaking towards the ache in his groin.

"Will you be mine?" Stephan whispered.

"Yours."

Stephan's fingers found his hardened flesh. Henry moaned. He buried his face in Stephan's shoulder. Stephan stroked Henry slowly. He shifted to lie on top of him, their bare chests pressed together. Henry ran his hands up and down Stephan's back, gripped his buttocks, desperate to have him close.

They thrust against each other, hearts pounding. Low moans crept up from their throats. A wave of warmth gripped them both and Henry saw fiery stars and more passion than he had ever known.

~ ~ ~

HENRY DRESSED QUIETLY, NOT wanting to disturb Stephan's deep sleep. He looked at his lover. Suddenly, guilt sent a shiver up his spine and made his hands tremble. *His lover.* He ran a finger along the leather chain round his neck and touched his cross. A whispered prayer slid from his lips. "Dear God, why did you bring this joy to my life if it is wrong?"

Closing the door carefully behind him, Henry caught sight of Allan bounding around the corner. From the looks of him—blond hair clinging to his damp forehead, cheeks flushed from the August heat—he must have run all the way from the palace.

"Sir Henry!"

"Shh!"

Allan grinned. The boy was bright. A shush and a quietly closing door? Henry knew Allan suspected Stephan was there. At least he was smart enough to hold his tongue.

"Master Robin asked me to deliver this letter to you, my lord," Allan said, nearly breathless. "And I'm to remind you of the council meeting."

Henry stared at the letter.

"I'll be off now. Would you tell Sir Stephan about the king's summons if you should see him?" When Henry didn't respond, he cleared his throat. "Are you well, my lord?"

"Stephan? Yes. Fine. I am fine." Henry shooed Allan away, his eyes glued on the letter. It carried his father's seal. News from England. The parchment was well worn. Who knew how many hands it had passed through, or how long its journey had been?

Henry chewed his lower lip. This could not be good. He cracked the seal, unfolded the letter with sweaty palms. His father's handwriting was slanted with neat, crisp letters but some were smudged—with tears? Almost illegible. Henry read the words and fell back against the wall.

nineteen

STEPHAN WOKE SLOWLY, REVELING in the memories of Henry's voice brushing his ear. Words of love, sounds of joy, of passion, freely given and heartfelt. He rolled over to reach for his lover, sitting up abruptly when he realised the spot beside him was cold.

Shouted orders rang in the streets outside the house. A dozen horsemen trotted past.

Stephan's gaze darted around the room. Henry's clothes, sword, boots—gone. He cursed softly. It had been too soon. He'd known it. Witnessing those executions made Henry vulnerable.

Stephan buried his head in his hands. Damn fool. *Why I am so weak?* He'd let Henry's words, oh God, his touch... He'd let the feel of the only man he'd ever loved push him to do something he should have known Henry wasn't ready for.

Stephan dressed and stepped outside, squinting into the bright summer sun.

"Out of the way," someone shouted above the thunder of hoofbeats.

Knights on horseback charged down the road. Stephan stepped out of their way and tripped, smacking his head against the wall.

A knight at the back of the pack reined in. "Morning, York."

"Wessex." Stephan rubbed the bruise blossoming on the back of his head.

"Quite an evening," the old knight said with a grin.

Stephan looked up sharply, took a deep breath. He'd only imagined that the noble knew he'd been with Henry.

Wessex swiped a hand across bloodshot eyes. "Do you think our men are anxious to see the king this morning?"

Stephan realised he'd been holding his breath, released it. "If their heads are pounding like mine, I imagine not."

"We all celebrated a bit too hard." Wessex laughed and spurred his horse, shouting back, "See you at the palace."

Stephan stared down the road feeling as lost as Henry had been when he'd found him on the beach. He joined the throng of soldiers shuffling through the streets. His stomach growled. For a moment he tried to convince himself that Henry might have gone for food. But this call to council— surely he'd have awakened him, not gone ahead on his own. *Christ! What have I done?*

"Saracens have pulled further to the east," a gangly man beside Stephan said. He reeked of ale from the night's celebrations. Dark stains splotched his brown tunic.

"I heard they march south," another said. "Destroying everything in their path."

A third man-at-arms scratched his scraggily beard and grunted his agreement. "What is worse? Seeing them camped on the far edges of the plains and in the hills? Or not seeing them but knowing they are there?"

The man beside him laughed nervously and quickly changed the subject. He complained about the heat and the ache in his head.

"Do not worry, Peter," his ale-reeking friend said. "Won't be no achin' heads on the march south. The king will have watered the ale down so much there will be no way to get drunk."

They hugged the walls to let another dozen mounted riders trot by.

"And no women," the scruffier of the men shouted over the noise.

"Did you say no women?"

"The commander said the king means to keep them here."

Peter scoffed. "Did ya' hear that?" he asked Stephan. "Guess that will keep the priests happy."

Stephan could have said that he'd not be bothered by that decision but he only nodded his agreement.

Just ahead, Little John and Allan stood at the palace gate. Allan's grin looked more mischievous than usual. "Sleep well, my lord?" he asked.

Stephan looked at him, suspicious, but he was too worried about Henry to muster a witty reply. All he could think about were the hours he'd spent in Henry's arms. And how foolish he'd been to let it happen.

The boys followed Stephan into the courtyard. Spurs clinking against the old stone floor masked the normally soothing sounds of water spilling from the fountain there.

"Have you seen Sir Henry?" Stephan asked Little John.

"Not today, my lord."

"I saw him," Allan said. "Master Robin sent me to his lodgings to deliver a letter. He was headed out the door, makin' me keep my voice down. You would think he'd left someone sleeping there." Allan nudged Little John.

Stephan ignored the insinuation. "A letter? From Robin?"

"I think it was from England, all sealed up proper and such, my lord. He paled a bit when I handed it to him."

Stephan clenched his jaw. England—Alys—that could ruin everything.

John of Rotherham slapped Stephan's back. "York!" he cried.

Momentarily forgetting Alys and England, Stephan tipped his head. "Sir John."

"Shall we finally be off to Jerusalem?" Rotherham waved his hands at the knights gathering. "We are too soft with the pleasures of the city."

Despite his concern for Henry, Stephan managed a smile for Sir John. The short, balding noble would be the first to admit his pleasures of drink, fine food, and lusty ladies.

Stephan followed Rotherham towards the far side of the courtyard but stopped to turn back to Little John. "Check Sir Henry's lodgings to see if he needs anything. I will meet you at my room after Council ends. I have a feeling we shall be packing up today."

"It's all done, just as you'd asked yesterday, my lord."

"Fine," he replied more shortly than he'd intended. He sighed. "Just check on Sir Henry."

Stephan pushed through the crowds. He ignored the animated conversations around him that heated the air. Speculation about Saladin's next move, the king's plan. What did that matter?

Damn that letter. Stephan's throat tightened and he could hardly breathe. If Henry regretted that they'd lain together, would news from home push his heart further away?

"Home?" Stephan muttered. When his father died, when his brother suggested he was neither wanted nor needed in Yorkshire, England had been no more than a place he once lived. Odd that he'd suddenly thought of England as home. That came from loving Henry. And every step closer to Jerusalem meant a step closer to home. It also meant Henry and Alys would marry. There'd be no way around that no matter how either of them felt now.

Yours. Henry's words when he'd asked, "Will you be mine?" He had to believe they could still have that.

The king appeared on the balcony. A hush came over the courtyard.

"His Holiness the Pope called us on this pilgrimage. We have one objective—Jerusalem." Richard's red-gold hair still shimmered though his recent illness had thinned it. Sunlight glinted off the jewel-encrusted crown on his head. He raised his sword, waving it across the crowd and towards the southeast. Planting it across his chest, he said, "I have sought the council of my commanders. It is time. Tomorrow I return to my headquarters in the camp. Ready your men. Ready the wagons. We begin the final leg of our journey by week's end."

Stephan expected a huge roar of approval, but enthusiasm drew up slowly like a gentle wave on the sand. His own heart pounded, muffling the sounds of the voices around him. He was desperate to see Henry's face, and hoped their love might survive that letter and the war ahead.

~ ~ ~

STEPHAN STOPPED AT HENRY'S lodgings. Still no sign of him. He hurried down a dusty alleyway to his own rooms. Arabic voices boomed from the kitchen, insults from the tone of them. Armour rattled in the hallway. He skirted past a dozen or more servants and squires packing up their masters' belongings. Swords clanked around the corner.

Geoffrey of Wiltshire called as Stephan turned into the hallway, "Watch out, York."

Geoffrey swung at Guy Fitzhugh. Guy's sword pressed downward. "Just showing Wiltshire," he said, slipping his weapon beneath the other knight's and lunging forward, "how that Saracen nearly took my arm off."

"The man carried no shield. Do you believe these infidels?" Geoffrey asked, breathless.

Stephan had been as surprised as anyone by the lightly armoured enemy, but he wasn't in the mood to discuss sword-fighting techniques. "Enjoy yourselves, my lords." He offered a quick bow and hurried to his empty room. It was so quiet he could hear the spider skittering across the marbled floor.

Stephan slammed the door and turned, giving it a kick. Leaning forward, he pressed his forehead against the wall.

A knock startled him. "Henry?" he said, flinging the door open.

Little John shrugged. "I am sorry, my lord. I cannot find him. No one has seen him."

Stephan paced across the room. "You checked his favorite tavern? That baker's shop that sells the sweet pies?"

Little John looked nearly as forlorn as Stephan. "And down by the harbour. The camp, too."

Stephan stared at his bed remembering what had happened in Henry's room a few hours earlier. He plunked down hard on the straw-filled mattress, bringing his hands to his face. *Henry...* He could still feel their fingers grasping each other's, still smell the musky scent of him.

"I never should have... What was I thinking? He is not one to take this lightly."

"He is scared, my lord."

Stephan looked up. He'd forgotten Little John was in the room.

"He will be back," Little John said. "He would not leave you. Not like that."

"Leave me?"

Little John's brows rose. "I heard that some wear their hearts on their sleeve. That's you, my lord."

"Does the entire army know?"

"Not many I'd wager. And you do not have to worry about me talking. I know the priests preach against it. But I am of a mind that thinks we should leave judgment in God's hands."

Stephan sighed. "Aren't you too young to know of love?"

"It's feelings. I do have them, my lord."

"You are right." Stephan frowned at his own insensitivity. Little John's reaction came as no surprise. He was a great observer of people, but he did not judge them. "I do not mean to dismiss you so lightly."

Little John laid his hand on Stephan's shoulder. "You are not yourself, my lord. You have Sir Henry on your mind."

"Still, you should not have to listen to the woes of my heart. Go find yourself a young maid. No wait—you are too young to be thinking of women, or men, that way."

Little John smiled. "But I can dream."

Stephan laughed. "Yes. Yes you can."

"Your heart is big and belongs to Sir Henry. You care for him. And he cares for you."

"I've frightened him off. I let passion sweep my head under a pile of hay." Stephan walked to the window and stared outside. "Where could he be?"

"I will keep looking, my lord."

"No. Robin expects me at the king's table tonight in the camp. Prepare my tent and move my things. I will send a squire from the king's mesnie to help you with Henry's goods."

"Shall we place Sir Henry's belongings in your tent?"

Stephan coughed. "There is no harm if our tents sit side by side but let's not give the priests any fodder for their preaching."

"They might just pray for you."

"They— Pray?" Stephan pounded the wall. "That's it."

"My lord?"

"I know where Henry is."

twenty

THE DOOR GRATED OPEN. Henry ignored the flood of light, ignored the footsteps treading across the old stone floor of the chapel.

Stephan sat down beside him. The wooden bench creaked beneath his weight. "Do you know how many churches there are in Acre?"

Henry nodded. He'd been surprised to find dozens along the main streets and hidden alleyways in the weeks after the knights quartered in the city. Many had been desecrated during the siege but within days of the peace, priests, masons and carpenters began repairs.

"I wish you had roused me before you left this morning." Stephan kept his voice low though no one else had come to find solace in the quiet of the place. Candles flickered in the niches illuminating tapestries depicting Christ and his apostles.

"You looked peaceful." Henry fingered the parchment in his hand. "I had intended to get some food and ale and return to wake you."

Stephan placed his hand on Henry's. When Henry didn't pull away, he asked, "The letter? From England?"

"From my father." Candlelight glinted off the moisture in Henry's eyes. He lowered them, and stared at Stephan's hand. "Alys is dead."

Stephan blew out a breath. "I am sorry."

Henry's head shot up, his eyes narrowed. "Is that all you have to say?"

Stephan squeezed his hand. "I love you."

Henry jerked away.

"Henry—" Stephan reached out, but didn't try to touch Henry again. "What else is there? It is a sad thing but you did not love her. What do you want to hear from me? Should I tell you my heart breaks for you, for this news? I wanted you to forget her. She has—had—a hold on you. Would you ever forget that she was waiting for you? Would marry you?" Stephan groaned. "She could give you the one thing I could not. A child, an heir."

Henry saw the tightness in Stephan's jaw and the way his hands trembled. He felt Stephan's hurt more than he wanted to admit, but he would never say that aloud. "That is what marriage is for." His voice sounded cold like a north winter wind. "That is why two men cannot love each other."

"You said you were mine. We—"

Henry met Stephan's eyes, enraged. "Enough!" He covered his face with his hands. "Go away. Get out of here."

Stephan would not be brushed off so easily. "You gave me hope that we might always have each other."

"If you think that then you are a fool." Henry couldn't face Stephan. Flinging horrible words at him was painful but it had to be done.

"I do not believe you. I saw your eyes. Saw into your soul, Henry de Grey. You cannot tell me that you do not love me." Anguish filled Stephan's voice. "Look at me, damn you!"

"What will it take for you to leave me alone? I used you. I needed to bury the horrors I saw yesterday in mindless fucking," Henry spat. "It is something you know well, something you have done for years."

Moisture pricked Stephan's eyes. He searched Henry's face. "No. You would not...could not."

"I did," he snarled. The lie was like a blade ripping his chest, but that cut hurt less than the look in Stephan's eyes. *Walk away, Stephan. Put us both out of this misery.*

Stephan did not move, didn't say a word.

Why must you make this so hard?

Sweat beaded on Henry's face. He looked at the gash on Stephan's jaw from yesterday's battle. What if he'd been killed? Henry's heart ached at the thought but he steeled himself, shot Stephan an accusatory glare. "We have nothing. There is no love between us."

"I felt it. And I know you did. Last night—"

"I cannot feel anything."

"She is dead, Henry. Why must you pretend nothing happened between us?"

"I know what we did. I am not proud of it. It was wrong. Wrong because my betrothed waits...was waiting for me. Wrong because it is against the laws of God. It is—"

"No, that is not it! You think you betrayed her? You are the only man I have slept with who would suffer those feelings. Look at those who find pleasure with their whores. The ones who swive me and relish the feel of it. They go home happily to their wives. You are not like that." Stephan reached to touch Henry's cheek, but Henry moved away. Stephan scowled. "What was I thinking? You are right. I am the fool. I'd never be free of listening to your confession that your flesh was closer to mine than it had ever been to hers."

Warmth raced through Henry. Guilt brought a flush to his face. Stephan's kisses. His breath. That calloused palm wrapped around his flesh. He'd thought of no one, of nothing, but Stephan.

Henry stared at the writing on the parchment. *I am sorry, Alys.*

Henry thrust the letter at Stephan. "A plague swept my village." Stephan took his hand but Henry tugged it away.

Numb, he didn't move. "My mother is dead. Twenty others died. There was nothing to be done."

"Christ, Henry. Your mother taken away? This is wretched news. What of your father? Your sister? They were spared?"

Henry glared at him. "Stop pretending that you care. All you care about is yourself." Henry stood abruptly and stormed to the front of the church. "This is my fault."

"What?"

"God is punishing me for this sin."

Stephan jumped to his feet. "Don't dare say those words. Do not think them!" He drew up beside Henry. "How can loving another person be a sin?"

Henry stared at the cross on the altar. He'd prayed for his mother's soul. Prayed for Alys.

"I defied God's laws," Henry said, his voice sounding dull and flat. He didn't want to believe it. He'd prayed to God. Argued with Him throughout the morning. He asked why and heard nothing. God had already given his answer. But he'd not asked God to forgive him.

Was there truly anything to forgive?

Stephan gripped Henry's head between his hands. "That plague was months ago. Their deaths are not on your hands or mine."

Henry shoved Stephan away. "Leave me alone, Stephan. There will never be anything between us." A sneer twisted his face. "Find someone else to fill your perversion."

Stephan recoiled as if slapped. He turned and walked away woodenly. The church door closed with a thud behind him, its echo deep and mournful.

Henry fell to his knees and gazed at the golden cross hanging above the altar. "Is this what you want?"

twenty-one

HENRY STOOD IN FRONT of the tent, arms folded across his chest. "This will not do."

Little John's mouth twisted and he scratched his head. "Sir Stephan ordered me to see it was set up next to his."

"He would." Too tired to show outrage, Henry could do no more than shake his head, but anger simmered behind his eyes. Anger with Stephan, not with Little John. Hours had passed since they had argued. Surely Stephan would have had time to reverse his order.

"It was late this morning, my lord. He was worried when you missed the council meeting with the king, especially when he heard you'd had news from England."

Stephan worried? God's wounds. Henry kicked at the dirt. Stephan's worry would have been that the letter was from Alys. A reminder of Henry's betrothal, of home. He had only been thinking of himself, had as much admitted his jealousy.

The thought of his tent next to Stephan's was hard to stomach. Avoiding Stephan during the day would not be too difficult. But God forbid should he have to listen to him with men he brought to his tent to pleasure.

"Find another place for it."

Little John's dark eyes grew wide. "The sun's long since down, my lord. Can it wait until morn—"

"Another place, Little John. Now." Henry's voice was stern. He sounded like the old village priest in Greyton. He cringed, remembering Latin lessons. One word mispronounced and Father James' leather rope cracked against Henry's wrist, a strike painful to think about, even years later. And now, he deserved so much more for his sin.

"There is no need to take that tone with the boy," Stephan said.

Henry turned sharply.

Stephan drew up beside Little John and clapped a hand on his back. "He was only doing as I'd asked. Go on," he told the boy. "Find someone to help you so it can be done quickly."

Little John shot towards the main pavilion.

Henry looked at Stephan. "It will be better this way."

Stephan walked away without a word.

Henry's heart felt heavy, heavier than it felt when he'd read the news of Alys' death. *This is not right!* How could it hurt more to push Stephan away?

Stephan stopped, glanced over his shoulder. "You are wrong, Henry. So wrong."

Henry straightened and was ready to deny his feelings, but Stephan had already continued up the road. Henry turned, frustrated, and pushed aside the tent flap. He searched amongst his belongings in the dim light. His father's letter spilled from his sleeve. Staring at it, he trembled violently, remembering the cruel message it carried. He crossed himself and slowly retrieved the parchment, placing it in his pack where he found his cloak. It was the Lincolnshire green woollen one his mother had made. He gently pulled it out and brought it to his face. Breathing in, he tried to recall the smells of home that had long since faded. He wrapped himself in the cloak, fixed the clasp at his neck, and headed towards a huge bonfire, in the opposite direction from Stephan.

A fire lit the night shooting sparks and reddish-gold flames into the air. Winchester warmed himself by the fire, sharing a flask of brew with one of the tradesmen. Henry plunked down next to them and pulled out his wineskin. The strum of a vielle nearby did not soften yesterday's battle and the executions. It did not erase Henry's sin. He could only hope those thoughts would intrude less as the days wore on.

Henry closed his eyes. Stay alive. Concern yourself with that. Stay alive, take Jerusalem, go home. England's green made him smile. The manor at Greyton. A warm fire in the hearth.

The bonfire crackled. A spark landed on Henry's hand and his eyes flew open. He stared at it burning his flesh, ignored the sting. When it sputtered out, he sighed deeply. Home? Would it ever feel right or true?

Winchester raised a drink to him. Henry tapped his wineskin to the older knight's and stared into the flames.

~ ~ ~

MEN HAD BEEN TRICKLING back to the camp after weeks in the comfort of the city. They drank less, whored less, and grew cranky. Robin insisted on drills every morning. In the late August heat that only made them crankier.

On the twenty-second day of August, King Richard ordered the army to move out. Supply and baggage wagons rattled along the old Roman road on the seaward side. Men-at-arms, laden with their heavy packs and weapons, marched on the eastern flank closest to Jerusalem and to the enemy. "Closer to heaven," they quipped.

Knights patrolled the eastern flank. Like the men-at-arms, they were first in the enemy line of sight, exposed to Saracens entrenched in the hills. When not on duty, the knights spread throughout the ranks. Most graced the center column between the wagons and men-at-arms.

The army advanced slowly the first two days, covering four miles to get accustomed to the heat. Saladin tested their mettle as they marched, ordering short, swift attacks and harassing the French at the rearguard. The enemy cavalry broke through Burgundy's infantry once, coming down upon them shrieking and with drums pounding. The French wagons were attacked.

King Richard, with his Poitevins and Templar knights, joined the fray and helped to drive the enemy off.

The army rested a day, but on the fourth day the king roused them before dawn. Henry had seen the map. He knew the day's objective was the town of Caiphas, eleven miles south. They would march until the early afternoon when the heat became too much for man and beast.

Henry trotted alongside soldiers bringing up the rear of the Anglo-Norman battalion, the men charged with guarding the king's standard. Stephan's duty kept him towards the front of their division. Henry could barely see him through the glare of the sun and the dust churned up by the caravan. And that suited him just fine.

The day had been quiet. Too quiet given the pattern of minor skirmishes of the first days' marches. With each step south, tension grew. The men anticipated an attack and watched the hills nervously. Earlier in the day the Saracens could be seen shadowing their movements. Nothing stirred there now but scraggily bushes brushed by the wind.

A ginger-haired bowman who stood a head taller than the men around him gaped towards the front of caravan. "The vanguard must be pitching their tents by now."

"Can you see ahead, my lord?" one of the men-at-arms asked.

"Nothing to see but the dust," Henry said, swiping at the sweat on his brow. "Keep your eyes to the east."

"Mayhap we'll get through one more day without loosing an arrow," a bowman named Aedric said. His arrow bag still brimmed with shafts. The enemy cavalry hadn't come close enough to the Anglo-Normans to make it worth expending even one shot.

Henry heard the beat of horses' hoofs and twisted in the saddle. Two of Burgundy's men galloped from the rearguard.

"Devil chasing them?" another soldier asked.

Henry tightened his grip on Sombre's reins, stroked his neck. Nerves prickling, he watched the Frenchmen pass.

Rumblings sweeping up from the rear made him stand in his stirrups for a better look.

"You spoke too soon, Aedric," Henry said.

A cloud of dirt and dust rose behind the Anglo-Normans. A trumpet blared, then another.

"The king!" someone shouted.

Horses snorted and pranced nervously. Sure enough, King Richard and his Poitevins, with Robin and the two messengers from Burgundy, charged towards the rearguard. Henry drew in a long breath to calm himself. If he closed his eyes, he would swear there was thunder in the air.

Robin slowed as he passed. "We are under attack," he shouted above the noise. "Guard the king's standard."

Henry tugged his hood onto his head. He seated his hand in his shield and unsheathed his sword, aware of orders shouted to set a defensive line. The men-at-arms near him turned to the northeast and kneeled where they stood. Shields were planted in the ground. Sharp lances were held ready should the enemy break past the king's charge. Henry and the knights around him pivoted their mounts. The commander ordered them to hold.

Henry strained to get a glimpse of King Richard through the thick brown haze. The enemy seemed to fall away from the king's sword, so many taking their last breaths by his hand. Henry's heart beat faster—he lost sight of the king in the melee. Robin emerged from a cloud of dust and wheeled his mount to help a knight surrounded by three Saracens. Henry wished he could do something to help. His gaze swept from the fighting to the king's standard and he sat straighter, for it was a great honour to guard Richard's banner. Henry and the men of the Anglo-Norman battalion held as ordered.

Steel crashed against steel. Men and horses fell. The soldiers around Henry cursed or prayed, their voices so loud Henry could only imagine the screams of the wounded and dying.

Henry pressed the hilt of his sword to his chest where his crucifix lay beneath mail, padded gambeson, and tunic. He whispered a prayer of his own. No bolts flew from the Anglo-

Norman ranks and the Saracens never came close. The fighting remained confined to the rearguard.

~ ~ ~

CASUALTIES WERE LIGHT that day. The army forged ahead and set up camp. By nightfall, Saracen campfires freckled the foothills. Crusader scouts scurried in with reports from north and south. On the morrow, the roads would narrow, and the bushes and thorns along the coast would bite into their skin. And the Saracens would attack. Knowing what lay ahead, more prayers fell from the men's lips, whispers sounding like a mournful song of the dying. Others drank the watered wine and ale and complained. About the heat, the godforsaken desert, the lack of female flesh.

As the men prepared to bed down, a public crier rallied them with the call, "Holy Sepulchre, help us!" The troops joined the shouting, repeating it with a fervor that renewed their resolve and gave them hope and strength for another day. And then the drums sounded. Henry could not get used to the drums. If not the enemies' that beat incessantly each day through the night along with their trumpets and cymbals, it was the drums in the pilgrims' camp. Thumping all night to frighten away the scorpions and tarantulas.

And sleep? There was little of that. Curses, men crying out from their own nightmares, and the moaning—the sounds of men fornicating—intruded into Henry's thoughts. Was one of them Stephan?

The days cycled by in endless repetition. Each night Henry crawled into his tent. He drew his knees to his chest. He buried his head beneath his arm. He hummed to drown out the harsh racket. Still, the drums beat. Even when he slept, he heard them in his dreams. He heard the war cries, the trumpets, and the last breaths of the dying.

His nightmares would fade for a short while before the sun cast its eye on Richard's army, and then he would rise with the men and do it all again.

northofArsuf
3september1191

twenty~two

THE ARMY HAD MADE camp for the day. Others might be unpacking their belongings, but Stephan was not off duty yet, having been assigned to scout the road south. He tramped through the maze of tents. Sword, long dagger, arrow staves in his belt. Bow case slung over his shoulder. Approaching the corrals, he nearly stumbled on the uneven terrain, kicking up a shower of pebbles that added to the dust on his boots.

Rounding a corner, he jerked to a stop. "You?"

Henry acknowledged him with a nod. He hung his bow case on a hook on Sombre's saddle. "You are late."

The two horses were saddled, tied to one of the wagons that formed a makeshift corral. Henry grabbed Sombre's reins and mounted.

Stephan strode forward, ignoring the jibe. Acre lay three weeks and some sixty miles behind them. The distance had not soothed Henry's coolness.

Untangling Hawk's reins, Stephan wrapped them around his hand and swung up onto the horse's back.

Damn Robin. The man had an evil streak, assigning him to this scouting mission with Henry. Stephan wondered if Henry felt the same way. It was hard to tell because Henry would hardly meet his eyes these days. Now he perched atop his horse—did he just feign indifference? He looked too serious, too formal. Like a haughty noble. His hauberk did not show a speck of dust from the day's march. It would probably gleam in the moonlight, Stephan thought. As for his own, dirt covering his mail chausses made them look more brown than grey. His white cloak was streaked with grime and the tunic he wore beneath his gambeson and hauberk was torn. Stephan swiped at his chausses and then spurred Hawk after Henry.

Clouds cast shadows on the reed-covered coastline where they rode, and they were forced to slow to a walk. The reeds were sharp, reminding Stephan of Henry's stinging words. Try as he might, he couldn't banish the hurt from his heart. Still, he couldn't bring himself to hate Henry. No matter what the man said or didn't say, Stephan still loved him. That was what hurt most of all. He would never love again. He was certain of that. The thought of being with anyone else, even to satisfy his physical needs, made him gasp for air. How could he lie with another man knowing what he felt, what he'd had so briefly with Henry?

Stephan's thoughts were broken abruptly when Henry reined in and said, "This way is treacherous." Here, less than a mile south of the army's camp, the coastal road turned marshy. It narrowed to a wagon's width, the sea to their right and a cliff wall rising on their left.

Stephan shook off his misery. "The wagons will never get through," he said.

Backtracking, they turned inland and entered the Forest of Arsuf. It was thickly wooded, a mile deep and at least ten times that long. Rumours had spread through the camp that Saladin would set the forest ablaze if the army marched through. Or that his soldiers would hide amongst the oaks and strike out.

"It is no wonder so many attended mass this afternoon," Stephan said.

"Shh."

"The priests were pleased to see—"

"Quiet."

"You think the Saracens do not know where we are?"

Henry glared. "They will if you keep talking." He rested one hand on the hilt of his sword and spurred Sombre.

Stephan watched as Henry cantered ahead, knew what he was thinking. Thousands of men would have to pass this way. It would take hours. Would Saladin trap them here?

Stephan nudged Hawk forward, alert for any movement in the trees. Thick shadows blanketed the road. He listened for the snap of a twig, the setting of a crossbow, or the sounds of horses.

When they emerged at the southern end of the forest, the way ahead was flat but edged with jagged outcroppings of boulders. The rocks rose to different heights along the road and trailed towards brownish-red mountains. A river snaked down from the hills. A plateau, mayhap a mile wide, lay on the far side of the river. To the west, the land dropped off sharply into the sea.

Henry took in a deep breath and leaned forward in his saddle. "Why would God have his only Son born in this land when He could have had the greens of England?"

Loosing his wineskin from the saddle hook, Stephan chuckled. "Mayhap He had known He'd not find twelve disciples among the wilds there."

Henry laughed.

Stephan brought the flask to his lips and thought how good it was to hear that sound again, to see that smile. He took a swig of ale, letting the warm brew coat his parched throat. He pointed towards the mountains. "Perfect place for an ambush. They might charge as the first battalion comes from the forest."

Sweat dribbled down Henry's forehead. He batted at the moisture stinging his eyes. "Robin says the enemy has twice our numbers."

Stephan twisted in the saddle, considering their options. They could scout further inland, though that route risked cutting access to supplies, and the army was already low on food. Jaffa was fourteen miles south. That might mean a week's journey at the speed the army had been moving. Securing Jaffa was crucial. Supplies brought through its harbour would replenish the army on the inland journey to Jerusalem. But Arsuf lay in its path. Stephan doubted King Richard would agree to turn further east. Saladin knew they must pass this way. He would put this wretched landscape to his use.

Stephan glanced sidelong at Henry. "But we have many brave and good men."

Henry smiled again. "We have King Richard."

That look warmed Stephan's heart. "We just might survive this." *And mayhap our friendship has not been lost in this hell.* "Listen," he said.

Henry glanced around nervously. "What?"

"The quiet." Stephan pointed to a flock of gulls over the water. "Just the birds looking for a meal. And rushes caught on the wind."

"No creaking wagon wheels," Henry said. "No grumbling from the men."

"No armour clanking." Stephan felt more at ease at Henry's side than he'd felt in weeks. Almost like the old days. Before Acre. Before that letter from England.

"No screaming Saracens." Henry snarled, breaking the lighthearted banter. "No drums." He tugged at the cross round his neck, fingering the leather cord that held it. "We should get back and report."

Stephan pounded the pommel of his saddle. He couldn't let this moment pass. He had to find a way to prove to Henry that what they had was good, and right. "Why do you think Robin assigned us this patrol?"

Henry turned crimson. He'd known exactly what Robin was up to. "His matchmaking is for naught."

"Mayhap he knows more about you and I than—"

An arrow whistled through the air. It struck Henry mid-thigh.

Henry cried out, "Stephan!" His eyes rolled back in pain.

Sombre looked ready to bolt. Stephan grabbed the animal's reins. "Hold on, Henry." He led them into an alcove in the rock outcropping. Dismounting in its shadows, Stephan grabbed his shield and unsheathed his sword. "Pray there is only one." He glanced over his shoulder. Blood from the wound coated Henry's chausses and spilled onto his horse's coat.

Henry slid down from Sombre. He landed hard, collapsing to the ground with a groan.

"Henry!"

"I am fine."

Stephan kept his shield raised, watching for a sign of their attacker, and looking furtively at Henry. "You are losing a lot of blood."

"Take care of that Saracen." Henry's voice cracked. He bit down on his lip, grabbed the shaft of the arrow, and yanked. His face twisted in pain. The arrow came free and he gasped but didn't cry out.

Even in the shadows Stephan saw Henry's face grow pale, watched him press his tunic against the wound to staunch the flow of blood. Stephan turned away, desperate to find the infidel before he struck again. He heard nothing save for the wind blowing the brush and Henry's breathing, which grew more labored as each second passed.

Stephan drew up beside Henry. He worked Henry's long dagger from his sword belt and used it to cut a strip of cloth from his tunic. He wadded it up, pressed it to Henry's wound. "You must hold that down." Stephan held out the long blade to Henry. "You cannot expect me to take the man alone."

Henry smirked at him, a good sign. "My bow?" he asked.

Stephan glanced at the blood pooling on the ground by Henry's leg. His throat constricted in dread, but he wouldn't let Henry see his fear. Shaking his head, he said, "You cannot nock and loose an arrow and keep pressure on that wound at the same time. Just make sure your aim is good with the dagger."

Henry waved the weapon shakily and smiled. "I shall only get one chance."

Stephan croaked. "I know."

"God be with you."

"I will be right back."

Henry smiled again. "Not going anywhere."

Shield and sword in hand, Stephan ducked out of the alcove. He hugged the rock wall. It was rough, pock-marked. He scanned for perches along its ridge, eyes darting to the forest and back.

"I know you are out here," he said quietly.

He followed the curve of the wall and slipped around it cautiously. The rock ledge above him cast shadows at his feet. A bush there was stirred by the wind. A larger shadow moved. Stephan jerked back. Too late. A Saracen swooped down on him with the grace of a hawk. A hawk with a very large sword in its claw.

Stephan tried to get out of the way, stumbled. The raised blade missed his head by an inch and the soldier straddled him. The pommel of his sword found Stephan's face.

Stephan felt bone crunch. He reeled from the blow. His sword slipped from his hand. Frantic, he reached for it but was struck again, a fist slamming into his jaw. Stephan raked his nails across the Saracen's face, dug his fingers into the man's neck. He shoved him, forcing them into a roll across the rock-strewn ground. Stephan's shoulder met a boulder the size of a sow. Shooting pain coursed down his back. Still, he managed to knock the sword from the man's hand. "Christ, you're a strong one."

His attacker pinned Stephan to the ground. The man's round, black eyes mocked him. He spat something in Arabic. Allah, sultan and a guttural khatala—kill—came through loud and clear. His intentions needed no translation. He dug his fingernails into Stephan's wrist, drawing blood. Sweat glistened on his huge quivering arm muscles. He landed another solid punch against Stephan's jaw.

Stephan's head snapped to one side. Blood pooled in his mouth. He gagged and then spat into his foe's face. The Saracen wrapped his hands around Stephan's neck. Bucking violently, Stephan struggled to throw the man.

Cannot breathe. Must not let him take me. Henry...

Stephan flailed wildly and felt the Saracen's grip on his throat loosen. Stephan whipped his head up, butting the man's nose. He heard a crack. Warm blood dripped onto Stephan's face, but his hands were suddenly free. He drove his fist into the man's temple. When the Saracen lurched back, Stephan grabbed his dull black hair and yanked it as hard as he could. The Saracen screamed and released his hold. Stephan propelled them into another roll, and stood shakily when they stopped. He blinked the blood from his eyes, sidestepped when the Saracen barreled into him. He wasn't quick enough and the wind exploded from his lungs when he hit the ground.

The Saracen's face burned a deep scarlet and his eyes grew wild. Sweat dripped from the man's hair and mingled with the blood on Stephan's face.

Coughing, Stephan tasted salt and copper choking him. His arms burned with exhaustion. His ears were ringing. *Cannot give up.* Henry wouldn't stand a chance against the infidel. Not with that leg.

Stephan saw his sword an arm's length away. He reached for it, but the Saracen got to it first. He brought it up, ready to impale Stephan with his own weapon.

With a sudden jerk, the Saracen gasped. He stared, eyes raised to the sky, and then slumped to the ground. Henry's long blade was buried to the hilt in his back.

Henry leaned against the cliff wall. His left leg was drenched with blood. "I owed you one," he said.

Stephan wheezed as he stood, wiping away blood dribbling down his chin. "What took you so long?"

Henry tried to smile. "You look awful." His eyes rolled back and he collapsed.

"Henry!"

Stephan stumbled to Henry's side, his legs barely holding him up. "Stay with me," he said, running his hand along Henry's forehead. He ripped Henry's chausses off and tore a strip from his hose to make a tourniquet. Satisfied with the crude bandage, he retrieved their horses. His head swam. His face felt numb. Trying to lift Henry, he gasped and nearly keeled over.

Henry moaned.

"That's right. It hurts. Keep that up so I know you are alive." *So much blood...* "Henry, do you hear me?"

Henry answered with another groan.

"We must hurry back to the camp. The Hospitallers will tend to you. Henry, I need your help." Stephan tugged at Henry's arms, tried to pick up his dead weight, and collapsed over him.

Stephan drew in long, slow breaths. Resting his head against Henry's chest, he felt tears stain his cheeks. "Do not leave me, Henry. Please, do not leave me."

Stephan wrapped his arm around Henry. His head was ringing but he was certain he heard riders approaching. Was that his name they called? "Sir Stephan...Sir Henry..."

Stephan's strength waned. The world swam around him, and then he fell into darkness.

Acre

twenty-three

LITTLE JOHN INSPECTED A cart piled with fresh fruit. He picked up an orange and held it in both hands like it was a precious jewel. It was smooth and dimpled, and as large as his fist. "Sweetest thing that ever came from a tree."

The shopkeeper huffed and snorted. His olive-skinned face wrinkled around the eyes, wary of Little John's deliberations to choose the best of the fruit and watchful of Allan's antics near the cart of dates and lemons.

Little John tucked the orange into the crook of his arm. He'd never seen any near its size in the markets in London. Wouldn't have had a penny to pay for even one back then. Picking up two more, he breathed in the luscious fragrance. "There is nothing that smells so wondrous. How many should we buy?" he asked Allan in between sighs.

Circling the other cart, Allan paid no heed to Little John's question. It would have been a tactic the two boys employed to distract a vendor on London's streets. Allan grabbed hold of the cart and stopped. He stared past Little John.

"Allan, how many—" Little John started to turn. "What are you looking—" A young street urchin knocked into him.

Grunting, Little John felt a roaming hand reaching for his coin purse. "Don't even think about it," he said, smacking the hand away. The boy couldn't have been any older than Allan had been when Little John first met him in London. A botched attempt to grab a sweet had turned them into lifelong friends.

Little John tossed the barefooted boy one of the oranges. "Now be off."

The shopkeeper growled what must have been, "You will pay for that one." He paraded up to Little John with the handle of his broom held like a weapon.

Allan said, "We have enough for two meat pasties and six oranges." He pretended to inspect the dates and lemons, but his eyes shifted from the cart to the crowded street.

"Good. Four for us, one for Queen Joanna, and one for Queen Berengaria." Little John scrunched up his face, deep in thought. "Six, that's sebha. No, wait." He looked at the shopkeeper, glanced at the two on his arm, and began counting in the Arabic that one of the palace maids taught him. "Wahid, ithnain, talatha—"

"Thalatha," the shopkeeper corrected him, watching Allan suspiciously.

"Thalatha," Little John repeated. "That's the one I gave away so three, not four, for us."

Allan nudged Little John. "Hurry," he said, handing the man a penny for the fruit.

"We've no need to get back to the palace. Queen Joanna told us to enjoy our afternoon." Little John still marveled that an orphaned thief might serve in the royal household. A few hours wandering Acre's markets each week meant more than the freedom he had roaming the English countryside or living on London's grimy streets. He picked up two more oranges. "Arbaa, khemsa—"

Allan elbowed Little John. "He's back. Look by the baker's shop."

Little John handed the sixth orange to Allan. "Sitaa," he said, glancing sidelong down the road. At midday, the marketplace was just busy enough for someone to mingle with the crowds and not be noticed. But Robin had often spoken of the need to keep a close watch anytime they ventured out. And the boys' previous lives picking pockets had been good training ground. In Acre, dark-haired men wearing light brown robes were numerous enough to form a scouting party. One man with silvery hair? He stood out like a golden lion on a red shield.

"What shall we do?" Little John asked. They'd seen the same man following them two days earlier.

"Split up. We will be long gone when he decides which of us to follow. I will meet you back at the palace gate."

Little John nodded. "Ready?"

"Run!"

Allan shot up the road to the north. Little John ran into an alleyway, headed east. A few minutes later, they rendezvoused at the palace. Winded, their gazes swept the streets and they laughed, juggled the oranges, and congratulated themselves.

"That was like dodging the soldiers in London when you got caught with that ruby red purse after King Richard's crowning!"

"I did not get caught. That was you."

"Was me who kicked the man behind the knees that had hold of you."

"I did not—" Little John stopped, nearly dropping the fruit. "God's bones, Allan."

"What?"

"We forgot to buy the pasties!"

near the
Foresto[Arsu[

twenty~four

STEPHAN REMEMBERED NOTHING OF his rescue by Robin and a handful of knights. He'd awakened hours later in a Hospitaller tent to men groaning and wind buffeting the thick canvas walls. It was long past sunset. The tent flaps were down to keep out the cool night air. The respite from the desert heat would have been welcome but for the hundred wounded and dying. Their sickbeds were lined up in four straight rows. Henry was one of those men, unconscious on a cot nearby.

King Richard hovered at Stephan's bedside. A sputtering candle reflected gold specks in his eyes. He offered Stephan a sip from his wineskin and questioned him as he would any able-bodied soldier. He appeared oblivious to the moans of the sick and to the putrid smell of gangrenous flesh.

Stephan gave his account of the lay of the land. Richard listened, stone-faced, and wringed his hands. It confirmed information provided by other scouts and local inhabitants. Satisfied with Stephan's report, Richard stood with some effort. He pressed one hand to his side. A grimace crossed his face, though no one but Stephan saw it.

"Are you well, sire?" Stephan asked.

Richard rubbed a spot near his waist. "It is nothing. A small wound from an enemy dart during today's skirmish."

Richard's "small wound" might have put a less stubborn man in bed for a day or two. He'd made light of it, so Stephan steered the conversation towards Saladin's hit-and-run tactics. "Robin told me the infidels' attacks on the rearguard grow bolder."

"We lost more brave men today. The Templars were hard hit. Many of their horses fell from the rain of arrows and darts. The knights will be marching alongside the men-at-arms."

There'd be no new animals brought from Acre by sea until the army reached Jaffa. Stephan had overheard the healers speak of greedy men selling the meat of the dead horses. He started to ask about fights erupting over the high prices when Richard tapped his cot. "I shall see you in my Council tomorrow. Rest well. We will need your courage and your sword."

"You will have both, sire."

On his way out, Richard took a moment to lay a comforting hand on a man receiving last rites. He crossed himself and then turned to speak with another wounded man. The priest, his prayers for one done, shuffled off to the next soul needing his attention. His feet crunched against the dusty gravel floor until he stopped by Henry's cot.

"Get away from him!" Stephan shouted.

All eyes turned to Stephan.

The priest remained calm, not flustered by the outburst. "All souls crave absolution before passing from this—"

"Not that one, Father." Every eye in the room shifted to Richard. He snorted, amusement tingeing the strength, resolve and friendship Stephan saw there. "I ordered him to live. He would not dare die."

"If God calls him home—"

"He will not. God shall keep him here to suffer this war with his friends." Richard nodded at Stephan. He strode from the tent leaving a confused priest in his wake.

The night was long. Stephan watched the Hospitallers administer to Henry, watched them remove the bodies of those who'd succumbed to their wounds or to disease. The air smelled of vomit and blood. It was stale with death, but Henry thrashed in his cot, fighting back.

Stephan finally dozed, startled awake when Henry cried out. Stephan stumbled across the tent. He laid his fingers on Henry's brow and flinched. Heat poured from Henry's feverish face. Stephan grabbed the cloth in the washbowl beside the cot and gently sponged Henry's cheeks and his forehead. "You heard the king's order, Henry. You will live."

Stephan pressed his lips to Henry's and slid his fingers beneath his palm. He watched Henry's breathing slow, and felt comforted when Henry fell back to peaceful slumber. He hadn't realised he'd fallen asleep himself until two squires dragged in another knight wounded in an early morning skirmish.

Stephan struggled to rise. He paced back to his cot, retrieved his sword belt, and tugged it round his waist. The healers protested, insisted he stay, but he ignored their advice. Henry was in good hands and King Richard expected him at Council. He knelt beside Henry and whispered, "Keep me in your prayers." Henry's eyelids fluttered. Stephan touched his cheek. Still warm, but not burning. He smiled and then hurried outside into the September sun as fast as his shaky legs would allow.

~ ~ ~

"WE MUST NOT LET them goad us into attack. It would surely be the end for us." King Richard's voice resounded with a heat that rivaled the temperature of the breeze blowing through the pavilion.

Knights crowded every bench. Skepticism filled many faces. "Not attack?"

Stephan craned his neck to see who'd spoken. He groaned from that simple effort. His mouth curled in pain and the split on his lip reopened. With much greater care, he dabbed at the blood there with the back of his hand.

Richard paced, tapping various points on the map secured to the tent wall. As Stephan and Henry expected, there'd been no questioning the army's route south through the Forest of Arsuf and onto the plain. Richard finally paused and traced a line with his long dagger along what would mark the army's eastern flank. "The knights must not charge until my trumpeters sound. Let the Saracens harass us. You know their strategy is to attack quickly, turn, and run."

"That does not make it any easier, my liege," one of the Hospitallers said.

Robin grabbed a wood figure from the table and waved it in the air. "If our knights charge too soon, the Saracens win. We will be scattered. Weakened." He scanned the stifling tent. Would any knight dispute his words? Apprehension filled their faces. "We are stronger as a whole."

"This is insanity," a Pisan knight in a dark red cloak muttered scornfully.

"We cannot endure repeated attacks," one of his compatriots grunted.

"How many more men and horses will we lose?" another shouted.

Robin held up his hand. "It is the only way. The bowmen and men-at-arms will protect the knights. The Saracens will wear themselves down with their pattern of attack and retreat. They want to draw the knights out."

Behind him, Richard nodded. "But we shall not let them. Their repeated offensive moves against us will be their downfall."

The Duke of Burgundy stepped towards Richard. "You are so certain Saladin will not attack us in the Forest?"

"It shall take us a day to pass." "Narrow roads…" "Is there no other way?" Questions and disagreements erupted from all corners of the pavilion.

Richard pressed the tip of his sword into the dais and waited for the arguments to die down.

"You would have us trek east into the mountains and meet them there?" he finally asked. "With wagons and near twenty thousand men? Every battle commander with half a wit knows that to be a fool's mission." Richard exhaled sharply through his nose. "I have sent a messenger and propose to meet with Saladin's brother on the morrow. While Saphadin takes my terms for peace to the sultan to consider, we will march. By mid-afternoon, we shall be making camp on the south side of the Forest, near the river they call Rochetaille."

One by one, the commanders approached the king. Kneeling before him, many bristled, but each man swore his support. Still, they strode from the pavilion disgruntled and complaining bitterly.

Robin grabbed a jug of ale and two mugs and slid his arm across Stephan's shoulder. They walked outside and planted themselves on a bench in the shade that faced the endless sea. Robin poured their drinks. He guzzled his down in one long slug. "How is Henry?" he asked.

"Feverish." Stephan eyed his ale, wishing he could drown his fear in it and knowing that Henry might still succumb. He took a drink. "He woke during the night in his own Hell, but seemed better this morn."

Robin palmed Stephan's hand. Stephan nodded, grateful for Robin's friendship. Tipping his head towards a group of Hospitallers deep in conversation further down the road, he asked, "Will the commanders hold their knights back?"

"They'd better," Robin said. He refilled his mug, staring out across the sea. "We shall all be dead if they do not."

theBattleOfArsuf
7 september 1191

twenty-five

AN ARROW AIMED AT retreating Saracens flew from the ranks to the front and left of Stephan.

"Hold steady," Stephan ordered, tightening his grip on Hawk's reins. The destrier shifted restlessly beneath him. "Do not waste your shots. They are out of range."

"Give them a few minutes. The bastards will be back," someone scowled.

Nervous laughter punched the still desert air. Stephan nodded his agreement, his gaze sweeping the landscape. Hospitallers in the rearguard. The men of the fourth battalion around him. He'd been relieved as any man when their divisions passed without incident through the Forest of Arsuf the day before and the army's tents rose by the River Rochetaille. When darkness fell, they'd watched the enemies' campfires glow on the opposite bank. And then Richard roused his men in the black of night and the march south resumed.

The first assault had come three hours later. Saladin's cavalry charged from the hills like a dark pitching wave of shrieking men and beasts. Arrows arced high, speeding towards the sea of Hospitallers. The enemy might not pierce a crusader shield, but the horses were unprotected. The rearguard took the brunt of it—again—but true to King Richard's orders, they did not charge.

Wave after wave, the Saracens struck. Thousands of them. Attack and retreat. Trumpets blasted and cymbals crashed, an ungodly melody accompanied by the war cries, "Allah Akbar!"

Frustrated when their tactics failed to provoke the Hospitallers, Saladin's cavalry broadened their assault and struck along the length of the army's eastern flank. Arrows rained down, striking horses, finding a shield slightly misaligned to reveal a less fortunate foot soldier. Those who plodded forward tried not to think of the men who'd fallen at their feet. Tried not to trip over the dead in their path.

The knights rode in formations so tight their legs brushed. The men-at-arms marched shoulder-to-shoulder. "I might fall asleep on my feet," one joked, "and still move forward."

"Dear God, save us," a man the others called Ox muttered during one of the lulls in the fighting. He lowered his shield to stretch, revealing the reason for his nickname. He was huge, broad-chested, with arms that looked like he lifted full-grown oxen for sport.

"Do the Saracens just spring from the desert sands?" a crossbowman croaked, his throat parched by the heat.

"I do not doubt that they do," Stephan said. He didn't need to repeat that he'd heard the Saracens were twenty-five thousand strong. Others said two or three times that number. It was enough to see the infidels retrench in the hills after a charge, almost ghost-like through the thick haze of dust kicked into the air.

"Tighten up," Stephan added. He craned his head, looking south. The army stretched so far that he couldn't see the men in the vanguard. "Stay close."

Beside him, Thomas of Winchester chuckled. "I do not doubt the men are tired of hearing that, York."

Stephan smirked. "Mayhap they would enjoy your voice over mine? What was that song that sprang from your mouth at the baths in Acre?"

The men around them laughed but a hollow feeling plagued Stephan as soon as the words passed his lips. He remembered that night when he'd held Henry in his arms.

Winchester moaned. "My head still aches, you need not remind me. And looking at your face makes me hurt all over," he said. "Shouldn't you be on one of those stretchers with your friend?"

"It looks worse than it feels."

Winchester's brow rose. "And my name is Saladin."

"Do not worry, Winchester. The infidel did not wound my sword arm."

"Good. I shall count on you and all these fine men."

Ox rapped his shield and lifted his lance to Winchester. "God keep us all."

The others around Ox drummed their shields repeating his call to the Almighty. Stephan glanced over his shoulder towards the wagons carrying the wounded. His throat tightened. He thought of Henry. *God keep you, my friend.*

Stephan wished he could escape the tight formation. He felt useless. Weak. Knowing Henry was surrounded by dying and wounded men, mayhap at death's door, made that feeling worse. Why hadn't he asked Robin to place him with Champagne's or Burgundy's knights? He'd much prefer riding on the eastern flank. This closed in feeling was maddening.

His gaze swept round. The king's standard flew high over their battalion. Stephan's conviction swelled. He and the Anglo-Normans would keep that golden lion aloft at all costs. He'd endure. Henry would live.

"The devils are back," Winchester said.

"Shields!" Stephan bellowed.

The black wave of Saracens had turned. The dust rose again and the sky darkened. An arrow clunked off Stephan's shield. "Steady," he shouted as dozens more struck around him. One hit Winchester's horse. The animal screamed, its blood spraying Stephan as it sidled into his horse. Nearby horses danced aside as Winchester's stumbled and fell, nearly rolling over Winchester.

"Keep moving," Winchester ordered as he got to his feet and ripped his sword across the animal's neck to end its suffering. Stephan steeled himself against that last cry, and brought his shield up as more arrows rained down. He heard Ox curse, heard him choking on the blood in his throat. Stephan's hand tightened on his shield strap. He cursed to himself as Ox fell and the men stepped over him, around him, and raised Ox's call again, "God keep us, God keep us."

The knights held back as ordered. The men kept moving forward, marching until early afternoon when the pitch of the war cries reached a new crescendo.

The rearguard commander charged past the Anglo-Normans towards the king. Stephan recognized Garnier de Nablus. The knight had argued with King Richard during many council gatherings. Two more horsemen followed in his path. Panicked voices swept up from the rear. Stephan turned. The Hospitaller battalion had broken ranks. Their infantry had opened a gap and the knights charged, forsaking the tight cohesion that might keep them alive.

Above the din, a rallying battle cry rang out. "St. George!"

"Dear God, help them," one of the Norman knights near Stephan shouted.

"The king has not given the signal," another man said.

"Turn, turn! For St. George," a third voice beseeched.

Stephan exchanged a glance with Winchester, on foot with the men-at-arms. "The Hospitallers cannot stand alone against the Saracens," he said. They'd not held out as long as King Richard had wanted, but even he must realise there could be no delay now.

"Where is the king?" Winchester asked.

Trumpets sounded in response to his question. Cavalry shot along the eastern flank. "There!" Stephan shouted. The king led the charge. The knights of the second and third battalions turned to join the battle.

"Holy Sepulchre, help us!"

"For St. George!"

The cries drowned out the enemy drums. The men-at-arms around Stephan opened a path. Stephan kicked Hawk into the fray. Hawk's hoofs beat the ground as the enemies' arrows whooshed by. A knight went down beside Stephan. Saracen swords flashed a few lengths ahead. An eye blink later, Stephan's shield took the brunt of a blow. Still moving forward, he swung his blade, felt it rip into flesh. A club arced towards his head. He ducked. Behind him, all around him, there was the *clank clank* of steel and the blur of swinging weapons.

Sweat burned Stephan's eyes. His arms ached. And he swung his sword again. Everywhere he looked the plain was littered with bodies of men and horses. The ground turned red. Blood caked the dirt and men stared blankly at the sky.

The Saracens retreated and Stephan felt a surge of hope. But they wheeled their horses and charged again, their banners held high defiantly and flapping in the hot wind. And each time they charged, King Richard was at the fore, leading his men.

As darkness fell, Stephan readied his shield and sword waiting for the Saracens to charge once more. His hands trembled. He was too tired to think or feel. But the field of battle grew quiet as the first stars appeared. Stephan lowered his arms and rested his weapons over the pommel of his saddle. The fighting had finally ended.

Jaffa
10 september 1191

twenty-six

IT WAS SAID THAT Saladin lost thousands of men at Arsuf. There'd been little time to mourn the seven hundred crusaders who had died. The men spent the day after the battle scouring the plains for their wounded, burying the dead, and getting what rest they could. Bodies and spirits were bruised, but Richard's sheer will pushed them onward.

On the third day after Arsuf, Stephan patrolled the length of the Anglo-Norman's eastern flank. He watched the Saracens in the hills mirroring their march. Would Saladin order another assault?

A mile or so ahead, the vanguard would be settling at the port town of Jaffa, the day's objective. Saladin had abandoned the fortress there. Mayhap he expected he could not hold the town, especially after his defeat at Arsuf. Still, Saladin had the advantage of knowing this land. He'd strike in his own time, and at a place of his choosing.

Though the sweltering sun beat down on them, the men's pace quickened the closer they drew to Jaffa. Their conversations grew animated. They spoke of fresh baked goods in the town's shops, or roasted meat rather than the salted and dried pork that made up meals most days. The king's ships would anchor in the harbour. There'd be supplies from Acre and fresh horses for knights who'd lost theirs to the Saracens.

"Do you see the towers, Sir Stephan?" one of the bowmen asked.

"Where's the fortress? Shouldn't we see it by now?" another asked.

Stephan stretched in the saddle. "I see...tents. Thousands of them."

The men near Stephan grew quiet and strained to look ahead. They'd expected to see the king's red and gold lions flying from Jaffa's city towers. One of the Hospitallers had told them of a grand fortress overlooking the harbour. But there were no towers. Only rubble. Not one wall remained intact. Saladin had ordered the town razed.

The army camped in the fruit and olive groves next to Jaffa. By nightfall, orders to rebuild the fortress had been issued and King Richard convened his council to plan for the next phase of the march.

Knights crammed the pavilion, packed as closely as they'd been on the march to Arsuf. Tempers were rising. Goals that seemed so clear to the king were met with opposition, mostly from Burgundy and his French supporters.

"We must take Ascalon," Richard argued.

"The town is three to five days march south. We shall be harassed by Saladin along the way," Burgundy said. "How many men and horses will we lose when the better move is to turn east to Jerusalem now? We came to secure—"

"We cannot expect to hold Jerusalem if Ascalon is not in Christian hands." Richard's voice remained steady but his large hands gripped the edge of the trestle. "Reinforcements for Saladin's troops will come through that port."

"All you have is the word of some Saracen scouts. What proof is there of this mighty force from Egypt?" Burgundy asked. "You place far too much trust in men who have betrayed their own."

"Likely working for Saladin," another Frenchman scoffed. There was mumbled agreement from the section of the pavilion near Burgundy.

Stephan leaned close to Robin. "Will he give way to the French demands?"

"They are being short-sighted." Robin stabbed the orange in his hand with his dagger, and dug it into the fruit to draw out the juice. He pointed his blade at the map behind the king. "Is it not plain for all to see? Are they deaf?"

Richard threw his hands in the air. "You wish to take a chance? Then let us march towards Jerusalem," he said and unsheathed his sword. He tapped the map, nearly slicing a long gash between Jaffa and the Holy City. "We turn inland. Saladin strikes from north *and* south. He will come in behind us. Cut our supply lines from the coast. And then what?"

"It is but rumour, this force from Egypt," Burgundy repeated.

Richard dug his blade into the trestle. "Send your own men south to Ascalon. Let your scouts verify these reports." He swung the sword, scattering the parchments there. "These *rumours* speak of ten thousand soldiers."

Voices groused from one end of the pavilion to the other. "March to Jerusalem. Now!" someone shouted.

Robin whispered to Stephan, "We must take Ascalon. Stop them there."

Stephan needed no convincing. "Take Jerusalem now and we shall be overrun by Saladin's reinforcements. His men will have re-stocked and rested in Ascalon."

Robin drew a line in the dirt with his dagger. "Even without them, and despite Saladin's losses at Arsuf, they outnumber us still. Can we endure another long siege at Jerusalem? Because that is what we will face. Like Acre."

Stephan glanced around the tent at the war-weary knights. He thought of the archers and men-at-arms who'd endured so much. Thought of Henry, still abed with fever and in the healers' care.

At the front of the pavilion, another sword was unsheathed. A hush fell over the tent. The Duke of Burgundy glared at Richard. "Fortify Jaffa. It will serve to keep the army supplied. We must turn east to Jerusalem now. Forget Ascalon. Else my men and I will sail north on tomorrow's tide." The French noble turned and stomped out of the pavilion, twenty others at his heels.

Richard closed his eyes, clenched his fist. He could not take Ascalon without the French. He had no choice. Jaffa would be rebuilt. The army would march to the Holy City.

~ ~ ~

THE SUN HAD SET and the air turned cool by the time Stephan left the pavilion intent on seeing Henry. In the few hours since the hospital had been set up and the wounded moved in, the place already reeked of festering wounds and rotted flesh.

Stephan jerked to a halt halfway into the Hospitaller tent. A priest knelt by Henry's cot. *No!*

Trembling, Stephan took a step forward, pausing when he heard the priest talking and not in prayer.

"I shall seal this letter to your father and see that it goes out on the morning tide. Is there anything else I can do before you leave?" the priest asked Henry.

"No, Father," Henry said, his voice weak. "Your words of comfort for my mother and my betrothed will see me through. It eases my mind knowing I will not be alone in my prayers for them."

"I will pray for you also, my son. Your pain for this loss is greater than that from your wounds. God knows your troubles. Turn to Him. Let Him help you through it."

"I will, Father."

"Rest now." He touched Henry's brow and turned to leave.

Stephan started across the tent. The priest caught his arm and hauled him back outside.

Stephan jerked away from the priest. "I must speak with Henry."

"Sir Henry does not need to see you now. He is weak and must sleep."

Stephan stared past the priest and into the tent. "I…I care for him."

The priest laid a gentle hand on Stephan's shoulder. "Let him be. He has enough pain."

"What? What did he tell you?" Stephan asked, but the priest turned away without another word.

Had Henry confessed? There was nothing to confess! *Henry, I will never believe it is a sin to love you.*

~ ~ ~

STEPHAN WOKE FROM A restless sleep and squinted at sunlight pouring through the tent flaps. He jumped from the bed. "If I am too late…" He'd done as the priest asked against his better judgment and later discovered Henry would sail north with other wounded. If he'd missed the chance to say goodbye—his heart clenched at the thought.

Rushing towards the harbour, Stephan was relieved to see the line of wagons lumbering slowly down to the docks. He ran from one to the next looking for Henry. Someone called his name. Stopping, he turned, heard it again, and followed the sound of that sweet voice.

Henry smiled up at him from the hospital cart, a two-wheeled wagon that held three other men stretched out like fish on a plank. "I thought you might not come to wish me well."

"You should not insist on travel ere the sun is up, friend." *I was so afraid I would never see you again.*

"It has been up near an hour, Stephan."

"Little John's dislike of early mornings wears on me."

Henry chuckled. "I told the healers I would stay, but they would hear none of it. I am not nearly as bad as some of the others." Henry turned his head towards the unconscious soldier next to him. The man's patched shoulder and chest were blackened and reeked of a fetid odor that made him turn away.

"The healers know best. You will be more comfortable in Acre."

"I tried to walk this morning. If Brother Ambroise had not been there to catch me, my face would look like yours." Henry grimaced. "You look terrible."

Stephan turned from side to side. His left eye and nose were not as swollen as they'd been the day before. "Adds a bit of character, don't you think?"

Henry couldn't help but grin. "You have more than enough to rival the king *and* Robin."

Stephan's eyes lit. "Are you trying to flatter me?"

Henry coughed violently, his face reddening.

"Are you well?" Stephan asked.

Henry waved away his concern, winced when the cart hit a rut in the road.

Stephan gripped the side of the wagon to steady it. "You are still weak. Give it time." He cleared his throat. "You gave confession yesterday."

"I spoke with Father Eustace. He was kind enough to write a letter for my father. So much happened after…" Henry pinched his lips, squeezed his eyes shut as if to block the memory. "I'd not responded to my father's letter. I wanted him to know I had received his news."

"I would have written it for you had you asked. You did not tell the priest—"

Henry held his hand up. "Father Eustace knows that I hurt you, nothing more. I asked God's forgiveness for that, and for what I did."

Stephan leaned over the side of the cart. "What *we* did. Not you. We, Henry," he said, his voice low. "The two of us. It is as special a bond as any your God allows between two people."

Henry closed his eyes again, his face wracked in pain. Not pain of the flesh but pain of the soul.

Stephan's heart cracked again. How could he be standing so close to Henry yet feel the distance between them?

The wagon stopped near the end of the docks. The driver jumped down to help unload the dozen others lined up in front of his. Wounded men were carted one by one aboard the galley.

Henry finally looked up. He reached out and touched Stephan's cheek. Stephan cupped Henry's hand against his face and then kissed it. Henry shook his head sadly.

Grief overwhelmed Stephan. His heart pounded so fiercely he was certain he'd collapse from the pain. He hated to think that Henry would always be consumed by guilt.

"S'cuse me, sir." A boy with long stringy hair who couldn't have been much older than Little John looked from Stephan to Henry. "Cap'n says we must hurry to move this one on board so she can catch the tide."

An older man helped pull the stretcher from the wagon, jostling Henry. He winced in pain.

"Careful there," Stephan said. Walking alongside Henry, he said, "I did not have a chance to thank you. I'd have been done for by that Saracen had your aim not been true."

Henry brushed his arm and smiled. "Do not take the Holy City without me."

Stephan squeezed Henry's hand. "I shall be waiting for you."

Stephan watched the ship sail. Hundreds of people milled about near the docks but he'd never felt more alone.

Acre

october 1191

twenty-seven

HENRY FORCED HIMSELF TO walk the stone floors of the hospital. He'd needed help the first week. The steps did not come easy. By the end of the second week, his leg felt like it had been pinned beneath a siege engine. Yet that pain was nothing when his night terrors invaded his days. The hospital's cream-coloured walls pressed in around him. They shut out Acre's blazing sun but couldn't soothe Henry's thoughts. The moans of the wounded echoed in the hallways and mingled with the voices in his mind. Enemy war cries. Messina, Acre, the march to Arsuf. Stephan…

So Henry prayed to God. *Help me understand.*

"This place allows all sorts inside, my lord."

Henry startled. He turned sharply towards the door.

Beaming, Allan bowed. "Sir Henry, I cannot believe my eyes." His deep blue and gold silk tunic heightened the green of his eyes. It was quite the contrast from the scruffy thief Henry remembered in Tours. Time spent in the queens' household made Allan hesitate, unsure how formal he should be.

Henry struggled to sit and then smiled, offering his hand to Allan. "It is good to see a familiar face."

Allan drew to his side and gripped Henry's hand tightly. "Sir Robin had sent word you'd been transported to Acre to recuperate. The healers have provided daily reports of your progress to my lady queen. You are to be her guest at the palace if you are ready to leave this place. I have a carriage waiting outside."

Henry stood, grateful for Allan's help. Allan snagged the sword belt looped over the bedpost and fitted it around Henry's waist. He fastened Henry's cloak at the neck with a large red and gold clasp. Henry reached for his walking stick. He moved slowly at first but felt steadier by the time the October sunshine washed their faces.

Henry let Allan help him climb into the carriage. It was a covered one with soft green cushions and shades that could be rolled down to block the sun or unwelcome onlookers. Something fit for a king or a queen. "You have come up in the world," Henry said.

"Not what I would have chosen for you or me, my lord. But we were not sure you would be up to mounting a destrier just yet."

Henry chuckled. "A wise guess."

The carriage rumbled down the street. Henry took a breath, glad for a whiff of local life rather than the stink of the hospital. He stretched his wounded leg between the seats.

The driver shouted to scatter animals being herded and people ambling at too leisurely a pace. Markets brimmed with shoppers lining their baskets. The colourful fruits and vegetables were a stark contrast to the cool greys and ambers of the hospital.

"What news is there from the south?" Henry asked.

"I hoped you would tell us. We hear little but Acre's gossip."

Above the clatter of the wheels, curses streamed from the mouth of the driver. Without warning the carriage stopped abruptly, nearly jolting Henry from his seat. Two Templar knights drew up on either side of the carriage. Henry hadn't noticed the broad-shouldered men accompanying them. He leaned out and asked, "What's amiss?"

Shouting and the clank of swords answered him.

One of the knights scowled. "Another fight over Jerusalem's fate. Follow us," he told the driver. His companion pointed at something beyond Henry's line of sight and then signaled a brown-robed figure on the street.

Allan sucked in a breath.

"You recognize that man?" Henry asked as the carriage whipped away. A troop of mounted knights thundered past to quell the violence and bells pealed throughout the city.

"I swear he spied on me and Little John in the market. And that was not the first time we'd seen him."

"The Templars seemed to know the man. Did you report your suspicions to the queen's guard?"

Allan scuffed his foot on the carriage floor, ran a hand along the scabbard of his long dagger. "We never saw him near the palace. We did not think to report it. If he is with the Templars—"

"Report it."

"Why would someone be watching us and working with the Templars?"

"There may be a reasonable answer but you do not know that. Now, tell me what you *do* know about the fights here in Acre."

"It gets worse every day, my lord. Bloody fistfights, out and out brawls. More dead than I can count on my hands. Why do they fight about who will rule Jerusalem when it's Saladin we need to worry over?"

Henry had overheard the healers as they went about their work at the hospital. The recapture of Jerusalem might be no closer than when Henry had been with the army near Arsuf, but the question of who would rule it stirred violence between the supporters of two rivals, King Guy and Conrad de Montferrat. Guy's wife Sibylla had inherited Jerusalem's crown during the reign of King Richard's father. She named Guy king-consort. When Jerusalem fell, he and his supporters took up the siege of Acre. Conrad, supported by Duke Leopold of Austria and Philip of France, married Sibylla's rightful heir Isabella. He'd claimed kingship when Sibylla died. Henry had paid little attention to either side's claims. He still despised politics, yet Allan had made a very astute point.

"If a boy—er, a young man your age sees this, why can't they?"

"I do not understand it, my lord."

Henry scratched his jaw. "And little news of King Richard?" he asked.

"Only the barest of details." Allan held up an invisible parchment and pretended to read. "Advanced three miles. Fought off the Saracens. Captured a handful. Lost a duke."

Henry wished he could laugh. "The king does not want to worry his queen. Believe me, my young friend, add the blood, illness, and death and the accursed roads and you might only imagine the true hardships."

"I had not meant to make light of it."

"I know that. But tell me, it has been weeks. Are they at Jerusalem yet, or at least marching on the eastern road?" A wistful smile crossed Henry's face. "I told Sir Stephan he must not take the Holy City without me."

"No worries, my lord. The last word shared with us just yesterday said they'd not ventured from Jaffa."

Still? Why hadn't the army turned inland if Jaffa had been secured?

~ ~ ~

LITTLE JOHN COULD HARDLY conceal his excitement when Henry joined Queen Berengaria and Queen Joanna for the midday meal. Little John stood behind Joanna holding a jug of wine, refilling her goblet when it was half full. His eyes danced between Henry, the queens, and Allan. Henry was impressed by both squires' awareness of their place in the royal household.

"Will you return to England, Sir Henry?" Joanna asked. Her deep emerald gown enhanced the green of her eyes.

"I think not, my lady. I may move slowly but in a week's time I shall be fit as any man in the army." Henry saw the queens exchange a look. The women had their suspicions of the condition of those men despite the dearth of information from the king.

Berengaria lifted her goblet to Henry's health. "Allan and John have leave to see to your needs while you are here."

"That is very generous of you, my lady. Both will have me dancing to fend off their swords in no time."

The squires grinned, breaking their royal servant facade. Berengaria smiled and her eyes softened. Her dark hair glistened with beaded pearls laced through her braids, matching ones offset by rubies on the gold trim of her dark blue gown.

Footsteps echoed on the marble flooring outside the great hall. A knight paused at the door and bowed. Silhouetted by light streaming in from the courtyard, Henry could not see his face, but the king's crest was emblazoned on his surcoat. When Queen Berengaria waved him in, Henry noticed his shock of silvery hair and the long brown cowl draped over his arm. Allan perked up, noticed it, too. It was the man from the street, the one the Templar had signaled.

The knight bent close to the queen's ear. His skin looked leathery, tanned and aged by the desert sun. After a moment, she nodded and he bowed again before departing as quickly as he'd come.

"One of our 'observers' in the city," Berengaria told Henry. "Sir Gregory was born here after his father served Louis of France and Queen Eleanor during the last Holy War. He speaks the language and has been of great service to my lord husband."

Joanna agreed. Gregory's reports informed the queens and the guard left behind to safeguard them and Acre. Messengers took his news to King Richard on a daily basis.

"Do those messengers bring back news of the army's progress towards Jerusalem?" Henry asked. "Allan tells me they have not ventured from Jaffa."

"That is our understanding." Joanna offered Berengaria a sympathetic look. Mutual respect and friendship had blossomed between the two women in the few months they'd known each other. "My brother is not forthcoming with many details. We did hear there was pressure from the French to fortify the city before the army turned east."

"I am anxious to join the king again," Henry said.

Joanna scoffed. "You have been here but three weeks, Henry. You must gather your strength. And what of your friend whom Little John speaks of so highly? We understand Sir Stephan was injured as well."

Henry felt heat creep up his neck. He cleared his throat, could feel Allan and Little John watching him closely. "I saw him ere I departed. He looked to have been trampled by a horse."

Henry immediately regretted the image he'd given the ladies. They might be aware of the casualties of war. They'd witnessed life in the camps, but that was nothing. Had they seen a charge, watched arrows fly? He could hardly picture them, hair coiffed, bejeweled in their sumptuous gowns, watching men die. "Apologies—"

Joanna ignored his concern. "No need. The servants do their best to keep the war from us, but we hear their whispers. We have seen the wounded, brave men battered by this war. And this struggle in the city between King Guy's supporters and Conrad puts more men in the hospital."

"And in their graves," Berengaria said. "Speaking of that rivalry, my lord husband's business settling this matter may keep him in Acre for weeks to come. Mayhap you will be well enough to return south with him."

"The king is here?" Henry asked.

"No, no, not yet. We expect him any day."

"His steady hand is needed," Joanna added. "Men and their politics." She snorted, most unladylike. Allan snickered. Henry shot a fleeting grimace at him, and was taken aback when Joanna grinned at them both.

Berengaria sipped her wine. She looked past Henry through the arched window. "It will be a wonder if these pilgrims do not kill each other before they march upon the Holy City."

"Has it truly come to that, my lady?" Henry asked.

She nodded sadly, the only sign of distress Henry had seen on her face.

Allan started to pour more wine into Berengaria's goblet but she held her hand out. Crooking a finger, she prodded him closer and whispered into his ear. Standing, she rested her palm on Allan's arm, eyes fixed on Henry.

"Enough of this political drudgery," she said. "I know two young men who are anxious to hear your tales of the march. Allan will check that your room is prepared and I promise to send him back here straightaway."

Little John drew to Joanna's side and offered his hand. Henry gripped the table, rose slowly, and bowed.

"Stay," Joanna told Little John. "Keep Sir Henry company."

When the door closed behind the departing ladies and Allan, Little John flew to Henry's side. He grabbed him in a brotherly embrace. "How are you, my lord? And Master Stephan. He is well?"

Henry held Little John tightly, glad the boy couldn't see his face. "All save his broken heart." He released him reluctantly.

"You are the only one who can mend that," Little John said.

"I cannot."

"Then I will be stuck trying to cheer two miserable people."

Henry sat down hard. He fiddled with the crumbs of bread on his plate. "You are not responsible for our lives. We are grown men, which is more than I can say about you."

Little John stared at his feet.

"I am sorry," Henry said. He tapped the chair next to his, urging Little John to sit. "You are more grown than many men I know."

Little John still didn't move. "And you should act like one, my lord. Admit you are wrong. I can't help wanting what's best for you. When me and Allan lived on London's streets we saw so much pain. Horrible things. People did not truly care for each other, 'cept where it got them a meal or a coin in their pocket. Mayhap a warm bed. But I see you and Master Stephan. There is respect and concern and love. And look what you have done for me and Allan. You've taken care of us. I must take care of you." He finally sat down, his cheeks flushed. "Even if you do say stupid things—" he paused, looked Henry straight in the eye, "my lord."

Henry laughed but inside his heart was breaking. He'd hurt Stephan, said things he didn't believe, hadn't really meant.

Little John saw the troubled mind behind Henry's smile. "Listen to your heart, my lord."

Henry's smile disappeared. He sat, unmoving. Stephan had been so kind and gentle when he'd seen him off at the docks in Jaffa. And it had naught to do with Henry saving his life.

Stephan had forgiven him.

Can I forgive myself?

twenty-eight

HENRY SETTLED INTO A routine at the palace. Mass with the queens and a dozen others just as the sun rose each day. Breakfast with the knights. Midday meals with the queens. Within days, he wielded his sword in daily practice with Allan or Little John.

Henry would have enjoyed another week to rest, but when King Richard arrived Henry accompanied him on his rounds. There were councils with the commanders of the guard, meetings with local officials, and inspection tours of the city. The king's negotiations with Guy and Conrad's supporters and reports from the army at Jaffa consumed each day.

Henry's disdain for politics grew at the rate his respect for Richard increased. When the day's business was done they'd review it over a meal with Queen Berengaria and Queen Joanna. At times that meant they dined by candlelight. In less than a week, they celebrated a successful agreement between the rival factions.

Joanna shooed the servants from the great hall when her brother and Berengaria finally retired for the evening. "At last. Peace and quiet," she said and smiled at Henry. "I know you would not say it, so I shall. I grow weary listening to my brother hour after hour. Do your ears hurt like mine?"

Henry tried to remain serious but Joanna's honesty made him grin. "Politics can be tiresome, my lady."

Joanna laughed. "A man after my own heart."

She had a lovely smile, reminding Henry of her mother, Eleanor of Aquitaine. But Joanna's hair was reddish-gold like her brother's hair, her green eyes were fiery, mischievous and calculating, like his.

She stood and Henry rose expecting to be dismissed. He was surprised when Joanna studied him, her gaze so intense that Henry blushed.

Joanna extended her hand. "Come, walk with me." She led him to the verandah. They settled beneath palms swaying in the breeze. A bright moon illuminated the smooth flagstone flooring and the shadows of the trees danced across it.

Joanna tugged at her cloak to ward off the evening chill. "I must say, you hardly seem the man who dined with us a few short weeks ago."

"That hobbling old man with the bad leg? Thanks be to God, the pain is gone."

Joanna looked at him again. "Is it?"

Henry shifted uncomfortably.

"Forgive me," she said. "I lived with my mother eleven years and, in that short time, I picked up her bluntness."

Henry chuckled. "I admire Queen Eleanor for that very reason. And I would say you have many of her fine qualities."

"I shall take that as a compliment. But I did not mean to turn the talk to my family. We have hardly spoken of your burden. I have watched you, Sir Henry, seen you distracted during practice with Little John and Allan or when my brother carries on a bit too long. You have suffered a great loss. Did you know her well? Your betrothed?"

Henry looked away. He could not tell Joanna that it was guilt about Stephan that plagued him more than Alys' death. His fingers tightened around the edge of the bench seat. "I am…was six years older than Alys, but we had been in each other's company since my tenth summer. We were friends."

"How lucky for you. A friend and lover. That is a great gift from God."

Henry met Joanna's eyes. "A gift from God?"

"So often our fathers decide our marriage fate with nary a thought for love." She sighed. "Oh, to find love and marry a friend. How wonderful. He knows what makes you smile, knows your favorites places, shares your stories. He is part of your life in ways no other ever can be."

Thoughts of Stephan raced through Henry's mind.

Joanna gazed at the moon. "I never had a chance to dream of that. To sit under the stars and stare at the heavens, feeling him close. Warm and secure." Joanna's voice ached with yearning. She paused, turned to Henry. "But wait. I have presumed too much, haven't I? You did not love her."

Henry rubbed his eyes, shook his head. "How did you know?"

Joanna tapped his hand. "You are like me. Tied into a marriage for political reasons."

Henry chuckled. "Politics in Lincolnshire are not near the plots and intrigue of the courts of kings and queens, my lady. May I ask…"

"Of course."

Henry knew of Joanna's arranged marriage. She'd left her parent's court at the age of eleven to marry William of Sicily. "Did you come to love your husband?"

Joanna clasped her hands in her lap, ran a thumb across the band on her ring finger. "I did. He was kind and thoughtful. I was happy."

"I would lie awake at night trying to imagine if I could be happy with Alys."

"Ah. So your burden is that you cannot feel more at her death?"

"Yes." Henry forced himself to keep his eyes on Joanna's face though his heart pounded. She spoke true, but there was so much more to his guilt. Could she see through him as plainly as Stephan did?

"Oh, Henry," she said shrewdly, "you are troubled because your heart belongs to someone else."

It does not! It cannot...

Henry said nothing.

Joanna palmed his hand. "Would that I might yet be fortunate to give my heart to a good man."

A good man? Stephan was that, and more. *God help me.* "It was wrong of me to be with another while betrothed to Alys." *And if you knew...*

"That is of no consequence now that Alys has passed." Joanna spoke so resolutely, as if it were a command. "You truly are blessed to have found love and friendship. Not many people do."

A steady thrum beat in Henry's head like the Saracen chants and their drums that brought the war to life in his dreams. *Two men cannot love each other. It is wrong.* He buried his head in his hands.

Joanna rubbed his back. "You say Alys was a friend. Would she want you to be happy?"

"She would," Henry admitted. "But I am afraid my father will have found another suitable wife before I return to England. He would not understand."

"Fathers rarely do." Torchlights flickering in the palace lit the smile on her face. She released a long, slow breath. "Nor do brothers. Be thankful you are not related to a king seeking political alliances."

Henry's brow rose.

"Richard would have me renounce my faith, become Muslim, and marry Saladin's brother."

"He would not!"

"I told him he'd lost his mind."

"You are not—"

"No, absolutely not." She eyed Henry mischievously. "It is a shame you have given your heart to another."

"My lady, would that it were possible, I would be honoured to be your consort."

"Do not tempt me, Sir Henry." She brushed his cheek with a kiss and extended her hand. Henry led her back inside. Bowing, he bid her goodnight and went to his room.

Henry fell asleep with Stephan on his mind, but the drums had gone quiet.

Jaffa
october 1191

twenty-nine

STEPHAN WALKED ALONG THE battlement behind Robin. He wished for news of Henry and had hoped there might be word from Acre. Messengers came daily by sea and land with updates on the king's negotiations or logistical news, but nothing of Henry. Stephan had convinced himself that Henry had sailed for England. He pretended that it didn't bother him, but Robin knew him too well and found a never-ending supply of work for him to oversee to keep his mind off the knight from Lincolnshire.

Stephan inspected the reconstructed parapet, glad for the distraction. "King Richard will be pleased at the progress."

Weeks earlier, one stone barely touched another in any part of Jaffa. The destruction wrought by Saladin had been thorough, but the men labored tirelessly to rebuild the town in the king's absence. Little encouragement was needed when ships put into the harbour daily laden with food and ale. And whores.

Shouts from one of the towers made both men turn. Robin glanced instinctively to the northeast expecting to see a cloud of dust raised by enemy soldiers. Minor skirmishes plagued

Richard's troops. Scouting parties would venture out and as sure as the sun would rise, they'd gallop back with Saracens on their heels. The crusaders would charge to meet them. Arrows flew, swords clashed, and the enemy retreated. But this day there was no one beating a path towards the fortress.

Stephan elbowed Robin. "Ships."

Robin turned, squinted against the sun's glare. "More supplies. I hope they've brought horses for the Frenchmen. I tire of their complaints. You would think they were the only ones to lose their stallions at Arsuf."

Stephan wouldn't argue that the French protested more loudly. He didn't approve of their laments of horses cut down by Saracen arrows. It was contemptuous when more than seven hundred men had died that day.

A tower guard with graying hair drew up next to Stephan. "What a blessing to see the boats." The man crossed himself. "Helps me remember we are not alone out here."

"Alone? With ten or more thousand men as your companions?" Robin asked with a chuckle. "I would be grateful for some time without the noise."

Despite the presence of the army, Stephan was hounded by a peculiar sense of loss, a strange silence of the heart. He released a deep breath. "What is your name?" he asked the soldier.

"Walter of Worcester, my lord."

"You are right, Walter. When I look up at the night sky and see the stars in the heavens, this land seems a place so large that you feel lost in it."

"Aye, sir. But I do feel closer to God here."

Stephan's beliefs in the mystical Almighty hadn't changed. He gave less credence to Him after these many months in the Holy Land, even more so after Henry's rebuke. But his admiration of the one the true believers called the Son of God remained. "Jesus might have stood here where we are and watched the sea," he said.

Walter's eyes grew wide. "I'd not thought of that, my lord. I shall find comfort in that when I sleep tonight."

Movement on the galley caught Stephan's eye. He shielded his eyes from the sun as it dipped towards the horizon.

On the boat, two figures ran from stern to bow. Both stopped and hung over the rail.

"Robin, is that…?"

"Little John and Allan." Robin laughed. He pointed to the banner flying from the bow. "The king's standard." Turning to Walter, he said, "Alert the harbour master to prepare for King Richard's arrival."

Robin waved his arms in the air, delighted when the boys returned his greeting. "I have missed those two. And it appears someone else we know has accompanied the king." Robin clapped Stephan's back.

A familiar figure had come to rail. The man's gaze followed Little John's outstretched arm, pointing towards Stephan and Robin on the battlements. Stephan held his palm up slowly. Henry waved back. Stephan felt his throat tighten. He stood rooted in place, legs weak, unable to move.

Robin scrambled down the stairs two at a time.

"Stephan!" Robin shouted.

He was halfway across the bailey when Stephan caught his arm. "We're still of one mind? The boys will stay in Jaffa?" Stephan asked. There might be a time when Allan and Little John would take up arms, but Stephan saw no need to push them to that life yet. "I do not want them on the march."

"We'll see no harm come to them," Robin said, mounting one of the horses a squire held ready. "They shall stay here."

On the galley, Little John and Allan stood to either side of the gangway as it was lowered. Allan fidgeted, flashed a grin at Robin. He straightened as the king came into sight of those on the dock. Richard greeted Robin and Stephan with a wave then glanced over his shoulder. A moment later, Queen Berengaria, dressed in a brilliant gown that matched the turquoise of the sea, took his hand. She recognized the familiar faces awaiting them and smiled as he led her down. Behind them, Queen Joanna appeared on Henry's arm.

Stephan attempted to focus on the king and queen, but his eyes kept returning to Henry. And Joanna. She held Henry's arm tightly, taking slow cautious steps, looking up to him for more than physical support on the wobbly plank. Dressed in golds and browns, the two of them looked near as resplendent as the royal couple. Henry was at ease at Joanna's side. More than that, he seemed to belong there.

Stephan bowed to Richard, Berengaria, and Joanna. He caught Henry watching him, noticed a confidence that he'd not seen since before Roger's death.

Allan and Little John followed them down the plank. Perfectly behaved young gentlemen, they were almost too calm for Stephan.

Robin bowed. "Sire, we did not expect you. We have no carriage prepared."

Richard waved off Robin's apology. "I should have sent word ahead." He pointed at the horses Stephan and Robin had ridden down from the town. "Those will do."

The royal ladies agreed. They mounted with the knights' help and the entourage walked towards the city gates. Conversations buzzed about Acre's politics and the coming campaign. Word had spread quickly from the harbour. Inside the city gates a huge fanfare greeted the royal retinue. Cleared of the drunkards and the whores, the great hall sparkled. Tables dressed in the king's golds and reds overflowed with food and drink.

Stephan and Henry hadn't exchanged one word until they'd settled round the table. Henry broke the silence. "You kept your promise."

Stephan looked at him quizzically. A moment later he remembered Henry's parting words and smiled. "You feel ready—strong enough—to take Jerusalem?"

"I do." Henry stretched, then lifted his ale to his lips and took a drink. "I was glad of news of the victory at Arsuf."

"You were there!"

"On a stretcher." Henry laughed but grew somber so quickly that Stephan shivered. "I remember very little of that time, but the king has spoken of your bravery."

Stephan glanced towards Richard, towards Joanna. He ignored the opportunity to boast and changed the subject. "You seem comfortable at Queen Joanna's side."

Henry saw his question. "Queen Berengaria insisted I stay at the palace after I left the hospital. Queen Joanna and I spent many hours together speaking of our homes, of her late husband. Did you know she was but eleven summers when she married? It made me realise I had little to complain—" Henry shook his head. "Pay me no mind."

Stephan sat back. What was that he heard in Henry's voice? An attraction brewing between Joanna and Henry? Surely she couldn't resist his charm and good looks. Stephan remembered his fingers tangled in Henry's dark curls. He gripped his goblet tightly and banished that thought. "The queen is cultivating your allegiance before you return to Lincolnshire," he said.

"It was Allan's doing," Henry said, glancing at the far end of table where the young squire stood behind Berengaria.

"I should have guessed."

"That boy hears everything. He had tracked me down at the hospital. I am certain he convinced the royal ladies I needed a room at the palace."

Stephan laughed. "Robin may have had a hand in that. But next we shall hear that Allan has talked the queen into arranging royal marriages for himself and Little John." His smile vanished and he turned to Henry. "I am sorry. I should be more thoughtful of your loss."

"When Queen Joanna learned of Alys' death she thought to cheer me."

"Christ. You did not confess anything to her?"

"I told her I was saddened but not aggrieved by the loss of someone I did not love. She understood and we spoke of arranged marriages. That my father would look to find another suitable wife for me."

Stephan glanced towards the dais. Henry had found friendship with the queen. Love could follow, and more than anything, Stephan wanted Henry to have both—even if it wasn't with him. "The queen is not much older than you," he said.

Henry drew back, frowning. "What?"

Stephan thought how odd it was that he'd been insanely jealous of Alys, yet now was ready to walk Joanna down the aisle and hand her over to the man he loved. "You cannot tell me she has no interest in you."

"A small estate holder in the midlands of England?" Henry asked. "No, I think not. What match would that be for the dowager queen of Sicily, sister to our liege lord?"

"A lucky match for her," Stephan said wistfully. "And not as uncommon as you might think."

Henry buried his head in his hands.

"Are you all right?" Stephan asked.

"You…" He met Stephan's gaze. "She is a perceptive woman. She saw in my eyes, heard in my voice, that my heart was torn."

Stephan stared at Henry. His tongue felt frozen. There might have been a thousand people in the hall, but to Stephan it was empty save for Henry. He heard nothing but his own heartbeat. The man before him was not the confused or angry knight who'd spurned him in the church two months earlier. But was he seeing more than he should in those eyes?

"We must talk," Henry said. "But not here."

When Stephan closed the door to his lodgings a few hours later he willed his hands to stop trembling. Henry had insisted they come here. Despite what he wanted to believe, Stephan swallowed back his dreams. He wandered across the room and lit a candle to chase away the darkness.

Henry hadn't strayed from the door. Stephan turned, saw Henry weighing whether it was too late to leave. Did the room remind him of that morning in Acre when they'd made love? It was still and quiet. The candle flickered, brushed by a warm breeze off the sea.

Henry drew in a breath, took one step forward. "I must...I cannot tell you how sorry I am. I said such hateful things, things I did not truly believe."

Henry's words had hurt, but even then Stephan had known Henry's last bit of innocence was crushed when the prisoners were executed in Acre. Henry had been vulnerable, and the news from England shredded what faith he had left. All Stephan could think of was the moment he'd awakened to find Henry gone. "I should not have let you—"

"No, let me finish," Henry said.

Stephan remained very still, like Henry, frozen in place.

Henry stared past him. "While I recuperated in Acre I walked across the plains where we butchered those innocents. I wandered down to the harbour, thought of returning home."

"But you did not."

"No. I had to see you. Tell you how wrong I was to say those things. I needed to know without doubt that you might forgive me. I would rather die than live without your friendship."

"There is nothing to forgive, Henry."

Henry sighed deeply. "But I cannot love you. Not like that." When Stephan didn't respond, Henry jerked around and slammed his fist into the door. "Would you speak?"

Stephan hid the ache in his heart. "You will always have my friendship," he said.

Henry's shoulders relaxed and he turned slowly. "You spoke those words long ago, but after what passed between us I was not certain you would want even that."

"I shall be at your side and only regret that we cannot share—"

"Please don't...do not speak it."

Stephan accepted Henry's last words with a nod, but there was something he needed to know. "Do you still believe God is punishing you?"

Henry shook his head. "No."

"Good then," Stephan said. "And the king has not pledged Queen Joanna to you?"

Henry chuckled. "No. And thank you." He took the three steps it required to cross the small room and wrapped his arms around Stephan.

Stephan leaned close. He took in the scent of Henry and for one moment remembered how it felt to have their bare flesh pressed close. He blinked back the moisture in his eyes, clapped Henry's back, and pulled away. "Welcome back, my friend."

toBeitNuba
november1191-january1192

thirty

THE WEEKS IN JAFFA wore on. A round of peace talks begun after the battle at Arsuf had stalled. King Richard suspected Saladin drew out negotiations to delay the crusaders' advance. He grew tired of the sultan's games. Spies brought confirmation that reinforcements from Egypt were indeed headed to the Holy City. Richard gathered his advisors once again. Defeating Saladin's existing garrison in Jerusalem would not be easy, but if Richard's army waited, it might prove impossible. The crusaders moved out.

The journey east across the plains of Ramla gave no man, not even a king, respite. Cold rains and blustery winds beat down on them in the days after the army marched east. Saladin chose not to muster a concerted strike as at Arsuf, but his warriors rained their repetitive attack and retreat tactics. The crusaders advanced, rebuilding two more casals—smaller fortresses—along their route. Setbacks plagued them. Squires sent out to gather fodder for the horses and pack animals were overwhelmed by a thousand Saracens on one awful day. The Templars who guarded them couldn't turn back the enemy cavalry until King Richard joined the charge. Many men died.

And still, messengers came and went between Saladin's peace envoys and the king.

Like the enemy, the weather was unrelenting. One numbing day after another. The king's pavilion offered a respite from wet, cold days and dozens of men berthed there at night. Not all slept peacefully…

"Henry, wake up." Stephan hovered over him. The fire nearby had been banked, but the air was smoky. Stephan laid his hand lightly on Henry's arm. "It's just a dream."

Henry sat up. His physical scars from the attack near Arsuf had healed. But he found no escape from the ones that ravaged his soul and made him cry out in his dreams. "The drums. I heard them pounding. And the war cries." He stared at his hands, seeing the blood of the innocent men massacred in Acre.

Stephan calmed him with a gentle touch. "All is quiet. No Saracens. No attack." He found Henry's wineskin and offered him a drink. "You were dreaming."

Henry sipped at the watered-down ale and lay back on his pallet. Stephan tugged the blanket up under his chin. "Go back to sleep."

Henry did sleep and rose before the sun with the other men to march another day. The war took a toll on King Richard's army, but the men were fervent in their desire to free Jerusalem, so certain God was on their side.

At the end of yet another day, Henry and Stephan patrolled east of the camp. The bitter wind grabbed Henry's hood. Flat on his stomach on a rise overlooking a wide valley, his cheeks stung from the cold. Stephan shifted closer. He tugged the hood back over Henry's head.

"I remember the stories you told of the campaigns against the king's father," Henry said.

"Are you going to remind me that I was a braggart and a bore?"

"No, I would not." Henry's voice reeked with indignation and then he laughed. "Was?"

Stephan jabbed him with an elbow. "Ha!"

Henry said, "I was thinking you never spoke of patrols like this."

Stephan studied the village in the valley. It was called Blanchegarde. "The more experienced knights were entrusted with this job. I was squire to Robin, mayhap a few years older than Little John," he said, digging at a rock that jabbed his ribs.

"Experienced?" Henry chuckled. "Robin has much faith in us when we barely survived our last mission."

Stephan scowled, clawed at the ground. A sharp rock finally gave way and he tossed it aside. "Indeed he does! There shall be no repeat of that today."

King Richard heard Blanchegarde had been razed. While the camp was being set he'd ridden out with a small troop of knights to investigate. He'd turned back, sensing danger, but not before deciding that Henry and Stephan might draw up on the casal without being observed.

Dressed in Saracen clothing and with captured coursers, the two knights could pass as Saladin's soldiers from a distance. Their cloaks were ragged and filthy, splattered with dried blood of the men who'd once worn them. Heads wrapped, hoods drawn, only their faces and blue eyes would give them away.

Grey clouds raced to hide the sun and the village fell into shadows.

"The reports were wrong," Henry said. "Saladin has not destroyed the town."

Smoke rose from neat rows of rooftops. There were barns and long, narrow structures. Fenced corrals held a small number of horses. Weeks earlier, scouts indicated the casal bustled with trade and had a population of several hundred.

"The streets are half-empty, but do you see how the people make haste? There are few women amongst them. And those men—" Stephan pointed to several different groups scattered around the town, "talking there, facing these hills."

"It is as if they know we watch them."

Stephan nodded. "They know. If our army can take the casal before Saladin lays waste to it? What a prize. Let's see what we will be up against."

Henry and Stephan backed down the hill and hurried towards their horses. A light rain began to fall. It came sideways when the wind kicked up, and then quickly turned to sleet. Henry tugged his scarf tightly around his face, blinked against the stinging moisture. The storm sent Blanchegarde's villagers scurrying indoors. Unobserved, Stephan and Henry rode in and left their horses tied up behind a building on the outskirts of the village.

Henry crept along the side of the building. Stephan kept a look out a few feet behind him. Henry lifted a latch and inched the squeaky door open, glad for the howling wind. He wasn't sure what he expected to see. When his eyes adjusted to the darkness a few moments later he pressed his palm to his crucifix. "Fodder," he said. "Packed to the rafters."

Stephan signaled to him and darted across an alleyway. He peered inside another building. "More feed."

Checks of three more structures revealed enough feedstuff to keep hundreds of animals well fed for weeks to come.

"Did you hear that?" Stephan scanned the streets.

Henry leaned further the shadows, alert for enemy soldiers. Stephan struck off before Henry heard the whinnies of horses carried on the wind. The sounds didn't come from the corrals. It was from one of the large outbuildings.

Henry shot after Stephan. He drew up to him behind one of the barns. "How many?" he asked.

"Dozens. We'd best check the others. Saladin must have half his cavalry here." Stephan may have been exaggerating, but a quick investigation revealed their worst fears. Not half the enemy cavalry, but more than enough horses to mount a severe blow against Richard's army on its way to Jerusalem.

The knights headed for the hills. They'd not gone far when Henry reined in his horse. Sloughing off the sleet in the scruff of his beard, he rubbed his face to bring life to his frozen cheeks. Behind him, torchlights flickered in the village, barely visible through the storm. A low drone—voices—caught his ear. "Riders coming."

"Did I mention this was a good place for an ambush?" Stephan indicated a spot overlooking the road. "If there are only two, we can take them there. Prisoners to interrogate. Another nice prize for the king."

Henry turned a mischievous grin on Stephan. "You just want to show off." He pivoted his mount before Stephan could dispute the accusation.

Stephan crouched low on the north side of the road. Two riders came into view. He signaled Henry, in position on the south side. Like wolves, they pounced, knocking the Saracens from their saddles. All four men went sprawling to the ground.

Stephan rolled to his feet and laid his sword laid across one Saracen's neck. Stunned from the fall, the man dragged his hands beside his head and surrendered.

Henry straddled the other man and swung his fist, battering the infidel's jaw. The man's head snapped to the side. Henry struck him a second time, drawing blood. The Saracen spat in his face.

Stephan's captive cried out in Arabic.

"Quiet," Stephan ordered, pressing the tip of his blade to the man's cheek. He gaped at Henry. "You all right?"

Henry's breaths came hard. Pent up rage and hate poured through him. He remembered Stephan, bruised and bloodied, and the two of them nearly killed. He wanted this man to hurt like that and he raised his fist to strike again.

"Henry!" Stephan shouted.

Henry's swing stopped an inch from the Saracen's jaw. Fist still clenched, he lowered his hand. He stared at it until his heart calmed. As he stood, he reached for his sword and pointed it menacingly between their two captives. "Get the rope. Tie them up."

Stephan backed towards the horses. He retrieved the rope and made quick work of restraining the men. Within moments they were mounted and headed towards the camp—the Saracens on their own horses being led, one by Henry, the other by Stephan. Sleet swirled around them. The wind strengthened to a gale-force storm.

"God help us," Henry shouted. He shielded his face with one hand, held the reins in the other. Their captives weren't so lucky. Behind him, the Saracens grasped the bows of their saddles and kept their heads down.

"This storm will knock me out of the saddle," Stephan called over the wind.

There was no place to seek shelter and they pressed on. The sleet turned to hail. Ice pellets the size of grapes bombarded them. The horses snorted, ears pressed back. Suddenly, one of the Saracen's horses pitched forward throwing its rider.

Stephan's horse reared. "Christ!" He calmed the animal, and then jumped down to check the fallen man.

Henry drew his sword to send a clear signal. He'd take no chance that either bound Saracen might attempt to run or to attack Stephan.

The downed Saracen screamed when Stephan grabbed his arm. "Broken." Stephan pointed at his other arm, extended a hand to help him up. He pushed the injured man towards his companion's horse. Hands cupped, he nodded. "Up you go. You must ride with your friend."

"How much further?" Henry asked, wiping sleet from his brow.

"That outcropping ahead looks familiar. Not far, I think."

It was dark by the time they encountered four Templars on the eastern edge of the camp. "You did not tell us you were bringing guests for dinner," one of them called out above the howling wind.

"Might have to scrape the meat off their bones," said another with a laugh.

Henry would have chastised the knights but his anger had faded and he was too numb from the cold to think clearly. Robin trotted up to them as they approached the king's pavilion. "Squires," he shouted. Henry and Stephan dismounted and turned over their horses and the prisoners to the three young men who appeared.

In the pavilion, ale was passed around. It warmed Henry's body nearly as much as the fire. The two captured Saracens had the luxury of neither drink nor warmth at the other end of huge tent. A healer, an interrogator, and the king surrounded them. The interrogator, a Templar who spoke Arabic, threw questions at the captives rapid-fire. The injured man remained silent. His face grew paler as the healer poked and prodded his arm. The other Saracen answered the interrogator defiantly and spat into his face before he finally quieted.

Richard was in the line of fire. "Well?" he asked, wiping the man's spittle from his tunic.

"He has choice words about you, sire," the Templar said.

"He's not the first. Let us try this again." Richard drew a dagger from his sword belt, and pressed the tip to the Saracen's cheek. "My mother gave me this blade. I should hate to see it covered in Saracen blood. Now, shall we begin again?"

The Templar translated Richard's words. Richard met the rebelliousness in the Saracen's black eyes with a look just as defiant. He applied increasing pressure to the blade and almost drew blood when the Saracen finally spoke. Richard lowered the dagger, listening as the man's speech came haltingly. Smoothing his peppered beard, the Templar looked at Richard gravely. "God protected Sir Henry and Sir Stephan, my liege, and let them return to us with news that Blanchegarde still stands. Our prisoner claims the casal is a base for a group of Saladin's elite troops."

"How many?" the king asked.

"Over three hundred men."

The healer gripped the wounded man's shoulder and jerked his arm hard. The Saracen shrieked. The healer turned to the king. "Apologies, sire. His shoulder was dislocated. I have corrected that."

Richard nodded, looked back at the Templar. "What else does he say?"

~ ~ ~

"WELL DONE," ROBIN SAID when he squeezed between Henry and Stephan by the crackling fire. The Saracens had been placed under guard in another tent. The trestles and benches were stacked along the edges of the pavilion. Many men had unfurled their pallets and bedded down for the night. "It was good the king listened to the nagging in his head. Was it not a sign from God, an angel whispering in his ear, that he turned back and only sent you out to patrol?"

Stephan said, "I would have guessed a hundred or more men, not a group of Saladin's elite troops plotting to ambush us."

"And we have learned he has sent many of his emirs home," Robin added, "thinking we'd not advance with winter setting in. If we can move whilst Saladin's army has shrunk—"

"Except he watches from the hills and has many men holed up in Jerusalem." Stephan snorted impatiently. "There are still thousands of them."

Henry rubbed his hands over the fire. "Robin, our men grow weaker. Supplies of fresh food and water are low. The horses, the pack animals—this brutal weather takes its toll."

"The land is unforgiving. Villages along our route cannot sustain an army of ten or more thousand, especially when Saladin lays waste to each as his troops withdraw. The roads are near impassable. Can our own wagons get through from Jaffa?"

Robin drummed his fist against his thigh, slow and steady. "Look at them," he said, eyes sweeping the pavilion. "Thoughts of this holy mission sustain these knights."

"And when that mission is fulfilled? Then what?" Henry hated the doubt growing in his mind. "How many will choose to return home? Who will stay behind to keep Jerusalem in Christian hands? To hold the ports where our ships come in?"

"The king knows this, Henry. He speaks of it every day."

"And the council convinces him to ignore sound reasoning." Henry's anger mounted. "You know I believe in this pilgrimage. In my heart, I believe we shall see the Holy Sepulchre, the True Cross, and those places most holy to all Christians. Even Stephan, who scoffs at the priests, wants to step where Jesus walked."

Stephan nodded. "As long as the Lionheart leads us there."

Robin slid his arms across the knights' shoulders. "For the king."

~ ~ ~

SIX DAYS INTO JANUARY in the year of our Lord 1192, the army had advanced to within twelve miles of Jerusalem. Every mile they'd gained brought more hardship and more death. They had trudged through torrential rains, mud, and high winds. Tents were torn to shreds. Mail rusted. Food rotted.

Richard convened his council once again and then gathered his knights.

Stephan nudged Henry. "Burgundy is not here."

Henry searched the room. None of the French were present. Another schism among the ranks?

"The barons have offered counsel," Richard said. "We have listened to the advice of our brothers who have lived in this Holy Land and know it better than those of us who journeyed thousands of miles to free Jerusalem. This decision is one I make with a heavy heart, but it must be done."

Henry palmed his cross, a movement Richard noticed and one that made his gaze intensify. A strong wind raged outside and the map behind him rippled.

"We are so close to the Holy City," Richard said.

"Twelve miles," a voice near Henry mumbled.

"Our supplies grow low. Many of us are in no condition to move forward." Richard looked weary but eyed the men resolutely. "Many may not survive."

"Leave them," someone shouted.

"No!" Richard's supporters cried. "Send them to Jaffa."

"We must go on." A chorus started to swell. "Jerusalem, Jerusalem."

"Quiet!" Richard's voice boomed. The room grew still. The whistle of the bitter wind was all that could be heard. "What do you think? Jerusalem will not be so easily taken. It will be another Acre. A long, drawn-out siege. Again I say, look at the men. Our ranks are spread thin. Saladin's forces outnumber us."

Richard pointed at the map of Jerusalem and its extensive city wall. "Gaps in our offensive lines will allow the infidels to route supplies to replenish the City. The circuit of Jerusalem, so far as we hear, is very large, and if we were to attempt to close it in on every side, our numbers would not suffice for the siege. Our own supply lines from Jaffa will be vulnerable to attack. Would not this, I ask you, be our utter ruin? How many men will we need to safeguard them?" Richard ignored the grumbling. "On the morrow, we retreat."

Henry drew down on one knee, crossed himself, and brought his crucifix to his lips.

Shock and disappointment etched faces from one side of the pavilion to the other. Far from home, these men had come to this Holy Land for a cause they believed in. That belief had kept their spirits high despite the enemy, despite horrendous conditions. Jerusalem was within their reach. Yet now, they were compelled to turn back.

Ascalon
march 1192

thirty~one

THE COURTYARD OUTSIDE HAD grown quiet. Hammers that clanged during the day had been put away. Weeks had passed since the army left Beit Nuba and seized the port of Ascalon, just as King Richard had urged months earlier. Rebuilding the razed fortress had been swift, especially after the arrival of skilled masons. Watching the common folk, clergy, and even nobles sink their energies into the construction had restored Henry's faith. He'd needed that.

Henry lay back on his blanket, stretched muscles aching from the day's labor. A feather pillow filled with dried flowers would have been nice, but his Lincolnshire green cloak worked near as well. He smiled up at the wooden beams in the ceiling of the great hall with a bit of pride. He'd a hand in fitting those in place.

The keep's hall served as sleeping quarters at night, as banquet or meeting hall during the day. Servants had put away the remains of the evening meal. Rushes were scattered on the floor. Their usual fresh scent was marred by the sweat of forty filthy knights who shared the room.

Henry rolled onto his side. "I should not like to be a king."

"Why do you say that?" Stephan spread his blanket out. He unbuckled his sword belt and placed it at the head of his pallet. He noticed the small parchment that had rolled from Henry's stomach to the ground. "What's this? A letter from home?"

"A note from Queen Joanna. She has invited me to visit her in Jaffa."

"You should go. There's time before we march east again." Stephan turned quickly. Henry couldn't see his face but saw him struggle to remove his tunic before he tossed it into the corner with a frustrated breath. Stephan glanced back. "You could tell Little John that I miss him. My mail is not nearly as clean as by his hand, and I have a hole in my hose that needs mending."

Henry smirked. "I am sure he misses you, too."

"Quiet," one of the other knights nearby complained. "Go to sleep."

Stephan grunted. He plopped down on his makeshift bed. "You would be a fair and just ruler."

Henry drew up on one elbow and rested his head against his palm. "My patience thins each day we are here. How does the king manage to hold his tongue? Joanna finds great humour in my desire to beat heads in. But if the king cannot convince the French to return…" He scrubbed a hand over his face, rubbed his eyes. Burgundy's supporters had been the most vocal of the retreat from Beit Nuba. Many had departed for Acre and Tyre; some to Jaffa. They'd been little help in the rebuilding of Ascalon.

"You've written to her of this?"

"That. And more." Henry enjoyed the letters they'd exchanged. He wished he could write his little sister in this fashion. But Beatrice lacked Joanna's worldliness. She was a woman who could speak of allies and enemies, of kings. Bea would know of sheep and horses, of wool, and of the village shops. Mayhap she'd be married when next he saw her. It was hard to think he'd return to England and might not even know her.

Stephan's brows rose. "And what of the news from England? What does Queen Joanna think of her youngest brother's intrigues there?"

Henry tried not to grin. "Her language is…colourful. Count John may be her brother but that does not hold her back. She is outspoken and claims she is too much like her mother in that manner. Mayhap I should leave it at that." Henry rolled to his back. One of the knights snored so loudly Henry was certain it flared the flames of the torches on the far side of the room. He chuckled, watched the hall pitch into darkness when a squire extinguished the lights.

"Saladin must revel in the king's bad fortune." Henry knew the threats to the realm from France and his brother John weighed heavily on the king's mind though Richard rarely spoke of it. "We have fewer men now than when we retreated from Beit Nuba in January."

Stephan rubbed his sore muscles and yawned. "I try to forget that march. At least supplies from Jaffa and Acre arrive regularly now that the winter storms have eased."

"Do you think we shall head towards Jerusalem soon?"

"Aye. In the scorching heat rather than snow, hail and rain."

"But the French—"

"Go to sleep, Henry," Stephan said. "King Richard will convince the French to return."

Henry closed his eyes. *Jerusalem, will we see you?* A noise startled him. He gasped and his eyes flew open.

"What is it?" Stephan asked.

Henry listened, heart pounding. He clenched his blanket. His fingers dug a new hole in the tattered wool. Sweat beaded on his brow. *The drums. Please, God, make them go away.*

"Henry?" Stephan repeated, his voice low but cracked with worry.

Henry slammed his fist into the floor. The drums, the war cries. They invaded his sleep every night. It was one thing to hear them in the heat of battle when he felt the power of his warhorse beneath him, had sword and shield in his hands, and saw King Richard's knights around him. But at night, he was naked. Weaponless. Always alone.

"Will my nightmares ever end?" he asked quietly.

Light from the moon cut a path across Stephan's face. He exhaled, a breath filled with Henry's pain. He reached out, brushed a hand on Henry's brow but quickly pulled back. "Mayhap when we are thousands of miles away with the greens of England beneath our feet."

Henry pressed the corner of his cloak to his nose. He let the sounds and smells of Greyton fill his mind. Sheep grazing in the field. Mary's roast pork sizzling in the kitchen. The trees. He rubbed a hand across his forehead and met Stephan's gaze. "What will you do when we go home?"

"Fight the French. Defend the king against his enemies, wherever they may be." Stephan struggled to remove his boots, tugged at one impatiently. "I am a soldier, Henry. I have no home. Think you that my brother will share my father's estate? Remember, he threw me out years ago. My home is with King Richard."

Stephan stretched out on his pallet. He turned his face to the wall.

Henry stared into the darkness. Home. Lincolnshire. He could go back there when this all ended. He had a manor, tenants to manage. He'd served the king well.

Stephan's breathing slowed. The man could fall asleep anywhere he put his head down. Henry teased him about it often. He would miss that.

Henry drew up on his elbow and watched Stephan sleep. His thoughts turned to England. How would he feel knowing that Stephan would not be there? Could he live a lie, sleep with someone whom he might never love? What kind of home was that?

near Jerusalem
june 1192

thirty-two

THE WINDSWEPT CLIFF STOOD like a lone sentinel guarding a gate. The horses pawed the ground nervously. Henry stared across the darkened valley. Lights glimmered on the horizon to the east like a thousand torches guiding them home. Jerusalem.

Henry tightened his grip on Sombre, wound his hands through the reins. For the second time in six months the army lay within reach of the Holy City. Twelve miles. A day's march, mayhap two. His heartbeat quickened, and he thought he heard the war drums…but it was only the whispers of the knights around him.

King Richard was silent. He wore a white surcoat with the Templar cross over his mail. He'd pushed his hood back to the dismay of his companions. His crimson cloak billowed out in the wind, revealing a gilded scabbard and the jewel-encrusted hilt of his sword. Watching him, Henry could see that Jerusalem might well be a hundred miles away. A thousand. A sudden sadness, mayhap regret, tinged Richard's eyes.

Robin dismounted and drew up beside the king. Richard heaved a heavy sigh. He slid from Fauvel, his Cypriot warhorse. Robin took the reins, handed both mounts to Henry's care.

"Saladin mocks us." Richard's powerful voice carried on the wind. He swept his hand to the north. "He sees us. Knows we grow weak. He might swoop down and cross the plains at any moment, cut our supplies from Jaffa."

"But why risk his men?" Robin asked.

Richard stood motionless, a deep frown creasing his face. Henry knew the answer before the words spilled from the king's tongue.

"He will not," Richard said. "He needs only to wait us out. I would swear that he whispers into the ear of Burgundy and his French, blotting out all sense of reason. They will not heed the advice of the Templars and Hospitallers. Why should the French believe those who have lived here twenty or more years? What reason would those men have to suggest that laying siege to Jerusalem is foolish?" Richard grabbed the hilt of his sword. "Yet here we find ourselves within a few miles of the Holy City. If we advance, Saladin will poison every watering hole from here to there. Our animals will die. He can strike from the north, from the east and at our rearguard. Then what will we have gained?"

Nothing, Henry thought. Only more dead. Each stronghold the crusaders took, like the one at Darum a few weeks earlier, made little difference in Saladin's daily raids. The king's scouts estimated Saladin had fifteen thousand men in the hills and thousands inside Jerusalem's walls. Keeping the lines of supplies and communications open between the port cities and the casals along the route to the Holy City was a deadly business.

Richard had not expected an answer from Robin. He'd settled it in his own mind. "In the morning, we shall convene the council and put an end to this."

Henry sat rigid in his saddle. Was this journey truly over? He tipped his head eastward. "The lights of Jerusalem flicker like a candle in this wind."

"A beautiful sight," Stephan said. "It reminds me of nights on the galleys when we would see lights from villages along the coasts."

"A candle?" Richard eyed the Holy City. "Saladin would squash that flame. He could destroy all that is holy to us and we would be left here in complete darkness." He whipped back into his saddle and spurred Fauvel west towards the army's campsite. Robin grabbed his reins from Henry, swung onto his horse's back and galloped after the king.

Stephan scanned the star-studded sky. The waning moon washed the knights in pale golden light. "We can remember we stood here under the same stars that light Jerusalem."

"And what of the men who died?" Henry asked. "Was all this for naught?"

Stephan shook his head. "They trusted their king. And their God. And, if I am to believe you, they have found heaven."

"And you?"

"I trust my king. Heaven?" Stephan's eyes reflected the soft light of the moon. "Is it not here, with friends like you?"

~ ~ ~

THE ARMY RETREATED. Saladin's cavalry did not let up. They hounded the crusaders every step of the way. Back to Jaffa. North to Acre. The eastern hills were a shifting ominous mass, the sky clouded with dust and dirt. The enemy mirrored the army's trek beneath the hot summer sun. Arrows flew. Lances punctured mail. Swords pierced flesh. And more men and horses fell.

In late July, King Richard's army marched through Acre's gates.

Acre
july 1192

thirty-three

STEPHAN WASN'T SURPRISED BY the lavishness of the banquet celebrating the army's return. The palace courtyard glowed with the lights of hundreds of torches. Minstrels strolled through the crowd, strumming lively tunes. Richard wanted no doleful songs. The knights' voices rose in chorus in songs of spring, of May days, of fools and lovers. When the singing quieted, conversations turned to the negotiations with Saladin and the men's imminent returns to Normandy, Anjou, to England or wherever they called home.

Looking for Henry and Robin, Stephan snaked his way through the room. His eyes were everywhere except where his feet were taking him and he plowed into a juggler. "Sorry," he said, helping the man retrieve his juggling balls.

A gentle laugh made him turn. Queen Joanna's light green gown and emerald necklace highlighted the sparkle in her eyes.

Stephan bowed. "Good afternoon, my lady." He winked at Little John standing beside her and tossed the ball in his hand to the juggler.

Joanna pretended not to see the playful exchange and merely smiled. "Sir Stephan."

"How was your journey back to Acre, my lady?"

She laughed lightly again and looked across the room. Stephan's gaze followed hers. Henry was speaking with her brother and Robin. "I just asked Henry that same question. He cannot put his feelings into words. He seems torn."

Henry. Not "Sir" Henry.

Looking at him now, proud, straight and tall—almost regal—it would be impossible for most people to guess Henry's thoughts. But Joanna's voice, the way she watched him, like Stephan, she knew him well.

"He is disappointed that Jerusalem remains in Saladin's hands." Stephan wrapped his hand around the scabbard hanging at his side, remembering Henry's passion for the pilgrimage when they'd first met.

"My brother's decision is not easy to accept. I know Richard still struggles with it himself. But for Henry, it is more than that, is it not?"

Little John pinched his lips together, stared towards the sky. He shifted his weight from one foot to the other, straightened the cloth lying across his arm. Stephan would have elbowed the boy if Joanna hadn't been standing there. He knew far too much.

Stephan hesitated, nodding. "Henry raised his sword for the king, for God. He is as fervent in his beliefs as any pilgrim—Jerusalem must be in Christian hands. Yet, he hates the war, the senseless killing. Has he spoken to you of his nightmares?"

Joanna winced. "He only tells me they awaken him in a cold sweat. He spares me the horrors though I wish he would not. Do all the knights suffer as he does? Do you?"

"Not all. And me? I do not dream of the battles or the sounds of war." *Christ help me. My nightmare is losing him.*

"Henry will miss the camaraderie. His close friends."

"He told you that?"

"For certes, he did. Look at him. He attends my brother and Sir Robin with such pride. He speaks of you with great affection."

Stephan pressed his eyes closed. Why did those words remind him of the few hours he'd spent in Henry's arms? *Christ, that was a year past. Leave it there.* Henry and his affection—it was friendship and no more.

A sigh escaped Joanna's lips. "He worries about his father."

"I do not envy that reunion."

"Will you go to Lincolnshire with him?"

Stephan turned towards Joanna abruptly. *No, she cannot know.* Little John stared straight ahead, mouth still pursed tightly.

Stephan cleared his throat. "I had planned to stay at the king's side, my lady."

"War with France." Joanna scoffed. "My brother can manage without you for a few weeks, Sir Stephan."

"I am not certain my presence would be of much help to Henry."

"A friend at your side can be a great comfort, whether in good times or bad. I think he will need you there."

Stephan could not help but look at Henry. "His father wants a match that brings property and power—and heirs." His voice cracked. "Henry must do what is expected of him."

There was pain in his words and Stephan was certain Joanna heard it. Still, he couldn't take his eyes from Henry. When the truce was signed, they'd go their separate ways, lead lives that wouldn't cross again. And that was a good thing. *I will find a way to forget...*

Stephan excused himself and made his way across the room.

~ ~ ~

JOANNA WATCHED STEPHAN. SHE glanced sidelong at Little John. "What do you think of those two, John?"

"Sir Stephan does not have many close friends. He hates to see Sir Henry hurting. I am glad you told him to accompany him to Lincolnshire."

"He cares more than he will admit, does he not? I wish I had a friend who thought so much of my happiness."

"You do, my lady. Sir Henry is a good friend to you."

"You are right, John. It is not often I have found someone to confide in and to laugh with. It is a shame Henry loves—" Joanna's jaw fell open. "Oh my."

Little John looked at her, alarmed. "Are you well, my lady?"

"I must think." Joanna stared at her hand, twisted the band on her finger, and then looked up sharply. Her eyes darted from one end of the courtyard to the other. "Wine. I need wine."

Little John slipped away, reappearing a few moments later. "My lady?"

Joanna took the goblet and sipped at the drink. Green eyes narrowed to slits, she scrutinized Henry and Stephan. *Look at them.* They joke, pound each other on the back. She watched Richard. He did the same with Robin, with other knights he called friends. That was the camaraderie she'd seen a hundred times. Men at war. They'd been to hell and back, lived in such close quarters. But this…

Stephan's eyes sparkled. A slight blush. That affection Henry spoke of. Yet…is it more? Does no one else in this room see the way Sir Stephan watches Henry?

Oh, how complicated. Henry loves someone whom his father will not approve. And Stephan's concern goes well beyond friendship.

Joanna sipped at her wine again. Is that love on his face? Or jealousy? Stephan is jealous that Henry loves another. Does Henry know?

Stephan leaned close to Robin, whispered something.

Joanna noticed the furtive glance Henry cast at Stephan. She blinked. *Oh my.* Does Henry's heart belong to Stephan?

Joanna's heartbeat quickened. Her gaze became a wild-eyed stare. Henry would forsake a life with her for…another man?

She tossed back the rest of her wine. "This cannot be." She pressed the goblet into Little John's hands and thrust her way through the crowd. The wine heated her veins as much as the insult that reared against her sense of womanhood. How could he?

Disbelief struck her like the fury of a sudden storm. *What am I thinking?*

Henry. Thoughtful, sweet, gentle Henry. *Why am I jealous?*

When she thought Henry loved another woman, she'd not given it a second thought. She'd never wed him. She knew that. She could enjoy the courtly love between a royal lady and a knight. Why shouldn't two men have those same feelings or more? There'd been a poem recited at the court in Aquitaine— her mother had wept over the tale of unrequited love between two knights. Eleanor would approve of Henry and Stephan, and Joanna was her mother's daughter.

Joanna slowed to a more leisurely pace, her heart finding its normal beat. By the time she drew close to her brother and the knights, her anxiety fell away. If she was right about Henry and Stephan—and she hoped she was—their love came from all that was true. It was conceived in friendship, with desire that blossomed from the soul. Wasn't that what most women craved? Closeness born of shared experience, of joy and pain.

Joanna suddenly found herself with an ache for the two knights. She knew of ceremonies where two men had been united in marriage, but the Church now spoke against such unions. Henry and Stephan would not be able to declare their love aloud.

She pressed herself between the king and Robin. "Richard," she said in that same authoritative tone he frequently used, "these good knights have listened to you from near Jerusalem to Jaffa and back to Acre. You should let them enjoy this celebration."

Richard looked at the men surrounding him. "They have food and drink. What more do they need?"

"I am fine, sire," Robin said.

The others agreed though Joanna saw the smiles behind their eyes.

She pressed next to Henry and slid her arm through his. "They must dance." She whisked Henry to the center of the courtyard, calling back to Richard, "Find your wife, my brother!"

~ ~ ~

HENRY WHIRLED WITH JOANNA on his arm. He realised it was the first time he'd danced in more than three years, and that had been with his sister on a warm midsummer's eve.

Joanna was the more experienced dancer. Henry tried to follow along. Two steps to the left. Palms touch. Two steps to the right. A bow. Repeat. Joanna laughed as he fumbled, tried to go right rather than left.

"The men will be jealous, my lady. And surely one or more," he added with a grin, "will want to prove their prowess in the dance is as good as their mastery of the sword."

"A handful of women and a hundred or more knights. You do not think I shall need to dance with them all, do you?"

"It may be a long night."

The strum of the vielle softened. Joanna's eyes flicked from Henry to Stephan and back again. "I am...confused."

"How may I help, my lady?" Henry asked.

"When two people are in love, why should they be denied?"

Henry coughed, felt the colour leave his face. Another two step in the dance and he was relieved they were back to back.

"We have spoken of your father's wish for you to marry."

"We have."

"Your heart... Christ," she muttered and stopped dancing. She turned to face him. "Why won't my words come? This...person you care for deeply?"

Henry lowered his eyes, didn't answer her right away. "My father will never understand."

Joanna tipped his chin. "You realise I would never suggest you live outright with a lover whilst you marry another. My own mother was devastated when my father lived with his...with that other woman."

"I could not do that. If I cannot marry the person I love, than I shall marry no one."

Joanna started to pace away. She swung about abruptly, grabbed Henry's arm and pulled him to the marble seating at the fountain.

Henry didn't know what else to say, didn't know what she expected of him. The sound of the water cascading should have soothed him, but he could only think that a huge wave was about to bury him in the cold depths of the sea.

Joanna placed her hand atop his. "You have not been honest with me."

A cold chill ran up Henry's spine. "I have told you no lies, my lady."

"But you have not told the whole truth. Not to me. And mayhap, not to yourself? If you must keep your love secret because the Church—"

Henry pulled away.

Joanna tugged him close again, turned Henry so they could see Stephan across the courtyard. "He does love you," she whispered.

Henry froze. "Did he tell you that? Because there is nothing between us."

Joanna frowned, ran her thumb along his cheek. "He did not need to say anything. And neither do you," she said, wrapping her arms around him.

Henry buried his face in the soft curls of her reddish-gold hair. "I cannot love him."

"Then you do care." Joanna stroked her fingers through his hair. "What are you afraid of? You cannot show it in public, cannot tell your father, your friends. But when the door closes..."

Red-faced, Henry jerked from her grasp. "My lady!"

"I told you I was forthright like my mother. I speak what I think, especially with my friends. I am not a naïve woman, Henry. In Sicily, there were men at William's court who lived openly with other men. Don't you see? How many people ever find the kind of love that is true?"

"But it is wrong."

She scoffed. "Because the priests tell us so?" She caught him watching Stephan. "Do not let him go."

"I may love him but I cannot be his lover."

"Why not? Because of the Church? Your father? Do you question whether you feel love or lust? If you were home, back amongst your friends and family, would you have these feelings for Stephan?"

"It is war that does this to men," Henry said without conviction.

"Do not be a fool, Henry. Men who seek a few minutes solace in the arms of another man, or with a whore for that matter, do not have the feelings that Stephan has for you, or you for him. War may have brought you together, and the feel of flesh may spin your head, but the heart does not lie."

Henry started to protest but Joanna's fingers flew to his lips to silence him. "I have watched the two of you. You worry for each other. Is he in your thoughts every minute of the day, and in your dreams when you sleep? Do not let go of that, Henry."

Henry shook his head. "My lady—"

Joanna stood, held her hands out. "Let's finish that dance. I want to imagine that someday I will have what you have."

Henry danced, and later watched Robin and Stephan take a turn with her on the cool roughened stones of the courtyard. Joanna made it sound so simple, but his mind whirled. It didn't matter what he felt for Stephan. All he could see was the heartache that lay ahead.

Acre
october 1192

thirty-four

HENRY LISTENED TO THE waves gently slap the sides of the boats. Horse hoofs clattered on the wooden planks on the dock. The animals snorted, their heads sawing the air.

"He is a might skittish, he is," Allan said as grooms urged Sombre on board.

Henry could look Allan straight in the eye now. The boy—the young man—brimmed with confidence. He looked every bit the noble in his dark green tunic and chausses.

"Are you ready to go home?" Henry asked.

King Richard had signed a three-year truce with Saladin at the beginning of September. There had been some good in the terms. The crusaders held Jaffa and coastal towns north to Acre. Christian pilgrims could enter the Holy City without fear and they could trade throughout the region. Ascalon was a casualty of the agreement, a fate difficult for the king to accept. The city he'd rebuilt had to be destroyed.

"Queen Joanna said I must visit her in Poitiers," Allan said. The two queens had set sail ten days earlier. They might be nearing landfall in Sicily if the winds were in their favor.

"Robin says we shall go there. And he plans to go to Lincolnshire."

Henry smiled. "Have you convinced Robin to see Marian?"

"He is like Sombre, my lord."

"What?"

"Robin. He is nervous, needs a bit of a push and gentle handling when it comes to Marian."

Henry chuckled. It was hard to imagine the warrior Robin shying away from anything. But Allan may have pegged him right when it came to that reunion with Marian. "Be careful about comparing Robin to a horse."

"He shall not hear it from me, my lord. And as for Marian, she should be glad to have him back. I will tell her that myself," Allan added. "He has a boy there, you know. When I heard that, I gave him the orders. Told him what a fine father he would be."

"Robin would not believe it from any tongue but yours."

"He is a good man, my lord. He will do right by his son, by Marian. As for me, I have no place to call home except at Robin's side, whether in England or fighting alongside the king wherever we find his enemies."

Henry's smile faded. "What will you do when the king's enemies are vanquished?"

"I'd not thought much of that, my lord. I shall be content to serve Robin all my days."

"No manor of your own?"

"I would not dare dream of that."

"Cavorting around the palace at Poitiers. I will be surprised if the queen does not find a fine wife for you."

Allan laughed, his voice suddenly husky.

"Why do you laugh?" Henry asked. "You are squire to a noble lord. You have served two queens faithfully for over a year. Do not forget Robin had humble origins."

"He was neither orphan nor common thief. Moreover, serving the king or a great knight leaves little time for home and marriage. And who would have me?"

"People will see the young squire Allan, as Queen Berengaria does. Tall and handsome, a jewel-encrusted scabbard and sword at your side. I saw that magnificent warhorse the king gave you. Allan riding into Winchester, Nottingham, Lincoln, or York. The young ladies at the great manor houses will swoon."

A familiar laugh drifted up from the dock. Henry turned and found Stephan.

Allan followed his gaze. "At least I will not have to fight you for them." He winked, blue eyes sparkling mischievously.

"There is nothing—" Henry laughed. Deep down, his heart fought the thoughts in his head. He remembered his conversation with Joanna. He cuffed Allan's neck playfully. "You scoundrel."

Stephan smiled at Henry, a look that made his pulse race. He would be back in England soon. He could lie on a hillside with tall trees over his head, sunlight dappling the ground around him. He could look up into a clear blue sky and feel...feel what? Alone. Empty. Would a look from any woman ever send a rush of warmth through him, the kind he felt when he was with Stephan?

Was the lady Joanna right?

~ ~ ~

THE *FRANCHE NEF* SLIPPED from the harbour. Henry stood transfixed by Acre bathed in the light of the moon. The oars scraped against wood, slapped the water in a beat that reminded him of Saladin's drums. But no smoke rose over the city. There were no sounds of siege engines. For this moment, there was no war, no blood of men on the sand. He could imagine street vendors selling their wares, smell bread baking in ovens, and meat roasting. The city was at peace. Could he say that of himself?

War might be behind them, but the nightmares still invaded Henry's dreams all too frequently. It had been both a blessing and a curse that he and Stephan had shared the same lodgings after he'd recuperated from the attack near Arsuf. He could not count the number of times Stephan would be at his side, hold him when he cried out. Stephan's calloused palms would wipe away the cold sweat plastering hair to his cheek. He'd whisper soothing words, stroke his forehead. No man ever had a truer friend.

A barrel slipped from its ropes and crashed to the deck. Henry startled, looked aft.

"Watch out!"

"Get hold of that thing," the captain shouted.

Crewmen shot after the loosed container. Three men corralled the barrel before it smacked the rail. At the stern, the king and several of his knights clapped their approval. Henry brought his hands together to join them but stopped, breath catching in his throat. Across the deck, Stephan laughed as the sailors jostled the barrel back into place.

That smile. Henry loved that smile, his laugh. Stephan's eyes, a brilliant blue, like the sky. There was nothing more he needed than to wake every morning to see them, and God help him, he could not push away the thought of the intimate moments they'd shared.

Henry closed his eyes. *I cannot love another man. Go away, Joanna. And Allan. Little John.* He breathed in the crisp sea air and set his meddling friends to the back of his mind. He was going home. He'd not had another letter from his father and could only hope that meant that no bride-to-be would be awaiting his return.

"You should visit your home," he'd told Stephan. "Invite King Richard to Castle l'Aigle. Think how jealous your brother will be."

Henry remembered how they'd laughed over that. The thought disappeared as quickly as it came, snuffed out like the flame of a candle by a gust of wind. When they touched the shores of England, it might be the last time he would ever see Stephan. That would be for the best.

Henry closed his eyes again, felt the cool breeze brush his cheeks. A strong hand clapped his arm. He knew it was Stephan by his touch.

Stephan leaned forward, hands pressed against the rail. He looked past Henry towards Richard. "The king is tired, but glad of the truce."

"He should have gone to the Holy City."

"Do I hear regrets that you chose not to see the Holy Sepulchre?" Stephan asked. "God called you on this pilgrimage. You could have accompanied others to Jerusalem, yet you leave Outremer behind without laying eyes on it."

Henry wrapped his fingers around his crucifix. How could he enter the Holy City when he had not asked God's forgiveness for his sin, when he wasn't sure anymore whether it was a sin. "I question the king's choice but not my own."

Richard turned, facing the coastline. He shouted for all to hear, "I now commend You to the Lord God! May He lend me time enough, if He so will, that I may yet relieve your ill! For still I think to succor you."

Henry gripped his cross tightly. The king and the men around him were solemn and several bowed their heads in silent prayer.

"The Holy Land lies in the past." Stephan looked to the west and grimaced. "Thinking of the weeks ahead on this ship makes my head pound."

"When did you ever suffer from the rolls and dips that make others ill?"

Stephan punched Henry playfully. "You know of what I speak. Stuck in the hold with forty or more knights. We shall have the dark of night and no privacy."

Henry stared out over the water. "Have you an eye on one of the Templars?"

Stephan groaned. "You!"

Henry suddenly wanted to run but he grabbed the deck rail. At times, friendly teases became too much to bear. He didn't want to hurt Stephan ever again.

Stephan reached out to him, pulled back and shook his head. "Henry, I— There is no one, has been no one…"

"You do not need to tell me that." Henry lowered his voice. "Find someone else. Someone who can be with you, love you, in that way." He closed his eyes against the heavy ache in his heart.

Robin hustled up beside the two knights, breaking the tension. He slung his arm across Stephan's shoulder. "Are we truly leaving this place?"

Henry's eyes swept the city one last time as the galley turned towards the open sea. Acre began to shrink behind them. "I was thinking of the day we came into the harbour." Sun had glinted off the rooftops. Henry pictured a sword raised, gleaming in the sunlight, cutting the desert air. Suddenly blood flashed before his eyes and he swallowed back the bile rising in his throat. "We are different men."

"That is a good thing," Robin said. "Think of the stories we will share of the brave men we know."

Henry scoffed. "Of dead men. And innocent blood shed."

Stephan's face softened. "Henry—"

"No, Stephan. You and Robin may colour the tales with the glory of war. But it was ugly, brutal. I will never forget the things I saw."

Robin pulled his wineskin from his sword belt and uncorked it. He waved it at the coastline and grew serious. "This land changed us all."

Stephan searched Henry's eyes. "I would like to think something good has come from it."

Henry didn't flinch.

"To you, my friends. To home." Robin gulped down his ale. Henry and Stephan pulled their own flasks and raised them. Robin clapped their backs, slugged down more ale, and then trotted aft to join the nobles gathered around the king.

"Where is that young squire of yours?" Henry asked.

"Where do you think?" Stephan tipped his head towards the mast.

Henry watched Little John and Allan sitting atop the mast, feet swinging, faces turned eastward. "Something good *has* come from this journey," he said. Sailors hanging onto the rigging surrounded the two squires. Henry wanted to think of them as boys—had they even passed sixteen summers? Little

John was broader now, all muscle, and a head taller than Henry. Allan was lean but strong. They had seen more than anyone their ages should, were wise beyond their years, but thank God, they'd not seen the worst of it.

"I see a bright future for them," Stephan said. The galley crested a wave then dipped. He grabbed the rail to steady himself. "Assuming we survive this leg of the journey."

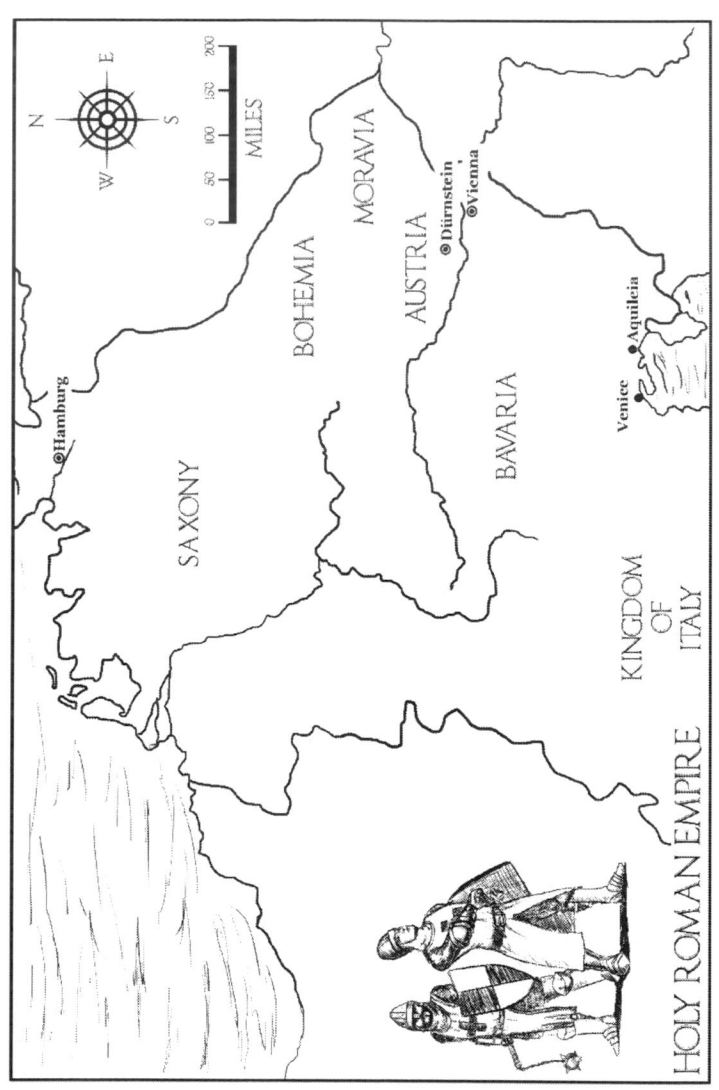

HOLY ROMAN EMPIRE

Corfu - Aquileia
november-december 1192

thirty-five

THE MORNING AIR WAS chilly but more than that, it was the stench of the galley's hold that made Henry tug a coarse blanket over his nose. That stink and his queasy stomach turned his thoughts to politics.

Within days of nearing Sicilian waters, King Richard had ordered his ships to turn back. Messengers sent word that Philip of France had allied himself with the Genoese and Pisans, masters of the waters from Sicily to Marseille. No safe landfall would be found there. Sailing the open sea to the coast of Aragon would be just as risky. Fall storms had already hampered the fleet's progress west and would only get worse— the sailing season usually ended in November.

The king now planned to identify a port where the knights could embark and journey overland to Saxony, the home of his late sister and Henry the Lion. Matilda had passed the year Richard was crowned King of England, but Henry was an ally who would offer them safe haven. From there, they'd make to a port on the German Sea and gain passage to England.

"Do you think we shall make landfall today?" Henry asked.

Stephan tossed and turned beside Henry. A few feet away someone retched. The hold was sour with sweat and vomit. The men had been confined below deck more than two days. The galley plunged and rose, pummeled by winds so strong that men used to swinging swords balanced in a saddle could find no foothold. The storm made it too dangerous for anyone but the most-experienced sailors to risk the waves crashing over the rails.

"Surely we're near Corfu," Stephan said. The crew had spoken of the island as they'd warily watched dark clouds racing towards them before the storm hit.

Little John moaned. "Is that near Saxony?"

"It is a long way. Hundreds of miles," Henry said, recalling the route on a map Robin had shown to him.

"Will we start overland from Corfu?" Allan asked, drawing up on his elbows to see over Little John's chest.

"We will not know until the king confers with the locals there." Groggy from sleep, Stephan yawned. "We may sail much further north."

"And then journey through Duke Leopold's territory," Henry added darkly.

"Will the duke's men have forgiven the king?" Allan asked. He wasn't the only one who'd wondered if the trampling of Leopold's banner by the English after Acre's capture might be forgotten.

Stephan chuckled. "If you can find one man amongst us who would bet they have, I shall polish Robin's sword for you for a week."

"That is not a bet I might win, my lord."

The ship and Henry's stomach churned violently in the choppy sea. Henry rolled onto his back. "We have journeyed thousands of miles." He stared at the beams above his head, imagining them to be roads to nowhere. "Marched through heat and snow. Watched friends die."

"Nearly got killed ourselves," Stephan added.

Henry rubbed the wound on his leg. "I will not believe God made us endure those hardships only to let us perish on these dark waters."

"It's nearly light," Stephan said.

Henry grunted. "Good. We will be able to see each other drown."

A man nearby groaned and a low husky voice in the shadows cursed. Others invoked God's name in prayer. Somehow, a few men slept, their snores rattling the rafters.

Stephan grimaced, rolled over. "Quiet," he whispered. "Go back to sleep. If we are going to drown, I do not think I want to be awake."

~ ~ ~

TWO DAYS LATER, THE fleet anchored at Corfu. Henry eyed the tidy row of buildings along the wharf, the cottages nestled into terraced hillsides. It looked peaceful enough. Fishing boats, larger sloops, and another galley the size of the *Franche Nef*, crowded the harbour. The water was calm and reminded Henry of a scene from one of the tapestries hung at the palace in Acre.

Henry wished he could say he'd never been so glad to see land, but Corfu could be as dangerous for King Richard as any port to the west. The only friends they could count on were the men on the king's boats.

"He will be recognized."

As if he'd heard Henry, Baldwin de Béthune shifted anxiously. Standing next to Robin, the knight glanced over his shoulder. He wasn't the only one of the king's closest advisors who'd seen the gathering of the curious on the docks.

Stephan fingered the scabbard hanging from his belt. "At least the locals do not have their swords brandished. But you are right. Take the royal red and gold robe away, remove the crown—he still looks like a king."

William de l'Étang, another of the king's loyal knights, refilled the goblet in Richard's hand.

Henry cocked his head towards the dark-haired knight. "Especially with his men doting on him."

De l'Étang's desire to see to Richard's every need matched his ego. No one might chastise the man and even Richard made no move to stop him.

Stephan chuckled. "Robin said they find it hard not to call him 'sire' and catch themselves midway into a bow."

"There might be some humour in that until you realise the king's life may depend on their behaviour."

The captain shouted orders. Sailors scurried across the deck, grabbing ropes and lines. The orders echoed into the hold. The oars' steady rhythm slowed then stopped and the anchor dropped. The smaller boats in the king's retinue encircled the *Franche Nef* like a protective shield.

Henry rapped his fist against the deck rail. How could they expect to conceal King Richard's identity with a display like this?

~ ~ ~

THE KING WENT ASHORE with Baldwin, two other advisors, and four of his Templar knights. Robin paced the deck watching for their return as the day wore on. Henry tried to convince Robin to take a meal. After his second attempt failed, he tugged Stephan aside. "He has not eaten since breakfast. Talk to him."

Knights at the port rail beside them were engaged in a game one had referred to as hit-the-bird. Stephan pulled an arrow from one of their bags.

Henry frowned. "I said get him to eat. What are you doing?"

Stephan swished the arrow in the air, waved him off. Grabbing a bow, he plodded towards Robin and tapped his arm with the shaft. "We must show them how it's done, Robin."

"It is a waste of arrows."

"Mayhap for them, but not for you. This is for dinner. Come, let's give it a try."

Allan ran up to them. "Bets?" He tugged a coin from his pocket. "I shall wager that Sir Stephan will kill the most birds. Who will take my bet?"

"A penny that Robin will best us all," one of the other knights said.

"Robin," another shouted.

"I've already potted two," Hugh of Sussex called.

Henry chuckled. Leave it to Allan.

Fingers digging into purses made coins clink. Allan looked at Robin. A grin curled Robin's lip. "Go ahead, bet, but leave me out of it."

Allan rushed round the deck, jumping over rope and past crewmen to collect wagers. Robin finally relaxed when Little John appeared with food and ale and coaxed him to drink.

It was nearly dark when Richard returned. He supped on the fragrant ginger and cinnamon spiced birds, laughed when told of Allan's gambling scheme. But the conversation turned serious when their bellies were full and the king laid out plans for the next part of the journey home.

Later, Henry huddled with Stephan and Robin on the deck.

"Pirates?" Stephan whistled a sigh. "He has agreed to pay them to sail *some* of us to a port further up the coast?"

"Twenty knights and squires, including William and Baldwin, a clerk, and the chaplain Anselm," Robin muttered, his tone as incredulous as the looks on their faces. "Count yourselves lucky that we are to be amongst them."

The Lionheart's reputation and silver coin had saved the fleet from the fate usually suffered at the hands of pirates.

Henry eyed the brightly lit streets of Corfu. Music drifted across the water from taverns near the docks. Gambling dens would see silver from the king's deal with the pirates tonight. "I cannot believe he would do this," he said.

Stephan frowned, exhaled sharply. "How much has he paid them?"

Robin gripped the deck rail, knuckles whitening. "That is not for us to worry over."

Henry grimaced. *No, not worried at all.*

"There will be so few of us to protect him." Stephan's jaw tightened. "I understand that it is far better for us to leave this galley behind, to steal into a harbour to the north. Still—only twenty knights?"

"Surely more could follow?" Henry asked.

"The king's orders are that the others are to hold here or in Sicily until the winter storms cease, or sail to Italy and find their way overland." Robin rubbed his temples. "I do not trust these pirates. Keep your eyes on the king."

To Henry's relief and Robin's surprise, the pirates were true to their word. But storms slowed progress north through the Adriatic and the weather nearly did them in. In early December—some two months after they'd departed Acre— the galley ran aground and sustained damage east of Venice. As water rushed into the hold and the boat listed sharply, the king and his companions grabbed their belongings and prodded the horses into the shallows to escape unharmed. They found refuge in the town of Aquileia. Within a day, a German translator named Otto was hired to accompany them across enemy territory.

But the king had reconsidered. "We must part company here, my friends."

The tavern where they'd supped was crowded and noisy, and the language was unfamiliar, but wary eyes observed them.

Robin's brows rose. "But sire—"

Henry kicked him under the table. Robin glared at him but realised his mistake. It *was* a hard habit to break. Richard's robes and crown had been ferreted away, but the king remained.

Robin released a deep breath, lowered his voice. "We had agreed to protect you. See you safely to Henry the Lion in Saxony and from there, to a galley bound for Dover."

"You look like a gaggle of guards." Richard grunted. He waved his arm at the men around the table. "Look at them."

It was impossible to mistake Templars with the red cross emblazoned on their white surcoats. Aquileia was a busy port. Foreigners were a common sight. But twenty knights in the company of a wealthy-looking merchant?

Richard downed his ale. Without a second thought, one of the knights sitting beside him in the crowded tavern refilled it. Richard batted his hand away.

"I have decided that William, Otto, and two Templars will accompany me. Without so many, we shall travel at a swifter pace and draw less attention to ourselves. It will be easier to find lodging along the way."

"We need not stay at inns," Robin said.

Stephan nodded his agreement. "Remember the campaign near Le Mans? Barns served us well. And churches." His eyes lit mischievously. "I have heard these Germans are savages. But godless? Surely they would allow weary travellers haven in their holy places."

Richard chuckled, but before he could respond, Henry chimed in. "We've lain in tents on the cold desert, trudged through rain, mud, and snow at your side. Fought off tarantulas and Saracens."

Pride shone in Richard's eyes. "We have been to Hell and back, no? I am honoured to have you at my side but there are too many of us. You know this to be true."

Robin sighed. "If you should be recognized, your Templars' sword arms are not nearly as strong as mine."

Richard grinned. "Trying to start a fight, Robin?"

"Si—"

Richard held up his hand. "My companions and I are pilgrims, granted safe passage by His Holiness."

Stephan scoffed. "I would not trust that the Pope's decree might protect you from your enemies."

Richard lifted his ale to his mouth, eyed his men over the rim of the mug. He guzzled down a large swig and said, "This is my wish. You, Baldwin, and the others will remain here to keep the locals' attention. Duke Leopold will hear of these pilgrims spending lavishly. Soldiers will be sent to investigate. We shall go our separate ways in the morning, and be miles away when they realise it is not the king of England they have found."

"It is a good plan though it will not put them off for long."

"You worry too much, Robin. You have my leave. Go home. I shall see you all in England." Richard bid the knights goodnight and trudged up the stairs of the tavern.

Stephan elbowed Henry. "It is surprising the king cannot be convinced of more sound reason." He looked at Robin. "He usually listens to you."

Robin frowned. "His mind is made up."

"He can be reckless," Henry added when Stephan failed to crack Robin's troubled mood. "How many times have we seen the king and a handful of knights charge into a skirmish against four times their number?"

"But you have also seen him strategize, debate, and negotiate with only his men in mind." Robin's fist met the table. "He knows his enemies are not interested in us. They want a king. Our king."

The route north was the wise choice and Henry knew this. Mountain passes to the west were higher, more treacherous in the winter and closer to Philip of France and his allies. Henry still found it hard to believe that Richard's enemies would risk excommunication, for the Pope had granted safe passage to all pilgrims who took the Cross. Was the offer of silver, of holding the king prisoner, worth Hell?

Robin chewed on the last of the roasted chicken on his trencher. He spat it out in disgust and rapped his fist on the table again. "What I do not agree with is his determination to be accompanied by so few."

Stephan's gaze trailed across the room. The Templar knights stood out like a bright candle in a darkened room. "The king is right to leave most behind."

"What will you do, Robin?" Henry asked.

"He may only want his four companions, but I will shadow them."

Stephan lifted his ale, tapped it to Robin and Henry's goblets. "We shall be at your side."

"I cannot ask you to do that. Wait out the winter storms and go home as he ordered."

"He is our king. We will not desert him now." Stephan yawned. "Where shall we meet in the morning?"

Robin started to protest but he saw the determination on Stephan's face. He lowered his head, rubbing the weariness from his eyes. He looked at Henry. "Is he always this stubborn?"

"You have known him longer. Why would you ask me?"

"Because you two—" Robin noticed Stephan shaking his head. "I thought…"

Heat rose on Henry's neck. He knew why Robin believed he and Stephan were lovers. They'd been near inseparable since Jaffa. They'd shared rooms. But they had not shared a bed.

Robin looked from one man to the other. "You aren't… But why not? God's bones! Mayhap I am wrong about the more stubborn one." He wagged his head, resigned. "I shall see you at the stables at dawn. We will depart ere he does, journey north then wait until he passes. We shall watch his back."

"He will be angry if he discovers us," Henry said.

Robin grinned. "We shall say it was Allan's idea. He wants to learn German games to share with the queens."

"Blame it on the boy?" Henry asked incredulously.

Stephan stood and nodded. "A good plan. I am off to sleep. Goodnight, Robin."

"Sleep well, my friends."

Bavaria
mid-december 1192

thirty-six

DAYS PASSED. A WEEK. The knights and their squires journeyed steadily north following on King Richard's tracks.

Stephan reined in and the others stopped beside him. In the valley below, smoke rose from cottages that lay in the shadows of a castle of timber and stone. Squared towers and a large keep loomed above its grey walls.

"It's a pity we are in enemy territory," Stephan said.

"Aye." Little John shivered. "Even a drafty old castle would be better than a barn."

"I am not so sure of that," Robin said. "I have slept in some nice warm barns."

"Better than the streets." Allan stretched, groaning.

Stephan chuckled. "Stiff arse, Allan? You must get used to long hours in the saddle."

"Is this what it takes to be a knight?" Allan asked, rubbing his backside.

Robin twisted at the waist, encouraging the kinks away. "You two have been spoiled by life with the queens."

"A cold barn is better than the snow-covered ground," Stephan said. "And no tarantulas here. No Saracen drums."

A grimace crossed Henry's face, his thoughts as clear as if they were Stephan's own. The storms at sea, the pirates, and riding along this mountain road hadn't dimmed Henry's memories of the Holy Land. The nightmares still came and Stephan felt powerless to help.

"We will make the village before nightfall. Might we stay at an inn tonight?" Allan asked. "Eat at a tavern?"

"What? You do not care to huddle round a fire and savour salted pork with your closest companions?" Robin teased.

Allan rolled his eyes.

"Roast chicken," Little John said, smacking his chapped lips.

Robin roared with laughter. "Tonight we shall do as the king has done. No hard ground, no barn. We'll find a modest inn and a good meal."

Sombre pranced, rocked his head, impatient. Henry stroked his neck. "The castle may have a contingent of Duke Leopold's soldiers."

"We've not much choice in our route north, especially at this time of year. And we want to stay near the king." Robin urged his mount forward slowly. "We shall do a bit of reconnaissance, check the area as best we can. And then, my friends, there will be warm beds tonight."

Allan hooted and spurred his horse, kicking up more mud than snow. Little John cantered after him. The knights caught up quickly, but within a few minutes, they'd all slowed to a walk. Snow began to fall hard.

"I can barely see a horse's length ahead," Allan said. He swiped at the flakes on his brow, wrapping his face with a scarf against the stinging snow.

"We will be lucky not to plow right into the king," Stephan shouted above the bitter wind.

Robin passed Allan and took the point. "Keep your eyes open."

Wind whipped the snow into drifts along the road. Ankle-deep one moment, hip deep the next. An hour earlier, the king's tracks were like the North Star on a clear moonlit night. The tracks were obscured now.

~ ~ ~

IT WAS DARK BY the time the weary travellers found a room. Robin ordered them to take a meal while he perused the taverns in the village. He spotted the king's Templar, Algar of Rouen, lurking in a doorway up the road. The knight had his eye on five men huddled outside one establishment. When a sixth joined them, Robin drew closer. A short, round man spoke fast, tugged at his hair and pointed to his ring finger. Robin didn't understand one word of the conversation. He did not need to. They'd recognized King Richard.

Robin skirted past the men and into the tavern. He'd not seen Gilbert, the other Templar, but trusted that he, too, was keeping watch.

Embracing the shadows, Robin pulled his hood low. He found an empty chair in a darkened corner, ordered an ale, and sat back.

Richard sat close to the hearth with the knight William and his German translator. Richard's woollen cloak was tossed over an empty chair. The golden threads and intricate embroidery on the sleeves and shoulders of his brown tunic set him apart from other customers.

Platters of food and a jug of ale were delivered to Richard's table by a stocky server. The silver-haired man tried to fill the king's mug, but William grabbed the jug from his hands. He sampled the brew, glared fire at anyone who dared look their way. Satisfied the ale had not been poisoned, he poured a good portion for Richard. He tasted the meat, chewing thoughtfully before scooping a heaping portion onto the king's trencher.

Robin sighed. *He is no merchant. Anyone watching sees that.*

The king ate sparingly. He spoke to his companions, even laughed. Robin was too far away, and the tavern too noisy, for him to hear their conversation. When Richard stood and stretched, Robin sank deeper into the shadows. He saw the feet scuffling towards him on the old stone floor and concealed his face with a hand over his brow. He had no need to look up. He recognized the rich leather boots, their gold stitching fouled by the grime of the road.

Richard slid onto the bench across from Robin. Ale from the jug in his hands sloshed on the table. He ignored the mess and poured a mugful for Robin. "I thought I had ordered you home."

Robin lifted his head. It rankled a bit that the king had spied him. The war was far from over and Robin resolved to be more cautious.

"You did." This was serious business, but Robin struggled to keep from grinning. "And we *are* headed home."

Richard fingered his drink. Robin pointed at his hand. "Your ring." Firelight glinted off the large ruby. "Travelling merchants and simple pilgrims do not wear jewels as large as strawberries. I wish you would put it away."

Richard scowled. "William said the same thing."

"You were concerned that twenty knights attracted too much attention. You and your companions manage it quite well on your own. That boy—the one who speaks German—is he listening to the conversations around you? Has he told you that they are speaking of you?"

"I do not need Otto's translation to know they keep a close watch."

"Yet you do little to lower their suspicions."

Richard shrugged.

"Some of the locals know you are here," Robin added.

"My knights keep watch. I imagine they have seen *your* men by now. Mayhap they are sitting by a warm hearth losing their silver to Allan in a game of dice." There was a fond gleam in Richard's eye. "How are the boys? I hope you have found a warm room for them tonight."

"Little John insisted."

Richard cracked a smile. He guzzled down the rest of his ale and wiped his sleeve across his mouth. "My men are nearby. We have paid off the mayor—"

"What?"

"One of his subordinates recognized me. I convinced the man not to inform the garrison commander, so we shall sleep without threat tonight."

"He is not the only one who might alert the guard, my liege."

Richard grew impatient. He glared at Robin, his narrowed eyes throwing off heat like the flames in the hearth. "I might take your lands and your title, Robin. You deliberately disobeyed my orders."

"You told us to go home. I saw no harm in following you. At a discreet distance, of course. Five more pairs of eyes on the road."

"Discreet? Five more men to be spotted. Why do you think I left Baldwin and the others behind?"

"I thought it was worth the risk."

Richard sighed, his anger dissolving. "I will thank you when we cross into Saxony. We shall entertain my late sister's husband with news of King Philip, of my dear brother John, and then plan for the rest of the journey home."

Robin heard the cynicism in the king's voice but merely tipped his head. "I am your faithful servant."

"Oh, Robin, would that our allies might remain so true."

"Their memories are long, sire. The hate never fades."

"Our children's children, and theirs one or two hundred years hence, will pay for our sins."

"Is that not the way with men?"

"So it seems." Richard poured himself another mug of ale, swallowed a gulp down. "What shall we do after we set my brother straight and squash Philip's plans to take my lands?"

"If I might take my leave of you for a short while? Go to Lincolnshire."

"Do you still have family there? You rarely speak of them."

"In truth, I do not know. My father still lived when Sir Henry left England, and he told me of a woman in his own household—"

"Robin, did you leave a maiden behind when you came to Aquitaine? Did you break a heart?"

Robin stared past the king, his eyes on the flames in the hearth. "I may have."

"This is a story I should like to hear. I remember you had a falling out with your father. But a woman? You have kept this from your king." Richard laughed. He ran the back of his hand across his forehead. "But not tonight. We shall save this tale for a night in Saxony. I am tired, Robin. I bid you goodnight."

Robin watched heads turn as Richard strode from the room. He eyed them, ready to intercede if anyone followed. His thoughts turned to England. To the girl with the long, dark hair, round cheeks, and dazzling deep brown eyes. Marian. And his son, the child he'd never seen, had not even known about. For the first time in months, Robin let himself think of them. He smiled and made his way back to the inn where he and his companions had taken a room.

"He knows we follow him," Robin said after he closed the door. He set his pack on one of the beds and tossed his cloak atop the blanket there.

Surveying the street from the window, Stephan chuckled. "Caught you unawares, did he? You are losing your touch, Sir Robin," he said, drawing a snicker from Allan.

Henry rolled up the map he'd been studying and tucked it into his pack. In other circumstances, he might have joined the teasing. "We can rest easier knowing his men *are* keeping watch."

"But we must not let our guard down." Robin flopped onto the bed. "Speaking of that, who wants first watch?"

"I'll do it," Little John offered. "I need to move about after sitting on that beast all day."

Allan crawled past Robin and ducked under the blanket, his back pressed to the wall.

Stephan tugged off his boots, stretched out on the other bed. "I will take a turn after Little John."

Henry looked at the space Stephan left and shifted uncomfortably.

Little John scowled at him. "I slept beside my master in the barn last night. He is quite safe. And warm."

Everyone burst out laughing. Henry relaxed, kicked off his boots, and climbed over Stephan. Stephan stopped laughing when Henry's thigh brushed his.

Henry cleared his throat. "Wake me when you return."

Robin ignored the way light from the tallow candle by the bed showed the colour in Henry's cheeks. "Allan, the pre-dawn watch after Henry's is yours," he said. "Off with you, Little John. The rest of you, to sleep."

Little John grabbed a leg of chicken and stuffed it into the sleeve of his tunic. He swallowed the last of his ale and adjusted his sword belt.

"Hold, Little John. I stopped for supplies before the shops closed. I have something for you." Robin rifled through his pack.

Little John looked at him curiously.

Robin produced two pairs of dark leather gloves lined with fur. He handed one to Little John, tossed the other to Allan.

Little John tugged them on. "I never owned such a fine pair. Bless you, Sir Robin."

Allan sat up in the bed. "Mayhap my fingers won't go so numb. Thank you, master." He reached to shake Robin's hand and pulled him into brotherly hug. "You are far too good to me and Little John. No one has every cared for us the way you and Sir Stephan and Sir Henry do. Why do you do it?"

Robin's thoughts drifted back to England, to his first meeting with Eleanor of Aquitaine, an encounter that led him to Richard's court. "The kindness of one person changed my life, Allan. I wanted to do the same for you and Little John."

~ ~ ~

ALLAN NURSED HIS ALE, his face barely visible in the shadows of his closely-drawn hood. The trickle of customers into the tavern had kept him awake in the pre-dawn hours. His watch was drawing to a close. He imagined Robin would be awake already, wondered if his master actually slept. When Henry had woken Allan for his watch, Robin had stirred, asked for an update, and then pretended to snooze while Allan pulled on his boots and grabbed his cloak.

Allan drank the last bit of his ale and started to rise. Footsteps creaked on the old wooden stairs. It was William, the king's companion. Allan slinked back into his darkened corner and watched William wander up to the bar. He ordered food from the old barkeeper and left as quickly as he'd come.

The scent of bacon and warm bread filled Allan's nostrils. His mouth watered. There wouldn't be time for a hearty breakfast if the king and his companions planned to depart before the sun was up. He sighed, hoping Little John hadn't eaten the last of the chicken.

Allan hurried to the door. It flew open just before he reached it. Four snow-covered men burst into the room. The red and white colours of Duke Leopold emblazoned their cloaks. One of the soldiers shoved Allan aside. Allan careened into a table. A goblet of ale splattered, its owner growling when the eggs and bread on his trencher were soaked. Cursing, the man stood and knocked Allan to the floor.

Allan bit back the sharp words on his tongue. *Do not bring attention to yourself.* He brushed himself off and pulled his hood over his head.

The soldiers paid no mind to the ruckus or to the man who came in behind them. The newcomer reached a hand down to Allan.

"Robin?"

"Shh." Robin leaned close, helped him up. "Go upstairs," he whispered. "Tell our friend to leave now. Take him out the back door. We've horses for them. You will see Little John across the street."

Allan nodded. Robin swayed, feigning drunkenness, and Allan scurried away. Glancing back, he saw the soldiers questioning the barkeeper. One looked at Allan as he started up the stairs.

A diminutive woman with huge, round cheeks appeared from the kitchen heavily laden with food. She shouted a greeting to the soldiers. Robin stumbled into the woman. The platters in her hands crashed to the floor. Robin apologized profusely and loudly.

As Allan treaded down the deserted hallway, Robin's voice was quickly lost to the snores emanating from behind closed doors. A mouse squealed beneath Allan's boot. He muttered a curse, but hurried to the king's room and knocked.

"It's me—Allan," he whispered, watching the stairs. It had grown far too quiet. He desperately wished to hear Robin's voice.

William cracked the door open. "What are you doing here?"

"Soldiers downstairs," Allan whispered.

William hooked his fingers into Allan's tunic and whisked him into the room.

Allan bowed to the king. "My liege, Sir Robin suggests you leave now."

Richard remained calm, took his sword belt from William's outstretched hand and fixed it round his waist. Otto helped him don his cloak and handed him an embossed leather pack. "How many soldiers?"

"Four downstairs. Robin has horses for you nearby. You'll need to follow me."

Richard nodded to William. "Check the stairs."

William peered into the hallway and moved out cautiously.

"They are likely no more than thirsty and hungry travellers," Richard told Allan, unconcerned. He tossed the pack over his shoulder. He adjusted his belt, tapped the hilt of his sword. His green eyes beamed, ready for the sport of the chase.

But this was no chase. It was a hunt, and Richard was the fox.

William reappeared in the doorway. "The way is clear, sire."

Richard strode from the room. William and Otto followed on his heels.

A voice boomed from the front staircase.

Richard stopped. He glanced back at Allan bringing up the rear. "Is that Robin?"

"He is creating a diversion, sire."

Metal scraped, swords unsheathed. The barkeeper began shouting. Whether curses or pleading, Allan could not tell.

~ ~ ~

ONE OF THE SOLDIERS aimed his blade at Robin's chest. "You oaf," he shouted in German.

Robin tossed a lopsided grin at the man, shrugged, and swayed. The barkeeper cursed and pointed at the mess. He stabbed a finger in Robin's direction and then towards the stairs.

Before the soldiers had a chance to think, Robin fell against another table. Robin and the table spun. He grabbed a chair for good measure on his way down. The barmaid gave him a black look. Getting to his knees, he met the barmaid's eyes. "I'so sorry. Lemme help you." His words sounded slurred. He wondered how they sounded to German ears.

A gap-toothed soldier spouted off. Robin understand one word—English—said in a tone that had to be a curse. Robin sized up his opponents. The tallest one would have been dwarfed by King Richard. Two of the men, including the one with the missing tooth, had drawn their weapons. The others stood at the bar calming the owner, and no doubt hearing about the wealthy merchant with the strawberry jewel.

Still on his knees, Robin swayed picking up one of the spilled goblets. He lurched forward. His aim was off and he missed the girl's tray. She slapped his hand. Undaunted, Robin leaned closer and kissed her. Surprised when she didn't pull away, he deepened the kiss, felt her fingers comb his hair. There were whistles and table smacking until the barkeeper shouted. He flew from behind the bar, cutting a path between the two armed soldiers.

Rage burned in the barkeeper's eyes. The girl saw him—her lover? She broke the kiss and screamed, shoving Robin hard. He fell back, smacking his arse on the floor. Rolling away, he drew his sword as he stood and scrambled towards the door.

~ ~ ~

"HURRY, MY LIEGE," William urged.

Richard saw Allan look back, saw his shoulders sag. He met the boy's eyes with a confident nod.

Allan appreciated the gesture though it did nothing to ease his concern for Robin. Clanging swords and furniture smashing made him shudder. He wanted to help his master but knew what Robin would say. *Protect the king.*

Outside, Little John waved Richard and William across the street and led them through the narrow lane next to a potter's shop. Alerted by Robin, the Templars, Algar and Gilbert, signaled the king as he approached their rendezvous point. William and Allan helped Richard mount. The king waved a salute to the boys and spurred his horse.

Little John started towards the livery where Henry was saddling their horses, but Allan had other plans. He'd done his part to protect the king. Robin needed him now.

As Allan approached the tavern the back door flew open. He hung back in the shadows. One of Leopold's soldiers appeared and eyed the fresh footprints in the snow. The sounds of steel meeting steel reverberated in the still of the cold winter morning. The soldier hesitated, and then ran towards the noise. Allan scrambled after him.

The swordfight ceased and the streets grew quiet. "Leadin' them on a chase, are you, master?" Allan peered around the corner. No Robin. No soldiers.

Suddenly, Robin rounded a shop on the opposite corner. He tore past Allan. The men pursuing Robin shouted, "Halt!"

Allan stepped out, determined to help. "Rob—"

A strong arm grabbed Allan, covered his mouth. Another yanked him back into the alley by the waist, keeping him caged.

"Quiet!" Stephan whispered, removing his hand when Allan recognized him.

Allan turned a pleading look on Stephan. "Robin needs our help. There are four of them, four of us. We can take them."

Shouts erupted down the street. Stephan hauled Allan further into the shadows. Allan started to protest, but the pounding of hoofs interrupted him. Six cavalrymen thundered past.

The fight attracted more than the soldiers' attention. Though it was barely dawn and snow had begun to fall from grey skies, dozens of people stepped out from the shops and cottages along the main road to watch.

"What can we do?"

Stephan shook his head.

Robin cut a path through the onlookers and ducked inside an unbarred door. Two mounted riders halted in front of the house. The other four shot up a side street to cut Robin off should he exit through a back door.

Stephan tapped Allan's shoulder. He pointed to Henry and Little John, mounted and waiting for them a short distance up the road.

"We must go."

Allan's face reddened. He struggled from Stephan's grip. "We have to make sure Robin is all right."

Robin sprinted back onto the street. Soldiers behind him, cavalrymen pressing in from all sides. Surrounded, he tossed his sword into the snow and raised his arms into the air. He fell to his knees, lowering his head.

The soldiers' taunts echoed up the street. Allan gaped in disbelief.

"Robin has given the king a bit of head start," Stephan said. "With luck, this snow will cover his tracks."

Moisture stung Allan's eyes. Angry, he shoved Stephan away and ran to his horse. He whipped up into the saddle, spurred the stallion, and took off to the north.

Stephan stared after him. He kicked at the snow on the ground.

"Stephan, we must go," Henry called.

Little John held Hawk's reins out to Stephan. Stephan took the distance between them in a few long strides. "What about Sir Robin?" Little John asked.

Henry looked determined. He knew what they must do and that resolve on his face gave Stephan hope.

"We cannot help him," Stephan said. He climbed onto his horse and met Little John's gaze. "Our duty lies with King

Richard. Once he is safe, we will seek his allies' aid to discover Robin's fate."

thirty~seven

THREE MORE DAYS PASSED. They rode hard. One village began to look like the next. It was bone-numbing cold. King Richard's tracks blended with others trekking northeast through the never-ending snowfall. He showed no sign of stopping, a good thing. Better yet, there were no signs of Leopold's soldiers on their trail.

Stephan was glad to see thatched roofs, smoking chimneys, and bustling streets ahead as they emerged from a narrow mountain pass. The shops and taverns felt familiar, a scene reminiscent of Normandy. It was the largest town they'd encountered since disembarking from the pirates' galley. The king and his companions could get lost in it if they tried.

Allan hadn't said a word since Robin's arrest. Sulking behind the scarf covering his nose and mouth, he glowered at Stephan. His eyes were cold and unforgiving. Little John looked as miserable as Stephan felt. Shoulders sagging, frost on his brows.

Henry tipped his head towards the town. "I'd wager there is a good chance the king has found rooms for the night here."

"What say you, Allan?" Stephan asked. "Shall we take bets? See who finds our liege lord first?"

Allan stiffened, tugging his cloak round his body and sending a shower of snowflakes into the air.

Stephan noticed Allan staring at the snow melting against the dark gloves Robin had given him. "I know you are worried," he said.

"Robin is my friend." Allan's voice trembled. "I thought he was yours."

"Of course he is."

Allan twisted in the saddle and glared at Stephan. "You would not be so calm if it had been Sir Henry they'd arrested!" He dug his spurs to his horse's flanks and cantered down the road.

Henry shifted in his saddle. He couldn't bring himself to look at Stephan.

Little John eyed the two knights. "He is right you know." He shot after Allan.

Henry stared after the two young men. "We are doing what Robin would have us do and we both know that."

Stephan blew out a hard breath. Henry was right. Allan was right. Pointing that out to Henry would do him no good. He spurred his mount and rode on.

Allan and Little John had slowed to a walk as they crossed an ancient stone bridge. The creek flowing beneath it had a thin layer of ice and water gurgled over rocks near the snow-covered bank. Beyond the bridge, neat rows of shops and houses fronted the town's serpentine roads.

Henry nudged his horse up next to Little John. "I say we get a room, a warm meal and ale in our bellies, and then uncover the king's whereabouts."

"I like that idea," Little John said.

Allan chuckled. "You like the food and ale part."

Little John grunted.

Bringing up the rear, Stephan smiled, glad to hear a bit of the old Allan. He silently thanked the stars for Allan's honesty. Memories of Acre sent an ache through his body. His cheeks grew ruddy. His cloak suddenly seemed far too warm. He was more certain than ever he could not deny his feelings for Henry even knowing he'd never win the man back into his arms.

~ ~ ~

THE TRAVELLERS ENJOYED A nice hot meal. Two burly-looking men turned keen eyes on Stephan's lavish gold and red trimmed cloak and rich brown tunic, and to his manner. Stephan and Allan flashed their coins. Allan lost at dice—on purpose, of course. Little John exaggerated his servant routine. If their goal had been to attract attention, to rouse speculation that the blond, wealthy-looking traveller might be the English king, they'd done that. Get their attention...and then divide it.

Henry and Allan slipped from the tavern without fanfare. Stephan and Little John stayed a while longer.

"The fish is quite good. Different spices than Badiah used in Acre." Stephan sniffed at the food on his trencher, looked at Little John. "Did you taste this?"

Little John stood stiffly at Stephan's side. "Not yet, my lord."

Stephan shoved his trencher to the empty place at the trestle. "Here, try this," he said. Little John started to sit when Stephan added, "And pour me more wine."

"Yes, my lord." Little John finished his task and sat, looking grateful yet meek, for the benefit of their audience. He'd taken one bite of the fish when the tavern door flew open. The flames of the oil lanterns danced in a gust of wind and tossed shadows on the walls. Two soldiers strode inside.

Shifting uncomfortably, Little John tapped Stephan's leg. The taller soldier scratched his neatly-trimmed beard and scrutinized Stephan. At the bar, his companion ordered their drinks. He leaned forward to look past his friend to get a better look at the Englishmen.

Little John manoeuvred closer to Stephan and whispered, "They are staring at you, my lord."

"Do not tell Henry."

Little John's brow furrowed.

Stephan smiled. "I would not want him to be jealous."

"I wish that was the reason for their interest, my lord."

Stephan tapped his mug to Little John's. He raised his ale to the soldiers, nodded politely. Too bad he'd never learned any German.

"I hope you have filled your belly, Little John. We may not be staying long."

"And I was counting on that warm bed tonight." Little John sighed. Four pieces of bread disappeared into one arm of his tunic. He pulled a cloth from his other sleeve and wrapped two legs of chicken to add to his stash. Looking innocently at Stephan, he said, "It's for Allan."

Stephan retrieved a handful of coins from his pouch and tossed them on the table. "Why don't we go deliver it?" He lowered his voice. "Mayhap Henry and Allan have had luck spotting our friend."

Stephan downed the last of his ale and stood. Little John helped him with his cloak. Stephan ignored the stares, sidled past tables. He focused on the door before him and Little John's steps behind him.

Outside, voices bellowed at the far end of the street. Stephan turned towards the commotion. He saw the two white cloaks and elbowed Little John. "That's the king's Templars." Swords clanked. "Do you see the king?"

Little John scanned the gathering crowds. "Too many people."

"Let's get closer."

They'd gone no more than a dozen feet when Henry appeared across the street. He acknowledged Stephan with a nod and jabbed his finger in the direction of the fight. Allan was running right into the middle of it all.

"What is he doing?" Little John cried.

A skinny fellow turned his head sharply towards Little John, eyes wide at the foreign tongue. Little John smiled politely at the man but moved past him, tugging Stephan along.

Stephan lost sight of Allan. "Can you see him?"

A few feet in front of Stephan a cloth-wrapped package flew into the air. Its owner tried to stay upright, but careened into an elderly couple. All three staggered and smacked the ground. Just beyond them, a man whipped his cloak back and patted his hipbone where a pouch once hung. His head jerked, inspecting the ground around his boots and the people surrounding him. "Diebin!" he cried.

Thief? Stephan saw the cloak-wrapped perpetrator. *Allan.* Two men bulled after him through the crowds. Stephan tore off on a parallel course, turned to intercept, and plowed into them. At the edge of Stephan's vision, Allan plunged into the shadows of an alleyway.

"I almost had him," Stephan said apologetically as he helped the men up. He twisted and turned alongside them, pretending to look for their thief. Words from their mouths sounded harsh. Stephan shook his head, held his palms up. The older man frowned, jostled past him and resumed the search with others on his heels.

Little John appeared at Stephan's side. "What has happened?" he whispered.

"Go back to the room," Stephan said sharply.

"But—"

"That is an order." Stephan made no apologies for his tone and strode towards the alley. By the time he tracked Allan down on another street, he was seething with anger.

Allan was leaning against the wall of a church. He fingered three pouches in his hand, smiling. Stephan marched up to him. His fist swung round and landed a solid punch to Allan's jaw. Allan reeled, his head smacking the stone facade of the church.

"What were you thinking?" Stephan shouted, his fist ready to knock Allan again.

Allan rubbed his jaw. "I was trying to help the knights. Why did you hit me?"

"The Templars provided enough of a distraction."

"I thought they needed help," Allan said. He turned to walk away.

Stephan dug his fingers into Allan's arm. "If I had not been close those men would have you now."

Allan glared. "So what if they did?" He yanked his arm away from Stephan.

Stephan clenched his fists at his side. Cold sweat tickled his neck. "Christ, Allan. You *want* to be arrested?" He didn't even want to think what the punishment might be for thievery in this country. His anger faded.

Allan's eyes grew teary. "I thought they might take me wherever they held Master Robin. I want to know what happened to him. I want to help him."

Stephan placed a hand atop Allan's shoulder. "He is well. We must believe that. And he would not want you to risk arrest for him."

"He is like a father to me."

"I know."

Allan slumped over, all the fight gone from him. He buried his head in Stephan's chest. Heaving sobs racked his body. Stephan held him close.

"I am not angry with you," Allan said when he calmed.

Stephan tipped Allan's chin up. "No lies. You know you would be happier if it had been me and not Robin who had been captured."

"Well…aye."

Stephan smiled.

Allan rubbed the last tears from his eyes. "Though I would hate to watch Sir Henry fret over you."

"There you are!"

Stephan and Allan startled at Henry's voice.

"Allan, what were—"

Stephan waved off his concern. "Everything is fine, Henry."

"Fine? The king's men have been arrested. Will he ever learn?" Henry looked past them, eyed a group of young men rounding the corner. They laughed, chatted away, oblivious to the foreigners in their midst. When they were beyond earshot

Henry asked, "What is it with kings? They believe they are untouchable."

"King Richard has no fear," Stephan said. "This is a challenge to him. The rush of blood a soldier feels in the heat of battle. The thrill of the chase. Anticipating victory." *It is like the game of seduction I used to play in the camps...before Henry.*

Heat rose on Henry's neck as if he'd read Stephan's thoughts. He cleared his throat and said, "Little John said you were angry." He noticed the bruise blooming on Allan's jaw and frowned. "You hit him?"

Stephan lowered his head and stared at the ground. The disappointment in Henry's voice was worse than a punch in the gut.

Allan gave Stephan no chance to respond. "Where is Little John?"

"He was headed to the inn," Henry said.

Stephan eyed Allan. "At least some people follow my orders." He regretted his tone immediately when he noticed the expression on Henry's face. That glare could cut stone.

"He will be worried," Allan said.

Henry ruffled Allan's hair, brushed the bruise on his cheek gently. "Then let's not make Little John wonder if we have all been locked up in a dungeon. The king will be here... somewhere. We shall keep watch and move out in the morning. This might be the last chance we have for a decent sleep until we cross the border into friendly territory."

Vienna
17–19 December

thirty-eight

ANOTHER HUNDRED MILES. A grueling two-day ride. It had been an awful, inhumane pace, and Henry had to say good-bye to Sombre on the second morning when he found him lame. God's bones, that had hurt more than he thought possible. The destrier had been a gift from his father when he'd been knighted. He'd been with him through all the trials of this journey.

It was near dusk when they crested yet another rise. The land before them was a canvas of taverns, shops of every kind, and hundreds of cottages. Duke Leopold's banners fluttered atop the bridge tower on the riverbank. A church sat alone on a distant hill, its bell tolling to call the faithful.

Henry remembered the stone marker they'd passed miles back. "This must be the outskirts of Vienna." He imagined the ancient city wall the Templars had spoken of would be beyond the church and over the next ridge. Duke Leopold's palace would be inside its walls. Henry had no desire to be anywhere near the king's bitter enemy, but their proximity to Vienna meant they were within reach of the border and more friendly territory.

Stephan pointed to a familiar figure crossing the road on the opposite bank of the river. "Is that the king's translator?"

Young Otto disappeared into a livery. A faded picture of three horses adorned its weathered sign and it swung in the breeze.

"Allan, Little John—find another place up the road to stable our horses," Stephan said, dismounting. "And get us a room for the night. Henry and I will follow the German boy."

Henry slid from his horse and followed Stephan across the bridge. They crept cautiously to the rickety doors of the stable. The sign creaked above their heads. Inside, Otto was saddling one of the coursers.

"Where do you suppose he goes?" Henry asked.

Stephan threw up his hands. "Let's find out, shall we?" He shoved the door open and crashed into the room.

The dark-haired boy jumped, but grunted when he recognized the knights. He finished adjusting the barrel strap.

"Where are you going?" Stephan asked.

"I must find a healer's shop."

"A healer? Why?" Henry's gaze shot towards Stephan, then back to Otto. "Is the king ill?"

"Yes."

Henry's throat tightened, his mouth felt dry. King Richard had not looked well when they'd left the pirate galleys behind near two weeks past. He'd pushed himself mercilessly in the days since. They'd had little sleep, had fought the bitter cold and snow. It was no wonder he'd not recovered.

Stephan saw the dread on Henry's face and tried to give him a look of reassurance. "Where is he?" he asked Otto.

"At The Stag."

"We shall keep watch there until you return. Go!"

~ ~ ~

HENRY WAS ON DUTY when Otto reappeared. The boy shucked off his cloak and scarf and sent a spray of snow flying. Men in its wake cursed or turned an evil eye on him unless they were too inebriated to care.

Pounding the table, the boy shouted for an ale. The barkeeper ignored his rude behavior. A coin in his pocket from a jackass was as good as one from a gentleman. He filled a goblet from the cask and smacked it on the bar top.

A serving girl in a drab grey dress retrieved the overflowing mug. Otto reached into his pouch to pay. Dozens of coins spilled out. He swore loudly, and took the opportunity to pinch the girl when she squatted down to retrieve silver that fell to the rush-covered floor. She squealed and thrust her large, round hips at him.

Otto enticed the girl onto his lap and slugged down some ale. His free hand slid around her waist. He lifted the mug to her mouth and she giggled, licking her plump lips in long, slow strokes. The boy looked so young, but he knew his way with tavern wenches. With a kiss to thank him, the girl wiggled her arse suggestively before darting away to tend to other customers.

Henry shot from his seat. He crossed the tavern, sat down, and grabbed Otto's wrist. Grumbling, he wrenched his arm from Henry's grasp.

Henry shifted closer. "Why are you sitting here nursing yourself with drink? If you brought herbs to soothe our friend, go. He may need them."

"He was asleep when I left."

"He may be awake and waiting for you. When you are done, come back and tell me how he fares."

Otto stood, cursing Henry beneath his breath. He slipped from the room with no one giving him a second glance.

~ ~ ~

STEPHAN LEANED AGAINST THE door of the livery watching for a sign of King Richard and his companions. It had been two days since Otto's return and Stephan had been glad when the king finally sent word that he felt well enough to leave Vienna. The streets still slumbered beneath the swirling snow. Stephan had hardly slept between the others' watches at The Stag, but he did not mind being up before the dawn if it meant they'd be riding towards the border.

"Why haven't they left yet?" Little John asked. He'd tired of sitting on his horse and had dismounted.

Henry fidgeted in his saddle. "Could we have missed them?"

Allan frowned at Little John. "I didn't close my eyes even once on my watch. I would have seen them."

Little John glared at Allan. "Are you saying that I fell asleep? I swear I did not."

"We are not saying anyone slept on their watch," Stephan said.

"Are we certain?" Henry asked.

"There is one way to find out." Stephan waved Little John over. "Check on their horses."

It was nearly light and a few of the shops showed signs of life. Little John disappeared around the corner and couldn't have been gone more than a few minutes when Otto emerged from The Stag.

Stephan called over his shoulder at Henry. "It's the boy." He slinked back from the stable door, still focused on the inn.

"Any sign of the king?" Henry asked.

Stephan scuffed his boot into the dirt, shifting anxiously when neither Richard nor the knight William appeared. "Nothing." He wouldn't let concern creep into his voice but the longer King Richard remained in this place, the more likely he'd be discovered. "Do you remember hearing him inspect the camp in the early morning hours?" he asked. Speaking of the past might let them forget the present for a short while.

Henry groaned. "Morning? The sky was dark as pitch and the moon hung high overhead. We would be on the march well before the sun rose."

"And you," Stephan said, tossing an accusatory scowl at Allan, "you were indulging in life at the palace."

"That was not my idea, my lord. I remember being ordered to stay—"

"There! The boy is off again." Stephan took two long strides, grabbed his horse's reins from Allan, and mounted. "I'll follow him."

Otto's behavior confounded Stephan. He rode into the heart of Vienna, some ten or more miles, took breakfast at a small tavern and seemed in no hurry to move on. When he finished eating, he perused merchandise in one shop after another. He inspected flasks, fine gloves, and spurs. Nothing seemed to satisfy him and he'd scoffed, words flowing from his tongue.

The merchants tried to appease him. They'd smile, hand him something more expensive. He merely waved them off, caressing the pouch hanging from his sword belt. It clinked and rattled, heavy with coins.

Stephan wanted to throttle the idiot. He didn't need to understand a word of German to see the way the shopkeepers acted around him. Polite, talkative—like the saddler who asked many questions. Otto answered them with an air of arrogance that made Stephan cringe.

When the merchant's apprentice appeared outside the shop with two leather saddlebags and an exquisite saddle, which he seated on Otto's horse, Stephan flexed his fist. Enough of this, he thought.

Stephan started towards the boy. He held back when the merchant emerged from the shop and exchanged a few words with his apprentice. Tipping his head, the man bid the translator a friendly good day. He slipped up the street, glancing back anxiously.

This is not good.

Stephan strode up to Otto, bumped him, and nearly knocked him to the ground. The boy shouted as Stephan reached for him, his mouth open in mid-curse when he recognized the knight.

"You talk and flaunt your wealth far too much," Stephan said angrily whilst smoothing the boy's cloak. "The saddler is—" He paused, catching sight of two soldiers on the heels of the merchant.

Stephan released his grip on the boy and turned up the street. *This is very bad.* He forced himself not to look back until he rounded a corner.

The soldiers questioned the boy. Otto looked nervously in Stephan's direction. There was no doubt in Stephan's mind that the boy would give up the king's location.

Stephan fled up the street. He cut through narrow alleys, jumped two low walls, and made his way back to the stable. His short stay in Vienna wasn't questioned when he tossed the farrier an extra coin. He wouldn't have understood the German anyway, and was glad when the man turned to tidy up his forge.

Curses spilled from Stephan's mouth rhythmically, matching the gait of his horse as he galloped down the road. The priests would tell him he'd find a fiery place in Hell speaking those words. That was the least of his worries. He'd not go to Hell in any afterlife. Nothing could convince him it existed. It was like heaven. As he'd told Henry when they saw the lights of Jerusalem from Beit Nuba, heaven was here on earth. Hell? That was Acre, the desert marches. That was nearly losing Henry. Yes, that was his Hell.

~ ~ ~

THE STAG WAS CROWDED with customers who'd begun to celebrate the approaching winter solstice. Stephan plowed through the room. He acknowledged Henry with a nod but did not beckon him to follow. Heading up the creaking staircase, he nearly tripped over a man and woman cuddling there. Upstairs, Stephan knocked on the king's door.

After a moment, William cracked it open.

Stephan checked the hallway for other eyes and ears. "Your German translator was arrested by soldiers in Vienna. There is a good chance he will tell them where you are."

William opened the door to let Stephan in. Tallow candles lit the room and barely masked the scent of sweat and sickness.

Stephan approached the king. Richard was stretched out on the bed. His cheeks looked sunken and flushed, his red-gold hair thinning. It reminded Stephan of days in the Holy Land when the king suffered from the Arnaldia.

"Sire, you must leave."

Richard green eyes looked dull. "I must rest a few more days."

William shook his head at Stephan.

Stephan palmed the hilt of his sword. The king had always appreciated blunt honesty, especially when advisors often told him what they thought he wanted to hear. "You do not have a few days, my liege. Tomorrow at the latest, I would guess. We shall see soldiers here by then. Please, sire, we are not far from the border. Two days if we ride hard."

"All right. Tomorrow." Richard looked past him. "Who else is with you?"

"Sir Henry and our squires."

"Where is Robin?"

Stephan shifted uncomfortably. "Arrested."

"Robin? Beaten? That is hardly the Robin I know. If there is a way to escape, he will find it." Richard tugged the woollen blanket up to his chin. "Until tomorrow. Stay close to us if you can."

"That is our intention."

~ ~ ~

PACING BETWEEN THE BEDS, Stephan eyed the bags he'd ordered Allan to pack. He paused at the window, certain he'd see soldiers galloping down the road any moment. It would be dark soon.

He cursed under his breath. They could've been on the road hours earlier. He regretted that he'd not dragged the king out, even if the man couldn't sit upright. He should have tossed Richard over the back of a horse and be done with it. Anything to get him away from this place. If Stephan had been a praying man, he would've asked God that Leopold's troops not steal into town until the morrow. Would they be lucky enough to escape before anyone arrived to capture the king?

Allan finally convinced Stephan to lie down. He didn't realise he'd fallen asleep until Henry gently pressed him awake. Henry had come off his watch and sent Little John on his way.

Henry tossed his cloak on the bed and plopped down next to Stephan. He pressed his hands together for warmth. "I hope we have done right by the king."

Stephan sat up, rubbed the sleep from his eyes. "He promises he will head north on the morrow. But he is deathly ill, Henry. I am not certain he can sit in the saddle more than three or four miles."

"If we ride double—"

"In this weather?" Stephan couldn't hide his frustration. "We'd not get far."

"This is hopeless."

Stephan stroked Henry's back, felt him relax for a moment. Henry stood and pulled aside the oilcloth on the window to look out.

"Are they still there?" Stephan asked, noticing Henry's gaze was not directed at the streets.

"Who?"

"Not who. You are staring at the heavens, aren't you? The stars?" Stephan asked. "Are they still there?"

"Twinkling like jewels against a cloudless sky." Henry glanced at Allan snuggled beneath two blankets on the other bed. The moon caught Henry's face in a soft glow, its light reflected in his eyes and on the smile that suddenly bloomed on his face.

"What are you thinking?" Stephan asked.

Henry looked at him pointedly. "What if we switch rooms with the king?"

Stephan perked up. "Bring the king here?" He jumped from the bed like the room was on fire. "We can do that. Quietly, so the innkeepers here and at The Stag aren't aware. It will buy us time, mayhap a chance to steal him away." He shook Allan awake. "Up, now, Allan. Get up! Go tell Little John that we shall need a distraction when we bring the king in."

Allan rolled over and yawned. "What?" He was fully awake by the time Stephan finished repeating the plan. He looked between the two knights. "There is a back way through the kitchens."

"You've been to the kitchens, have you?" Stephan asked.

Allan licked his lips. "One of the serving girls showed me."

"Did she?" Henry's mouth curled. "Should I ask what else you were doing with the girl?"

Stephan laughed. "Get dressed. We've work to do."

thirty-nine

HENRY SCRUTINIZED THE JEWELER'S wares. He picked up a ring, letting his eyes follow the swirls of its design. A silver crucifix caught his fancy and he placed the ring down. He fingered his own cross, fondly remembering his mother placing it round his neck. The carved wood and leather cord weren't ornate, but he treasured the gift.

Henry examined the simple lines of another chain, pausing when voices outside the shop grew animated. Ignoring the conversation, he listened for the clatter of hoofbeats, of armour, and heard nothing, yet still felt no relief. Duke Leopold's soldiers would come. It was just a matter of time.

Banging from the back of the shop startled him. The chain slipped from his hand, clinking against a display of rings. Henry looked apologetically at the shopkeeper and sighed. Allan would have used the distraction to slip a jewel into his pocket. Henry kept the grin from his face and picked up a sparkling silver chain. Perfect for Allan, he thought. He'd already decided that both young squires deserved more than a place to sleep, more than food and a good horse. But what might he give to Little John? The young man's faith was strong. A crucifix seemed ideal.

Henry found a simpler cross like his own. He handed the items to the shopkeeper and then thought of Stephan. A gift for the squires. A gift for Stephan. No cross for him. It was the intricate filigree on one of the rings that captured Henry's eye. Stephan was strong and bold. He had a tender side, hidden from all but those who knew him well. The filigreed design symbolized that.

Henry paid twelve marks for the lot, a hefty sum, though not unusual for a wealthy pilgrim. The merchant would remember him, just as he'd intended.

Stephan was already making a nuisance of himself when Henry arrived at The Stag. Stephan pilfered a mug of ale from one of serving girls, laughing loudly when she slapped his hand. He apologized in a German accent so horrible it caused a halt to many a conversation.

Stephan looked magnificent. Like royalty. No crown, but dressed head to toe in the finest of the king's clothes. The wine-coloured tunic was lined with black fox fur. It set him apart from the others in the room. Firelight blazing from the hearth reflected off the large emerald on his finger.

Henry forced himself not to stare. But Stephan's laughter brought back memories. Their first meeting in Southampton. That first kiss. Henry touched a finger to his lips. His heart pounded so hard he worried that the men in the tavern might notice. Their plan to shuffle the king stealthily from one inn to another would be ruined.

The king's companion William stood at the top of the stairs. Henry shoved back his disdain for the man. Why hadn't he thought to secure lodging in a place that offered more than one way out? The front door would be their only exit.

Henry tipped his head. Stephan grabbed a serving girl walking past his table. She shrieked, and while all eyes were on her, William led King Richard down the stairs. He hunched over to conceal his height. The hood of his cloak covered his flaming reddish-gold hair that far too many eyes might know as well as the Lionheart's banner.

Henry and William did their best to block the line of sight from the crowded tavern to the door. Henry checked the street and they hurried outside, skirting the building and fleeing into the alley.

Allan awaited them at the back door of their lodgings. When he saw the royal retinue coming, he ducked his head inside but reappeared within seconds. He waved an "all clear" to Henry.

Allan bowed as the king drew near. "My liege."

"Are my knights treating you well, young Allan?"

Allan held the door to let the king pass. "Not as well as your lady wife, sire."

"I shall have a word with them later." Richard's breaths were short after the jaunt from The Stag. Still, he managed a wink and glanced back. "How is it that you have procured our way through this back entrance? Won another game of dice?"

Allan grinned and scooted past Richard. "The cook's daughter has dragged him from the kitchens to speak with a customer. The bacon here is not fit for a pig, or so I've heard."

"I shall be sure to avoid it during my stay." Richard followed him through the narrow passage. "This girl—your friend? I did not know you spoke German."

"A man need not say a word when enjoying a lady's company, sire."

Bringing up the rear, Henry coughed.

Richard laughed. "Charming serving girls now, are we? I shall not tell the queen."

The kitchen was deserted as planned. Allan grabbed two loaves of bread, tossed one to the king, and held up his hand. Words raised in anger bit the stale tavern air. Curses flew from a man's tongue and a woman invoked the name of *Gott*.

"That's my girl." Allan beamed. From the doorway, he signaled to Little John.

Little John reached for the basket of bread left by one of the servers. His arm knocked over two goblets filled with ale, splattering him, the old man sitting across from him, and the table. Little John jumped up and cursed loudly. He pounded the trestle, sending both mugs and half a roasted chicken to the floor. "You clumsy old man! Look what you have done. This is my best tunic."

The man's dark eyes widened. He might not understand a word Little John uttered, but he had no intention of taking the blame. Shouting, he pointed at the mess and poked Little John—a brave thing to do considering John stood more than a head taller. The serving girl glared at Little John and joined in the old man's curses, her argument with the cook and another customer forgotten.

Henry moved unobtrusively from the kitchen. He waited near the bottom of the stairs while the king made his way slowly up the steps with William's help.

Henry took another quick look in every direction. Little John's argument had died down. He'd bought a drink for the old man. The cook and serving girl brushed past Henry to return to the kitchen.

Henry wasted no time and joined the king a few moments later. Richard sat on edge of the bed. He shooed Allan back downstairs. William stood at the window watching the street. Richard waved his hand, indicating Henry should sit on the other bed. "Well done," he said.

Henry bowed but chose not to sit. "I should return to The Stag, sire. We must keep up the appearance that you are still there." Henry cleared his throat. "May I speak freely?"

"Of course."

"This plot may buy you time but Stephan and I cannot help but worry. The duke's soldiers might arrive at any moment."

Richard unbuckled his sword belt. "William," he called. The knight turned just in time to catch it flying across the small room. William hung the belt, and then moved to the king's bedside.

Richard lifted his foot to let William remove one muddied boot. He stared past Henry. "Soldiers following us from the south. Soldiers coming from the north. We are like a bug about to be crushed beneath a heavy boot," he said as William nearly fell backwards struggling to free his foot.

The king was right but Henry wanted to raise his spirits, and needed to raise his own. "Remember the road to Jaffa, sire? Saladin harassed us from the van to the rearguard, yet we were the strong ones." Mayhap it wasn't the best example. Henry held his breath waiting for a response—good or bad. But no words came. To Henry's eyes, Richard looked haggard. His skin was flushed, his eyes red. Henry dreaded to think of the snow and cold, the hard ride ahead.

"May I get you anything before I leave?"

Richard picked up the loaf of bread that he'd placed on the coffer between the beds. "This will do for now."

Henry turned to William. "We shall make the horses ready before the sun rises. One of us will come for you, and then we'll be on our way."

Richard nodded wearily. William followed Henry into the hallway. He closed the door, looked warily up and down the corridor. "I do not think he will be able to travel on the morrow."

"Do what you can." Henry leaned close and whispered, "And for God's sake, do not let him show himself downstairs. Even ill, he looks and acts like a king."

Henry hurried away and slipped back outside. The skies were grey and snow had begun to fall. Back at The Stag, he strode across the room. It was noisy, crowded, and he wanted nothing more than to crawl into the shadows.

Bowing to Stephan, he eyed the platter of mouth-watering beef dripping with deep brown gravy. "Hungry?"

"Sit. We are not going anywhere."

"I know." Henry sat opposite Stephan. He tugged a dagger from his boot and used it to scrape meat from the platter to his trencher. "Why haven't the soldiers come?" he asked, picking at the meat.

"Mayhap the German boy has not revealed the king's whereabouts yet. He is better at weaving stories than we had thought?"

"I would like to believe that, but he is a fool. We warned him…" Henry's hands started to tremble. He willed them to steady and filled his mug with ale, then refilled Stephan's. "If the soldiers come, I will rouse the king and we shall head towards the border."

"Mind the back doors. They will be watching."

"But they will be *here* at The Stag on the German boy's confession. You shall keep them occupied. They will be observing the back door of this inn, not the one at the far end of road."

"His horses—"

"We have worked through this." Henry and Stephan had been over every detail a dozen times. Second thoughts had to be banished. "It is a good plan. Little John will saddle the animals as we'd agreed. Ours will have to serve the king, even though he may complain he is forced to ride a common rouncy."

Stephan chuckled. "I hope he is well enough to complain."

"He shall have his stallion back when you catch up with us."

Stephan's knee brushed Henry's. "You know that may not be possible."

Henry felt the breath knocked from his lungs. Of course he knew that. Still, he could not bear to think of losing Stephan. He swallowed hard. Stephan would be fine. He had to believe that.

"Do not fight them," he said, his voice barely a whisper. "Robin was arrested because he drew his sword. Just keep them busy with talk."

"The chances of them believing I am the King of England are not good."

Henry squeezed his eyes closed for a moment. "What happened? We should be near home by now."

"And that would mean fighting his enemies there." Stephan shrugged, drank some of his ale. "Instead, we await them here."

Henry leaned closer. "Promise me you will do nothing rash."

"Me?" Stephan had that mischievous look that oftentimes made Henry squirm. Or laugh. "You know I would never—"

Henry growled. He wasn't in the mood for playful banter. "I know you too well," he said seriously.

Stephan must have seen his fear. His face turned solemn. "Do not worry. I shall remind them I am under the Pope's protection. A pilgrim from the Holy Land. They will release me, I am sure of that. I shall be on the road behind you as soon as I am able." Stephan brushed Henry's hand, the touch so gentle that Henry shivered. "Your friendship these last few months has brought more joy to me—"

"Quiet. You speak as if we might not see each other again."

"Listen to you," Stephan said.

Henry could no longer deny his feelings. He wanted to tell Stephan, but the words wouldn't come. Every memory of being with Stephan came flooding back to him. Stephan's gentleness. His fierce loyalty. His understanding. He had been there for Henry through the worst of times. Roger's death, the massacre at Acre, the nightmares. That letter from England. Stephan comforted him. There was no one more caring. And loving.

"No, I should have listened to you," Henry said. "I have wasted so much time ignoring my heart."

Stephan was speechless. "What?" he finally said, his voice trembling.

Henry fumbled with the silk purse tied to his belt. Coins clinked as his fingers rummaged through its contents until he found the silver ring he'd purchased. He did not hesitate, did not look to see if the tavern's customers were watching. He seized Stephan's hand and slid the band onto his finger.

Stephan stared at the ring, and then met Henry's eyes. He slipped his hand beneath the table. Henry found it there and held it as if he would never let go. They caressed each other with that simple touch and nothing more than a look.

The evening passed quietly. Henry worked out details of the watches with Allan and Little John. They reviewed their plan to help the king on his way in the morning. The day had been one of the longest he could remember. All he wanted now was to close his eyes and sleep.

But sleep wasn't in the plan. Not yet.

Henry returned to the room they'd switched with the king. He opened the door. A dozen candles flickered. Stephan was stretched out naked on the bed. He smiled as Henry latched the door. "What took you so long?" Stephan said. "It is cold in here."

"I think I might fix that." Henry flung off his cloak and tossed aside his sword belt. His tunic sailed through the air and landed on the other bed. He straddled Stephan and kissed him.

Stephan ran his hands through Henry's dark, wavy hair. "I feel warmer already."

Henry moved against Stephan slowly. "I will not stop until you are on fire."

"Promise?"

Henry kissed him again, lost in feelings of passion and love. The future was uncertain, but tonight—no, forever—his heart belonged to Stephan.

Vienna
20 december 1192

forty

A COCK CROWED. Henry cracked an eye open and reached out for Stephan. He found only the ruffled blanket and a cold spot. Stephan was at the window looking through a hole in the oilskin covering.

Stephan heard him stir, glanced back. "It is so quiet."

Henry could just make out noises emanating from the kitchen. The cook was starting the fire downstairs. "Better this than the sounds of war," he said.

Stephan rubbed his eyes.

"Did you sleep?" Henry asked.

Allan snored and they both laughed. He'd come in from watch sometime during the night. Henry remembered hearing him, but had only buried his head against Stephan's chest and drifted back to sleep.

"People. We need more people out there. It is easier to hide a king on a bustling street. Where are they all?" Stephan spotted a familiar figure. "Little John is on his way."

Henry threw his legs over the side of the bed. He stood up, stretched. "Time for us to get on the road."

Stephan eyed Henry's muscles. "So soon? Can we have one more moment?" He took the three steps needed to move from the window to Henry. He put his arms around Henry and rested his chin on his shoulder.

Henry would be happy to stay like this. He buried his nose against Stephan's neck, felt the damp scruff of his beard. He breathed in the musky scent of him mixed with rose water from the washbasin.

Stephan tilted his chin back, kissed him. When he broke the kiss, he whispered, "I would take you right now, here, if I could."

A fiery ache sped down Henry's spine. His knees weakened, but he pulled away. Sighing deeply, he pointed to Allan.

"He can sleep through anything." Stephan dragged Henry back into his arms. A knock on the door made them both jump.

Little John was frowning as Stephan opened the door to let him in. "The king will not leave," he said. "William says his fever has risen. His cough is rattling the doors of the inn."

Stephan looked ready to rattle a door with his fist. "Good Christ."

Henry tugged on his dark woollen hose, and grabbed his sword belt. He dreaded to think what might happen next. "I will go talk to him."

"Why bother?" Stephan asked. "He has made up his mind."

Allan rolled over and peeked out from beneath his covers. "If that's the case, may I go back to sleep?"

Stephan paced back to the window and pulled back the oilcloth. "When the soldiers come, I will tell them the king is far beyond their reach and try to convince them that whatever Otto confessed is a lie. Mayhap they will believe me if no one saw our little switch."

Henry whacked Allan playfully. "Out of bed. We shall let the king rest but when the soldiers arrive, you must help William get him to the stable. Ill or not, he must leave this place."

Allan moaned and patted the straw-filled pillow. "Might be the last nice bed we have for a while. I will wager that the duke's prison cells are cold and dark."

"We are not going to get arrested," Henry said.

Allan sat up, looked from the knights to Little John. "Shall we take bets on that?"

~ ~ ~

TWO DOZEN SOLDIERS GALLOPED into the village three hours later. Their horses snorted and whinnied, complaining of the hard ride.

Allan signaled Henry with a nod. Henry had begun to move up the street and away from The Stag. They'd left Stephan in the tavern. Little John was waiting at the stables.

It was time to get King Richard. Allan sauntered into the inn, but once inside, he took the stairs two at a time. He knocked on the king's door. No response. He knocked again, calling out for William. Pushing down the latch, he opened the door. The room was empty.

"They are going to kill me. I've lost the king."

Allan traced his steps back downstairs. The tavern wasn't busy. Five men hovered over dice at one of the tables, but neither the king nor William sat with them.

Strolling into the kitchen, Allan smiled broadly at his serving girl friend. A noise by the hearth made him turn. The cook, no, the cooks—Allan halted dead in his tracks. There was no mistaking King Richard. "God have mercy on us all."

Allan shot out the back door. He stopped, gawked down the street. There was no sign of Sir Henry. Mayhap he's chosen to keep watch on The Stag, waiting until the last possible moment to meet at the stable, and trusting Allan to get the king to their rendezvous.

Allan skirted around the building. Back on the main road, he slowed, not wanting to draw attention to himself. The mounted soldiers had reined in at The Stag. Just as Henry and Stephan assumed, the German translator had provided the king's location to his captors. Allan joined the curious crowds approaching The Stag hoping Henry would see him. He was halfway up the block when Henry grabbed him.

"Why aren't you with the king?" Henry asked.

"Sir Henry, you will not believe it. He must be mad."

"It's not wise to call—" Henry paused. He noticed the near terror on Allan's face. "What has happened?"

"He was not in his room. I found him in the kitchen."

"What?"

"He is huddled over the fire putting herbs on the birds roasting there. Basting the meat," Allan repeated, trying to convince himself of what he'd seen.

"What is he thinking?" Henry stared past Allan, his shoulders sagging. Energy seemed to drain from his body. He began to pace, and then a slow smile curled the edges of his mouth. His eyes brightened. "I suppose it might work. He is not a guest, but a cook."

Allan waved his hand in front of Henry's face. "A cook wearing a ruby the size of a boulder."

Henry groaned. "God's bones."

Allan peered around the corner. "Guards at the front door. A dozen still mounted, waiting for orders."

"I counted six of them going into The Stag," Henry added. He started to pace again. "They will have found Stephan by now."

Allan watched Henry knowing that he'd try not to think of Stephan. Henry finally leaned against the wall, looked at Allan. He said, "We shall follow the plan as we had agreed. We cannot interfere with the soldiers questioning Stephan. I will talk to the king."

~ ~ ~

"YOU ARE NOT THE King of England." The captain was a tall man with a long, straight nose and piercing black eyes. He stood stiffly in front of Stephan. His French was halting, but good. Excellent compared to Stephan's German. He was courteous. King or not, enemy or ally, he had no desire to take chances if he was wrong.

"You have seen me before?" Stephan coughed, brought his bejeweled fingers to his face. He flicked his hand across his chest to wipe away the ale he'd spilled when the soldier first approached him.

"No, I have not. Nor have I seen the English king. But you are not him."

"You did not take the Cross with Duke Leopold?"

The captain cleared his throat. "That has naught to do with whether I believe you are the King of England. You are too young. And though the light is not good here, I see no red in your hair."

"Everyone knows I have golden reddish hair, do they?"

"Yes, but you are not the king. You must tell me where he is hiding."

"Rumours run rampant." Stephan looked up, amused. This was far too enjoyable. "Do they also say I breathe fire and my valiant steed is a dragon that whisks me high above the infidels?"

The captain's stern facade cracked, but only for a moment. He must wonder if he was dealing with a madman. His sergeant stared straight ahead, stone-faced. He hadn't understood one word.

The captain placed his hands behind his back, turned his full attention on Stephan. "Where is the king?"

Stephan swallowed the last of his ale. He looked past the captain. "Gustaf, my goblet is empty. Another drink!"

The barkeeper jumped at the order. Stephan certainly sounded like a king.

The captain straightened his shoulders. He watched the barkeeper refill Stephan's mug, exchanged a few words in German with him, and turned back to Stephan. "You will not cooperate?"

Stephan waved at the empty chair. "Please, sit, captain. Gustaf," he called again, "bring an ale for my friend."

~ ~ ~

HENRY PEERED PAST ALLAN'S shoulder towards the door into the inn's kitchen. This was insane. "More soldiers. It will only raise more questions if I enter through the back. I am not exactly fitted out to look like the help. I shall have to go in the front."

"What would you like me to do?" Allan asked.

"Keep watch on The Stag. If that captain tires of our fake king and orders a search of the town, warn me—but only if it is safe."

"And you?"

"I will protect the king. If that means a fight, so be it." Henry looked around the corner again. He drew back sharply, suddenly remembering the gifts he'd bought. He tapped the pouch hanging from his sword belt.

"What is it?" Allan asked.

"I have something for you and Little John." Henry gently drew the silver chain from his pouch and placed it over Allan's head.

Allan fingered the links, slid his hand round the chain and palmed it. "It...it is the most beautiful thing I have ever owned. Thank you."

Henry dug into the pouch again. He tugged at the leather cord that held the cross and lifted it out. "Would you give this to Little John?"

Allan pushed it back into Henry's palm, curled his fingers around it. "You give it to him later."

Henry tucked the cross into his purse. "Should our plan fall through, you and Little John take the horses. Head north just as we had planned. Ride hard. Go to England. Queen Eleanor must be told what has happened." Before Allan could see the moisture pricking his eyes, Henry shot away.

Another contingent of soldiers on horseback trotted into town scattering the peasants and merchants. The streets suddenly swarmed with red tunics, all mustering near The Stag where Stephan entertained their captain.

Henry slipped into the tavern, tipping his head at Allan's friend. He found the king sitting at the hearth in the kitchen, firelight glimmering off his hair like a beacon. Richard had borrowed a ragged brown cloak that was thrown across his shoulders. He didn't turn, did not lift his head.

Henry saw the ruby on Richard's finger. *Damn that ring.* He drew down on one knee. "Sire, there might be time to get you away."

Richard looked up, his eyes watery, bloodshot. His cheeks glowed ruddy from the fire, if not from fever.

The old cook shuffled up behind his "assistant" Richard to scrutinize his work. His jowls swayed like a loose pudding. He breathed in the fragrance of the succulent birds. Pointing to the short trestle by Richard's boot, he grunted something in German.

Richard picked up the bowl there, held it below the short man's nose. "More herbs?"

The cook nodded curtly. Richard set aside the basting spoon and plunked his fingers into the mix. As fat and juices dripped and sizzled on the fire, he sprinkled the fresh and dried green and brown flakes over the chicken and then whisked his hands.

If Henry hadn't been witness to this moment with his own eyes, he'd never believe it.

Glancing at Henry, Richard said, "Face the truth, Henry. It is time to stop running. We cannot fight our way out of this. There are too few of us to stand against the duke's men."

"Five of us not enough? We do have Allan and Little John, sire."

Richard chuckled. "Mayhap Allan could play them a game of dice for my freedom?"

"We would be headed north in no time," Henry said with a smile. He could almost believe that Allan might pull that off.

Richard turned serious. "See that those young men live through this, Sir Henry. Get them back to my queen."

"I believe the squires have other ideas. They expect to fight at your side. Whatever may come, whether against the French king or your brother."

"They are good men."

Henry rested a hand on the hilt of his sword. "Let me stay with you, sire."

"No." Richard's voice sounded harsh.

"Where is William?"

"I sent him back to the room. Now go. You must get to England."

Henry stood, forced himself not to bow. He was nearly out of the kitchen when Allan plowed into him. "They are taking Sir Stephan," he said.

"God's wounds," Henry muttered darkly.

Richard looked up. "Can you help him?" When Henry shook his head, Richard ordered, "Leave now. One cook's helper might not draw attention."

Henry prodded Allan towards the back door. The serving girl blocked their way. Allan exchanged a glance with Henry and started to push past her. She clutched Allan's arm, pointed towards another door, and spoke in a quiet, urgent tone. The words were in German, but her eyes conveyed her concern. She slipped her hand into Allan's and looked at Henry. He nodded and said, "Go."

She led them into a large storage room where trestles and chairs were stacked against one wall. Another wall had hooks holding a variety of cook's tools. The girl grabbed an iron kettle from one and held the pot out to Allan.

"What are you doing?" Allan asked her.

She ignored his question and pressed the kettle into his hands. She grabbed hold of the hook and tugged hard, straining with the effort. Suddenly the wall moved. She smiled at Allan as a secret door creaked open.

"Do you trust the girl?" Henry asked as she urged them to follow.

"She helped us earlier. Should we go back for the king?"

"He will not come. He sees no use in running."

They passed through the secret entrance and climbed a narrow, darkened staircase. At the top, they found a musty room stacked with fine oak barrels and crates. Henry ran his hand along one, gave it a shove. It didn't budge. It must be a private stash of goods, he thought, hidden from the tax collectors.

Henry crossed to the small window overlooking the street. A half dozen soldiers remained mounted outside The Stag; others guarded the door. Henry turned to thank the girl for her help, but Allan had taken that into his own hands. He kissed her full on the mouth. She pulled back and scurried away, so quiet she'd not disturb a mouse.

Henry raised an eyebrow at Allan, and then without a word, resumed his reconnaissance. There was no sign of Stephan. *God, please keep him safe.* "Did you see what direction they'd headed with Stephan?"

Allan scrubbed a hand across his forehead. "Sorry. I should have—"

"It's all right. Mayhap Little John did." Henry noticed two soldiers emerge from The Stag. The taller of the two commanded the attention of the men gathered there. "The captain of the guard is issuing orders," Henry said.

A few moments later, the soldiers dispersed into smaller groups. They marched briskly to each tavern, inn, and shop along the road. Their search was methodical and thorough. Henry could hear the shouting and the frightened cries of innocent townsfolk.

A handful of soldiers approached the tavern where King Richard played assistant cook. Henry beat his head against the wall. "I forgot to remind the king to remove that ring."

"I do not think it would make much difference," Allan said.

Shouting erupted downstairs. German voices—the cook or the innkeeper—Henry couldn't tell. But then Allan's girlfriend shrieked, "Nein!" and all grew quiet. Henry held his breath. What was happening? Allan looked at him worriedly, but Henry just shook his head. *My God, have they killed King Richard?*

Boots and spurs struck heavily on the floor below them. Two soldiers ran from the tavern shouting, their swords drawn. In a matter of seconds, the rest of Duke Leopold's men converged on the building.

"Is he alive?" Allan asked.

Henry stood frozen by the window. If the soldiers had killed the king, what would happen to Stephan? Rubbing the ache in his temples, he let his mind drift. The mountains loomed above the town like the curtain wall of an ancient fortress. Stephan would be imprisoned out there...somewhere. *God's wounds. I cannot help Stephan and I've failed King Richard. Why did I let him talk me into this?*

"Sir Henry," Allan whispered, "I hear him. It's the king. He's alive."

Henry listened. The voices were muffled but there were two—one halting, hesitant; the other speaking steadily and with increasing volume and agitation. "Don't you have anyone here who speaks French or Latin?" a familiar voice boomed.

Henry looked toward the heavens and blew out a breath, relieved. "You are right, Allan. The king is alive."

Soldiers moved in and out of the tavern. Guards waved away one customer after another. A knight chatted casually with the baker from the shop across the street.

Hours passed. "What are they doing?" Allan asked. "Why are they taking so long?"

"King Richard must be negotiating the terms of his surrender."

"Pity the poor captain with that job," Allan said, eliciting a smile from Henry.

It was well past midday when three of the duke's men hurried from the tavern, mounted their horses, and galloped north towards Vienna. Henry could only hope that was a sign of progress.

Allan had drifted off to sleep atop one of the crates. Like Stephan, Henry thought, the young squire could sleep soundly anywhere. Mayhap he'd learned that in his old life on the streets of London or as a camp follower. Henry realised he knew little of that time and set his mind to see what Allan might share. But when Allan woke, he didn't give Henry a chance to speak. "Would it be all right if I check on Little John?" he asked.

310

Henry shook his head. "You'd never get out of here unseen. There are too many soldiers. Little John is fine. We would know if something happened." If Little John had followed orders, he would have moved the horses hours earlier from the livery near The Stag to one away from the main road. Henry tapped his fingers against the wall, winked at Allan, hoping to ease his concern. "It's Little John."

"I know he can take care of himself," Allan said unconvincingly. "He will be worried for Sir Stephan."

Henry padded lightly across the room and placed his hand on Allan's shoulder. "We all are. And about Robin," he said. "Why don't you keep watch for a while."

Allan took his turn at the window. He'd not been there long when noises in the street caused Henry to hurry to his side. Allan blew out a long deep breath. A low whistle escaped Henry's mouth.

A large gilded carriage rattled down the road. Four knights led the procession. They sported shiny helmets and breastplates that reflected the sun. A dozen cavalry on black warhorses trotted behind them, decked out in Duke Leopold's colours. Red and white banners fluttered in the afternoon breeze, and people scurried out of their way.

"Has the duke himself come?" Allan asked.

They watched the carriage halt in front of the tavern. Two men stepped out, one in a rich brown cloak with ermine trim. Henry remembered seeing the duke one time in Acre. He was tall, though not near the king's height, and looked to be Richard's age. From his vantage point, Henry thought he spied a slight paunch beneath the cloak. The duke's hair was dark, barely visible beneath the ermine hat perched on his head. He stood stiffly outside the carriage and waited. His companion entered the tavern.

"The one by the carriage—that is Leopold. The king must have insisted the duke come personally to accept his surrender."

Allan palmed his fist. "It is over. All this. The Holy Land. The suffering, the deaths."

"You have been listening to me far too long, Allan. It is not over as long as King Richard lives."

"But they have arrested Master Robin and Sir Stephan, and now they have the king." Allan pressed his back against the wall. "What will keep them from arresting us if we are found?"

"Nothing. We have done nothing wrong, Allan. And we are not worth ransoming. The king will insist they release us." Henry tried to sound confident. Surely the king's word and the Pope's protection would keep them from a castle dungeon. If these were men of faith, they'd let them go.

Henry forced his hands not to tremble. He wasn't sure he believed that any longer. These "men of faith" had captured the king. Still, he couldn't destroy Allan's hopes that they'd be freed, as would Robin and Stephan. "We will carry on," he added.

There was a tap at the door. Another tap. "Bitte," a familiar voice called quietly. The hinges creaked when Allan opened the door. The girl had a platter of food and a jug of ale in her arms. She placed it on a chest and kept her voice low, rattling off a stream of German words.

Henry shook his head.

She pointed to her ring finger. "Friend."

Henry looked at Allan. "Have you been teaching her French?"

"Just a word or two."

"Does she have a name?"

"I call her 'my beauty' but I cannot say that she knows what I am saying."

Henry chuckled. "I would bet she does, but it would not do me well to call her that." He looked at the girl, pointed to himself. "Henry."

She grinned, placed her hand near her heart. "Gisela." She spoke rapid-fire and pointed to the street.

"Friend," Henry said. "Where are they taking our friend?"

Before she could say another word, a racket arose outside. Henry shot back to the window. Swords drawn, the soldiers stood at attention to keep away curious onlookers and enemy rescuers. A moment later, King Richard was escorted outside. William stepped out behind him. Their hands weren't bound, but Henry knew Leopold wasn't ushering the king to a feast.

William must have retrieved Richard's sword and fancy cloak, for the king had shucked the poorer one Henry had seen him wearing in the kitchen.

Henry waved Gisela over. He pointed at the king. "Our friend."

Gisela nodded and sighed.

Richard unsheathed his sword, stretched out his arms, and laid the tip of the blade atop his left wrist. He bowed to Leopold. Leopold returned the courtesy and then took the weapon, handing it to his companion. He waved his arm towards the carriage and urged the king aboard.

Gisela's eyes darted around the room. Rather than spill more words she knew they wouldn't understand, she finally spoke just one. "Dürnstein."

"They are taking the king to Dürnstein," Henry said.

Gisela nodded but Allan's brow furrowed. "Where is that?"

"It is west of here." Henry remembered seeing it on their map. "Not far."

Henry wrapped his arms around Gisela. Her dark eyes lit up and she kissed him before he relinquished his hold on her.

Allan tapped her arm. "What about me?"

Gisela giggled. Allan tugged her close and gave her a kiss.

"All right. Enough of that," Henry said. He watched the carriage bounce down the road. "Let's eat, but save some for Little John. Once all the soldiers leave, we shall find him. Tonight, we stay here. At first light, we follow King Richard's orders and head for the border."

~ ~ ~

HENRY STARED OUT WINDOW eyeing the brilliant stars against the black of the night sky. Allan was sleeping soundly but he heard Little John stirring on the bed and glanced down at him.

"He is fine," Little John said, fingering the cross that Henry had given him.

Henry rubbed the chill from his arms. "I hope he is warm."

"If he is thinking of you, like you think of him, he will be. I am sure of that." Little John rolled over, draped his arm across Allan's back and fell asleep.

Henry crawled beneath his blanket. The memory of Stephan's fingers tracing across his forehead, his temple and through the scruff on his jaw made him shiver. Nestling his nose against the pillow, he breathed in the scent that lingered there and he slept peacefully, his dreams nothing but Stephan.

2 December 1192 -
1 January 1193

forty-one

TWO DAYS. THAT WAS all they'd needed to get to friendly territory. If only the king hadn't been ill.

Henry watched their backs on the journey from Vienna. He prayed he'd see Stephan. His heart ached each time a stranger galloped up from behind and passed them by. When they stopped for the night, he'd sit in the tavern until the wee hours of the morning hoping to see that familiar face walk through the door.

He struggled to stay strong for Allan and Little John. Each day was harder than the last as their path took them further north. He and Stephan had survived the Holy Land, survived Henry's doubt. But for what? To be left alone with only memories when he wanted so much more? God, how he missed him.

King Richard's brother-in-law Henry the Lion of Saxony had welcomed them and offered safe passage to Hamburg. From there, the weary warriors boarded a boat and sailed downstream to find passage to England.

From the doorway of the inn, Allan frowned at dark clouds rolling overhead. He muttered a curse about the puddles in the streets. Driving sheets of rain cascaded from skies so black that night and day were barely indistinguishable. "Will this winter squall ever end?"

Little John leaned out the door. The weather had calmed earlier that afternoon and he'd escaped the confines of the inn. But the reprieve had lasted only a short while. He shifted impatiently and gave a low whistle. "We won't see England 'til summer."

"Could be worse," Henry reminded them. "We've a warm room, food and drink."

Allan chuckled. "It is better than the camps in the desert or the barns with holes in their roofs where snow comes in."

"And there are no enemy soldiers trying to capture—" Little John paused, glanced over his shoulder where Henry stood behind him.

Henry appreciated their efforts not to mention Stephan. He knew they felt his loss—and Robin's—strongly.

Drawing up next to Little John, Henry peered outside. "I heard someone say that the New Year will be upon us soon. Can it be that we left Acre nigh on three months past?"

Little John sighed. "I hardly remember when we left England."

"What do you mean? It weren't that long ago," Allan said.

"The days fade one into the next."

"You are right, Little John," Henry said. "I met Stephan in Southampton three years ago come March." He looked at the sign above the tavern across the street. It swung wildly, battered by the wind and the rain. That was how he felt. Beaten. Guilt swept through him. Guilt that he'd waited so long to be honest about his love for Stephan.

Henry shook off his melancholy and palmed his coin purse. The silver clinked. "And we met you two scoundrels in Tours a few weeks after that."

Allan grinned. "Will you be buying us dinner tonight, Master Henry?"

"Why is it I always pay for your roast chicken?" Henry winked.

Little John's eyes twinkled mischievously. He rubbed his belly. "Fish. We should have fish tonight. That place with the sign of the boat down the road serves up a good one, or so the innkeeper told me."

"There is dried beef in our packs. Or I would not mind going back to The White Wave." Henry licked his lips, remembering the taste of the herb-roasted pork that melted in his mouth the night before.

"Not there again." Little John crossed his arms. "Fish sounds better."

Allan looked at him curiously. It wasn't like Little John to be so stubborn.

"Never want to eat dried meat again?" Henry asked.

"I think the taste is finally leaving my mouth."

Henry laughed, clapped a hand on his shoulder. "Fish it is."

Allan shielded his face from the rain with his cloak and led the way down the street. At the tavern, Little John tugged the door open. A cold draft swept the room. Candles flickered and the customers groaned. He strode into the room like a bear following the scent of dinner.

Henry shed his cloak. Water puddled at his feet. When his eyes adjusted to the dim lighting, he looked at the faces huddled at each table, just as he'd done at every other tavern along the way from Vienna.

Little John's laughter rang out. He'd grabbed hold of someone.

Henry's breath caught in his throat. *Stephan!*

Words spilled from Allan's mouth but Henry couldn't hear them. He cut a path across the crowded room.

Stephan waved and shouted.

They wrapped their arms around each other. "I have missed you," Henry whispered.

~ ~ ~

THIS WILL NOT DO. Robin strained against the rope. Another day on the road. Another mile further from the king. He'd loosened his restraints but his captors made quick work of tightening them each night and binding his feet to ensure he didn't attempt an escape. The bloodied cuts on his wrists were numb. His fingers felt stiff and cold despite the fur-lined gloves the soldiers allowed him to keep.

He looked in far better shape than the two Templars. Algar's face was bruised, his nose crooked from being bludgeoned with the hilt of a sword. Gilbert had been toppled from his horse. He'd broken his arm in the fall and wore a sling of fabric ripped from his tunic. His other arm had been hastily wrapped in linen to staunch the flow of blood from a wound he'd suffered during the fight with Leopold's soldiers. The guards hadn't been gentle with him. He looked feverish and bright red blood seeped through his bandaged arm.

Eyes half swollen, Algar looked from their captors to Robin, gave him a short nod. It said, "Do what you must to escape."

Robin rolled across the hay. He pushed himself to a sitting position next to Gilbert. "He is going to die." Robin glared at the guard who'd lost the straw draw for the first watch of the night. To his trained eye, and given his captors' laxness and constant bickering, Robin wasn't so sure they were soldiers. Mercenaries? Or just riff-raff who would turn over their captives to slavers?

"Help me," Robin added.

The guard stared at him blankly.

"I need fresh bandages." Turning, Robin lifted his bound hands as best he could. "Untie me. Let me help my friend." He leaned down, tugged at Gilbert's soiled bandages with his teeth.

The guard reluctantly removed the rope on Robin's wrists.

"Use my tunic, Robin," Algar said.

"You need it yourself, my friend." Robin looked around for something else that might serve as a bandage aware of the lance aimed at his back. He had to bind Gilbert's wound before they attempted an escape. Gilbert might not survive otherwise.

Robin ripped a strip of cloth from his own tunic. He poured wine on the cut. Gilbert screeched and his eyes rolled back.

"Is he all right?" Algar asked.

The guard shifted further away. Squeamish, eh? Robin would've laughed but all he could do was thank God that Gilbert was still breathing. "He is not dead…yet."

He began to clean the cut. It wasn't near as bad as he'd feared, as Gilbert's groans had led him to believe. Gilbert cracked an eye open and Robin acknowledged him with a curled lip. He took his time, eyes tracing between the wound, his patient, and the guard. When he tied the bandage, Gilbert nodded his thanks. "Godspeed," he whispered.

The guard nudged Robin away from Gilbert. When he laid the lance down to tie Robin's hands, Robin butted him in the face. Blood spurted from the man's nose. Robin loosed a solid punch and cracked his jaw. The guard fell backwards, smacked his head against the horse stall, and lay still.

"Go, Robin," Algar said. "Go now."

Robin untied Algar's hands.

"What are you doing? Gilbert is not fit to ride."

Robin was already saddling the horses. "You are coming with me," he said. He grabbed the guard's blanket and placed it in Algar's pack.

Gilbert sat up. "We will only slow you down."

"Go, I will stay alongside Gilbert," Algar said, "and pray God that you find safety with friends. Let them know of our plight."

Robin grabbed the unconscious guard's sword. He recognized the crest on the scabbard and looked at Algar. "This is your sword."

"Take it. Give it to my family in Rouen."

"No. You give it to them." Robin pressed the sword into Algar's hand. "Tell them of your loyalty and bravery. And when we are next together, we shall have a great feast." Robin peered outside but pulled back from the barn door with a jerk. "Guard coming," he said. "May I borrow your sword?"

Algar tossed the blade back to Robin. He turned it in his hand, missing the heavier weight of his own sword. King Richard had given it to him the day he'd been knighted. He could still remember the feel of that hilt.

The approaching soldier called out and began whistling a tune. Inside the barn, the other guard stirred, grabbed his broken, bloodied nose, and moaned. The whistling ceased.

Robin cursed beneath his breath.

"Friedrich?" the voice outside called.

Algar punched Friedrich back into unconsciousness.

"I shall lead this one away," Robin whispered to the Templars. "You take those horses and ride hard. We cannot be more than ten or fifteen miles from the coast. God will watch over you, my friends."

The barn door creaked. "Friedrich?" The voice sounded wary now and the distinct sound of a sword loosed from a scabbard echoed in the cold still air.

Gilbert groaned loudly, imitating Friedrich. Robin shoved the door open. Friedrich's comrade reeled back, avoiding the swing of the door. He raised his sword and strode forward.

Robin gaped at the gold inlaid pattern on the crossguard of the man's weapon. "That is my sword," he shouted. He blocked the first blow, twisted away, and then lashed out with a powerful thrust. "And I want it back!"

~ ~ ~

STEPHAN'S LIPS BRUSHED HENRY'S cheek. They laughed, pounding each other on the back. He finally let Henry go and grabbed Allan in a bear hug.

Allan's eyes narrowed. "You knew?" he asked Little John as they settled at the table.

"Found him this afternoon."

Henry frowned. "And you waited—"

"It has not been *that* long. If I had brought Master Stephan back to the room, well... I knew you would need some food before..." Little John's blush matched Henry's. "Aye, so I waited. And it was the longest wait trying not to say anything."

Their laughter drew stares but Henry didn't care. He clasped his hand over Stephan's. "Did they let you go?"

Stephan gulped down his ale and told the tale. He'd been at Dürnstein when they'd brought King Richard there. "...and he secured my release. I bid the king farewell, assured him we would tell his fate to his lady wife and the queen mother."

"Thanks be to God, the king is well." Henry's shock seeing Stephan had faded but his heart still raced. "And you," he added, thinking how he dreaded the thought of not seeing those eyes or that face again.

Stephan tapped his tunic. "The duke's letter provided me safe passage. I knew where you would head, so I came straight away. I thought I had missed you. Figured you had sailed before this storm blew in."

"We have been here three days waiting it out."

"One of the old-timers says we shall see blue skies in two days time. The others claim he has not been wrong in ten years." Stephan downed his ale, stretched. "I had not found a room yet."

Allan winked, looking from Henry to Stephan. "I think you might find a warm bed with us."

"I am no where near ready for sleep," Little John said. He rubbed his stomach. "My belly is not full."

Allan waved at the boy clearing tables. He pointed to their empty trenchers. "Another platter of the roast pork and a jug of ale, please."

"And more fish," Little John called.

Henry looked at Stephan. He felt peace and a kind of fear, though it wasn't a fear of God's judgment or Hell. Hell would truly be *not* loving this man. He only knew he wanted to be at Stephan's side in the days ahead. He slid his hand beneath the table and pressed it to Stephan's thigh.

Stephan leaned close. Hot breath brushed Henry's face and his knees felt weak. Clearing his throat, he forced himself up and started for the door.

Little John grinned when Stephan combed his fingers through his hair and smoothed his tunic.

Allan lifted his mug. "Don't wait up for us."

~ ~ ~

HENRY LATCHED THE DOOR to the room. Stephan came up behind him, swept his arms around Henry. Henry rested his head against Stephan's shoulder. The familiar smells of musk and leather were more comforting than a woollen blanket on a cold winter's night.

"We are going home," Stephan whispered.

Henry turned in his arms. "Home is not England." He placed his palm to Stephan's heart. "Home is here. With you."

"Henry—" Stephan brought his mouth down hard on Henry's. He shoved Henry against the wall and nibbled at his ear. "Tell me again. How much did you miss me?"

Henry laughed, fumbling to tug Stephan's tunic over his head. Stephan helped between kisses and moans, as desperate as Henry to feel flesh. Tunics, hose and braises found the old wooden floor. There was nothing gentle in the way they moved against each other. Need consumed them until they climaxed in a storm of short, rasping breaths and hearts pounding like thunder.

Stephan held onto Henry until their heartbeats slowed. He tilted his head to capture his lover's mouth once again and then pulled him across the room and into bed.

They slept tangled in each other's arms until light crept through the shuttered window. Henry combed back strands of hair that had fallen across Stephan's face. After a while, he said, "You once said you wanted to do unspeakable things with a man." His gaze locked on Stephan. "I must confess I am not...I do not know...there is more to it I am sure..."

"There is," Stephan said.

"I have never... You must show me what to do."

Stephan kissed the tip of Henry's nose. "I will," he whispered. He nuzzled Henry's close-clipped beard, rested his head against his chest, and promptly fell back to sleep.

Dover to Winchester
january 1193

forty~two

THE OLD-TIMER HAD BEEN RIGHT. The weather cleared, the seas calmed, and four days later Dover's white cliffs loomed large under bright blue winter skies. The keep of Dover Castle should have been a welcome sight.

"Count John's supporters may control the castle," Henry said when Allan spoke of sitting round a fire in the keep. "We cannot risk being stopped by them."

"Have you been there, my lord?" Allan asked. "It is bigger than any I have ever been in."

"When were you in the castle?" Stephan asked.

"After King Richard's coronation."

Little John nodded. "We followed the train of nobles and knights who had taken the Cross and gathered here to go on pilgrimage."

"It was easy to hide amongst their wagons. And a good place to pilfer pockets," Allan said.

"We followed along, eating off their scraps," Little John added quickly.

"And you ended up in Tours." Henry smiled. "I think we know the rest of that tale."

Henry would not have believed how the story had unfolded had he not lived it. He recalled the pain and hardships—losing Roger, the executions at Acre. So many dead. The unrelenting desert and Saracen blades. Vienna.

Stephan's laughter made him turn. He watched Stephan, remembering how, in their own ways, they'd each been so alone. How different they were back then. Stephan, who went from one man's bed to another because he did not believe he'd ever love. *And me?* Naïve about war, and far too righteous. The times spent fighting at each other's side, celebrating each mile towards Jerusalem, towards England. *We were still alone, weren't we?* Henry felt a tug at his heart—love and passion had consumed that loneliness. How could he have ever denied his feelings?

"Get your horses and what supplies you'll need," Stephan said, interrupting Henry's thoughts. "We will meet you on the road just to the west of town."

The knights and their squires went their separate ways to avoid attracting attention. Henry quietly blessed Henry of Saxony for the silver he'd lent them. Within an hour of stepping off the boat, they rendezvoused and took to the road. Riding hard into the night and rising with the sun, they arrived in Winchester on the third day of their journey.

Queen Eleanor saw them immediately.

"Madam," Stephan said, "we bring the gravest of news. Your son, the king, has been taken prisoner by the Duke of Austria. He holds him at Dürnstein Castle, to the west of Vienna."

Eleanor reached back, grasped the arms of her chair to steady herself, and sat down slowly. "Richard? Captured? Tell me what happened."

The knights recounted their journey from Acre.

Colour rose in Eleanor's cheeks. It matched the red silk of her gown. "Duke Leopold must be insane."

"Yes, madam," Henry said.

Eleanor sat stiffly, her hands clasped tightly in her lap. "His hatred for my son is well known. But this?"

"Would that we had not needed to bring this news to you and Queen Berengaria."

Eleanor turned to her advisor and chief justiciar Walter de Coutances. The archbishop fingered the cincture at his waist with wrinkled hands. He'd served her late husband and transferred his loyalties to Richard when he'd become king. Henry recognized him. Coutances had been in the king's closest circle from Tours to Messina. He'd negotiated the peace after Richard captured Messina. He would have accompanied the king to the Holy Land if civil disturbance hadn't arisen in England. Sent back as a mediator, he'd been at Eleanor's side faithfully.

"See that a message is sent to Richard's wife."

Coutances' dark robes swayed as he bowed. "At once, madam."

"The queen arrived safely in Poitou, my lady?" Stephan asked.

"I am afraid not. Richard was not the only one eluding enemies at sea. Our contacts in Italy informed me that Berengaria and my daughter Joanna have taken refuge in Rome. The Holy Father is interceding on their behalf. God willing, the Count of Toulouse, mindful of obligations to pilgrims, will heed the Pope's request and escort the ladies to Poitiers."

Eleanor straightened, her green eyes meeting theirs. "We shall not solve this here and now. You have traveled far and look weary." She signaled her servant. "Show my friends to their rooms. Draw baths for them." She looked at the two knights. "Relax a while and we shall talk over a good meal after you have rested."

~ ~ ~

ELEANOR SENT HER APOLOGIES when business interrupted her desire to take the afternoon meal with the knights.

Henry smoothed the fabric on Little John's shoulder as they waited outside the great hall the next day.

Stephan eyed the two boys. "Remember to be on your best behavior. You are dining at the queen's table. Speak only when spoken to."

Allan grunted, tugged his tunic down and readjusted his sword belt. "We do not need a lecture. We have done this before."

"You were servants at the royal tables in Acre, not guests," Henry said.

"Not much different," Little John said.

Allan chuckled. "Do not try to refill her wine, my friend."

Little John scowled.

The door opened and a servant waved them in. The feast laid out was sumptuous. There was a spread of venison, pork and chicken, dozens of cheeses, soup and fish, the likes of which Henry remembered from meals he'd shared at King Richard's table at the palace in Acre.

Eleanor greeted them warmly, made special note of the boys. "Are you satisfied with the tunics my tailors made for you?"

"Very pleased, madam," Little John said.

"And surprised," Allan added.

Little John's tunic was the colour of Eleanor's sapphire blue woollen gown. Allan's green one matched his eyes. Both had cut their beards short and their hair had been trimmed.

Eleanor smiled. "I am glad. You look as handsome as any royal princes."

"Your generosity is overwhelming, madam," Little John said, a blush highlighting his cheeks.

"It is the least we could do for the men who tried to bring the king home." Eleanor smeared a chunk of bread with cheese and honey and the servants began to fill everyone's silver plates. Eleanor bit off a piece of bread and chewed. Her brow creased, her eyes suddenly narrowed. "I *have* seen you at court."

Allan stopped mid-chew, looked from Little John to Eleanor. He shook his head. "That could not be possible, madam."

"I know I am getting old, Allan, but my memory is quite good." She looked at him again. "The hair, and those eyes. I would not forget. Yes, it was at Westminster. At Richard's coronation. Sir William took after you when he saw you—"

Allan shook his head vehemently. "That was not me."

"Allan," Henry asked, "you didn't?"

"No, Sir Henry, I did not…we…me and Little John were just watching."

Eleanor burst out laughing. Her laughter was infectious, and Henry and Stephan had to wipe their eyes.

"What?" Allan asked, incredulous.

"Oh Allan, you must forgive me. Even if you had been pilfering purses during Richard's coronation, I could not hold it against you. Or you, John. Joanna's letters of the time she spent with you are so full of affection. My daughter is your most ardent supporter. She is proud of the young men you have become and I can see why she would feel that way."

Little John had turned a shade of crimson that rivaled the strawberries on his trencher. "Thank you, madam. Queen Joanna has been very kind to us. God bless her and see her safely to Poitou."

"And she has quite the talent for dice," Allan said with a smile.

"I hear she regularly beat her brother," Eleanor said.

"That is true, madam," Stephan said. "Allan is a good teacher."

"Good. Richard needs a comeuppance now and then. If there was time, I would have you teach me your tricks." Eleanor sighed, and then turned to Henry with a gleam in her eye. "Joanna also spoke with great affection of you, sir. You would make a good match."

Henry stiffened, not daring to look at Stephan. "She is a good friend and I care for—"

Eleanor waved her hand. "Yes, she wrote that you got along well and your friendship might easily be more." She sipped her wine.

Henry couldn't breathe. Had Eleanor's eyes flicked towards Stephan?

"However, Joanna knows, as we all do, that many of us do not have the luxury of love. Political alliances outweigh the feelings people have for each other." Eleanor laid a finger on Henry's hand. "You do understand? Richard would never agree to the match."

Eleanor withdrew her hand. She turned to Stephan, and her eyes danced mischievously from him back to Henry. "More so, she could not bear to come between you and your heart."

God's bones, Joanna told the queen mother…

The room had grown quiet. Henry looked for something to say. Joanna had claimed that her mother was open-minded but admitting out loud that he and Stephan were lovers was not prudent.

Eleanor gave Henry no chance to respond. She cleared her throat. "And Stephan, lest you feel ignored, Joanna said she had never met a knight so true."

"I will thank her for those kind words and wise thoughts when we meet next, madam," Stephan said.

The conversation drifted back to Richard's ordeal. Eleanor tapped the table with her finger, its rhythm waxing and waning throughout. She interrupted Henry and Stephan with dozens of questions.

"The archbishop and I studied our maps this morning. I do not remember this Dürnstein though it lies along the Danube River. You might know I took the Cross near fifty years ago after Turks captured Edessa. I was with Louis' army when we marched that route to the Holy Land."

Henry looked from Eleanor to Stephan, his face full of regret. "We should have followed Leopold's soldiers to confirm the girl's story."

"And done what?" Eleanor asked. "No, it was best you returned here. I am glad to have this news from Richard's men rather than from one of Leopold's stodgy, gloating messengers."

The door into the hall opened. Eleanor looked up sharply, perturbed at the interruption. A clerk entered and bowed.

"Yes? What is it?" Eleanor asked.

The long-legged man hurried to her side and leaned to whisper in her ear.

Eleanor's brow rose. She looked at him, "Indeed?" He bent low again to complete his message. Eleanor slapped the table. "I do not care how filthy he is. Send him in right away."

Flushed, the clerk departed with great haste.

Eleanor smiled wryly at Stephan and Henry. "Another messenger has arrived claiming to have news of the king."

"Is it William de l'Étang or someone from the duke's court, madam?" Henry asked.

Eleanor glanced towards the door as it opened and smiled.

"No," a familiar male voice boomed. "It is Robin du Louviers." Robin bowed. "Madam."

Allan forgot all decorum. "Master!" He jumped up from the table and ran to greet Robin, nearly bowling him over.

Robin wrapped his arms around the young man. "It is good to see you, Allan." He tipped his head at Little John.

Henry and Stephan were on their feet, all grins. "King Richard was right about you," Henry said. "He knew you could not be held. Thank God you are well, my friend."

"Welcome home." Stephan reached to shake Robin's hand, and then hauled him close for a brotherly hug. "I have never been so glad to see someone."

Robin pulled back, studying Stephan's eyes. "That is not true," he whispered and glanced at Henry. "I remember the look on your face the day Henry returned to Jaffa."

"We have come far since then," Stephan said.

Henry felt a tug at his heart but for once didn't blush when Robin looked between the two knights.

Eleanor was watching them, unawares of the whispered words but delighted by the joyful reunion. "Robin, come in," she called.

Robin handed his mud-caked cloak to the servant and smoothed the wrinkles from his tunic. "Madam, forgive my appearance. I have had to beg and steal through enemies' lands from Verona to Poitiers to Paris, but you will be most pleased of this letter I bring to you."

Eleanor fingered the parchment he placed in her hand. "Sit down, Robin." She snapped her fingers. Servants scurried to set a place for him and wine was poured.

Eleanor's eyes swept the words on the page. "I would say that I am outraged that the Emperor Henry plots with Philip of France to imprison my son, but this treachery does not surprise me." She looked up at Robin. "What were you doing in Paris? It's rather out of the way. When did you get this letter? And where?"

"I assume Henry and Stephan told you of my misfortune when I was captured along with two of the king's knights?"

"Do you have word of them?" Henry asked.

"Sadly, I do not know their fates as we parted ways."

"How did you escape, master?" Allan asked.

Robin's eyes softened when he saw the eagerness in Allan's. "That is a tale for another time." He turned to Eleanor and told of his journey to Poitiers. He'd arrived the week before Christmas. Rumours of Count John's dealings with King Philip were rife there, and Robin had learned that John might be at the French king's court. "I chose to steal into Paris to see by my own eyes. The taverns near the palace hum with word of King Richard's death and John's attempts to raise an army.

"Your advisor, de Coutances, has his spies watching the French court. Six days ago, I recognized one of them. We'd fought alongside each other in campaigns against your late husband. He'd acquired the letter you hold in your hands. When he learned I had been with the king in Bavaria, he entrusted me with bringing this news to you."

Eleanor faced Stephan and Henry. She scowled, waving the letter in the air. "Duke Leopold plans to hand Richard over to the Emperor Henry. No doubt he will be moved from Dürnstein."

"What shall you have us do, madam?" Robin asked.

"We might go to Dürnstein, intercept them when they depart," Stephan said.

Eleanor didn't respond. She swirled the wine around in her goblet, glanced at the tapestry on the wall depicting the Angevin empire stretching from England across the Narrow Sea to Normandy and beyond. "I must send envoys to the Emperor. And I will implore His Holiness the Pope to intercede on behalf of the king. Richard is a soldier of Christ and under the protection of God and the Holy Church. The Pope must not tolerate this vicious act. He cannot allow this barbarism to go unpunished."

"We are at your bidding," Henry said.

Eleanor smiled, studying the faces of her loyal knights. "You, my dear friends, would do anything for my son. I need you and soldiers like you, here, in England.

"John has asked for fealty from his brother's lords. They have not thrown their support to him. Robin, those were no rumours you had heard in the French taverns. My spies tell me that John has resorted to hiring mercenaries. I fear he plans to invade England."

Henry, Stephan, and Robin stood, lifting their goblets.

Henry nodded to Eleanor, to his friends. "To King Richard."

"To the king," they shouted.

Robin downed his wine. He lifted his brow, his blue eyes cunning. "Here is what we are going to do…"

nearDover
march 1193

forty-three

DAWN STRUGGLED TO BREAK the darkness. At least the rain had ended. Henry leaned against the turret wall, watching the thick fog roll in towards the beach. He shivered against the cool air and wiped the sea spray from his face.

A clank of mugs and the quiet rumble of Queen Eleanor's home guard wafted up from the bailey, where hundreds of brave men had gathered. They were a mixed company of experienced warriors fresh from the Holy Land, and Kentish peasants, gentry and noblemen mustered from nearby towns and villages. Along the battlements below Henry, commanders on the line began morning inspections. Their orders echoed off stone and timber walls that held secrets of battles from long ago.

Weeks had passed since their first meeting with Queen Eleanor at Winchester. Strategy planning had consumed the days there, but it was the quiet nights alone with Stephan that Henry kept close. Baths in soapy lavender water warmed their battle-weary souls. They collapsed on the softest of beds. Stephan would spoon his muscular body around Henry and they slept safe from stormy seas, their enemies, and war.

That world seemed foreign and distant now that he was guarding the southeast coast of England for the queen against her youngest son.

Pulling his hood down tightly, Henry stared into the fog. He was certain he heard a low, deep hum coming from somewhere on the water. Ships, troops—Count John's mercenaries.

Henry buried his head in his hands. His heart beat rapidly. The nightmares of fighting the king's enemies and the sounds of battle remained, painted vividly in his mind. How often had he awakened with sweat beaded across his forehead remembering the times they'd come within a whisper of dying?

Oh God, the chanting…stop the awful chanting. Saracen war cries, scars from that godforsaken desert. The sounds were as clear as if they'd come off the water.

Stephan drew up behind Henry, startling him. Stephan's arms enfolded him. His hair tickled Henry's ear. "Are you well?" Stephan asked, his voice tender. "You look like you have seen a ghost."

Henry pointed to the unseen forces out in the channel. "Their ships are out there." Strands of damp hair matted on his face. He smoothed them back and glanced at Stephan, refusing to tell his lover how much he dreaded facing another battle. Wondering whether these might be their last moments on this earth. And as always, afraid that Stephan would not see another summer.

"I am not mad."

"I did not say a word," Stephan replied.

Any other time those sparkling blue eyes might have eased Henry's fears. Not tonight.

Henry took a deep breath, released it. "I can hear them. It is like the Holy Land," he said quietly, voice trembling. "Do you remember the Saracen trumpeters, the incessant beat of the drums?" He closed his eyes against the memories. "Kept us awake half the night."

Stephan nodded against Henry's shoulder.

Henry shivered. "There would be that awful droning and chanting before they would attack our lines."

Stephan pressed closer. "Crying out 'Allah Akbar', thousands of them," he said.

Henry's eyes opened with a start. "Do you hear them? The drums?"

Stephan listened but shook his head. "It is all quiet."

The sudden clang of steel upon steel made Stephan a liar. Henry stiffened, relaxing only when laughter from familiar voices down in the bailey disrupted the early morning practice.

"The Frenchmen will hear us with all this revelry," he said. "Robin should order them to be still."

"The men are restless. Anxious for battle. We were like that once." Stephan gave him a squeeze.

"I know." Long before their arrival in the Holy Land, Henry had realised how full of bravado he'd been when he'd first left England to join the king's army. He fisted his fingers into the sleeve of Stephan's tunic. "I am just tired...tired of war."

Pressing his lips to Henry's neck, Stephan let his hands slip to his waist. He slid calloused palms beneath Henry's tunic. Henry's muscled flesh warmed at his touch. Stephan pulled Henry against him and his hands snaked downward to fumble with the laces of his hose.

Henry tried to squirm away. He whispered through a moan. "Not here!"

"No one will see. Not with this dark grey fog." Stephan's voice had a smile in it. "Besides, Allan and Little John are guarding the bottom of the stairs with orders to let no one pass."

"It is not the seeing." Henry gasped as Stephan's hands conquered the laces and palmed the flesh hardening beneath his braies. "It's the hearing!"

"Let me take care of that." Stephan turned Henry to face him and silenced him with a kiss.

Henry's gaze darted to one of the other towers. The darkness revealed a silhouette, another soldier with eyes on

Flanders. Feeling a little less conspicuous, Henry moaned into Stephan's mouth as the knight's hand gently stroked him.

Stephan's kisses trailed down his neck and across his shoulder. Every touch sent a fiery spark down his spine. Fire smoldered in the pit of his stomach, a longing ache that made him arch his back as Stephan's skilled hands caressed him.

Old battle scars faded in Henry's mind. He stifled a pleasurable groan as Stephan proved that his lovemaking rivaled his skills with sword and bow.

~ ~ ~

HENRY HELD STEPHAN TIGHTLY, his body shuddering in the final moments of his climax. His heart pounded in his ears like the waves crashing against the rocky beach far below them. He brushed his fingers along the scar that a Saracen blade had carved on Stephan's cheek and finally found his breath. "You do know I love you."

Stephan smiled. "I love you, Henry."

Henry pressed his forehead to Stephan's. "Thank you," he murmured.

"Why would you thank me?"

"The others never speak of the war. You listen. Let me remember. Help me forget the scars we carry, even if it is only for a few moments." Henry took a deep breath. "I thought we had put war behind us forever when we left the Holy Land. We were good soldiers. We gave ourselves to King Richard, to England. Those warriors we became should have been left behind in Outremer. But what happened? We fled enemies in Bavaria and now face others here. Reliving the nightmares of that Holy War every day, every night. Look at us. Fighting against the king's brother! It makes no sense."

"You are right," Stephan whispered, his hand tracing the frown lines on Henry's forehead.

"All I wish is to have our own table near a warm hearth, close to family and friends. Our stay with the queen mother was not just a dream."

Stephan sighed. "No, it was real."

As real as it could be behind closed doors.

"We will have that for ourselves. Soon," Stephan added. "The king will come home."

"The king is sitting in a dungeon in Bavaria. His brother wants his throne. If Richard is out, then we will have nothing," Henry said. "We shall be stripped of our lands, our titles. We might have nothing but the forest."

Stephan shook his head. "We will not let that happen. But even if we only have the forest, I will be by your side."

"Promise?"

"I do."

"I shall hold you to that." Henry looked at the man to whom he'd pledged his love and his life. "You will not get yourself killed today?"

"Or tomorrow." Stephan brushed Henry's lips with a kiss. "Or the next day." He released Henry reluctantly, wandering to the bailey-side of the turret to inspect the courtyard below. The swordplay had ended.

"That table, the hearth," Stephan said, glancing back. "You'll not tell your father—"

"How can I?" Henry covered his face with his hands.

Stephan drew up beside him again, wrapped him in his arms. "We will find a way. No one ever need know." He fingered the intricate filigree on the ring Henry had given him in Vienna. Guiding Henry's hand to it, he said, "You gave me this band after all."

Boots clattered on the stairs. Robin appeared, sword drawn, a sheen of sweat dampening his face.

"Did practice go well, my friend?" Stephan asked.

Robin shot a glance past Henry towards the sea then joined them at the wall. He rested his elbows on the turret, cocked his head back towards the bailey. "The knights are impatient with these coddled gentry who have rarely lifted a sword. They improve slowly. But," he said, turning his back to the water and looking from Henry to Stephan, "their hearts have the passion. We will turn back John's mercenaries."

Henry felt the heat rise on his neck. "Will they be so enamoured of war when they hear the last breaths of their friends? When they feel blood splatter like rain on their faces?"

Robin placed his large hands on Henry's shoulders, his eyes compassionate but determined. "No. They will not. But like you and me, like Stephan, they will see this fight through for king and country."

"Ships!" The shout rang out from one of the men on the battlements below them. A bell started to peal.

The three knights stared at four vessels breaking through the fog.

Robin threw his arms across his friends' shoulders. "And so it begins." He kissed each man on the cheek then moved to an embrasure closest to the battlement. Cupping his hands around his mouth, he shouted down to the troops gathered along the wall walk. "For England!"

The defenders responded back to Robin in one loud voice that reverberated in all directions—into the inner ward, over the castle walls, and out across the sea. "For England!"

Sunlight broke the dawn, chasing the fog away. Orders rang out. Robin threw a confident nod to the knights and darted down the stairs.

Stephan found Henry's hand. The two lovers kissed one last time as the pulse of drums grew stronger and fireballs screamed through the air.

AUTHOR'S NOTE

The history of the Third Crusade is well-documented by several chroniclers who provided slightly different versions of the events of the day. Some of the history was written in the years following King Richard's departure from the Holy Land after a three-year truce was signed with Salah al-Dīn. (In the novel, I choose to refer to him as most Christians did: Saladin.) I depended heavily on primary source translations, including Nicholson's *Chronicle of the third crusade : A translation of the Itinerarium peregrinorum et gesta regis ricardi,* and Riley's *The annals of Roger de Hoveden, comprising the history of England and of other countries of Europe from A. D. 732 to A. D. 1201.* I turned to those works and Weir's *Eleanor of Aquitaine: a life* for initial background information.

As I delved deeper into *Battle Scars,* my list of resources grew to include numerous biographies of King Richard I, other historical figures of the day, and general histories of and articles about society and culture in the Middle Ages. (Working at a large university library has its perks!) Miller's book, *Richard the Lionheart: the mighty crusader,* has a wealth of information about fleet and army logistics. The number of pilgrims, those we commonly call crusaders, varies wildly in reports from the chroniclers. Ambroise's *Estoire* and the author of the *Itinerarium* mention 100,000 Christians and 300,000 Turks (or Saracens as the term I chose to use to mean all those in Saladin's army). Both figures are greatly exaggerated. Actual estimates for the crusader army are closer to 20,000, with 6,000 horses. The Saracens numbered 25,000-30,000. The logistics of moving and feeding this 12th century army in a land far from home, especially under such adverse conditions as the weather, the terrain, and Saladin's scorched earth policy, are incredible. Miller estimates that man and beast required 67 tons of food and 180 tons of water per day, most of which had to be carried with the army. He also notes that "Actual quantities [of supplies] are seldom recorded in the accounts that remain...but surviving records showing that 50,000 [horseshoes] were provided by the county of Gloucestershire and another 10,000 by Hampshire." (p.168)

While the primary sources and others detail Richard's actions, I had no intention to recreate every moment, but rather tell the story through the eyes of two fictional characters: Sir Henry de Grey and Sir Stephan l'Aigle.

An early turning point for Henry and Stephan in *Battle Scars* occurs with an incident regarding the first reported fatalities. The armies of Richard and Philip of France had not even departed the European continent when a bridge over the Rhone River at Lyon collapsed in July 1190. Ambroise describes the scene as utter chaos with hundreds of people, animals and wagons plummeting into the rapidly-raging river. The chroniclers report only two deaths (or two bodies recovered per Ambroise) from that mishap. Scholars note that deaths among the "common" people often were not reported.

> "But those who in the morning passed
> Crowded the bridge so thick and fast
> Misfortune did them overtake.
> ...the arch fell and they tumbled in,
> and were shouting, groans and din...
> The water there so fiercely surges
> That little which falls in emerges."
> --*Ambroise, The crusade of Richard Lion-Heart*

Henry and Stephan are present for many of the events of 1190-1193. The joy of writing two fictional characters within an historical setting is that I am able to weave their fictitious lives around actual events. It gives me—without the benefit of being there myself—the chance to imagine what they saw and what they felt. Henry and Stephan are onlookers to the actions of the king. They have some intimate knowledge of King Richard's inner circle but other sights and sounds are strictly their own and mine.

So forgive me, dear readers, if I slipped in an occasional anachronistic phrase, if I inadvertently missed or barely touched on key moments, or altered a date or an event to allow my two young knights to be participants. I have done my utmost to stick close to the historical record.

I did incorporate the translations of some of Richard's words to his advisors, and in at least one instance, I placed those utterances on a different occasion on the road to Jerusalem for the pace of the story. I chose to use a fictitious character to deliver the news to Richard of Philip of France's decision to leave the Holy Land in July 1191. It lets me add a bit more drama to that scene while showing the nature of allies and enemies. The fictitious messenger is a "hat tip" to my coffee shop acquaintance, Mick, who gave me *The Book of Chivalry of Geoffroi de Charny*. De Charny, who must be France's equivalent of William Marshal (England's greatest knight), is Mick's 14th century ancestor. De Charny and his family (through his mother) had close ties to French kings in the 13th and 14th centuries. I decided to extend the family's relationship back to the 12th century with a paternal, rather than a maternal, connection.

The details of the Lionheart's journey after he left Acre in October 1192 are not as well-documented. Some events are debated among scholars so I admit I have taken poetic license. In my research, I have not discovered the names of all of Richard's companions as he journeyed through Bavaria. I chose one reported version of his capture because it added to the "adventure" of this novel. Queen Eleanor received news of Richard's capture in mid-January 1193 and my research of the literature did not indicate who delivered that news. Why not Henry, Stephan and their friend Sir Robin?

Though one of the underlying themes of *Battle Scars* is the relationship between Henry and Stephan, I do not refer to the question of King Richard's homosexuality. Twentieth century scholars suggested that Richard was gay, though more recent scholarship shows the "evidence" is circumspect. Like other forms of sex outside marriage, it was considered a mortal sin.

The late John Boswell notes severe punishment, including death, did exist in some countries in the Dark and Middle Ages. However, Boswell also cites evidence that the "crime" of homosexuality was dealt with no more harshly than other forms of adultery, with a fine or penances to be offered for as little as a year.

Lastly, I would like readers to know that the final scene of *Men of the Cross* was actually the beginning of this labor of love. At a weekly meeting of my writers group, I shared a short story with Cathy, Marie, and Mark. The characters struck a chord with them. The Robin Hood legend—my take on it—is birthed in the novel because of their encouragement. Why not include the man who becomes the legend rather than just have a "Robin-like" character? My writing group wanted to know more about Henry, Stephan and Robin. How did these men, who fought at Richard the Lionheart's side in the Holy Land, arrive at that moment on the battlements of a castle on the south coast of England in the early spring of 1193?

So I give you *Men of the Cross*, book 1 of *Battle Scars*.

As I closed in on completion of the first draft of *Men of the Cross*, plot possibilities for a sequel invaded my thoughts. It demanded to be written. As I publish Book I of *Battle Scars*, the second book in this series, *For King and Country*, sits in rough draft form on my hard drive (and in the Cloud because I am a huge believer in back-ups). The continuing story will follow Henry, Stephan and Robin in England as they reunite with their families and friends. The actual events in England of 1193-1194, when Richard languished in captivity and was held by the Duke of Austria and the Holy Roman Emperor, are well-known. My three knights will be part of that history, uncovering a plot by John, the king's brother, to usurp Richard's throne. I will expand the Robin Hood legend in Book II, including an explanation of Robin's family history in Lincolnshire. Many familiar characters become integral to the plot, but I will approach their backgrounds from my own perspective. I hope you will stick around for the adventure.

For a list of my reference resources and to monitor my progress on Book II, please drop by my website, http://charlenenewcomb.com.

ABOUT THE AUTHOR

Visit Charlene's website: http://charlenenewcomb.com

Follow her on Facebook,
http://www.facebook.com/charnewcomb
or on Twitter at http://twitter.com/charnewcomb

ALSO BY CHARLENE NEWCOMB

Keeping the Family Peace

A Certain Point of View
in *Star Wars: Tales from the Empire*

Shades of Gray: from the Adventure of Alex Winger
freely available via Random House
(linked from the author's website)

And numerous short stories in the *Star Wars Adventure
Journal,* published between 1994-1997.

11354272R00206

Printed in Great Britain
by Amazon